THE BEGINNING OF FOREVER

THE FOREVER SERIES

BOOK 1

MILLIE MICHAELSON

BLURB

It all began amongst the crowd of roaring fans during our high school homecoming week. Our fates collided in a way that neither of us expected. I met Reid Carter, and he had a quiet charm that captured my heart.

The moment our eyes met, our connection was undeniable. The magnetic pull between us defied all reason. Under the sweat and heat of the game, Reid Carter was the most handsome boy I'd ever seen. And it seemed like he couldn't take his eyes off me either. But we're from two different worlds.

I'm a spirited and strong-willed African American volleyball player, and Reid Carter is a gentle, quiet white basketball player. Despite our differences, we shared stolen glances and bashful smiles, growing into a passionate connection that defied high school norms.

We saw something in each other that would join us in ways that couldn't be broken. Developed a love so strong that we didn't know what hit us. Shared our hopes and dreams and imagined the life we'd build together. That's how strong our love was.

Love, however, has a way of revealing its complexities. As college acceptance letters arrived, we realized our dreams might pull us apart. We learn that love, especially young love, doesn't always follow a straight path. The challenges we face will turn our lives upside down, and I don't know if our love is enough.

"High school is like a daily sitcom where the drama is too real, the assignments are like uninvited guests, and the cafeteria food is a mystery that could rival any detective novel. Welcome to the hilariously chaotic rollercoaster ride, also known as teenage survival!"

FIRST DAY OF SENIOR YEAR

My alarm goes off, blaring so loud that it startled me out of sleep. I fling my arm out and reach wildly toward my nightstand to shut off the offending noise. With a groan, I roll over and hide under the covers, not ready to get up. It's the first day of school, and I'm finally in my senior year.

"Ugh, it should be illegal to get up this early," I mumble as I snuggle in deeper.

As I lay here, I reflect on the past three years of high school, and it's been a whirlwind. Freshman year, I felt intimidated by the older kids and had to prove myself. My sophomore year was a blur of classes, homework, and trying to fit in. The junior year brought the pressure of college applications, the SAT, and figuring out what I wanted to do in life. Now, senior year is here, and I'm ready for it. High school shaped me into who I am today.

At one time, my insecurity about being skinny was the main concern in my life. I could eat anything without gaining weight. I'm not sure if it was a blessing or a curse, but it gave kids plenty of fodder for gossip. People kept asking if I was on a diet or had some kind of sickness.

I kept insisting that it was just my genetics, but the whispers never ceased. As time passed, something inside me shifted, and I realized that their words or opinions didn't determine my worth. My confidence grew, and I saw myself in a new light. Today, I stand proud of who I am. I'm a confident young woman who doesn't let the opinions of others define her.

"Amelia! Get your ass out of bed!" Mom shouts, cutting through my thoughts. "You missed breakfast, and I'm leaving for work."

I pull the covers down and sigh. "I'm up. I'm up," I reply.

The morning sun paints a warm glow on my bedroom walls as I roll out of bed. Excitement flows through my veins, and anticipation fills the corners of my mind. Senior year, the culmination of my high school journey, holds both promises and uncertainties. The thought of college acceptance letters and the impending future weighs on my shoulders, but today, my initial conflict is simpler, though not insignificant. I don't know what the hell I'm going to wear to school.

I stretch and yawn, then shuffle to my closet to find the perfect outfit. As silly as it may seem, choosing an outfit for the first day of school is a big deal. It's another first impression I'll make on my classmates and teachers. Plus, it sets the tone for my entire senior year because kids can be brutal when teasing.

As I scan through my closet, I contemplate my options. Can't decide between a cute, comfortable look or dressing to impress. Ultimately, I go for a pair of high-waisted jeans, a flowy blouse, and my white sneakers. A perfect balance between casual and put-together.

I check the clock, realizing I only have thirty minutes to get ready before it's time for me to leave. With my outfit decision made, it's time for me to tackle the rest of my morning. After getting dressed, I descend the stairs with the aroma of freshly brewed coffee greeting me.

Mom greets me with a smile as she rushes around the kitchen, gathering her things. After a quick kiss on the cheek, she rushes out of the house, telling me to have a great first day at school.

With Mom gone, I turn to see Destiny nursing a cup of coffee at the kitchen table, with her eyes glued to her phone, no doubt scrolling through her work emails. Iris is still in her pajamas and stuffing her face with cereal. My older Destiny and younger sister Iris are polar opposites.

Destiny is the quintessential responsible sibling. She's always been the organized and focused one, diving into her work with an intensity that can be both admirable and slightly intimidating. She's a creature of routine, with her every move calculated and purposeful. Destiny loves her morning coffee almost as much as she loves her spreadsheets and pie charts.

Then there's Iris, who is a breath of fresh air with her ever-present laughter and carefree spirit. She's a social butterfly, always chatting, singing songs, or dancing with a carefree attitude. Iris lives in the moment and loves to explore new things. Her vibrant energy is infectious, and I can't help but smile when she's around. Despite their differences, I adore them both.

As different as they are, Destiny and Iris have shaped me in more ways than one. Destiny's disciplined and methodical approach to life taught me the importance of hard work and responsibility. She's often the person I talk to for making critical decisions. Her pragmatic view of things grounds me when my thoughts wander into the realm of idealistic dreams.

Beneath the serious exterior is a sister who would go to the ends of the earth for me and is always there to help me navigate the challenges in my life.

On the other hand, Iris is my go-to for anything pop-culture related. Her carefree spirit and zest for life are a constant reminder to live in the present and not take life too seriously. Her interests are as diverse as the colors of a rainbow, always changing and always vibrant. One day, she's deep into the world of K-pop, and the next, she's trying her hand at pottery or painting.

Her joy for life is infectious, and she often pushes me to step out of my comfort zone and try something new. Her laughter, unyielding optimism, and uncanny ability to turn even the most mundane days into an adventure make her a constant source of light in my life.

Their contrasting personalities balance me out. They are my reality check and my escape, my counselors, and my partners in crime. Despite our individual quirks and interests, we are really close.

"D, what's up?" I call out, using my nickname for Destiny.

She peels her eyes off her phone and gives me a once-over, her lips curving into a smile.

"Look at you, all grown up and ready to tackle your senior year," she says.

She was my rock during my high school years, always there when I needed advice or someone to vent to. It feels surreal to imagine being in her shoes a year from now, navigating the real world and finding my path. Iris drops her spoon into her bowl of cereal.

"Amelia, you're up! I need your help with something," she says around a mouth full of cereal, her voice filled with urgency.

I shake my head because Iris is always up to something and always needs our help to fix it. Destiny and I have gotten her out of trouble plenty of times. Even though she causes a fair share of headaches, I wouldn't trade her for the world. As the youngest, she adds a certain spark to our family dynamic that I can't imagine living without.

"Well, what did you do this time, squirt?" Destiny asks, her eyebrows raising in amusement.

"Oh man, I really messed up this time. I 'revamped' Mom's beloved high heels," she says sheepishly.

Destiny's eyes widen with shock. "No way! What did you do?"

"I used glitter glue, sequins, and all sorts of things. I thought they needed a pop of style," Iris replies.

I scrub a hand down my face before sighing. "You know how much Mom loves her heels, Iris. Why in the hell would you do that?"

"I know. That's why she's not exactly thrilled with the new look. I'm in big trouble," Iris says in a low and defeated tone.

Destiny pats Iris's shoulder. "Don't worry about it. I'll talk to Mom. When I'm finished, the most you'll have to do is clean them off and return them back to their original state."

"Thanks, D," Iris tells her with a smile.

"Any advice for me today?" I ask Destiny.

"Hmm?" Destiny says as she looks at me. "Oh, just be yourself, Amelia. You're a senior now. Own it. Keep all that shit from last year in the past."

She smiles reassuringly before her gaze slides back down to her phone, and she sips her coffee.

"Amelia, it's your last first day of high school! Aren't you thrilled?!" Iris says, her troubles long forgotten.

"I wouldn't say thrilled... maybe just really excited," I admit.

Iris gives me a comforting hug. "You'll do great. Remember, if anyone gives you any trouble, I'll deal with them."

I laugh, shaking my head at Iris's protectiveness. With a quick breakfast and a backpack filled with neatly organized supplies, I leave my house. The morning air is crisp, and the autumn leaves crunch beneath my sneakers as I make my way to school. My best friend Hazel couldn't pick me up this morning, so I'm taking the bus.

As the bus pulls up, I hop on and slide into a vacant seat near the back. Outside the window, the world moves past in a blur of colors as the bus rumbles down the street. Soon my stop arrives, and I rise from my seat and, with a slight hesitation, exit the bus.

My heart races as I step through the doors of Crestwood High School. It's a swirl of excitement and a dash of nerves, but the bustling halls and familiar faces put a smile on my face. My eyes roam the bustling hallway. Crestwood High is a relatively small school, so almost everyone knows everyone. High school has had its difficulties, but my experience has been mostly positive.

The hallways are a riot of color and noise. A sea of the school's signature blue and gold. I hear the far-off echo of lockers slamming shut and the low hum of chattering students filling the air. The smell of waxed linoleum floors and the faint aroma of cafeteria food mingled, creating a scent that was undeniably 'school.' The fluorescent lights overhead buzz softly, casting a harsh, white glow on the freshly waxed floors below.

Every so often, the intercom would crackle to life with the principal's voice filling the halls and classrooms with the first day of school announcements. The feel of cold metal lockers under my fingertips, the sight of familiar faces in every hallway... all of these made Crestwood High more than just a school; it's a vibrant, bustling microcosm, a world unto itself, shaping us and preparing us for the life beyond its doors.

As I walk down the hall, I spot Hazel at her locker and smile. She's organizing the books in her locker according to her class schedule, which she color coordinated. I walk up to her and lean on the locker next to hers.

"Hey, Hazel. How was your summer?" I ask her.

Hazel looks up, and her face lights up when she sees me. "Amelia! Oh my gosh, it's been forever!" she says, moving away from her locker to give me a quick hug. "My summer was awesome! I visited my grandparents in Florida and got this fucking amazing tan." She gestures at her sun-kissed skin, laughing. "How about you? How was your summer?"

Her enthusiasm makes me laugh. "Wow, your summer sounds like it was a blast. My summer was pretty low-key. I mostly spent the summer with family. You know how it is."

Hazel smiles as she knows how wacky my family can be. My mind thinks back to a crazy incident two winters ago when we got lost in the mountains. While we were trying to find our way, my mom noticed a car following us. To lose them, she made every turn possible, but the car continued to follow. Eventually, my mom pulled over and got out of the car with a sledgehammer and a hatchet, which she had brought on the road trip, just in case.

To our relief, the car just drove past us. We all laughed at our own paranoia and continued on our way until the police unexpectedly pulled us over. It turned out that the person in the car had called the police, reporting a crazy woman waving weapons on the side of the road. Thankfully, it was just a misunderstanding, and we could resume our road trip with a good story to tell.

"Ready for senior year?" Hazel says, interrupting my trip down memory lane.

"As ready as I'll ever be," I tell her.

I watch Hazel for a few minutes as she meticulously arranges her books and supplies in her locker, each item finding its perfect place with an almost surgical precision. Her attention to detail is something I have always admired, and it's fascinating to see her in action. As she continues her organization spree, an idea suddenly sprouts in my mind. I lean in closer, peering at the color-coded class schedule taped to the inside of her locker door.

"Hey Hazel, mind if I look at your schedule?" I ask casually, hoping the universe has aligned our stars and put us in some of the same classes.

To my delight, she hands me her schedule with a smile. As I scan through it, a grin spreads across my face. We had no one but three periods together this year: English, history, and lunch.

"Hey, do you realize we have third period, lunch, and seventh period together?" I ask her.

Hazel's brows raise. "Oh, really? Hell yeah! What classes are they?"

"Third period is European History with Ms. Peters, and seventh period is chemistry with Mrs. Ramirez," I say as I read the schedule.

Hazel catches on to my excitement and grins back at me. "Looks like we're going to have an amazing senior year together. What about your first period?"

"Ugh, it's art class," I reply with a sigh.

I can't help but roll my eyes whenever art comes up. I've never been good at it, and it's always been a personal struggle.

"I get it, you're shit at art," Hazel says with a laugh. "Don't worry, maybe you'll surprise yourself and create something fucking amazing!"

I frown as I do not share her optimism. "I hope so, but everything I make ends up looking like a pile of shit."

"You're right. I was trying to make you feel better about your terrible art skills," she says with a shrug.

As Hazel finishes her sentence, the warning bell rings through the hallways. The sound is sharp and resonating, cutting through our conversation and bringing us back to the reality of the new school year. Hazel quickly shuts her locker, the echo of the metal door clanging shut, blending seamlessly with the fading bell. She looks at me with her eyes sparkling with excitement and a bit of first-day nerves. Hooking her arm through mine, she gives me a reassuring squeeze.

"Well, here goes nothing," she says.

Together, we walk toward our first period classes. The hustle and bustle of the hallway is a clear reminder that the summer is over and the new school year has officially begun.

As Hazel and I navigate through the sea of students, I notice the once bustling hallway slowly thinning out. Students are breaking away from their groups, heading toward their respective classrooms. A few teachers have emerged from their rooms to gently usher the remaining stragglers along.

Mrs. Peters, the European History teacher with her cat-eye glasses perched on the bridge of her nose, is standing right outside her room, clapping her hands and calling out to students to hurry. Mr. Thompson, the Economics teacher with a reputation for his dry humor, is leaning against his doorframe, his arms folded and his eyes scanning the hallway for his first-period students. The excitement in the air is palpable as both the teachers and students are ready to embark on yet another academic year.

"Can you imagine how much homework we're going to have this year?" Hazel says as we walk down the hallway. "How are we going to have time to socialize? To go to parties?" She wiggles her eyebrows. "To date all the cute boys."

I roll my eyes at her. Hazel is definitely the more social of us. "I'm fine with the homework and studying. Not all of us want to party and focus on boys."

She frowns at me, and I can tell she wants to say something about last year, but decides against it. As we continue on our way, a harsh female voice pierces through the noise.

"Make way, slut coming through," she says, loud enough for people to hear. My heart skipped a beat. It's Jada, Kendra's little sister, who, on the first day of school, seems to be on a mission to make my life as difficult as possible. Kendra, my ex-boyfriend's fling, had caused a lot of problems for me and my ex, and Jada is a constant reminder of those painful memories.

"I'm not in the mood for your drama this early in the morning, Jada," I tell her. "Move along before I punch you in the damn face."

I'm trying to keep my composure. I want to start this year off on a good note, and kicking her ass is a sure way to get me on the principal's shit list.

Hazel pulls my arm. "Come on, Amelia. Don't pay the ugly bitch any mind."

Jada smirks, clearly enjoying this confrontation. "Oh, Amelia. Are you still heartbroken that your boyfriend left you for my sister? I didn't realize you were so sensitive. I thought you'd have thicker skin by now."

I yank my arm out of Hazel's hand and spin to get in Jada's face. "I have thicker skin but even thinner patience. Grow the hell up, Jada. Leave me the fuck alone, or next time, your friends will be picking you off the floor."

Jada's eyes widen, and I know she got the message. I'm not the meek little girl I used to be.

"Don't mess with Amelia," Hazel tells Jada. "Don't worry, though. I'll get to you before you get to her. Better watch your back, bitch."

With that, Hazel and I continue on our way, determined not to let Jada's presence disrupt our morning any further. Though the scars of the past are still fresh in my memory, I'm determined to rise above the drama and negativity that Jada seems intent on bringing into my life.

I tell Hazel I'll see her later as we arrive outside her first period class, which is Calculus with Mr. Martin. She gives me a quick hug and responds with an encouraging smile before disappearing into the classroom. Taking a deep breath, I turn in the opposite direction, making my way toward the dreaded art class.

"High school art class: where you discover the profound truth that the more abstract your masterpiece, the better your chances of convincing the teacher it's intentional." truth that the more abstract your masterpiece, the better your chances of convincing the teacher it's intentional."

CREATING A NEW ROUTINE

As soon as I step into art class, I'm greeted by the vibrant energy of Ms. Clark. She has a quirky style and infectious enthusiasm that radiates a fun and friendly vibe that instantly lights up the room. There she is, in all her quirky glory, sporting a dress that's as colorful as her personality. Her outfit is a kaleidoscope of bright hues with patterns that are daring, bold, and playfully eclectic.

It's a fascinating mix of polka dots, stripes, and everything in between that somehow comes together in a charmingly harmonious fashion. Her hair is a flamboyant cascade of vibrant pink waves, flouncing around with a life of their own, perfectly capturing Ms. Clark's playful spirit.

"Alright, folks!" she yells to the students as her eyes twinkle with excitement. "This year's art journey is going to be nothing short of amazing. We're kicking off with something really cool today. We're sculpting our own flower pots. So, let's roll up our sleeves and dive in!"

As she instructs everyone to don their smocks and gather their materials, her enthusiasm is unmistakable. I can't miss the broad smile on her face and the spring in her step as she guides us toward the back of the classroom to start our artful adventure.

I grab my clay and start to knead it, feeling the smooth texture between my fingers. As I work on shaping my pot, Ms. Clark goes around the room, offering tips and encouragement. She spots my frustration from across the room and quickly heads over to me, her cheerful demeanor still in place.

"Ah, there's beauty in working with clay, isn't it?" she says with a comforting smile playing on her lips. "Sometimes, it has a mind of its own. Don't worry, Amelia. Sculpting is an art of patience and resilience. Let me show you a little trick."

With gentle hands, she guides my fingers, helping me reshape the misbehaving clay into a beautiful pot.

Her voice elevates with genuine excitement as it starts to take shape. "See? There you go! It's coming along nicely. You're doing a great job!"

Her optimism and encouraging words help to soothe my irritation and make my struggles a little easier.

"Remember, there's no right or wrong way to do this," she says with a reassuring grin. "Just let your creativity flow and have fun with it!"

I can't help but feel a pang of frustration as I look around the room. My classmates seem to mold their clay as if they were born for this, their hands moving confidently as they shape their pots into various forms of beauty. I glance down at my own work to see a misshapen lump of clay that barely resembles a flower pot. It looks more like an abstract disaster, a far cry from the impressive creations I see around me.

Ms. Clark notices my disappointed look and walks back to my table with her eyes sparkling with warmth and encouragement.

"Hey there, Amelia," she says, her voice soothing. "Remember, it's not about making a perfect pot on your first try. It's about enjoying the process and learning along the way."

In spite of her words, I'm getting more pissed off by the minute. I never wanted art class, but I've avoided it my entire high school career, and it's required to graduate. I understand that it should be an enjoyable experience, a voyage of discovery and self-expression. However, at this moment, all I can ponder is how much I hate taking this class.

As I look around the room, my classmates seem absorbed in their own sculpting duties, their laughter and chatter adding a lively rhythm to the creative ambiance. The unexpected tap on my shoulder startles me from my thoughts. When I turn around, I'm met with the smiling face of Lawrence. Lawrence, a classmate I remember seeing around the school during our freshman and sophomore years but never really interacted with.

"May I?" he asks, gesturing towards my clay catastrophe.

His request surprises me, but I nod and step aside, watching curiously as he takes over the lump of clay. His hands move with practiced ease, reshaping the clay while he explains the basic do's and don'ts of clay sculpting. His instructions are insightful, and I find myself fascinated by the transformation of the clay under his hands.

"Alright, Amelia," he says with his fingers tracing gentle patterns on the clay. "One of the key things to remember is patience. Don't rush the process. Allow the clay to guide your hands."

I nod, watching how his hands smoothly manipulate the clay. "That's what Ms. Clark said, but what about the shape?" I ask him. "How do I make sure it doesn't collapse on itself?"

"That's a great question," he replies with a smile. "It's all about maintaining balance. Make sure the base is strong and thick enough to support the upper structure, and as you thin out the walls, do it evenly all around. The clay will follow your hands if you guide it right."

His fingers slowly dance around the clay and breathe life into it. "Oh, and hydration is key. If your clay starts to crack or harden, add a little water. Not too much, though, or it will become too sticky and hard to manage."

As Lawrence explains, he demonstrates each step on my clay pot, transforming it from a misshaped lump of shit into a beautiful, budding flower pot. His smile is contagious, and I find myself mirroring his expression as he jokes about his own first struggles with clay. Our conversation flows easily as his casual, friendly demeanor puts me at ease.

We exchange jokes, share laughter, and delve into a variety of topics throughout the rest of the class. As the bell rings, signaling the end of this torturous class, I look at the clay pot we sculpted together and can't help but smile.

I gather my things and carefully wrap my half-finished clay pot in a damp cloth as Ms. Clark had instructed. Lawrence is standing beside me, still wearing his mischievous grin.

"Thanks for your help, Lawrence," I say, looking up at him.

His smile widens as he bumps his shoulder against mine. "No problem, Amelia. I'm always happy to help a damsel in distress."

Raising an eyebrow, I meet Lawrence's gaze with a smirk. "I'm no damsel in distress," I reply in a sassy but playful tone. "I'll kick your ass the next time you say that."

As we make our way towards the classroom door, Lawrence turns to me.

"Can I walk you to your next class?" he asks in a voice full of confidence.

I frown at his request. I appreciate his help, and his company has been pleasant, but I don't want to give him the wrong impression. Maybe my playful demeanor made him think I was flirting, which I most definitely was not. High school has been a whirlwind of emotions, rumors, and raging hormones, and I've had my fair share of heartache. The memories of my first and only boyfriend and what happened last year still sting.

I was young, and I loved him, or at least I thought I did. I gave him parts of me I could never take back, only to discover he was cheating on me with his ex-girlfriend. Worse, he prided himself on sharing our intimate details with the entire school. Ever since then, I've kept myself on the sidelines of the dating scene. I'm a romantic at heart, and I still believe in finding *the one*, but I'm not in a rush. I'm waiting for the right guy to truly pique my interest.

"I appreciate the offer, but I can manage on my own. Thanks, though," I tell him with a friendly smile.

Walking into my next class, Social Studies with Mr. Jones, I brace myself for an hour of monotone lectures that have a knack for lulling even the most alert students into a trance. I take my seat and attempt to focus on Mr. Jones as he begins teaching, his words melding into a continuous drone. Despite my best efforts, my eyelids start to droop, and I find myself on the brink of sleep more than once.

Mr. Jones always has a few tricks up his sleeve as he's well aware of the soporific effect of his lectures and has developed a unique method of combating it. Just as my head starts to dip forward, a sharp shriek cuts through the monotonous hum of the classroom. I jerk up to see Mr. Jones holding a horn in his hand as he looks straight at me with a knowing smirk. The class erupts into laughter, and I'm wide awake, my cheeks burning with embarrassment. His little trick works every time, ensuring a sudden jolt of adrenaline keeps us alert, at least for a while.

Class continues on much in the same vein, with Mr. Jones'

strategic horn-blows jolting me awake a few more times. The laughter that follows each blare has become a familiar sound-track, and the embarrassment a predictable warmth spreading across my face. Soon enough, the clock on the wall signals the end of the hour-long class, and I gather my things quickly and then head to my next class.

Next up is European History with Ms. Peters, and the contrast couldn't be more pronounced. From Mr. Jones' monotonous, sleep-inducing drone to Ms. Peters' engaging and animated discussions. As I step into the classroom, the air is filled with the scent of history, and the sight of maps and textbooks immediately captures my attention.

Hazel waves at me from the back of the room, and I make my way toward her as a smile spreads on my face. Pulling out the chair next to Hazel, I sink into the chair just as she starts talking.

"Honestly, Amelia, calculus should be outlawed as a first class," she groans, her arms flopping down dramatically on the desk. "I'm already exhausted."

I chuckle and shake my head at her theatrical display. "I can't believe you're complaining, Miss Math Whiz. You love that shit."

"Of course I do. I'm a fucking genius," she says while tucking a loose piece of hair behind her ear. "Still, it's too fucking early." She pauses, her eyes taking in my bewildered expression. "Okay, spill. What's got that look on your face?"

"Nothing special," I tell her. "I just had an…interesting conversation with Lawrence in art class."

Hazel raises her eyebrows as her grin turns into a mischie-vous smirk. "Lawrence, huh? He's a cutie. Please, don't tell me you're not interested in him. He's a hot piece of ass. Why aren't you interested?"

"I am not going down that road again, Hazel. You know

what happened last time," I snap at her though I don't really mean to.

Hazel brushes off my attitude with a dismissive wave of her hand. "Not every guy is that asshole. Maybe Lawrence is genuinely a nice guy?" Hazel continues without giving me a chance to reply. "You should hit it and quit to relieve all that tension you have."

My mouth hangs open at the cavalier way she's talking. I get what she's trying to do, though. I am allowing my past to dictate my current decisions. Maybe Lawrence was just being kind, or maybe he does like me. I didn't really feel any interest while talking to him, but maybe I need to open myself up more. Only one way to find out, I guess.

Hazel's voice interrupts my thoughts, her playful tone making me smirk. "You know, for someone who doesn't date, you sure do flirt a lot. Maybe Lawrence thought you were into him."

I open my mouth to retort, but the sound of the door opening interrupts me. In walks Ms. Peters, her presence instantly commanding everyone's attention. The playful atmosphere evaporates as the class settles down, and Ms. Peters sets her things down on her desk.

As soon as Ms. Peters begins her lecture, I can tell it's going to be an engrossing one. Hazel and I never got a chance to revisit our earlier conversation as we were both too engrossed in the riveting tales of ancient civilizations and their impact on our present world. She has a knack for bringing history to life, and before I know it, an hour has passed. The bell rings, signaling the end of this class, and we gather our books to head to the next class.

I make it to my next period with seconds to spare, as it's on the other side of the school. Calculus class zooms by as Mr. Martin explains the lesson, and suddenly the bell rings, meaning it's time for my lunch period.

As I push open the doors to the cafeteria, a wave of chatter and laughter washes over me, a stark contrast to the quiet intensity of calculus class. The atmosphere buzzes with excitement for the first day of school. The long tables are filled with students huddled in groups, some engrossed in animated conversations while others simply enjoy their lunches. The smells of various meals intermingle in the air, creating a unique aroma that's simultaneously appetizing and overwhelming.

The clatter of trays against the metal lunch counters is punctuated by the occasional burst of laughter from a far-off table. The lunch ladies, in their white aprons, move efficiently behind the counter with their cheerful banter adding to the cafeteria's lively atmosphere.

I grab a lunch tray and head over to the counter, opting for a classic cheeseburger and a side of fries. Spotting Hazel at our old table, I make my way over, settling down in the seat opposite her. Hazel groans, placing her head in her hands.

"I have Mr. Jones's class after lunch. I just know I'm going to fall asleep with a full stomach," she complains, earning an amused laugh from me.

"Maybe don't overdo it with the food then," I suggest, biting into my burger.

Hazel snorts at my comment before rolling her eyes in mock disbelief.

"So, what are you up to after school?" she asks, changing the topic.

"I have volleyball practice," I reply before I take a sip of my drink.

Hazel hums in acknowledgment and starts delving into a new topic, her words flowing in a constant stream as I finish my lunch. The bell rings just as we're clearing our trays, and we head to our separate classes.

The rest of the day passes in a blur, the hours ticking by until the final bell rings. I find myself heading to the girls' locker room in anticipation of volleyball practice. As I change my clothes, I feel a rush of excitement. Despite the long day, I'm looking forward to ending it on the volleyball court.

As soon as I step onto the court, a surge of adrenaline fills me. Each time feels like entering a different world. During practice, I transition smoothly between the roles of setter, outside hitter, and middle blocker, thanks to hours of honing my skills. With precision, my fingers handle the volleyballs, serving, setting, and spiking them alongside my teammates.

Sweat drips down my face, my muscles ache, and my breath quickens. It's mentally and physically exhausting, but I wouldn't trade it for anything. The satisfaction of each successful play and point won is indescribable. The gym's dust and echoes fade away as I focus solely on the white ball, my teammates, and the exhilarating feeling of giving my all.

After the final whistle, the team congregates in the middle of the court, each of us catching our breath and exchanging tired smiles. Coach Thompson slowly walks towards us, a proud smile stretching across her face.

"Great job today, ladies!" she tells us. Her words resonate in the gym, bouncing off the walls and settling in our hearts. "If you keep up this kind of work, we may just make it to state this year."

Her words land among us like a spark, igniting a new surge of excitement. The possibility of making it to the state championship has been our collective dream, and I feel a rush of determination.

As Coach Thompson dismisses us, I make my way back to the locker room, change out of my sweaty volleyball gear, and back into the clothes I wore to school. After slipping into my sneakers, I stuff my volleyball gear into my duffel bag and sling it over my shoulder. Exiting the locker room, I step out into the corridor and start making my way toward the gym exit.

I don't even need to look around to know that Hazel will be there, leaning against her car with that trademark smirk on her face. True to form, as I step outside, I spot her leaning against her old, beat-up Ford, arms crossed and foot tapping impatiently. Her familiar blue eyes light up when she sees me, and a quick grin stretches across her face.

"Hurry up, slowass," she calls out before unlocking the car as I approach. "I've got places to be, people to see!" she teases.

We pile into the car and cranks the music up as we drive away, ending a good start to the first day of school.

"School spirit: because pretending to love pep rallies and dressing up for themed days is the only socially acceptable way to survive the academic circus. It's like being in a cult, but with more homework and less chanting."

HAVE SOME SCHOOL SPIRIT

As my senior year charges on, one day blending into the next until weeks have passed, I've found my groove. I'm balancing academics, athletics, and a decent social life. Before I know it, the leaves turn with hues of crimson and orange. September fades into October, bringing in the cooler air.

I rush downstairs to grab a quick bite before heading to school. I spot Mom casually sipping her morning coffee at the kitchen table as if it's a normal Sunday or something.

"Mom, shouldn't you be getting ready for work?" I ask.

She gives Iris a stern look, who's pretending to be engrossed in her cereal. "No, Amelia, I'm going to Iris's school today. Your sister has gotten herself into trouble again."

"Iris, what did you do this time?" I probe, trying to keep my voice steady. She's lucky Destiny could get her out of trouble the last time.

"Oh, nothing much," Iris nonchalantly responds, stirring her cereal as if it's the most interesting thing in the world.

"That's not what Mom thinks," I reply, my curiosity now thoroughly piqued.

Just then, Destiny walks into the room. "What's the daily disaster?" she asks, reaching for the coffeepot.

"Iris, apparently," I say. "But she's keeping quiet about it."

Iris finally puts her spoon down and shoots us both an annoyed glance.

"Fine, I may have poured glitter into Principal Brown's coffee cup. Only because he gave me detention for a dress code violation. It's called fashion, people," Iris says with irritation.

Destiny and I can't help but laugh at Iris's explanation.

"You know that's not how it works, right?" Destiny says between giggles.

"Yeah, you're lucky they didn't suspend you," Mom tells her as I try to hold back my laughter.

"I get that you're mad, Mom, but grounding Iris won't change anything," I start, trying to sound as diplomatic as possible.

"Yeah, Mom. It's not like Iris did something terrible. It was just a harmless prank," Destiny chimes in.

Mom looks at both of us with her eyebrows furrowed. "It's not about the prank, girls. It's about Iris respecting authority."

"Mom, think about it. Isn't grounding her like proving Iris's point? That she's unnecessarily policed?" I try, hoping a different point of view will sway her.

"Yeah," Destiny continues. "Maybe we should talk to her and explain why authority is important. Help her understand instead of grounding her immediately."

Mom frowns as she looks at us. "I'm a fan of grounding and whooping ass. Iris is old enough to know better, and you're not going to convince me to let her slide this time."

I share a sympathetic shrug with Destiny toward Iris with our eyes saying, 'sorry, sis, we tried'. Iris's eyes widen in disbelief as the gravity of her predicament finally sinks in. This might be the one time her big sisters can't save her.

"Uh, what are you wearing?" Destiny asks me with a quirk of her brow.

This week is spirit week at school, and me and Hazel have been totally into it. We're rocking the school colors, and we're totally nailing the themed days. Twin day was hilarious as we showed up in identical outfits that were so spot on you'd think we were actual twins, despite the color difference. We had fun for Pajama Day as we both went to school in full-body bunny pajamas. It's like we've turned school spirit into an art form.

"It's spirit week," I tell Destiny as I look down at my blue and gold attire. "I've been dressing up according to the themes all week."

Destiny smiles as she gets a thoughtful look on her face. "I remember those days. What's today's theme?"

"Oh, it's just blue and gold day today," I tell her with a wave of my hand.

Before she can respond, I grab a bagel and sling my backpack over my shoulder. I slip my feet into my shoes, give everyone a quick 'bye,' and stride out the door to Hazel's waiting car.

Hazel and I arrive at school with enough time to throw our things into our lockers and rush to class. Art class continues to be a disaster for me. Ms. Clark, with her eclectic style and infectious energy, decides it's a good day to teach us how to sculpt and mold faces. I can feel my creativity shrivel up and die as my hands struggle to produce anything close to a human face. What I'm creating looks like an alien potato.

Beside me, Lawrence flashes his charming smile as his hands expertly mold clay, and he cracks jokes to lighten the mood. He's always there to help when my frustrations get the best of me.

"Amelia, your face is uh... abstract. It's looking good," he teases, clearly enjoying my frustration.

His good-natured teasing should irritate me, but instead, I find myself laughing along with him. Despite his obvious interest in me, I can't seem to reciprocate the feelings. Lawrence is nice, funny, and good-looking. To the other girls, he's perfect, but in reality, there's just no spark. I'm careful to set clear friend zone boundaries.

"Thanks, Lawrence," I say, giving him a weak smile. "I think I'll stick to reading. Clay isn't my medium."

The bell rings, and just as I pack my stuff, Lawrence clears his throat. The usual smile on his face is replaced with determination.

"Amelia," he says with a different, more flirtatious smile. "Would you like to go to the homecoming dance with me?"

His words hang in the air, and suddenly the classroom, once filled with chatter and laughter, falls silent. His question catches me off guard, and I'm unprepared for the shift in our usual banter.

"Lawrence, I thought you had a girlfriend?" I ask.

I've heard the rumor from another student in our class. My question slices through the tension like a knife. Lawrence looks at me in surprise.

"No, I don't," he answers before taking a deep breath. He continues, his tone is now confident and cocky, "I was actually trying to ask you out. You could be my girlfriend."

The clay in my hand feels heavy, and I look at Lawrence in a way I never have before. Maybe I misjudged his nice and easygoing demeanor before. He says it like it would be an honor to be called his girlfriend, and now I want to smash this clay in his face.

"Lawrence," I say, careful to keep the irritation from my voice. "I'm going to have to say no. I won't go to the dance with you, and I don't want to be your girlfriend."

The words tumble out of my mouth as I meet his expectant gaze with a resolute one. The classroom is still silent as my words hit him. Then, to my surprise, he laughs. It's not the usual charming chuckle, but a loud, mocking laugh that echoes off the class walls.

"Damn, I really thought the good boy act would work," he says, wiping a tear from his eye. The laughter slowly dies down, and he fixes me with a smirk. "I told the guys I'd get you to put out by homecoming," he continues. "We remember what your last boyfriend said about you in bed. I can teach you a few things."

My face burns as his words hang in the air. His tone is a stark contrast to the playful banter we shared just a few minutes ago. I can feel the stares of our classmates, their whisperings like a gentle breeze rustling the leaves. I clench my fists, determined not to let Lawrence see how his words affect me.

With no further hesitation, I draw back my arm and deliver a sharp slap across Lawrence's smirking face. The sound echoes around the silent room while everyone's eyes widen in shock. The smirk fades off his face as he brings a hand to his stinging cheek.

"Eat a dick, Lawrence," I snap, and my voice rings out clearly in the silent classroom.

I hastily grab my things, not bothering to glance at the stunned faces around me, and march out of the classroom while holding my head high.

Fuming and with a slight sting of embarrassment, I find my way to the counselor's office for my next period. Upon walking in, I tell Ms. Riley that I need help with a couple of college scholarship applications, which isn't entirely false. While I applied to schools during my junior year, some are still accepting applications and issuing scholarships. I plop down at a small table and spread out the applications and the required documents.

In reality, I'm just seeking a quiet refuge away from the whispers and the prying eyes. Ms. Riley, always eager to help, pulls up a chair beside me. We spend the hour going over the paperwork, her calm and patient demeanor providing a welcome distraction from the tumult of emotions roiling inside me. Soon, the bell rings, and she sends me on my way to my next class.

"That's for Amelia, asshole!" I hear Hazel yell from down the hall.

As I turn the corner, I catch sight of her, and she's standing over Lawrence, who's doubled over in pain. She glares at him one last time before delivering a sharp knee to his groin. Lawrence crumples to the ground, gasping and groaning in pain.

Hazel straightens up, brushes off her hands as if dusting off invisible dirt, and strolls in my direction. She notices me and her eyes light up as she quickly hooks her arm through mine.

"Come on, Amelia," she says, a mischievous twinkle in her eye. "I heard about what that asshat said to you. I bet he won't say anything else to you from now on."

"Thanks, Hazel," I tell her.

She smiles and winks. "You know I got your back."

As we walk away from the scene, Hazel leans in closer, her voice dropping to a conspiratorial whisper. "I heard from Jessica that Lawrence has a small dick and a short stroke."

Her words ring clear in the silent hallway, triggering a ripple of laughter from the students around us. We stride into class, the sound of laughter following us like a badge of victory. My next two classes fly by quickly, and as soon as the bell rings, I pack my bag and leave the classroom.

I'm itching to make it to the cafeteria. I barely step into

the hallway when Hazel catches up with me, her cheerleading uniform practically sparkling with school pride. To say she lives for these moments is an understatement. Hazel practically bleeds our school colors. I glance at her cheerleading uniform looking like it's made of pure energy, with her school spirit radiating off her like a bonfire.

"Hazel, you know I think you're the most hardcore cheerleader we've got, right?" I ask, nudging her with a grin.

She's all about the game days, the pep rallies, the spirit week. Anything that involves showing off our school pride, she's there front and center, leading the charge. Her enthusiasm is just wild, but in a contagious way. It's like she's a walking, talking embodiment of our school spirit, and I can't help but be sucked into it. It's just impossible not to love her energy.

"Fucking right I am! Hey, did you hear about the basketball game against Rushmore High tonight?" she breezes, bouncing on her toes with excitement.

I make a noncommittal sound. "I don't really follow basketball," I reply, tugging my bag higher on my shoulder.

Hazel knows I'm more at home spiking balls over a net in volleyball than watching guys dribble them on a basketball court. That's the thing about Hazel, though. She lives and breathes school spirit. No matter how hard I try, I just can't seem to catch that same enthusiasm.

Stepping into the lunchroom, we're met with a wave of noise that's even more energetic than usual from Spirit Week's infectious enthusiasm. The unending chatter, the laughter, and the cheerleaders rehearsing their routines all give the room a kind of charged energy. Hazel's animatedly discussing the upcoming game while I grab an apple and a sandwich. We weave our way through the maze of tables until we finally find a spot by the window where the sun is streaming in, casting a warm, natural light that somehow makes the room seem even more lively.

"So, are you going to tonight's basketball game?" Hazel asks again as her eyes shine with excitement.

Her question hangs in the air with a school spirit that I just can't seem to catch. Her enthusiasm for school events is infectious, but today, my mind is elsewhere after the confrontation with Lawrence.

"I don't know, Hazel. You know that's not really my thing. I don't go to school games," I tell her.

Hazel's eyes widen in shock at my response. "Where's your school spirit?" she asks. "People come to see you play volleyball all the time. You should support the school."

"I have school spirit, Hazel," I retort back, my eyebrows arching in annoyance. "I've been dressing ridiculously this whole week in the name of school spirit. Isn't that enough?"

I gesture towards my outfit, the school colors glaringly apparent in every piece of clothing I'm wearing. "I support the school, just in my own way. You focus on cheerleading, and I focus on my academics and volleyball. It doesn't mean I have any less school spirit."

"Then continue with your school spirit and come to the game," she counters, crossing her arms over her chest.

The back-and-forth between us turns into a lively debate, our voices growing louder and our argument growing more heated, though not in an angry way. Hazel is relentless with her school spirit, pushing her to persuade me to attend and to experience the thrill of a school game from a different perspective, not as a player but as a supporter. I can see it's important to her. She breathes school spirit, but it's not as simple for me. I'm not one to sit on the sidelines, cheering for others.

In the end, Hazel's stubbornness wins out. Not because I'm suddenly brimming with school spirit, but simply because

I can't bear to listen to her nagging anymore. It's like she's a dog with a bone, refusing to let it go.

"Alright, Hazel. I'll go to the game, okay?" I say, my tone dripping with a hint of reluctance.

Hazel's grin widens at my agreement, and she's practically glowing with victory. Little does she know how much her relentless school spirit is shaping my high school experience by pushing me out of my comfort zone.

"Unexpected encounters are the serendipitous portals through which destiny whispers, and in the dance of chance, the steps taken in those fleeting moments may lead to the grandest chapters of our stories."

THE START OF SOMETHING NEW

I exit the bustling cafeteria with the chatter of my peers slowly fading as I stroll down the hallway. My next class is physics. A subject that both intrigues and challenges me, where we dissect, demystify, and present the laws of nature in mathematical form.

As I enter the room, my eyes meet those of Lawrence and his friends huddled in the corner, their laughter echoing around the room. Lawrence shoots me a menacing glare but doesn't speak to me. Unfazed, I smirk and raise my middle finger in a defiant gesture, which draws gasps from some of the other students. At that moment, the door swings open to reveal Ms. Allen, our stern yet approachable physics teacher.

"Settle down, everyone," she commands as her voice cuts through the chatter like a knife.

The room falls silent, and the day's lesson begins. Ms. Allen's passion for physics is evident in her every word and gesture. Her explanations are simple, concise, and accompanied by lively demonstrations that captivate the class. She makes complex concepts seem simple and encourages us to think critically about the world.

"Today, we're going to dive into the heart of physics, Newton's laws of motion," Ms. Allen says before turning toward the chalkboard.

"The first law, also known as the law of inertia, states that an object will remain at rest or in uniform motion in a straight line unless acted upon by an external force. Can anyone give me an example?"

A few moments of silence follow before a hand shoots up.

"Yes, Jeffery?" she says.

"Well, it's like when you're riding a bike and stop pedaling. You keep moving forward even though you've stopped pedaling because of inertia," Jeffery offers.

"Correct! Now, let's move to the second law. It tells us that the force exerted on an object is equal to the mass of that object multiplied by its acceleration. In other words, $F=ma$. What does that mean in real life?"

Another hand goes up.

"It means if I push a heavy object, it will accelerate slower than a light one," says a voice from the back.

"Exactly," Ms. Allen says with a pleased smile.

She continues teaching the lesson. "Last, the third law: For every action, there is an equal and opposite reaction. It's why when you jump off a boat, the boat moves backward. Or when you push the wall, your hand hurts. The forces are equal in magnitude but opposite in direction."

As the class continues, I listen attentively, occasionally jotting down notes as Ms. Allen continues her energetic delivery of Newton's laws. She made physics appear less like a complex maze of equations and more like an intricate dance of nature's fundamental principles. The bell finally rings, signaling the end of class. Gathering my belongings, I give Ms. Allen a nod of appreciation before exiting the room.

My next destination is the chemistry lab, the home to beakers, Bunsen burners, and Mrs. Ramirez. Renowned for her strict demeanor and clever demonstrations, Mrs. Ramirez had an uncanny ability to make chemistry both exciting and accessible.

Upon entering the chemistry lab, I immediately notice Mrs. Ramirez in goggles, gloves, and a smock, her protective gear signifying another exciting chemistry session. As more students filter inside, she claps her hands together, the sharp noise cutting through the chatter.

"Quickly take your seats, everyone," she calls out, her authoritative voice commanding instant obedience.

The room quickly settles into an orderly silence with all eyes on our stern yet passionate teacher.

"Good, let's begin," Mrs. Ramirez says as her stern facade breaks into a warm smile. "Today, we'll be delving into the mysteriously beautiful world of chemical reactions. These are processes where substances transform into new substances. This transformation is accompanied by energy changes and can be triggered by various factors."

With that introduction, Mrs. Ramirez reaches into a cabinet and pulls out two distinct bottles, one filled with a clear liquid and the other with a dense grey substance. She carefully measures and mixes the two substances into a beaker. A few moments later, everyone in the room gasp in awe as the mixture bubbles and then instantly transforms into a vibrant purple hue.

"What you're seeing, students," Mrs. Ramirez explains, "is a classic chemical reaction between hydrogen peroxide and potassium iodide. The reaction produces an exothermic reaction, meaning it releases energy in the form of heat, causing the solution to heat and decompose rapidly into water and oxygen. The purple color that has you all so enthralled is because of the presence of starch in the solution and its reaction to iodine."

The class sits in fascinated silence, captivated by the

remarkable transformation that had taken place before their eyes.

The rest of my day continues uneventfully, a blur of facts, figures, and faces. The steady rhythm of the school routine lulls me into a comforting sense of familiarity. It's a symphony of learning, where each class is a different melody, enriching the grand composition of my academic journey. As the last bell of the day rings, a sense of excitement surges within me. It's time for the much-anticipated basketball game with Hazel. Gathering my belongings, I make my way toward the gym.

Upon entering the gym, my heart pounds in sync with the echoes of the dribbling basketballs. The gymnasium buzzes with energy, filled with the excited chatter of spectators and the distinct squeak of athletic shoes against the polished wooden floor. As I step into the crowd, I feel the contagious energy wash over me, heightening my senses and quickening my pulse. I am ready for the thrill, the anticipation, and the unpredictable turns of the basketball game. I spot Hazel waving frantically from across the room.

"Amelia!" she yells, her voice slicing through the roar of excited chatter.

She points to an empty seat beside her, evidently saved for me, right behind the cheerleaders' court side. I can't help but roll my eyes at her overzealous display, yet a wide grin spreads across my face. The sight of Hazel's infectious enthusiasm is a reassuring constant amidst the ever-changing sea of faces in the crowd. With a sigh of resignation and amusement, I weave my way through the crowd of spectators toward Hazel.

"Amelia, over here!" Hazel yells again, her eyes sparkling with excitement. "I saved a spot right here for you, next to the cheerleaders, so you can't ditch in the middle of the game. I know you don't want to be here and I'm excited you are."

I laugh as my excitement mirrors Hazel's vibrant energy.

I take the designated seat. "Thanks, Hazel. This crowd is intense!"

"I know, right?" Hazel responds, a wide grin plastered on her face. "Just wait until the game starts. It gets even crazier."

She then stands up, her cheerleader uniform gleaming under the gym lights. "I've got to join the team now. We're doing our pregame cheer soon. You're going to love it, Amelia."

With that, Hazel gives me a quick wink before darting off to join the rest of the cheerleading squad. I sit back, admiring Hazel's spirited demeanor, and eagerly anticipate their pregame performance as cheerleaders.

With Hazel at the helm, the cheerleading squad files onto the court amidst a roar of applause. Their uniforms, a vibrant splash of the school's colors, shine under the intense gymnasium lights. The crowd falls into a hush as the cheerleaders lift their pompoms high in the air, with their faces radiating energy and enthusiasm. With a synchronized shout, they launch into their routine.

Go Crestwood, go Crestwood, don't you quit!
Reach for the stars, it's a perfect fit!
Eagles soaring high above the rest,
Showing all they meet, they are the best!
Shoot the hoop, make your mark,
Let your spirit ignite the spark!
Crestwood Eagles cannot be tamed,
This is our game to claim!
Go Crestwood, go Crestwood, hear our cheer,
With every shout, let your victory near.
Our pride is strong, our spirits high,
Crestwood Eagles, ready to fly!

The court comes alive with an electrifying mix of high leaps, intricate formations, and rhythmic chants that echo through the gymnasium. At the end of the performance, the crowd erupts into cheers, mirroring the cheerleaders' infectious energy. Hazel's eyes sparkle with excitement, and she leads the team off the court amidst continued applause. Her excitement is palpable as she slides back into the seat next to me.

"Ready for the game to start?" she asks while swaying her pom-pom in rhythm to the crowd's cheer.

Just as Hazel finishes her sentence, the loudspeakers crackle, and the announcer's voice booms throughout the gymnasium.

"Ladies and gentlemen, we appreciate your patience. The game you've all been eagerly waiting for is about to begin."

Hazel and I exchange excited glances as we continue our conversation, the air around us buzzing with anticipation. We talk about trivial matters, the latest gossip around the school, and the upcoming school dance, all while the announcer introduces the away team.

"Please put your hands together for the Rushmore High roaring Lions!"

The crowd applauds, albeit with less enthusiasm on our side. The Lions run onto the court, their red and white uniforms shimmering under the glaring gym lights and their faces set with determination.

Several minutes pass, filled with the increasing roar of chatter around us, until the announcer's voice interrupts us again.

"And now, ladies and gentlemen, the moment you've all been waiting for. Please welcome your own, our pride, Crestwood High Eagles!"

Hazel and I yell, our cheering joining the deafening roar of applause that shakes the rafters. As our players burst from the gym doors, their blue and gold jerseys a sharp contrast against the shining court, they're greeted by a wall of noise from their supporters. Loud cheering sounds after they announce each player's name, and the energy in the gym reaches a fever pitch. The Eagles line up opposite the Lions, the tension between the two teams clear and electrifying. The game is about to begin, and it feels like the entire school is holding its breath in anticipation.

As I sit there, staring at the sea of players on the court, I'm suddenly taken aback. My breath hitches in my throat, freezing me in place as my eyes land on the most stunning sight. There, amongst the bustling energy of the basketball court, stands the most handsome boy I have ever seen. He's tall, with an endearing touch of goofiness that only adds to his charm. His legs, thick and muscular, are the most attractive I've ever seen, exuding a sense of strength and agility that makes my heart flutter.

He's talking and laughing freely with his teammates. He's so naturally engrossed in his surroundings that he's oblivious to the fact that I'm staring at him like he's walked straight out of a fashion magazine onto the basketball court of our little school. My heart pounds in my chest with an intensity I've never known before. It feels as if everyone and everything in the gymnasium fades into a blur, leaving only him in sharp focus. His laughter rings through the air, reaching my ears as the sweetest melody. Every time he moves, his muscles ripple under his jersey, showing a strength that is both sexy and incredibly alluring.

From my seat, I watch as he moves fluidly across the court, his tall frame towering over the other players. His brown hair is lightly tousled from the pre-game warm-up, lending him an air of effortless charm. Though, it's his eyes that truly captivate me. They're a striking shade of green, the kind that makes poets write lyrical about emerald seas and verdant forests. Despite the distance, they seem to glint under the harsh gymnasium lights, like hidden gems catching the sun.

His laughter breaks through the din of the crowd again, and I find myself drawn back to those mesmerizing eyes brimming with joy and mischief. He's breathtaking, a beacon of light and vitality among the group of players on the court, and I can't help but feel a fluttering sensation in my chest each time he flashes that irresistible, boyish grin.

My breath catches in my throat as his eyes, those beautiful eyes, flicker across the court with a lively spark that I find captivating. I've never felt this way before. The fluttering in my stomach, the heat creeping up my cheeks, the magnetic pull I feel towards him - it's all-new, all-consuming, and entirely overwhelming. The sudden boom of the gym's loudspeakers snaps me back to reality.

Leaning forward, I tap Hazel on the shoulder, interrupting her conversation with the girl next to her. I point at the court, specifically the mesmerizing boy that caught my attention.

"Hazel?" I ask with a hint of curiosity in my voice. "Who is that? Number 19?"

Hazel follows the direction of my pointed finger and grins knowingly as her eyes twinkle with mischief. "That," she responds dramatically, "is the one and only Reid Carter."

"In that fleeting gaze, the atoms between us conspired, creating a magnetic field of undeniable chemistry —a silent agreement that our souls had met before our words ever dared to."

THE UNDENIABLE SPARK

Hazel's eyes sparkle as she turns to me with a wide grin stretching across her face.

"Amelia," she shrieks in a voice filled with an uncontainable excitement. "You're seriously crushing so fucking hard right now! On Reid fucking Carter!"

Her words float in the air, charged with the electric energy of a newfound infatuation. With a giggle, I swiftly place my hand over her mouth as my cheeks flush a bright shade of red.

"Shhh, Hazel!" I hiss, glancing around to make sure no one had overheard.

The last thing I need is for this to become the talk of the school, especially when I'm even sure about my own feelings yet. I'm still processing the powerful pull I just had toward Reid.

Hazel doesn't care as she's still grinning and wiggles her eyebrows at me. "So, you like a little creamer in your coffee, huh?" she teases, her voice laced with playful innocence. "He's a tall 6'3" white oak that I'm sure has a thick branch you can sit on."

"Oh my God, Hazel. Stop!" I say with a laugh.

She shrugs and gives me an innocent look. "What? I'm just saying, Amelia. That white boy's going to love taking a bite out of your chocolate skin."

My face turns an even deeper shade of red at the implication, and I feel a strange flutter of nerves in my stomach. I have big brown eyes with medium-length black hair. I'm tall with beautiful chocolate brown skin, and I know I'm pretty. However, I can't help but notice the stark differences between the white, blonde, long-haired beauties that roamed these halls and myself.

Sure, I know I'm not considered unattractive, but up against their golden locks and light eyes, I'm not so sure. Reid might not be interested in dating a black girl. I wouldn't be shocked as mixed couples aren't exactly a common sight around here, despite the changing times. The uncertainty of it all twists my stomach into knots, but I force a laugh, shrugging it off as best as I can.

Hazel's wild speculations dance around in my head, and I can't help but blush. I glance nervously around the gym, hoping none of the girls nearby have heard Hazel's teasing remark. I quickly turn my attention back to her with a frown.

"I'm not sure he'd be interested, Hazel," I finally murmur as I look at the players on the court. "We're very different."

Just then, Reid turns around, looking at the crowd of people in the gym. Our eyes meet for a split second, and my heart races. I avert my eyes so he doesn't see me blush again and try to distract myself from the nervousness that's bubbling up inside of me.

Hazel grabs my hand. "You are not different. Besides you being of the female population and him of the male population, you're just two normal people. I'll introduce you to Reid after the game."

She leans in closer to whisper in my ear. "Just so you know, you caught his eye. He's been staring at you, too."

"Really, Hazel?" I ask, my voice barely above a whisper.

Her smile widens, and she nods emphatically.

"Just remember," she says in another whisper. "You're beautiful, and he sees that too."

Her words linger in the air and help to push away some of the apprehension that was clouding my thoughts. Hazel's confidence is infectious, and for a moment, I allow myself to believe in the possibility that Reid might actually find me attractive. I feel a wave of nervous excitement wash over me. Perhaps things might not be as complicated as I thought. The game starts, and we dive back into conversation. The whole time she's talking, I can't stop thinking about Reid.

The game is a thrilling spectacle of athleticism and sheer excitement. Players sprint across the court with their shoes squeaking against the polished hardwood floor. The basketball is like a fiery comet, zipping from hand to hand, defying gravity as it arcs toward the hoop. Reid is a force to be reckoned with. His lean figure slices through the other players with elegance, and his eyes are always trained on the basket.

His every move is calculated. From his sharp passes to his powerful jumps that culminate in spectacular slam-dunks, sending the crowd into an uproar. Each swish of the net is like music to my ears, a rhythmic symphony that underscores my growing admiration for Reid. As the game progresses, my focus vacillates between the riveting game and the captivating player whose athletic prowess seems to mirror the strength and depth of his character.

The gym's fluorescent lights glint off Reid's sweaty form as he moves effortlessly on the court. The sheen of sweat that coats his skin makes him appear almost ethereal, a radiant beacon amidst the flurry of bodies. His movements are a practiced rhythm, almost like a dance. The basketball seems like an extension of his arm, moving where he wants it, when he wants it. Each shot he makes looks effortless, yet I know he must have put in countless hours of practice that lay behind every swish of the net.

Our school team is at the top of their game, the scoreboard showing a lead of ten points as the halftime buzzer sounds. The crowd roars in approval as their cheers echo off the high ceiling. All I can hear, all I can see, is Reid. His chest heaves as he catches his breath, his face aglow with satisfaction and excitement. The sight of his sweaty body and handsome face triggers an unfamiliar surge of lust within me.

"Hazel," I say as I lean toward her. "I'm going to use the restroom."

I can see that she wants to protest, to insist that I stay and watch them cheer with her for half-time, but I quickly cut her off.

"I'll be quick, promise. You go on and cheer, alright?" I tell her as I stand.

With a nod and a lingering glance at Reid, I push myself off the bleachers and head toward the restroom. As I make my way there, the basketball leaves the court to go to the boys' locker room. Amidst the group of players, Reid stands out with his tall figure cutting through the crowd. Then our eyes meet. In an instant, everything around us seems to blur into oblivion, as if the world lowered to a low hum. It's as though Reid and I are the only ones left in the vast gymnasium, caught up in a silent exchange that echoes loudly in my heart.

As we move in opposite directions, our eyes remain locked, a magnetic connection that seems to keep us tethered. I continue walking with my heart pulsating in a rhythm that matches each step Reid takes. His gaze is intense and unwavering, like a beacon guiding me through the busy gym.

Time seems to stretch, each second elongated under the weight of our shared gaze.

Our gazes stay on each other until, finally, Reid walks straight into the locker room door. The swift end to our visual connection jolts me back to reality, breaking the spell that had, for the last few moments, encapsulated us completely. The world comes rushing back in a rush of noises and colors, but the echo of that silent exchange remains, etched into my mind, as vivid as if it were still happening.

Reid steps back and winces in pain as he rubs his forehead. He looks at me again as his cheeks flush a deep crimson from embarrassment. He pushes the door to the locker room open and disappears inside, leaving me standing at the entrance to the bathroom with my heart pounding a wild rhythm in my chest. I regain my composure quickly before turning to continue through the door. Inside, I splash water on my face, trying to quell the tremors of excitement and apprehension that is fluttering within me. After a few minutes of calming my nerves, I leave the bathroom and walk back over to Hazel.

As I approach, I can see Hazel surrounded by a gaggle of cheerleaders, and their laughter echoes through the gym. She spots me, and her eyes light up with a mischievous glint in them. I brace myself for whatever she's about to say, knowing her all too well.

"Look who finally decided to join us," Hazel calls out, her voice carrying over the buzz of the crowd.

The cheerleaders shift their attention toward me, and their giggles blend into the ambient noise.

"Have a delightful walk, Amelia?" One of them asks.

I shrug and feign nonchalance. "Just needed a quick bathroom break."

Hazel's grin widens. "Oh, we all saw your 'bathroom break'," she says while making air quotes with her fingers.

"You and Reid couldn't take your eyes off each other. Reid running into the door was certainly funny."

My cheeks warm, and I force a laugh with another shrug. "Can't help it if the guy's got a knack for walking into doors."

There's a beat of silence before Hazel erupts into laughter, and the rest of the cheerleaders join in. As the laughter ripples around me, I can't help but smile. There's something between Reid and me, and everyone can see it, no matter how hard I try to say otherwise.

The second half of the game starts, and the tangible tension in the atmosphere is like a living entity. Both teams are charged with an almost animalistic fervor and are playing hard. The scoreboard reflects a neck-to-neck chase as the opposing team somehow leveled the points. The clock starts its relentless countdown, with the final two minutes ticking away. Spectators hold their breath, engrossed in the adrenaline-coated spectacle unfolding before them.

Then, suddenly, it all seems to go in slow motion for me as Reid gets the ball. His eyes scan the court before he pushes off, dribbling his way to the other end. He is a blur of motion, dodging defenders with an agility that is breathtaking. In a final burst of effort, he leaps off the ground, his long arm stretching toward the hoop as he executes a perfect layup. The ball whooshes, cleanly dropping into the net and upping our score by two crucial points.

The ball changes hands, landing in the possession of a player from the opposing team. He slips away from our players, moving with a grace that's almost envious. Dribbling around our players, he finds his shot and nails it with precision, once again tying the game. My heart pounds in my chest as the last thirty seconds of the game count down.

I squint my eyes to see one of our players, tightly guarded by the other team, as he tries to maneuver his way around them. The tension is high, the silence deafening, as he attempts to find an opening for a shot. Suddenly, he catches sight of Reid and swiftly passes the ball to him. Time seems to slow as Reid catches the ball with his eyes locked on the hoop.

With a swift, graceful jump, he releases the ball into the air. It arcs perfectly, landing effortlessly into the net, adding three more points to our score. The gymnasium erupts into cheers as the buzzer sounds, marking the end of the game and our victory.

The crowd roars in celebration, and their excitement echoes bouncing off the gymnasium walls. Overwhelmed by a surge of excitement, Hazel and I jump up and down in sheer delight. Our screams of glee blend with the uproarious clamor, creating a symphony of victory.

Almost instantly, the cheerleaders spring into action, tossing their pompoms into the air as they perform a victory cheer. Their infectious energy and harmonious chants add a sprinkle of magic to the already joyous atmosphere, amplifying the thrill of the win. Now the players line up for the traditional handshake line.

The players, still panting from their intense showdown, line up to cordially shake hands with their counterparts, acknowledging each other's commendable sportsmanship. One by one, they move across the court, each handshake sealing the end of an unforgettable game.

As the crowd filters out of the gym, the noise level gradually subsides into a steady low murmur. Hazel turns to me with a grin and her eyes sparkling with excitement.

"Wait for me here, I've got to change out of this cheer uniform," she says and, with a swift spin, darts towards the girls' locker room.

I find myself a vacant spot on the bleachers and wait for Hazel to return. My gaze instinctively drifts back to the basketball court, where Reid is surrounded by his teammates.

Their joyous chatter fills the air as they share laughter and playful jabs.

Reid stands in the center with his face flushed from the game and sweat glistening on his skin under the harsh luminescence of the gym lights. His eyes meet mine across the distance, and a soft smile graces his lips, causing my heart to flutter. Somehow, I'm able to smile back despite my nerves. Hazel returns a few minutes later, but by then, the basketball team had already retreated into the locker room.

"That game was intense," she says when she's closer. "The boys will be out soon, so we can wait here for them."

"Hazel, let's just head home. The guys are probably wiped out after the game," I say, trying to convince her there's no need to introduce me to Reid. Hazel, ever the romantic, is persistent. She shoots me a knowing grin.

"Amelia, we're not leaving until I've introduced you two. I know you. You won't say anything, and Reid, as cute as he is, doesn't seem like he's ever talked to a girl. You two need me to get the ball rolling. Trust me," she says.

I roll my eyes at her dramatic antics, but I'm unable to suppress my smile. Even though I don't share her grand vision for my dating life, I have to admit her unwavering determination is endearing. While we wait, we find ourselves wrapped up in a conversation with a few of the cheerleaders who are waiting for their boyfriends. They chat about the game's highlights, the after-party, and the latest school gossip, putting our previous discussion on hold, at least for the moment.

Suddenly, the hairs on the back of my neck stand up, and an inexplicable thrill courses through me. I turn to the source of the sensation and find myself looking at Reid and his friends as they emerge from the locker room. They're freshly showered, their hair still damp, and in a change of clothes that only accentuate their athletic build.

A hush falls over our little group as the basketball players make their way toward us. From the corner of my eye, I see Hazel's grin widen. She grabs my hand, her fingers lacing through mine in a reassuring grip, and with an excitement that's borderline childish, she drags me towards them.

As we approach the boys, Hazel greets them with enthusiasm. "Hey, Reid. Hey, Benjamin," she says with a smile.

Yet, the way she pronounces Benjamin's name is more like 'been jammin', a playful twist that has me laughing before I can contain it. The sound of my laughter, loud and genuine, echoes in the quiet gym, causing a few heads to turn our way.

A grin spreads across Reid's face at her play on his name, and his eyes twinkle with amusement while Benjamin throws back his head and joins in the laughter. As the laughter subsides, Hazel nudges me forward with a mischievous gleam in her eyes.

"Oh, by the way, Reid, this is Amelia," she says casually, as if we were just making small talk. "I figured I'd introduce you two so you can quit staring at each other."

I feel my cheeks heat with embarrassment, but there's no backing out now. Leave it to Hazel to make awkward with her straightforward approach.

"Hey, Reid. Nice to meet you," I say through my embarrassment and extend a hand toward him. "That was quite the game-winning shot you made."

He looks at me and shakes my hand, his grip firm and confident. "Thanks, Amelia. Nice to meet you, too," he replies, his voice quiet. "I was just lucky, I guess."

I can't help but smirk at his modesty. "Well, if that's what you call luck, then you must be the luckiest guy in the world."

At my flippant compliment, he did something I didn't expect - he blushed. The confident, game-winning basketball player blushed at a cheeky remark. It's such an endearing sight that I find myself laughing again, and this time, Reid joins me in the laughter.

Hazel grabs Benjamin's arm and pulls him to the side. "I have to talk to Benjamin. You two get to know each other a little better."

I shake my head at Hazel's obvious intent but decide to take her advice and talk to Reid about the game. During our conversation, I find myself lost in Reid's eyes. They're an unusual shade of green, like an emerald, with a hint of mischief lurking within them. His confident demeanor has softened, replaced by an air of humility that is downright captivating.

Then it hit finally me. I'm attracted to Reid. Not just physically, but also to his persona, his humility, and his charm, and if my intuition serves me right, there is a good chance he is too. The thought of it sends a flutter of excitement through me. I decide to take a chance and flirt with him, conveying my interest to see if he's really interested or just being nice.

"You look real nice, Reid," I say with a playful smirk on my lips.

"Uh...thank you," he stutters, as a flush creeps up his neck.

I can't help but laugh at his flustered state. It's amusing to see this confident basketball player blush at my teasing.

"You looked nice playing out there, too. It was a great game," I continue with my voice dipping low and my eyes locking onto his.

The blush on Reid's cheeks deepens, and I smile at the effect my words have on him. His disarmed, slightly embarrassed response is far more endearing than any suave comeback could have been. I lean in closer, eager to break through his shell and discover more of the boy behind the basketball star facade.

Just as Reid and I are delving deeper into our conversation, Hazel and Benjamin interrupt us, signaling that it is time to leave.

I turn my face up to look at Reid with a warm smile. "It was really nice meeting you, Reid."

He replies with a nod, his emerald eyes reflecting the same warmth. As we bid our goodbyes, the boys sauntered off, their laughter echoing in the now-empty gym.

Hazel is beaming at me as she slings her arm over my shoulder as we walk out of the gym.

"Amelia," she says, a hint of mischief in her voice. "The chemistry between you two was so hot, I was practically burning up just standing there watching you."

Her words elicit a laugh from me, and I shake my head at her dramatic description of our interaction.

"You guys are perfect for each other," she continues. She raises her hand in front of her as if visualizing a distant future. "I can see it now. I'll be the maid of honor at your wedding and the godmother to your children. Just wait and see."

Her tone is so sure, so certain, that I can't help but laugh again. She's letting her romantic side dictate my dating life, but the thought of getting to know Reid better fills me with a sense of excitement. Not the getting married and having kids part, but just genuinely getting to know him better. I'm far too young to think about that kind of stuff.

"Whoa, don't get ahead of yourself, Hazel," I tell her while laughing at her enthusiastic prediction.

We continue toward the parking lot, with the lights of the school slowly fading behind us. As we slide into the vehicle, the warmth wraps around me, a comforting contrast to the chill outside. As Hazel navigates us onto the road, the thought of Reid lingers in my mind, playing out like a reel. I find myself unable to suppress the smile that creeps onto my face, a giddy sense of elation fluttering in my chest.

Despite my teasing, Hazel's words resonate with me. The chemistry between Reid and me had been thick. It's an undeniable spark that left me both excited and nervous. I keep replaying our conversation, his laughter, his blush, his eyes locking onto mine. As Hazel turns the corner, heading toward my house, I realize that this sudden interest in Reid feels like the start of something new, something exhilarating that I've never felt before. It kind of scares me.

"IN THE ALCHEMY OF
DESIRE, YOUR GAZE
BECOMES THE POTION
THAT TRANSFORMS MY
INSIDES INTO A GARDEN OF
SENSUAL BUTTERFLIES,
EACH DELICATE WING
WHISPERING THE SECRETS
OF LONGING BENEATH THE
SURFACE OF MY SKIN."

FEELING CONNECTIONS

I'm lying in bed with my textbooks scattered all around me as I try to focus on my homework. All I can think about is Reid and our introduction from earlier tonight. It's like a movie scene stuck on replay in my mind. His voice, his smile, and his eyes...they're just lingering in my thoughts, making it impossible to concentrate on anything else.

As I think about meeting Reid, a warmth spreads through me, and my lips curve into an inescapable smile. It's like some magnetic force has lifted the corners of my mouth, and no matter how hard I try, I can't seem to suppress this spontaneous display of giddiness. The memory of our meeting stirs a delightful flutter in my heart, a sensation I can't quite place but one I wouldn't trade for anything.

With a heavy sigh, I close my algebra book with more force than necessary. My homework will just have to wait. I can't keep pretending to understand these equations when all I'm really doing is replaying that moment with Reid. A change of scenery is what I need, so I rise from my bed and head downstairs.

As I walk into our cozy little kitchen, I find Mom at the stove, her apron dusted with flour, stirring something that smells heavenly. Destiny is at her side, presumably helping but probably just sneaking tastes of what Mom is cooking. Iris is sitting at the kitchen table with her nose buried in a book. Since getting into trouble at school, there's been no TV, games, or electronics of any kind for her, though reading isn't really a punishment in my eyes.

"Hey Amelia, you've been grinning like a Cheshire cat since you came home. What's got you so chipper?" Destiny's voice pulls me from my thoughts, her teasing tone echoing around the kitchen.

"Well," Iris pipes up. "I bet it's because of a boy."

I feel my cheeks flame and my smile turning sheepish, but I can't bring myself to deny it. I hadn't realized I was still smiling. Iris's squeal bounces off the walls, filling the kitchen with a bubbly excitement.

"I knew it! Oh, I absolutely knew it!" she jumps up, her book forgotten, and her grin almost rivals my own.

"Girls, leave your sister alone," Mom chastises, but I can hear the laughter in her voice and see the amusement in her eyes.

Trying to play coy, I feign ignorance and raise an eyebrow as I reach into the refrigerator for a water bottle.

"I don't know what you're talking about," I tell them while attempting to suppress the grin spreading across my face.

I take my seat at the table, and the cool water does nothing to quell the warmth radiating from within me. Mom simply gives me that look, the one that says she knows exactly what's going on, and smiles softly.

"Amelia, honey," Mom starts, her voice filled with a motherly wisdom that I associate with moments like these. "I know my girls. I know every facial expression, every sigh, grunt, eye roll, and more. Here's a little secret. I know what they all mean, and that smile of yours? That tells me there's a boy."

The kitchen fills with laughter, the sound echoing off the walls, wrapping us in a shared joy. As much as I try to deny it, there's no fooling a mother's intuition. With a sigh, I finally give them the answer they're looking for.

"Okay, I did talk to a boy today," I confess, barely above a whisper. "His name is Reid, but we're just friends, nothing more. I literally met him today, and he's nice."

"Nice and cute, I bet," Destiny replies.

"Stop, D," I tell her as I put my face in my hands, shielding my embarrassment from her teasing.

Mom simply quirks an eyebrow at my rushed explanation. "I call bullshit, Amelia," she says, her voice soft but firm, her eyes never leaving mine. "You don't smile like that unless you really like someone."

Mom always knows more about us than we know about ourselves, and it makes it hard to get anything past her. I remain silent, surprised by her astute observation. I'm still trying to process these intense feelings that have suddenly come to life within me and I struggle to find the right words to explain them, mainly because I don't understand them myself.

Yes, I like Reid. However, I've never felt such intense attraction for a boy before, not that I have much experience in the first place, but Reid is different. Mom turns to me fully, places her wooden spoon down, and wipes her hands on her apron before offering me a small smile.

"Amelia, sweetheart, you don't need to explain anything to us," she says, her voice soothing the chaotic thoughts racing through my mind. "If you say you are friends with this boy, then fine. Friends it is."

She pauses for a moment, her gaze piercing mine with an

intensity that only my mother can muster. Then she gives me the mom look, that stern yet caring expression that brooks no argument.

"This is important, and I want you to remember because I remember being young, and I know how you young kids are," she begins, her voice firm. "Whatever type of friend he may be, he's not tappin' it unless he's wrappin' it, understood?"

Her words echo in the now silent kitchen, her motherly caution wrapped in love and peppered with humor.

"Mom!" I shriek with embarrassment.

"What?" she asks. "I'm giving my motherly advice. I know kids your age have sex and I'd be stupid to believe they're not. Whether you are or not isn't really my concern. It's educating you. If you are, protect yourself. If not, then fine."

I can only nod as a soft blush heats my cheeks as the weight of her words sinks in. That is not something I was thinking about. The kitchen erupts into laughter at Mom's blunt yet heartfelt advice.

I can't help but join in, despite the heat in my cheeks. The laughter soon fades into the comforting hum of our nightly routine. A rich aroma fills the room as Mom announces that dinner is ready. Iris and I gather a few plates and silverware to set the table while Destiny helps Mom with the food. We sit around the table, each of us contributing to the flow of conversation as we eat.

The food is as delicious as always. The warmth of the food, the comfort of my family's company, it all serves to soothe the whirlwind of emotions that had been stirring within me. After dinner, I cleared the dishes and bid everyone goodnight. As I retreat to the sanctuary of my room, I can't help but wear a contented smile.

As the week trickles down to its last days, the air at school is still charged with anticipation and excitement. The boys' basketball game was undoubtedly a thrilling event, but everyone knows it was just the prelude to the main event. I can feel the collective heartbeat of the school pulsating in rhythm with the upcoming homecoming football game, and after the game is the homecoming dance.

I step into my first period and navigate past the familiar desks, heading straight to my seat near the front. As I settle down, an unwelcome voice disturbs my bliss. Lawrence, every bit as irritating as he is arrogant, strides past me, muttering "bitch" under his breath. I'm quick to react, my middle finger shooting up in a silent retort. But before I can savor the moment, I freeze. My gaze strays past Lawrence to land on a sight that makes my heart skip a beat.

Reid's at the back of the room, sitting at a table alone. He's looking right at me, his eyes twinkling with a familiar warmth. He catches me looking at him, and I'm rewarded with a smile that makes my insides turn to jelly. My cheeks flush, and I can't help the silly grin that spreads across my face. Despite Lawrence's nasty comment, the sight of Reid and his smile made my day start off on the right foot.

Gathering my things, I rise from my seat with my heart pounding like a drum against my ribcage. With each step I take toward the back of the room, my anxiety rises, but there's a magnetic pull that I can't resist, a force that's drawing me to Reid. I stop at his table and take a deep breath as I must up my courage.

"Hey, Reid. Can I sit with you?"

His eyes meet mine, and a soft smile dances on his lips. "Hey, Amelia. Sure, you can sit with me."

The butterflies in my stomach take flight at his simple affirmation, but I keep my smile steady. Carefully, I set my things down and take the seat opposite him, my heart dancing with a silent victory. His gaze stays on me the entire time, almost like he can't take his eyes off me if he tries.

"So, Reid," I say to break up the awkward air around us. "How was your morning?"

He hums in response, a thoughtful expression coloring his face.

"Pretty good, actually," he replies, his eyes meeting mine. "Got a workout in before school, so that's a plus."

"That sounds great," I tell him with a smile. "I can barely drag myself out of bed in the morning. Can't imagine going for a workout."

My words elicit a chuckle from him, and I can't help but bask in the glow of his laughter.

"Well, it's not for everyone," he admits, a playful smirk pulling at the corners of his lips. "Some of us are just morning people."

His laughter is infectious, and it's not long before I'm joining in. The conversation flows more easily from there, the initial awkwardness fading into a comfortable familiarity. We move to the topic of classes, and I am surprised we haven't spoken before now.

"I... um, I didn't realize we were in the same class, to be honest," I confess, fumbling with the zipper on my bag to avoid his gaze. "I was... ah... too focused on trying to create art without making a colossal mess."

As the words leave my lips, I feel my cheeks heating involuntarily. I risk a glance up at Reid, only to find him watching me intently. His gaze is so intense, so focused. It's as if he's hanging on my every word. Blushing even more, I quickly look back down, my heart pounding wildly in my chest. Reid's eyes flicker to mine, his lips parting as he speaks.

"You're beautiful," he blurts out before a blush rapidly colors his face, and he hurriedly corrects himself. "I mean... your art... it's beautiful."

His deep red blush matches my own, and I can't help but feel a rush of warmth spread through me. His unintended slip, followed by his adorable embarrassment, leaves me momentarily speechless. I don't acknowledge his slip and continue the conversation. I don't want him to feel more embarrassed. As Reid and I continue our timid, yet increasingly comfortable conversation, I find out that he's enrolled in a couple of the same classes as me.

"Wait, you're in my sixth period, too?" I question, disbelief clear in my voice.

The surprise of this revelation creates a bubble of excitement in my chest.

"Yeah, I guess so," he chuckles, a shy smile playing on his lips.

The idea of sharing more classes with Reid fills me with an unexpected delight. It's a pleasant coincidence that seems to wrap us together, both in the quiet stirrings of the morning and the soft glow of the afternoon. Our conversation is interrupted by the entrance of our teacher,

"Alright, everyone, let's get started," she announces, her voice echoing through the room. Class begins, and I can't help but glance at Reid one last time with a smile tugging at the corners of my lips.

As I sat here, desperately attempting to mold the lump of clay into something remotely human, I can't help but sneak peeks at Reid. His own project isn't exactly a masterpiece, but at least you can tell it's supposed to be a face. Mine, on the other hand, bears a striking resemblance to a mashed potato sculpture, comically misshaped and devoid of any discernible features. I catch Reid glancing at me from time to time, and I wonder what he's thinking.

I can't focus on the clay in my hands, as I'm too attuned to Reid, and before I know it, Ms. Clark tells us to clean up. Reid and I put our sculpture in the back to dry and clean our table. Just as we're finished, the bell rings, and Ms. Clark tells everyone to have a great day. Reid clears his throat and breaks the stillness.

"I should probably get going," he says. "I'll see you in our next class."

I nod my head and follow him out of the class. I see Hazel perched by the door, waiting for me. She grabs my hand and drags me down the hallway through the masses of students hustling to their next period.

"This is not the way to my next class, Hazel," I tell her, wondering where the hell we're going.

"I know," she calls over her shoulder. "We're headed to the committee room. I have to finalize the results for the Homecoming court and the details for the dance. It's Wednesday, and the game and dance are on Saturday. We don't have much time to make sure everything is perfect."

"Um, okay, I get that, but what the hell does that have to do with me?" I ask her in confusion. "I'm not part of any of that."

Hazel stops and looks at me. "You're a part of it today. I need your opinion on everything. Come on, Amelia. It gets you out of Mr. Jones's boring ass class."

"Well, I don't want to hear that damn horn blaring every ten minutes, so count me in," I tell her with a laugh.

I follow her through the bustling hallways until we find our way to the committee room. The rest of the student committee is there, and they're talking in excitement about upcoming festivities. I am out of my element, as this has never been my thing. Hazel's always the one who takes part in facilitating fun activities for the students. With a mix of nervousness and eagerness, I take a seat at the table with Hazel to finalize the event.

"What is the slut doing here?" Jada says after we take seats. "She's not on the committee."

I hadn't realized she was on the committee. I can't stand

her, and I try to keep my distance, not because she scares me but because I don't want to deal with her drama.

"I asked her here," Hazel replies before I can. "If you call her a slut one more time, I'm going to beat your damn face in."

Everyone promptly ignores Jada and starts discussing homecoming. Everyone delves into the setup for the homecoming court reveal, carefully planning the perfect moment during the halftime break of the game. I give my input here and there, though I think it's going to look great. During the finalizing, a wave of laughter ripples through the room as we look over the names of the homecoming king, queen, prince, and princess. It's as if we all knew deep down who the winners would be.

With the reveal settled, we transition to the final stages of planning the dance, from the colors, vibrant ribbons, and balloons, to the vendors who will bring their vision to life, ensuring every detail is perfect. Every time Jada offers her input, everyone ignores her. I can tell she's getting frustrated, but separates herself with her snarky attitude.

"Alright, I think that's it," Hazel says when they finish. "I'm going to take this to Ms. Riley for approval."

Jada sits up in anger. "Wait a damn minute. You guys didn't listen to a word I said. What about my opinion? How does Amelia get input, and she's not even on the committee?"

I notice she doesn't call me a slut again, but I continue to ignore her presence.

"Nobody wanted you on this committee, Jada," one girl answers. "You didn't help this entire time, and you want to show up and tell us what to change? You don't get an input."

Everyone gathers their things to head to our next period. With the plans solidified and their collective approval in hand, Hazel and I stride confidently toward the teacher responsible for overseeing the committee.

The rest of the day whizzes past in a blur, the buzz of classes and hallway chatter fading into the background. As the final bell rings, I make my way to the locker rooms to change for volleyball practice. The adrenaline kicks in as I lace up my sneakers, my mind already on the court and the thrill of the game.

Stepping back out onto the worn hardwood, however, something seems off. Active 1: The boys from the basketball team have filled the usually deserted bleachers during our practices. Puzzled, I move over to one of my teammates, Jenny, who's tying her shoelaces.

"Hey, Jenny," I ask, nodding towards the bleachers. "Any idea why the boys are here?"

Jenny glances over towards the boys and shrugs, her attention more on her tangled shoelaces than my question.

"Their team is waiting for us to finish up in the gym," she explains, finally securing her shoelaces into a neat bow. "They have a practice scrimmage scheduled here before their next game."

"Ah, got it," I say, a smile playing on my lips.

It looks like our practice session just got an unexpected audience. Practice starts with a few warmups before the Coach has us play against each other to practice new plays. With every pound of my heart, every bead of sweat trickling down my face, every gasp of air I draw, it's not just the exertion of the game I'm feeling but the pulsating awareness of Reid sitting in the bleachers.

The thump of the volleyball against the court resonates within me, amplified by the knowledge of his gaze on me. Each time I leap to strike the ball, I imagine his eyes following my movements, and it sets my skin aflame, a hot, thrilling sensation that sends shivers down my spine. It's as if his gaze has the power to penetrate the layers of my jersey, reach my heated, sweat-slicked skin, and stir within me a pool of feelings I've never known.

There's a sweet ache in my muscles and an intoxicating thrill in my veins. Every glance in his direction, every fleeting contact with his gaze, is like a spark, igniting within me feelings I've never dared to explore before. His presence, rather than distracting me, fuels my energy and my desire to push harder and play better.

The room shrinks until it's just the two of us. Me on the court and Reid in the bleachers. His gaze is the invisible thread linking us, pulling me toward him with a force that's almost magnetic. The intensity of these emotions scares me, yet I crave it, this sweet torment of wanting and being wanted.

As I catch my breath, I steal another glance at Reid and find him looking right back at me, a soft smile playing on his lips. The look in his eyes is enough to have me soaring despite the fatigue gnawing at my limbs. The piercing sound of the coach's whistle slices through the air, marking the end of our rigorous practice. I gather my things and head to the locker room with my body drenched in sweat.

Without wasting any more time, I hit the showers, letting the lukewarm water wash over me and soothe my sore muscles. I change into my clothes and sling my bag over my shoulder.

As I step back into the gym, the boys have already taken our place on the court, their practice in full swing. I can't help but look for Reid, and my gaze finally lands on him. He's dribbling the ball effortlessly, his focus on the hoop ahead, but then he suddenly stills. He looks over, our eyes locking for a brief moment, and my heart skips a beat.

Reid lifts his hand and mouths a 'bye' to me, his smile reaching his eyes. I can't help but return his gesture, my lips curving into a soft smile as I wave back at him. His smile deepens, and I swear my heart flutters in response.

With Reid's goodbye still resonating in my thoughts, I step out of the gym, the cool evening air kissing my skin. As I make my way home, I feel as though I'm walking on air with my heart light and my spirits high. The day had been a whirlwind of emotions, but the sweet thought of Reid and his warm farewell left me with a fluttery feeling in my stomach.

"In the gallery of my heart, I've

painted a masterpiece of strong liking

for you, but the brush of hesitation

keeps me from adding the strokes of

romance, leaving the canvas

suspended in the beautiful agony of

unspoken feelings."

In the days that follow, I can't help but notice Reid more at school. We exchange friendly glances in the hallways, and our paths often cross between classes. I linger a little longer when our eyes meet, even if it's just for a fleeting moment.

We find ourselves engaged in small talk during our shared classes, discussing our teachers and classmates, and getting to know each other better. Our conversations become more frequent as we get comfortable with each other. I'm realizing how much we have in common, despite running in different social circles. Even though I'm the vivacious volleyball player and Reid is the reserved basketball player, we seem to mesh pretty well.

Our shared academic interests and growing friendship draw us closer. We walk to our lockers together, chatting about our previous class. Though we still move in different circles, we have a common ground that keeps us connected: Hazel and Benjamin. As Reid and I walk toward our lockers, he clears his throat.

"Amelia, can I maybe...um...get your phone number?" he asks.

There's a hopeful yet nervous look in his eyes, the kind that holds the weight of anticipation. The usual confidence in my stride falters for a moment, replaced by a fluttering sensation in my stomach. I turn to him, attempting to maintain my playful exterior.

"What, want to discuss chemistry equations at ungodly hours?" I say jokingly.

As I scribble my number on a stray piece of paper, I can feel my heart thumping in my chest. I hand it over, and our fingers brush briefly. The contact sends a small spark of electricity through me, leaving a blush creeping up my cheeks. His fingers close around the paper, and a look of what I can only describe as exhilaration and nervousness cross his features.

"Something like that," he says as he slips the paper into his pocket with a shy grin.

As Reid gazes at me, his blazing green eyes seem to glow with an intensity that makes my heart flutter. They're the most beautiful eyes I have ever seen, a mesmerizing blend of emerald and forest hues that seem to pierce my soul. Then, he gives me that small smirk, the one I adore so much. It's gentle and playful, a beautiful contradiction to the intensity of his gaze. It's a smirk that holds a myriad of unsaid words and unexpressed feelings, making me curious and nervous all at once.

I feel a warmth spread through me as I watch him, a sense of happiness that is inexplicably tied to that smirk. Then, just as quickly as it had appeared, the moment was gone. He turns around and walks away, leaving me standing there, heart pounding, as I watch his retreating figure.

It's finally Friday, not just any Friday, but the day of the annual football homecoming game. Still lost in my own thoughts, I'm startled as Hazel bounds up to me in the hallway.

"Amelia," she says, out of breath from her sprint across the hall, "Stop gazing after him like you'll never see him again."

I can't help but laugh at her dramatics. She has this uncanny ability to read my mind, or at least accurately guess my thoughts.

"Well, Hazel," I say, trying to seem nonchalant but failing miserably as a giggle escaped my lips. "I gave him my phone number."

Her eyes widen for a moment before a broad grin spreads across her face. Hazel claps her hands in delight, her blonde curls bouncing with her enthusiasm.

"Final-fucking-ly!" she shrieks. "You two have been dancing around each other for days."

Before I can reply, she quickly changes the subject. "So, about the homecoming game tonight..."

I sigh, knowing perfectly well where this is going. Hazel loves football games. I, on the other hand, prefer the peace and quiet of my bedroom.

"Hmm, I don't know, Hazel," I tell her. "I'm not really into all the hype around the homecoming or the game. I already went to the basketball game, isn't that enough?"

"Admit it. You loved it, and you met Reid. It's not just about the game," Hazel says with her eyes sparkling with excitement. "Think about it. The energy, the unity, the tradition... it's like the heartbeat of our school year."

I shrug, still unconvinced to go. "I just don't see the appeal. A bunch of people running around after a ball."

"That's a simplistic way of seeing it," she responds, sounding slightly exasperated. "It's about school spirit, camaraderie, community. It's about being part of something bigger than yourself."

"Ugh, alright. I'll go if you stop talking like one of the teachers," I say with a laugh. "No need to give me damn a speech about school spirit."

Hazel squeals in excitement, hugging me tight before rushing off to cheerleading practice before the game. I head home to change clothes and prepare for Hazel's overzealous spirit surrounding the game.

As the sun sets, casting a warm orange glow over the field, I head to the bleachers. The stadium buzzes with excitement and energy as students, parents, and alumni fill the stands. Searching the crowd for Hazel, I spot Reid sitting with his friends, laughing and enjoying the atmosphere. Our eyes lock for a fleeting moment, and I feel that familiar tingling surge through my body at the intensity of his gaze.

As the cheering crowd roars in my ears, every cell in my body yearns to go over and join Reid. Instead, I redirect my feet toward Hazel, who's motioning frantically from the top of the bleachers. The homecoming game starts, but my mind is elsewhere, my eyes constantly darting over to where Reid sits. I'm so engrossed in my thoughts, I don't even realize when our team scores a touchdown.

The blare of the halftime whistle pierces the air, signifying the pause in the game. Hazel turns to me, her eyes twinkling with excitement.

"I'll be right back," she promises before darting off into the swell of cheerleaders preparing for their performance.

Spotlights illuminate the field as the cheerleaders kick off the halftime show, their perfectly rehearsed moves a whirl of school colors under the bright stadium lights. The energy of the crowd is infectious, washing over me in waves of cheers and applause. As the cheerleading routine ends, Hazel steps up to the microphone to introduce this year's homecoming court.

"Ladies and gentlemen," she announces, her voice echoing around the stadium, "It's time to meet your homecoming king, queen, prince, and princess!"

The crowd's excitement is palpable as Benjamin, our homecoming king, steps into the spotlight. His contagious laughter rings out as he playfully performs an exaggerated, regal wave, eliciting a roar of laughter from the crowd. It's impossible not to get caught up in it, and I chuckle along.

Hazel continues with the introductions, the cheers from the crowd growing with each name. I must admit, it's a sight to behold, and I wish I'd gone to the games before my senior year. The cheerleaders rally one last time, their voices harmonizing into a spirited cheer that echoes across the field. The crowd joins in, their voices blending into a symphony of school spirit.

As the cheerleaders finish, the players reclaim the field, ready to kick off the second half. My gaze strays to Reid to find him looking at me. I'm so wrapped up in his eyes that everything fades away. As the final whistle blows, indicating our victory, I'm jolted back to reality. The crowd around me erupts into a frenzy of cheers and applause. I look back to Reid, and his green eyes look right back at me, and he has that iconic smirk on his face.

I find Hazel, and we leave the frenzied crowd behind and make our way toward the school for the dance. The moment we step in, a wave of soft music and subdued laughter washes over us. The school gym is now adorned with strings of fairy lights that cast a soft, ethereal glow on everything. Large strips of midnight blue and gold fabric drape elegantly from the ceiling, giving the impression of a star-studded night sky indoors.

Clusters of balloons in our school colors float around the room, bobbing gently in rhythm with the music. The dance floor, normally just varnished wood, shimmers under the magical array of lights, inviting all to dance and celebrate. Tables adorned with blue tablecloths and glowing centerpieces line the sides, offering delightful goodies and punch for the students.

Everything is breathtaking, but the most alluring sight of all is the giant, moon-shaped disco ball hanging right in the center. It casts a mesmerizing constellation of lights that dance around the room, adding a touch of magic to the romantic setting.

Students smile as the DJ plays an upbeat song, setting the tone for the night. The transformation amazes me as I see the students dancing to the rhythm, their faces beaming with joy and anticipation. The energy in the room is contagious, and I find myself swept up in it as well.

Hazel and I are in the middle of an energetic song, our laughter mingling with the music, when she suddenly stops and grabs my arm. Her grip is firm, her eyes wide as she glances over my shoulder.

"Amelia," she says, her voice barely audible over the pounding beat of the music. "Your white knight has finally arrived."

Her words send a jolt of anticipation through me. I turn around, and there he is. Reid, standing at the entrance of the gym, looks more handsome than ever. His gaze meets mine across the room, and for a moment, everything else seems to fade into the background. The music, the laughter, and the swirling lights. It's just him and me, our eyes locked in a silent conversation.

I watch as a group of girls slowly gather around Reid, Benjamin, and their friends, their interest in them palpable in the air. Giggles break out intermittently, punctuated by the boys' hearty laughter. For a moment, I feel a pang of something I can't quite put into words. But then, I make a conscious decision not to let it bother me.

Taking a deep breath, I muster up the courage to navigate through the maze of our classmates. Each step feels both electrifying and daunting as I move closer to Reid. As I approach, his conversation with friends falls to a hush, and all eyes turn to me. My heart pounds in my chest as I hold his gaze, hoping my nervousness isn't as transparent as I felt it to be.

"Reid," I start, trying to steady my voice. "Would you like to dance?"

The room seems to hold its breath as he studies me, his expression unreadable. He glances at his friends nervously before looking back at me. After what feels like an eternity, the corners of his mouth finally lift into a small smile.

"Um..sure," he replies in a voice barely above a whisper yet somehow reaching me clear as day. Relief washes over me, replacing the nervous anticipation that had built up. Without another word, I grab his hand, interlacing our fingers, and pull him into the pulsating crowd of students on the dance floor. The music envelopes us, the rhythm acting as our guide as we move to the beat, every step bringing us closer than we'd ever been.

Dancing with Reid is a dream come true. I can't help but smile as we sway to the steady rhythm of the music. His cheeks turn a deep shade of red as he tries to find the rhythm of the music. He moves with an endearing awkwardness, like he's not sure what to do with his hands.

I giggle at his bashfulness, which makes him blush deeper in response. At that moment, among the swirling lights and the pulsating music, everything else fades away. It's just Reid, me, and the rhythm of our hearts echoing the melody of the night.

As we dance, I see Hazel sauntering over with Benjamin close behind her, and I can't suppress a smile. I know she's coming over to make our dance even more awkward than it already is.

"Come on, Reid, show us your moves," she teases, turning

her playful gaze towards Reid.

The challenge seems to take him by surprise, and he glances at me nervously, his cheeks flushing a deeper shade of red. The sight is adorable. It's funny to think that Reid, in all his bashfulness, has no idea of the charm he exudes. He's so unaware of how his shyness only adds to his appeal, making him even more irresistibly sexy.

I gaze at him, an amused smile playing on my lips. He is the quintessential boy next door, yet there's something so captivating about him, something that just draws you in. The irony is not lost on me. Reid, my endearingly awkward dance partner, is the heartthrob of our homecoming night, and he doesn't even know it.

As the song shifts to a slow tempo, Reid and I instinctively move closer. There's an intimacy in our shared silence, the rhythm of the music dictating our movements. His hands gently rest on my waist, causing a flurry of butterflies in my stomach. I raise my eyes to meet his, and what I see takes my breath away. His usual playful spark is replaced with a serious intensity I have not seen before. It's as if he's seeing me, truly seeing me, for the first time.

His fingers trace small patterns on my back, his touch light but electric. It sends a shiver down my spine, and I inhale deeply at the sensation. His gaze never leaves mine, the depth in his eyes pulling me closer. The energy between us is a magnetic force that leaves us both helpless.

The room around us fades into a blur as Reid gently sways me to the rhythm of the music. He pauses, his green eyes locking onto mine, and his lips part slightly as if he wants to say something but can't find the words. The connection between us is undeniable, and it seems neither of us knows how to navigate this territory. Neither of us knows how to put into words what we're feeling. As we sway to the slow beat of the song, I lay my head on his shoulder, content to be in his arms.

"AS HALLOWEEN MASKS OUR FACES, MAY IT UNMASK THE COURAGE WITHIN US, ALLOWING US TO STEP OUT FROM BEHIND THE FAÇADE AND PURSUE THE DESIRES THAT LURK IN THE SHADOWS OF OUR HEARTS."

HALLOWEEN

Since homecoming, the connection between Reid and me has grown exponentially. We find ourselves immersed in late-night conversations and texts ping back and forth between us throughout the day. Our interactions become increasingly meaningful, and the spark of attraction between us grows stronger with each passing day. In European History, we shared notes, exchange whispers, and occasionally engage in playful banter. In chemistry class with Mrs. Ramirez, we partnered for experiments.

As the weekend rolls around, Hazel and I find ourselves sprawled across her bed, phones in hand, as we relax for the afternoon. The occasional giggle or gasp punctuates the silence in the room as we individually uncover the latest gossip through our screens. Suddenly, an unexpected shriek from Hazel jolts me out of my latest text.

"What's going on?" I ask, curiosity piqued.

With a wide grin, Hazel thrusts her phone in my direction. On her screen is an invitation to David's, one of our schoolmates, Halloween party tonight. Hazel turns to me, her eyes glittering with mischief.

"We're totally going!" she declares.

I look at Hazel, my eyebrows furrowing in disbelief. "Wait, Hazel, I don't even have a costume, and I'm really not in the mood for a party."

Hazel simply laughs, shaking her head at my reservations. "Oh, come on, Amelia!" she says. "You need to get out and have some fun. Besides, it's Halloween, and we can't miss out."

"Don't worry about the costume. We're heading to Halloween Depot right now. There's bound to be something left that we can jazz up for the night," she adds when she still sees the frown on my face.

After a couple of beats, I let out a sigh, resigning myself to the inevitable.

"Fine," I concede, pointing a finger at Hazel. "But if they don't have a costume that I'm willing to wear, I am not going."

Hazel rolls her eyes at my stipulation, her lips curving into a confident smirk.

"Oh, Amelia, you'll find something," she assures me, her voice brimming with certainty. "Even if I have to piece shit together myself."

Grabbing our jackets, we make our way out the door to head to Halloween Depot. As we step into the store, the first thing that hits me is the bustling activity that fills the store. It's swarming with last-minute shoppers, all rummaging through racks and boxes in desperate search of a perfect fright-night look. The line at the checkout counter is a winding serpent, twisting its way around the aisles. I glance at Hazel apprehensively, doubt gnawing at my confidence.

"Are you sure we'll find something decent here?" I ask, my voice barely audible over the noise.

Without waiting for her response, we plunge into the crowd, our eyes scanning the sea of costumes. We wander from aisle to aisle, scrutinizing the array of outfits. Hazel dives into the chaos with a gusto I can't help but admire, her eyes lighting up as she pulls costumes off the racks. She flits from one side to another, dancing around the other customers, her movements fluid and purposeful. I follow her, weaving through the crowd as I try to keep up with her relentless energy.

Suddenly, Hazel halts, her eyes wide with excitement. She spins around to face me, her arms loaded with an array of costumes. With a mischievous wiggle of her eyebrows, she thrusts the outfits towards me.

"Look at these!" she says, barely containing her excitement.

She shakes a brightly colored ensemble, complete with a cape and a mask. "How about a superhero? Or," she continues, holding up a black pointed hat and a flowy black dress. "You could cast some spells as a witch."

Hazel's eyes sparkle with mischief as she shuffles the costumes, revealing a pale, high-collared dress with a set of fangs. "Or perhaps you'd prefer to be a blood-sucking vampire?"

I pick up each costume she hands me, rolling my eyes at her over-the-top acting, but I can't help the laugh that escapes my lips. Just as I'm about to comment, Hazel holds up one last costume, a fitted white dress with a matching nurse's cap.

Hazel wiggles her eyebrows again, a devilish grin on her face. "Or, my personal favorite," she says, holding the costume against me. "A sexy nurse?"

I can't help but burst out laughing at the absurdity of it all, shaking my head at my ever-dramatic friend.

Still giggling, I manage to respond through my laughter. "Hazel, those are terrible costumes."

I shake my head, placing the nurse costume back in her

hands. We continue our search, sorting through piles of pirate hats, fairy wings, and zombie masks, until my eyes land on an elegant white dress adorned with golden accents and an elaborate headpiece. I feel a sudden surge of excitement as I pick it up.

"What about this?" I ask, holding up the costume to Hazel.

She squints at it for a second, then her eyes light up with recognition. "Amelia, that's perfect! You'll be Cleopatra. That dress will look great against your skin tone."

Her own search ends when she stumbles upon a flowy white toga-style dress, complete with a gold leaf headband. Hazel holds it against her body, spinning around to model it.

"I think I've found my costume," she announces, her eyes sparkling. "I'll go as a Greek goddess."

As we head to the checkout, costumes in hand, I can't help but feel a bubble of anticipation for the party. After checking out, we head back to Hazel's. As we step through the front door, her parents greet us with their warm smiles.

"Well, don't you two look excited? Big plans for tonight?" Hazel's dad asks, his eyes twinkling with amusement.

We nod, grinning, as Hazel holds up our bags triumphantly.

"Off to a Halloween party at David's," she explains, her voice laced with an infectious excitement.

Her mom's eyes light up at the mention of the party, and she wishes us a fun night ahead. With that, we scamper off to Hazel's room. Hazel plops onto her bed, fluffing up the pillows and patting the space beside her in invitation. I kick off my shoes and join her, sinking into the soft duvet. With a click of a button, the TV flickers to life, and we find ourselves engrossed in a new TV show.

As we watch, our laughter fills the room, mingling with the faint aroma of cookies wafting up from the kitchen. As the hours slip by, we finish one last episode before it's time to get ready for the party. We gingerly pick up our costumes; the soft fabric runs through my fingers as I change into the elegant white and gold ensemble. Hazel, on the other hand, slips effortlessly into her white toga, the golden headband crowning her long locks like a halo.

The transformation doesn't end there. Hazel, with a twinkle in her eye and an uncanny knack for cosmetics, takes control of our makeup. Her fingers dance over our faces, applying foundation, a dash of blush, a sweep of eyeshadow, the perfect winged liner, and a touch of lipstick. Luckily, I have makeup with me, and she works wonders on my face. As we gaze at our reflections, it's hard not to be awestruck by the stunning girls staring back at us.

"Reid is going to lose his shit when he sees you, Amelia," Hazel teases.

At the mention of Reid, my heart flutters and a blush creeps into my cheeks. Reid and I have been texting throughout the day. I know he's coming to the party too, Benjamin convinced him. I can't help but feel eager at the prospect of seeing him, of discovering what costume he has chosen.

With one last glance at the mirror, we pick up our bags and head downstairs. Hazel's parents, sitting in the living room, look up as we approach. Hazel's mom lets out a gasp of surprise, her eyes wide.

"Oh, you girls look stunning!" she says.

Her dad grins, nodding in agreement. "You sure do. Have fun, ladies, and remember to be careful," he adds.

We assure them we will, waving goodbye as we step out into the crisp autumn evening. The drive to the party is filled with laughter and anticipation. When we arrive, we're greeted by a lot of laughter and music. As we step inside, our eyes are immediately drawn to the array of costumes our friends have chosen. I spot Tom, who's normally quiet and reserved, transformed into a bright pink flamingo, complete with a beak and feathers. The sight is so comically absurd that Hazel and I can't help but burst into laughter.

Across the room, we see David, the host, has opted for a walking, talking sandwich costume, complete with a side of fries. His girlfriend, Chloe, is dressed as a bottle of ketchup. Their costumes are so unexpected and hilarious that we double over with laughter. The room is filled with other equally ridiculous outfits.

There's a guy dressed as a banana, a girl draped in a shower curtain - complete with a rubber duckie cap, and we even spot a couple dressed as a pair of dice. The atmosphere is jovial, and everyone's spirits are high. The sight of our friends letting loose and getting into the spirit of Halloween is infectious, and Hazel and I are giggling even before we join the throng of party-goers.

A little while into the party, an inexplicable sensation prickles over my skin, a feeling I recognize as Reid's presence. I don't know when or how I became so attuned to him, but it's as if there's an invisible thread drawing me towards him. I scan the crowd, my eyes wandering over the sea of costume-clad party-goers until they meet his across the room.

Reid is already looking at me, his gaze steady and unblinking. There's an intensity in his eyes that sends my heart racing. His lips curl up in a slow, appreciative smile, and the look he gives me leaves no room for doubt - he likes what he sees. My heart flutters with a mix of anxiety and anticipation.

Before I even have the chance to react to Reid's gaze, he makes his way over to us, with Benjamin in tow. I tear my eyes away from Reid's to see Hazel's eyes light up like fireworks when she spots Benjamin. A beaming grin stretches across her face, and she goes to meet them halfway, pulling me along with her.

"Oh wow, you guys look amazing," she tells them while looking them up and down. "Benjamin, your costume is great."

I follow her gaze, looking at Benjamin. He has transformed into a convincing Superman, right down to the curly lock of hair falling onto his forehead. His costume is a perfect fit, the blue and red suit accentuating his athletic build, with the iconic 'S' logo emblazoned on his chest.

"I could say the same about you," Benjamin replies, gesturing towards her outfit with a grin. "You make a pretty cute Greek goddess, Hazel."

Our attention then shifts to Reid. He's dressed as a pirate, complete with a black tricorne hat, a white ruffled shirt, a long crimson coat adorned with gold trimmings, and even an eyepatch. The costume fit him well, showcasing his tall, lean figure and giving him an air of danger and mystery.

"Reid, you make a convincing pirate," Hazel adds, trying to stifle her laughter. "I half expect you to start talking like Jack Sparrow any minute now."

Reid chuckles, adjusting his eyepatch with a playful smirk. "It was all I could find last minute."

The party is in full swing and the air filled with chatter, laughter, and the rhythmic pulse of music. Reid and I move almost instinctively towards the dance floor, drawn into the swirl of bodies moving to the beat. We fall into the rhythm as our bodies move fluidly and in sync with the music and each other.

There's an intense chemistry tugging at us, an electrical charge that dances in the air. His hand on my waist feels warm, and I feel powerful feelings for him in a way I've never experienced before. His gaze is captivating, almost hypnotic. All my senses seem heightened around him - the lingering scent of his cologne, the gentle pressure of his hand guiding me across the dance floor, the sound of his soft laughter in my ear.

As the night wears on, we find ourselves tucked away in a quiet corner, our fingers entwined. His thumb gently caresses mine, sending a shiver down my spine. Suddenly, a slow, sensual song plays, and the dance floor around us empties a little. Reid's gaze softens, and he guides me closer still, so our bodies are almost touching. The world seems to shrink around us until it's just Reid and me in the glow of the twinkle lights.

Our other hands rest on each other's waists, pulling each other closer. His eyes never leave mine, creating an intimate silence that feels like a shared secret. I rest my head on his chest, surrendering to the rhythm of the music and the beating of his heart. I close my eyes, letting the moment wash over me, the spark between us undeniable and over-whelming.

The rhythm of the music matches the pounding of my heart, and his soft, steady breathing against my ear sends shivers down my spine. I feel his fingers lightly tracing patterns on my back, his touch sending waves of warmth coursing through me. He leans in, his breath tickling my ear.

"I've never met anyone like you, Amelia," he whispers.

His words spark a flurry of butterflies in my stomach, and I can't help the smile that plays on my lips. I look up at him, drawn in by the intensity in his eyes. The gentle pressure of his hand on my back pulls me even closer, and my heart skips a beat. It's then that I realize this is not just an in-like moment, it's the beginning of something beautiful and terri-fyingly profound.

"Amelia," he whispers again, his voice quiet but filled with an intensity that sends my heart racing, "I can't explain it, but I feel this pull towards you that's hard to ignore."

I can't help but smile, and I squeeze his hand lightly. "I know exactly what you mean. Is it weird?"

"It doesn't feel weird to me," he responds. "It feels...nice."

I lay my head back on his shoulder. "I think it feels nice, too."

As the night winds down, it's clear that we're on the brink of something special. The connection, the chemistry, the shared laughter, and the moments of quiet intimacy have all contributed to creating a bond that feels both exciting and terrifying in its intensity.

He pulls me closer, our bodies swaying in time with the music. We stare at each other, trying to convey the feelings we're feeling. His eyes never leave mine. I can't tear my gaze away from his, lost in the warmth and intensity they radiate. I can feel the heat rush to my cheeks, my heart pounding in my chest.

The world around us blurs into the background, leaving only the two of us. It feels like we've created our own little bubble, a world where it's just Reid and me. The connection between us strengthens with each touch, each look, and each smile. Whatever this is between Reid and me is something neither of us can seem to ignore. As I gaze into his blazing green eyes, I realize that my feelings for Reid are growing, and it scares me.

"In the garden of desire, our hearts bloom like delicate flowers in the moonlight, each petal unfolding in the tender dance of a budding romance, where the language is written in whispers and the touch speaks volumes."

SMALL TALK

My phone buzzes just as I'm settling into the soft cushions of my couch. A glowing notification blinks up from the screen with Reid's name. I can't help but let a grin spread across my face as I swipe to answer.

"Hey, Reid," I say, doing my best to keep the excitement from my voice.

His customary greeting comes through the speaker. The low timber of his voice is like a warm caress, sending shivers down my spine. The sound of his voice... it's something I can listen to forever.

"How do you feel about the assignment from art class today?" I say, twirling a lock of hair around my finger. "I swear, Reid, I can't draw a straight line to save my life."

There's a chuckle on the other end, and I imagine the crinkle of his eyes as he laughs.

"Amelia, quit being so dramatic," he teases. "Last time I checked, you weren't that bad."

"You're just saying that because you're nice," I mutter, but I can't help the smile that tugs at the corner of my lips.

There's silence for a moment, comfortable and warm, like a soft blanket in winter.

"You know," I say, breaking the silence, "We've talked and texted a few times now, but I feel like we don't really know each other all that well."

I hold my breath, waiting for his response, hoping I haven't overstepped.

"Yeah," he replies, a hint of shyness in his voice, "I'd like that, getting to know you better."

A rush of relief floods through me, and I can't help but smile. "Well, I guess I'll go first, then. I have two sisters, Destiny and Iris. Destiny is the oldest. She's two years older than me and the total brainiac of the family. She graduated two years before me, and now she's got this job that she absolutely loves. It's full of numbers, pi charts, and all that jazz. She can't get enough of it."

Reid chuckles softly, and I can imagine his smile. "And Iris?" he asks.

"Oh, Iris," I laugh. "She's the youngest and what we like to call 'the hellion of the family'. She's in the eighth grade and always getting into trouble."

We share a laugh, and I feel my heart flutter. This is nice, sharing and opening up. We've been dancing around each other for weeks now, and it feels nice to break the awkward ice that keeps us from really saying what we want to say.

"Your turn," I prompt, shifting to get more comfortable on the couch. There's a slight pause before Reid replies.

"Well," he starts. "I've got two brothers. Logan is older, and he drives trucks for a living. He's always on the road, going from state to state." I can hear the fondness in his voice and the respect he holds for his big brother.

"And the other one?" I ask curiously.

"Nathan," he chuckles. "He's a little brat, and he's in eighth grade, too. He's always causing trouble."

A laugh ripples through me, mirroring his own, and I imagine a mini Reid causing havoc.

"Sounds like Iris and Nathan would make quite the team," I quip, and we share another comfortable laugh, both lost in our own worlds yet somehow incredibly together.

We continue to share tidbits about ourselves, from tales of childhood pranks to our favorite family traditions. After a while, our conversation flows into shared interests and hobbies.

Our conversation slowly winds down, both of us succumbing to the lull of late-night fatigue.

"Reid, I'm really glad you called tonight," I admit, my voice softening.

"Me too, Amelia," he replies, his voice sounding just as tender, if not more.

His words wrap around me like a warm hug, one that makes my heart flutter.

As we both say our goodnights on the precipice of ending the call, I surprise myself - and possibly him - by whispering, "I like you, Reid."

There's a prolonged silence that pricks at my anxiety until I hear him whisper back, "I like you too, Amelia."

As we hung up, I lay back on the couch with a silly grin spreading across my face. I can't help it; tonight's conversation was something right out of a movie, something I've always dreamt of. I replay his words in my mind, his confession making my heart dance with joy. I lie down and fall to sleep with a wide smile on my face.

As I walk down the hallway the next morning, I can't help but wear a smile that feels as wide as a mile. Hazel is waiting for me by the lockers, her eyebrows raise in question as I approach.

"Why are you all smiles this morning?" she asks, a teasing lilt in her voice.

"Oh, you know me," I respond, shrugging nonchalantly and trying to play it cool. "I always start my day with a smile."

She just shakes her head, a knowing look in her eyes as she chuckles. "Sure, whatever you say. I'm willing to bet that a certain cutie with green eyes put that smile on your face."

"Okay, he did. We actually admitted we liked each other last night on the phone," I tell her.

Hazel looks at her watch and then back to me. "It's about fucking time. My watch is telling me you guys are moving too slow to get this relationship rolling."

"It's not that simple, Hazel," I say. "He's different, shy and quiet. Not at all what I'm used to. Plus, after what happened last time, I'm taking it slow, getting to know him and really assessing my feelings."

"Both of you are scared to make a move," she says. "Don't be a punk, Amelia. Make the first fucking move."

After giving her very unwanted advice, Hazel tells me she'll see me in our next period together, and I head toward my class. As soon as I step into class, my eyes naturally gravitate towards Reid. I make my way over to him as the room buzzes with students settling into another day of learning, but Lawrence abruptly blocks my path. The scowl twisted on his face is far from friendly.

"Move the fuck out of my way, Lawrence," I growl, not in the mood to deal with his shit today.

"You're such a stuck-up bitch, Amelia," he snarls, his words echoing around the room. "You're just pissed boys don't want to touch you once they found out how much of a slut you are."

The nasty comment stings, and a few students nearby snicker at his comment. I'm about to shoot back a response, something to put Lawrence in his place, when our teacher walks in, her heels clicking against the tiled floor.

"Alright, everyone, find your seats," she orders, effectively ending the standoff between Lawrence and me.

So, instead of answering, I turn and move toward the table where Reid is sitting. My face is hot, and I'm pissed. I refuse to give Lawrence the satisfaction of seeing me upset, but I can't deny that his words had an impact. Not because they were true - they're not. I've only had sex once in my life, but that's the thing about rumors. The truth doesn't matter. It's what people believe that hurts the most. As I sit down, I can't bring myself to meet Reid's eyes. I'm too mortified, too embarrassed by Lawrence's words. Even though I know they're not true, they still sting.

Ms. Clark, ever the beam of sunshine, begins her lesson with an infectious enthusiasm. She discusses our upcoming art projects in her signature cheery tone, her passion for the subject filling the room. Though I'm usually drawn into her energy, today, I find myself unable to shake off Lawrence's words. The whispers and snickers from others act as a constant reminder of his comment, making it impossible for me to focus. So I fix my gaze straight ahead, refusing to look at Reid.

Suddenly, I feel the softest whisper of contact on my hand. Looking down, I notice Reid has edged his hand so close to mine that they are touching, just barely. His touch, albeit faint, sends shivers down my spine, the warmth from his hand seeping into mine. I raise my eyes to look at him, and he's looking back at me, his eyes full of something I can't quite decipher.

He leans over slightly, just enough to make sure our conversation remains between the two of us. "Don't let what Lawrence said bother you, Amelia. He's just trying to get a rise out of you."

His words offer some comfort, but it's the next act that really touches my heart. Gathering courage, Reid takes my hand in his, gives it a quick squeeze, and then releases it. His voice is barely above a whisper, yet it carries a conviction that surprises me.

"You're beautiful, and he's mad he can't have you," he says.

I blink, taken aback by his words, my heart fluttering at the sincerity in his voice.

As Ms. Clark continues to teach, Reid's hand remains over mine, offering silent comfort and reassurance. His touch, a source of safety amidst the whispers and snickers, holds me grounded in reality. The bell rings, tearing us from our shared silence, and he lets go of my hand. That smirk, the one I've grown so fond of, graces his face before he heads for the door, leaving for his next class.

I make my way to the next class, my mind still replaying Reid's comforting words. As I enter my Social Studies class, the surrounding buzz quiets down. Mr. Jones is already at the front of the room, wearing his characteristic serious expression. He shuffles some papers, adjusts his glasses, and then begins the lesson with a commanding voice that demands attention.

"Good morning, everyone," Mr. Jones starts, speaking in his usual monotone. "Today, we'll be exploring the branches of the U.S. government, a crucial aspect of our nation's governance. The United States has a system of checks and balances, with three separate branches: the executive, legislative, and judicial branches. Each branch has distinct responsibilities and powers, ensuring a fair and balanced government. Let's dive into the details, starting with the executive branch..."

His words reverberate throughout the room, and though lacking enthusiasm, they make me feel drowsy. Mr. Jones has to blow his horn a few times to snap me out of my drowsiness. Despite his efforts, the class seems to drag on endlessly. As soon as the bell rings, I rush out to my next period. My heart turns lighter at the sight of Hazel waiting for me at our usual spot, and we walk into class.

"Hey, Amelia. Do you want to come with me to the nail salon after school?" she asks, her eyes sparkling with the thought of a girl's day out.

I shake my head, a pang of regret at having to refuse her. "Sorry, I can't, Hazel," I say, a sigh escaping my lips. "I have practice after school, a big game tomorrow, and the coach wants us to do drills."

Her face falls slightly, but she quickly replaces it with an understanding smile.

Hazel smiles at me, a hint of determination in her voice. "That's okay. I'll wait till this weekend. And, you know what? I'm coming to your game. You guys may not have cheerleaders, but you'll have me cheering for you."

I can't help but laugh at her enthusiasm, my mood instantly lifting.

"That sounds like a plan, Hazel," I reply, my voice filled with warmth.

Our conversation is interrupted as Ms. Peters enters the classroom, the shuffle of her papers signaling the start of a new lesson. The rest of the day blurs by, the hours ticking away until the final bell rings, signaling the end of classes. I make my way to the girls' locker room with my steps quick and purposeful. The school is a flurry of activity, with students rushing to their after-school commitments or heading home. I unzip my bag and pull out my practice uniform. I had packed an extra set of clothes as well, always prepared for the unexpected.

As I leave the locker room, my shoes squeaking slightly against the polished tiles, I spot a familiar figure standing by the gym entrance. Reid. His signature smile lights up his face as he spots me, and it's like being pulled in by a magnet, our steps syncing as we move toward each other. We stop just a foot apart, and for a moment, everything else fades into the background. His eyes are soft, and he's looking at me with a warmth that sends a rush of butterflies through my stomach. For a moment, we just stand there, caught in our own little world amidst the bustle of the school corridor.

Just as I'm about to say something, Benjamin's voice interrupts our moment.

"Are you communicating silently or something because you're just staring at each other?" he teases.

Reid and I burst out laughing, the tension that had formed between us disappearing. I gesture awkwardly towards the gym.

"I have practice," I inform Reid.

He nods, understanding, and tells me he's planning to hang out with Benjamin. We find ourselves wrapped in silence once again, but it's not uncomfortable. Rather, it feels familiar, comforting even.

Benjamin sighs dramatically, breaking the silence. "Stop staring at her and kiss her already," he says, chuckling.

Reid blushes, a hint of red creeping up his neck and coloring his cheeks. He looks away, clearly embarrassed. Trying to ease his discomfort, I quickly changed the subject.

"Have fun with your friends," I tell him, giving him an exit from this now even more awkward encounter.

I lean forward and wrap my arms around him in a quick hug, catching him off guard. His arms come around me hesitantly before giving me a reassuring squeeze. We step back from each other, and I wave at him as I walk around him to the court. I can't help but smile, a sense of warmth spreading throughout me.

Practice is grueling, as expected. Coach Thompson is a stickler for detail and believes in pushing us to our limits. The gym echoes with the thud of volleyballs hitting the wooden floor and the sharp whistle of the coach, cutting through the noise. We start with a warm-up that comprises a few rounds of jogging and then stretching. It's crucial, Coach Thompson always says, not to jump into the drills without preparing our muscles first.

Drills follow the warm-up. We practice our serves first. Coach Thompson walks around, observing each of us critically. She corrects and advises, her sharp gaze missing nothing.

"Aim, Amelia. And serve! A bit more force next time!" she keeps repeating until she's satisfied.

Next, we practice setting. It's my favorite part of the game, the moment when I'm in control, deciding on the next move. The volleyballs fly around the gym, and we move in rhythm, almost like a dance. Coach Thompson's voice rings through the gym as she shouts instructions, her eyes assessing every move we make.

The final drill is the toughest. We practice our receives. It's the most challenging part of the game. You never know where the ball will come from, and you have to be ready - ready to drop to the ground, ready to lunge sideways, ready to jump. It's exhausting, but it's what makes a skillful player great.

By the end of practice, I'm drenched in sweat, my muscles screaming in protest, but this is what it takes to win. This is what it takes to be the best, and despite the exhaustion, there's a thrill that comes from pushing myself, a sense of accomplishment. I gather my things and head to the locker room, feeling more prepared for tomorrow's game than ever before.

Walking out of the school, my heart is light and buzzing with excitement. Not because practice is over or because the big game is tomorrow, but because of what awaited me at home: a phone call from Reid. There's something about his voice; a smooth, low timbre that rings clear over the phone, making every word he says sound like a sweet melody. It's a voice that can soothe my worries, lift my spirits, and ignite a fire within me all at once.

As I make my way home, the anticipation builds. I can almost hear his voice in my head. Those carefully chosen words delivered in that comforting rhythm, a conversation I am eager to be a part of. The thought brings a smile to my face, one that I can't seem to shake off, not that I want to.

"In the tapestry of love, ours is an explosive romance—a kaleidoscope of emotions that paints the sky with the vibrant hues of passion. Like fireworks in the night, our connection lights up the dark, leaving a trail of memories that linger in the heart's starry canvas."

The hours Reid and I spend on the phone are infused with revelations about our dreams and aspirations. We delve into the depths of our unique quirks, laughing at the differences that exist between us. Reid dreams of a world where technology has a human touch and where algorithms and codes evoke empathy. I, on the other hand, dream of becoming a teacher, teaching new generations that will grow up to change the world.

Our dreams diverge, but they come together in the shared passion we have for our pursuits. Through our open-hearted conversations, we discover the beauty in our differences.

As I'm strolling down the hallway, my mind is still swirling with the lingering echoes of Reid's last text. I'm lost in the enchantment of our shared dreams and aspirations, oblivious to my surroundings. Out of nowhere, an abrupt push from behind shakes me out of my reverie. It's Jada, flanked by her two constant companions, wearing their usual smirks.

Jada sneers, a snarl distorting her features. "I'd love to see you try to punch me in the face. Without Hazel around, you're not so tough, are you?"

I looked her straight in the eyes, refusing to be rattled by her intimidation tactics.

"I don't need Hazel to protect me, Jada," I tell her with a steady, bored tone. "I'm more than capable of fighting my own battles."

The hallway falls eerily silent as my words echo around us. I take a step closer to Jada, my gaze never wavering from hers. "Never touch me again, or you'll regret it," I warn her. "I assure you, if it comes to it, I won't hesitate to kick your ass."

Jada's smirk falls as my words sink in, replaced by a malicious glint in her eyes. Without warning, she lunges at me with her two stooges following suit. Reacting on pure adrenaline, I sidestep her, my elbow connecting with a thud to her stomach. I spin around with a swift punch, landing on the cheekbone of one of her sidekicks. The other made a grab for my hair, but I duck and counter with a swift knee to her midsection.

As our scuffle continues, I'm vaguely aware of a strangled gasp, followed by an "I'm getting a teacher!" from a bystander whose face I didn't bother to register. My attention is squarely on the three girls trying to tag-team me. I land a solid kick on the shin of the one clutching her stomach from my earlier blow.

Just as I'm about to land another hit, I see Jada lunging at me from the corner of my eye, but I'm ready. I quickly pivot and catch her wrist in mid-air.

"I warned you, Jada," I hiss through gritted teeth.

Powered by a surge of adrenaline, I pivoted quickly, swinging my fist straight at Jada's face. A sickening crack echoed through the hallway, followed by a shocked gasp. The sensation of Jada's nose giving way under my punch was unmistakable. Without a second thought, I hit her again, just for good measure.

Before her goons can react, I hear the familiar pounding of boots on the linoleum floor. It's Hazel. She's barreling down the hallway with her eyes blazing with fury. One-two and both girls were down, Hazel's punches hitting them with the force of a freight train.

She quickly grabs my arm, pulling me away from the crumpled figure of Jada.

"Let's get out of here," she hisses between clenched teeth.

The urgency in her voice snaps me out of my adrenaline-fueled haze. With one last look at Jada, I let Hazel lead me away.

As we dash down the hallway, I can hardly believe what had just transpired. My heart is pounding in my chest, each beat echoing the disbelief and shock. I can still feel the harsh impact of my fist on Jada's face, the sound of her gasp ringing in my ears. I looked over at Hazel. Her face is hardened with determination, her eyes focused on the path ahead.

As the day unfolded, Hazel and I went our separate ways to attend our respective classes, the echo of my last punch still reverberating in my mind. Each passing period filled me with a fresh wave of anxiety, dreading the call to the principal's office for the showdown in the hallway. But, to my surprise, the call never came. As the last bell rang, I couldn't help but think that maybe Jada felt too humiliated to admit what had happened.

Perhaps the bruising impact on her ego was more unbearable than the one on her face. With these thoughts swirling in my mind, I head to my locker, where Hazel is waiting, her face mirroring the relief I feel. Despite the turmoil of the day, nothing had happened. No reprimands, no detentions, no calls home. For now, it seems we are in the clear.

As I approach my locker, Hazel is already there, leaning against the cool metal facade, her arms folded over her chest.

"You okay?" she asks, her eyes searching mine for any lingering fear.

I nod with a small smile. "Yeah, I'm fine. Thank you, Hazel."

She responds with a half-smile. "Don't thank me. You handled yourself pretty well."

The fallen smirk on Jada's face flashes in my mind, making me chuckle. "I guess I did."

The conversation lulls into a comfortable silence. She seems to ponder something before asking, "Speaking of handling things, are you going to the basketball game tonight to see Reid?"

My cheeks flush at the mention of his name. "We're just friends, Hazel," I mutter before looking away.

Her laughter echoes in the hallway. "Yeah right, Amelia. You're more than friends, even if you haven't, you know..." She winked at me, the hint of mischief in her eyes.

I blush harder, shaking my head at her insinuation, but a small smile tugs at the corners of my mouth. The thought of Reid and me being more than friends makes moisture pool below. A feeling I've only felt once in my life.

Hazel and I make our way to the crowded school gym. The air filled with anticipation and the buzz of eager chatter. As cheer captain, Hazel quickly joins her team, their routines practiced to perfection, ready to rouse the spectators. The basketball team, with Reid as their star player, enters to roaring applause.

The atmosphere at the basketball game is electrifying. The gym is packed to the brim with students, teachers, and parents, all decked out in the school's colors, their faces painted with fervor. Deafening cheers and chants from the crowd fill the air and reverberate off the walls, creating a sonic wave of support for our team. The cheerleaders, led by

Hazel, own the floor during the breaks; their spirited routines adding to the exhilarating atmosphere.

The scent of popcorn from the concession stands wafted through the air, mingling with the aroma of sweat and anticipation. Every point scored by our team is met with an eruption of applause, with the crowd on their feet, hands clapping, and voices rising in unison. Amidst this hive of activity, the players on the court, including Reid, are the epitome of focus. Their eyes are locked on the ball, bodies moving with agility and precision, each pass, each shot, each strategy executed with a shared goal of victory.

As I watch Reid dribble the ball across the court, my heart mirrors his every move. Fast, unpredictable, and full of anticipation. There is an undeniable magnetism about him that draws me in every time he's near. His athletic prowess, his focused expression, the way his uniform hugs his well-built frame. All of that stirring feelings within me I had been trying to deny for so long. Every time our eyes meet, I feel a rush of emotions, a mix of nervousness, excitement, and a longing I can hardly understand.

As much as I wanted to dismiss these feelings as a mere crush, a part of me knew it was something more profound, more binding. It wasn't just about his looks or his popularity; it was about Reid, the person he was. His kindness, his humility, his passion for the sport - all of it was a part of the irresistible package that was Reid. Every stolen glance, every shared laugh, every late-night study session - they all added layers to my feelings for him, deepening the connection I felt. As I cheered him on from the sidelines, I couldn't help but wonder if he felt the same way about me.

The final whistle blows, and to our collective delight, we emerge victorious. While the crowd erupts into wild cheers, I find my eyes fixed on Reid. Despite the sheen of sweat on his brow and the clear exhaustion, his eyes shone with an unmatched intensity. I feel a surge of pride wash over me as he pumps his fist in the air, a triumphant grin on his face. Waiting for Hazel in the gym, I watch as Reid celebrates with his team, their camaraderie and shared euphoria palpable. As I watch on, my heart races, echoing the exhilarating energy of the room.

Steeling myself, I push through the sea of smiling students, making my way towards Reid. His back is turned to me as he's caught up in the euphoria, his laughter mingling with those of his teammates. I pause for a moment, watching him, before finally stepping forward and tapping on his shoulder. He turns around, surprise etched across his face as he recognizes me.

"Amelia," he says, his voice barely audible over the din of cheering students. I can't contain my excitement, with my nerves giving way to a playful glint in my eyes.

"You were amazing out there, Reid," I tell him, my voice barely more than a whisper.

His face flushes a beautiful shade of pink, his usual swagger replaced by a bashful stammer. "I-It was nothing," he says while scratching the back of his neck. His discomfort, so different from his usual confident demeanor, is endearing.

Before he can react, I muster my courage and plant a soft, lingering kiss on his cheek. I can feel the warmth of his skin seeping into my lips, the faint stubble on his face prickling my skin. The move surprises him, but he seems thrilled by my boldness, his face flushing an even deeper shade of pink. Our eyes lock, and for a moment, it feels as if time stands still.

The maddening noise in the surrounding gym fades away, replaced by the deafening silence between us. All I can hear is the sound of my heart pounding in my chest. In that instant, under the dimmed lights of the gym, amidst the echoes of our victorious cheer, Reid makes the first move. His eyes flick to my lips, then back to my eyes, and he leans down slowly, and his lips touched mine.

The kiss starts out slow. He is hesitant, taking his time. I take control of the kiss and cup his face as his hands go to my hips, holding me in place. The kiss deepens, and I can feel him growing in his shorts as he tugs me closer.

Suddenly, a piercing screech cut through the silence, startling Reid and me out of our little bubble. It was Hazel. She stands a few feet away from us with her mouth open, eyes wide in shock. The rest of the students cheer, their claps and whistles echoing through the room. The reality of what had just happened starts sinking in. We had just kissed in the middle of the gymnasium, in front of everyone.

I feel my face heat, and I bury my forehead into the comfort of Reid's chest, hiding away from the eyes that are on us. The embarrassment surges forward, but despite that, I'm aware of Reid's arms around me, a soft chuckle vibrating from his chest. We had lost ourselves in that moment, completely oblivious to the world. Hazel waves her hand back and forth in front of her face, her eyes wide.

"Whoa, that was hot as hell!" she says in a voice louder than I expected.

The crowd's cheers rise even higher, their excitement filling the room. I can feel my cheeks going even redder, if that was possible. Reid's grip on me tightens momentarily, and, despite the embarrassment, I can't help but laugh.

It's a ridiculous situation, but it's also thrilling, making a memory that I will never forget. I lift my head from Reid's chest, meeting his gaze. His eyes sparkle with amusement, and from the look of it, equal parts embarrassment. But mostly, they hold a tenderness that makes my heart swell. I give him a small smile, and, in that moment, it feels like everything is going to be okay. We shared our first unspoken yet profoundly meaningful kiss. The taste of the moment is sweet, a heady mix of victory, adrenaline, and newfound love.

Reid takes my hand, leading me through the throng of students and out into the cool night air. The clamor of the gym fades behind us, replaced by the serene silence of the outdoors. We stand there for a moment, caught between the exhilaration of our first kiss and the mundane reality that lay ahead. Just as I'm about to break the silence, a familiar voice ring out.

Hazel, seated in her car, rolls down the window, a mischievous grin on her face. "Hey, sexy, get your ass in the car," she teases, her laughter echoing through the quiet night.

I can't help but join in, my laughter intermingling with hers. Reid, ever the gentleman, merely shakes his head and tells me he'll call me later. With that, I give him one last lingering look before getting into Hazel's car, ready to face the inevitable teasing that awaits me.

As the car speeds off, Hazel's excited chatter fills the small space. "Amelia, I still can't believe what just happened! You and Reid, locking lips in front of everyone? That was epic!"

She gushes., her eyes sparkling with excitement. I can only blush and shrug, my heart still aflutter from the thrill of the evening. The entire ride home is filled with Hazel's endless chattering and my feeble attempts to shush her, though her excitement was infectious, and I can't help but join her laughter.

Before I know it, we were pulling up to my house. The lights are off, indicating my mom has probably turned in for the night. As I unbuckled my seatbelt, I turn towards Hazel with a thankful smile on my face.

"Hazel, thanks for tonight," I say, my voice just above a whisper.

She simply winks at me with a knowing smile playing on her lips. "Just remember, I want details tomorrow, Amelia!"

she teases, her laughter echoing long after I close the car door behind me.

Standing on the sidewalk, I watch her car disappear down the street, the faint smell of the night air hitting me. Tonight was a night of unexpected turns, but as I make my way towards the front door, the corners of my lips curl into a satisfied smile. With the taste of Reid's lips still lingering on mine, I knew everything had changed.

As I lay on my bed, replaying the night's events in my head, my phone buzzes from my bedside table. The screen lights up, casting a soft glow in my dark room. "Reid" flashes across the screen, and my heart races as I watch his name, the reality of what happened sinking in even more. I hesitate for a moment, my fingers hovering over the phone. Taking a deep breath, I pick it up and swipe to answer, pressing it against my ear.

"Hey, Reid," I say, trying to keep my voice steady, as the memory of our shared kiss is still fresh in my mind.

"Hey, Amelia," he says.

The line is silent, neither of us knowing what to say. The silence is deafening, a stark contrast to the noise that surrounded our kiss just hours ago. I can almost feel Reid on the other end of the line, likely mirroring my own thoughts. We're both navigating these uncharted waters of our newly altered relationship, fumbling for the right words that seem to elude us.

"I cannot believe we kissed in front of the entire school," I tell him, finally breaking the silence. "We're definitely going to be the main talk of the school."

He laughs a little. "Yeah, we did." He pauses for a moment. "That was...uh my...first kiss."

I'm stunned and silent because that kiss was everything. I've been kissed before, and it never felt like that. How could he have never kissed a girl before?

"Reid," I sigh softly. "I'm your first kiss?" He remains silent, so my tone turns to teasing. "I guess that officially makes me your girlfriend now."

"I guess you are," he says with a laugh. "I really like you, Amelia."

"I really like you too, Reid," I reply quietly.

"In the tempest of intense romantic feelings, we navigate the stormy seas of passion, charting a course through the unpredictable waves of desire, and discovering that, sometimes, it's in the chaos that the most beautiful connections are found."

AWAY VOLLEYBALL GAME

After that moment, we became the couple at school. Some people, even the teachers, couldn't stop talking about how cute we were. There were also some people who didn't care to see a white boy slumming it with a black girl. We didn't let those people bother us because we're too consumed by each other. Since that first kiss, it's like a switch flipped in Reid, and we can't keep our hands off each other.

Reid and I, we've shared countless kisses since that day, each leaving a sweet memory imprinted in my heart. Each one is different, yet each one is filled with the same electrifying sensations. As I let the memories wash over me, my lips curve into a wide smile, my heart fluttering just as it does every time with Reid.

The cafeteria is a hive of activity, its familiar hum a comforting backdrop to my thoughts. The clattering of trays, the bursts of laughter, the inaudible murmurs of gossip—they're all just noise. Yet, amid the din, I can still pick up whispers laced with my name and Reid's. It's hard to tune out the speculative eyes and hushed conversations, the barest hints of curiosity and judgment.

I glance over at Hazel, who seems to ignore it all, engrossed in her lunch. I wish I can lose myself in something as simple as that, but the whispers have a way of sticking to you. Like persistent little gnats, they buzz in your ears, echoing long after the actual words have faded. It's strange how something as trivial as schoolyard gossip can feel so substantial.

Being with Reid has brought such happiness and vibrancy into my life. His intellect, his charm, his wit—they add up to a person who I'm absolutely smitten with. Every moment together is filled with laughter, friendship, and a sense of mutual understanding. It's as if we've known each other for ages, even though our relationship is still fresh. That's the beauty of it. That's the magic of Reid and me.

Taking a chance on a relationship again, especially after what happened with Anthony, feels like a victory. Anthony and I started dating, and he was a year ahead of me. I was a smitten sophomore, and he was a charming junior. Our relationship carried on into the following year, and I thought I was in love. We had been together for so long that it just felt natural to take the next step. Unfortunately, that turned out to be the biggest mistake of my life.

The day after Anthony and I took our relationship to the next level, I was floating on cloud nine. I was certain that things between us would only get better. That we were on our way to becoming that high-school sweetheart story people always wanted to hear about. That blissful bubble burst abruptly when Kendra, Jada's older sister, found me at my locker. Kendra had this fiendish grin on her face, one that could make your blood turn cold.

With an audience of students, she taunted me, throwing around words like "cherry popping" and my name in the same sentence. My heart pounded in my chest, my face burned brighter than a thousand suns. I was mortified and utterly confused. I stood there frozen, perplexed as to how Kendra could have possibly known what happened between Anthony and me. The hallway echoed with laughter, but all I could hear was the sound of my heart-shattering.

As Kendra's laughter echoed down the hallway, I could only stare. Confusion and anger were fighting for dominance on my face. Her next words sent an icy chill down my spine, "Anthony told me, silly girl. We've been dating this whole time. You didn't actually think he was yours, did you?"

Her words hit me like a sharp slap in the face. It felt like the ground beneath me had evaporated. Anthony and Kendra? But...he had insinuated they were over when we started dating. Hell, he'd all but assured me they were. The room spun, and I could feel the bile building up in my throat. I had been played. The entire time, Anthony had been playing both of us, and I was the last to find out. The laughter in the hallway was now a dull roar in the background, drowned out by the pounding of betrayal in my ears.

Almost as if on cue, Hazel came barreling down the hallway, shoving her way through the students. She grabbed my hand, her grip firm and grounding, and dragged me away from the crowd. But not before turning to Kendra, her gaze as cold as ice.

"You're a dumb bitch, Kendra," she spat out, her voice echoing through the hall. The laughter seemed to die down at that, replaced by a stunned silence. "You're standing there proud that you're with a cheating piece of shit and then have the nerve to rub it in Amelia's face? You're a dumb bitch and when he leaves your ass, I'll be there laughing."

I allowed Hazel to pull me away, the eyes of the students becoming a blur as we moved further down the hall. I was grateful. Grateful for Hazel and her impeccable timing. Grateful for her fierce loyalty and grateful because, despite the humiliation, I was not alone.

In the days following that incident, I poured my energy into moving past it. It was tough, but with Hazel by my side, I had the strength to confront the whispers and glances at school. Over time, the whispers died down, the glances became less frequent, and the incident became a distant memory.

Then Reid came into my life. His presence is like a breath of fresh air, washing away the remnants of my past. Every moment with him is a revelation, a stark contrast to what I had experienced with Anthony. His intellect, charm, and wit are enchanting, but it's his respect and kindness that truly captivate me. With Reid, I feel valued, cherished, and understood. What I thought I had with Anthony feels insignificant compared to what I'm developing with Reid. It's like comparing a flicker to a flame. The magic between Reid and me is powerful and real. It's something I have never experienced before, and it is something I'm eager to explore further.

As I marinate in the nostalgia from those past events, Hazel's voice abruptly brings me back to reality. She seems to have a knack for interrupting my trips down memory lane. Her timing is always impeccable.

"Amelia, who are you playing in today's away game?" Hazel asks, her question slicing through my thoughts.

"We're playing Riverside Prep," I reply before shifting my gaze to meet hers.

The mention of the game brings a familiar excitement bubbling up within me. Her face falls slightly at my response, a frown tugging at her lips.

"Riverside Prep? That's on the other side of town. I won't be able to make it. I have cheerleading practice," she admits, her disappointment clear in her tone.

"It's okay, Hazel," I reassure her with a light tone. "There will always be another game. You don't have to worry about it."

She gives a hesitant smile before nodding her head. The rest of the class passes by in a flurry of discussions and note-taking. I find myself lost in the details of the lecture, my mind a million miles away.

The bell finally rings, pulling me from my thoughts. Gathering my belongings, I head towards the hallway, my steps taking me to my locker. The sight of Reid leaning against it, grinning casually as he waits for me, causes a smile to bloom across my face. His presence never fails to brighten my day.

He greets me with a warm kiss on the lips. "Hey."

A blush creeps onto my cheeks as Reid kisses me, the usual flutter of butterflies invading my stomach.

"Hey..." I respond, my voice barely a whisper.

Together, we retrieved our belongings, and with his hand in mine, we walked to class. Reid and I barely make it into class as the bell echoes through the school corridors, a loud proclamation of the beginning of another period. Our desks, situated near the back of the class, offer the perfect view of the entire room, filled with students settling into their seats, a flurry of chatter dying down. Ms. Allen, a woman with a warm smile and an infectious enthusiasm for physics, rushes to the front of the class. The echoes of the bell is replaced by the scraping of chairs as everyone gets ready for the lesson.

With her signature welcoming smile, she starts the lesson. "Good morning, everyone! Today, we'll dive deeper into the fascinating world of quantum mechanics. I hope you're ready for some mind-bending concepts."

Her excitement is palpable. It's hard not to get drawn into her love for the subject. I glance at Reid to see his green eyes mirroring the same enthusiasm. Without another thought, I sit straighter and dive into the lesson.

The day passes like a whirlwind, the usual humdrum of school life envelopes by my thoughts of Reid. Before I know it, I'm changing into my volleyball uniform, waiting in the gym with the rest of the team for Coach Thompson. As we sit in the bleachers, I can't help but watch the boys' basketball team, Reid included, as they prepare for drills. My eyes are inexplicably drawn to him, to the way he moves, to his infectious enthusiasm.

Coach Thompson's voice echoing through the gym, breaking me out of my Reid-induced trance. "The bus is ready, ladies!"

As we all clamber down the bleachers, Reid jogs over with a beaming smile.

"Hey Amelia, have a great game, okay?" he tells me, his voice filled with sincerity. The taut silence that follows is punctuated by the echo of our heartbeats in the gym.

"Have a great practice, Reid," I reply, my voice barely a whisper.

In the midst of our team's hustle and the boys' teasing, we share a sweet, lingering kiss. Benjamin, always the jokester, makes kissy noises from the back, drawing laughter from the others.

"Alright, that's enough!" Coach Thompson interjects, her stern voice silencing the gym. "School is not the place for that. Amelia, go get on the bus."

As I turn to leave, Reid and I share one last look, filled with promises and unspoken words. I take a deep breath, pick up my gym bag, and walk out of the gym, the echo of laughter and Reid's encouraging words trailing behind me.

The game against Riverside Prep is nothing short of an adrenaline-charged battle. Every strike, every block, every serve is met with grit and determination, echoing our resolve to conquer. Riverside Prep is a formidable opponent, their ruthless attacks a constant challenge. Still, we played on with enthusiasm, determined to win the game. As the final whistle blows, the scoreboard reads in our favor. The jubilant smiles on my teammates' faces mirrors my own as we hug, our victory cheers resonating in the otherwise quiet night.

Back on home ground, my mother is waiting, her face lighting up at the sight of us. In the car, I regale her with tales of our game, my excitement bubbling over with each vivid description of the intense game. She listens to every word, her pride clear in her warm smile as she congratulates me.

Once home, the day's exertions finally catch up with me. I take a refreshing shower and let the warm water soothe my tired muscles. After changing into comfortable clothes, I devour the plate of food mom had prepared, its homely taste a comforting embrace. Finally, I sink into my bed, the TV playing softly in the background, providing enough distraction to let my mind wander.

My phone buzzes, and a glance at the screen brings a smile to my face. Reid. My heart skips a beat at the sight of his name. I pick up the call with my voice soft, yet full of anticipation.

"Hey, Reid..."

"In the rearview mirror of regret, I glimpsed the silhouette of an ex-boyfriend, a chapter closed with lessons learned. Yet, in the embrace of new love, I found the healing balm that mends the fractures of a once-broken heart, turning the pages of pain into a story of resilience and renewal."

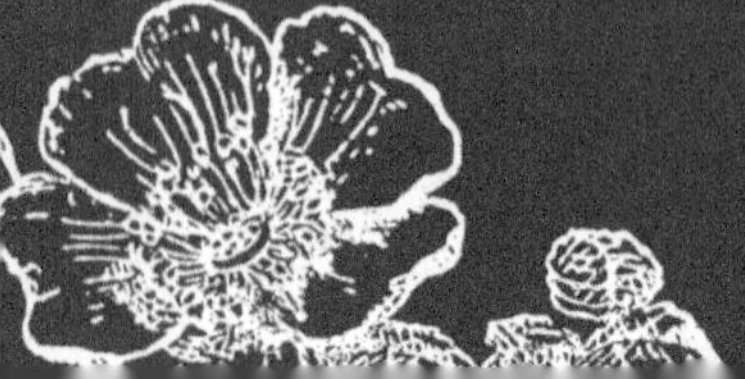

RUN IN WITH EX-BOYFRIEND

When I wake up the next morning, I'm all smiles. I can't help but think about the phone call with Reid last night, how his laughter echoed in my ears, and the way he said goodnight. I swing my legs out of the bed, my feet meeting the cool floor as I make my way to the bathroom. With a toothbrush in hand, I stand before the mirror, brushing away, still immersed in the memories of the conversation. Next comes the real task of taming my unruly curls. I sigh as I look at my reflection to see the curls having a life of their own. Dressed warmly in anticipation of the chilly weather, I descend the stairs, ready to tackle the day, my mind still playing Reid's laughter on a loop.

As I step into the kitchen, the tantalizing aroma of freshly brewed coffee fills the air, blending with the sweet scent of Destiny's vanilla perfume. I notice Iris, my youngest sister, still wearing her unicorn pajamas, with a milk mustache adorning her face as she enjoys her cereal.

"Good morning, everyone! What's so funny?" I inquire.

Mom, wiping tears of laughter from her eyes, points to Iris. "Your sister," she says amidst fits of giggles, "tried to do a

magic trick with her cereal! She thought she could make it disappear!"

"And now we have cereal all over the kitchen!" Destiny adds.

Iris simply shrugs, her mischievous grin revealing a mouthful of half-chewed cereal.

"Well, the kitchen needed some decoration anyway," she responds, mischief sparkling in her eyes.

Unable to contain myself, I join in the laughter. Grabbing a quick bite to eat, I give one last look at the breakfast chaos before heading out the door. The cool air nips at my nose as I make my way to school, Reid's laughter now replaced with the crunching of autumn leaves under my feet.

Upon entering the school, my eyes immediately find Reid waiting by my locker, just like always. His presence is a familiar comfort amidst the hustle and bustle of the hallways. My heart skips a beat as I walk up to him, and I can't help but break into a smile. I lean in, pressing a sweet kiss to his lips.

"Good morning," I greet him, the words coming out more like a soft whisper. He returns my smile, a gentle hand at my back as we navigate our way through the crowded hallway to the first period.

As the chatter in the classroom slowly quiets, Ms. Clark begins her lecture on the complexities of art, her excitement for the topic clear in her passionate discourse. I try to focus on her words, pen poised over my notebook, but I feel Reid's eyes on me. I turn to meet his gaze, and the intensity in his eyes takes my breath away.

Reid leans over, his voice barely above a whisper. "Amelia...you're beautiful." His words send a shiver down my spine, and I feel a blush creep up my cheeks.

"Reid..." I start, but he cuts me off.

"No, let me finish," he continues, his eyes searching mine. "Every day, I find myself... liking you more and more." His hand reaches over, gently brushing a loose curl from my face. His touch is electrifying, sending a jolt of energy through me.

His admission hangs in the air between us, both of us unsure of what this means for us. My heart pounds in my chest, but I find myself leaning into his touch, a silent acknowledgment of the unspoken feelings between us. As I meet his gaze, I see a mirror of my own emotions. Fear, excitement, and a hint of hesitation.

"Reid..." I finally whisper back. "I really like you too."

Reid takes a deep breath, his eyes momentarily drifting away before focusing back on me. "You know, Amelia, I've never had a girlfriend before. I've liked girls, sure, but never enough to do anything about it."

His voice trails off, and he swallows hard. "I've never had this kind of connection before." He rushes out the last words, a blush creeping up his cheeks that matches the sincerity in his eyes. "So, yeah. I just wanted to tell you I really like you."

A slow smile pulls at the corners of my lips. Reid, the guy who's been my rock, my constant, feels the same way about me. It's an unreal feeling, like I'm floating. Before I can respond, however, the sharp voice of Ms. Clark cuts through my stupor.

"Mr. Carter, Miss Campbell, if you two could pay attention, please? This will be on the final," she says.

I snap my eyes back to the front of the room, a blush now on my own cheeks. I can feel Reid's chuckle more than I hear it, and I can't help but join in.

As the bell rings, signaling the end of class, Reid and I gather our belongings and make our way to my locker. The sounds of shuffling feet and the high chatter of students fill the air, creating a familiar hum that is the soundtrack of our school days. I grab my textbook for my next class, the weight of the book a tangible reminder of the academic responsibilities waiting for me.

Turning to Reid, I lean in, pressing a quick kiss to his lips. "I'll see you after class," I tell him, my voice soft.

Suddenly, a voice echoes down the hall, instantly recognizable and causing the color to drain from my face. The cheerful chatter and the clanging of lockers fade into the background as I turn around to see Jada talking to her sister and Anthony.

As Jada, Kendra, and Anthony saunter towards me, an air of arrogance enveloping them, I can't help but notice the snide look etched on Jada's face. My heart rate quickens, and instinctively, I step back, my back colliding with Reid's broad chest. Instantly, his muscular arm wraps around my waist, providing a sense of security. I look up at him, his chiseled features looking even more striking in the harsh fluorescent light of the hallway.

His gaze is locked onto the approaching trio, a determination in his eyes that only intensifies my beating heart. The smirk on Jada's face doesn't waver, but underneath it, I can see a flicker of uncertainty, perhaps unaccustomed to the protective stance Reid has taken. His grip tightens slightly around my waist, a silent promise that he's here, he's with me, and together we can face whatever comes next.

As they stop in front of me, Kendra looks me up and down, her smirk twisting into a venomous grin. "Well, if it isn't little Amelia."

A wave of anger washes over me, hot and seething. "What do you want, Kendra?" I snap back.

My voice is strong despite the tremor that threatens to betray me. Kendra's mere presence is enough to resurrect feelings of past humiliations, but I refuse to bow down to that intimidation.

"You graduated. Why are you here? Shouldn't you be out doing your job and walking the streets?" I snap, taking in the surprise that flickers across her face.

My words have hit their mark.

"Don't talk to my sister like that," Jada snaps, coming to Kendra's defense. Before I can respond, Anthony breaks the uncomfortable silence.

"Amelia," he says, his gaze shifting from me to Reid, a knowing look in his eyes. "I see you've changed your... interests." He looks at Reid. "Has she opened her legs for you yet? I had to wait a long time to get between her legs. If you haven't, let me tell you, she's not worth the wait."

"You're a fucking asshole!" I snarl at Anthony, anger seeping into every word. "I can't believe I ever dated you. You're a piece of shit."

That felt good. Letting out all the pent-up aggression and pain, but their laughter, only fuels my anger. Kendra, Jada, and Anthony. They all laugh like it's the funniest thing they've ever heard.

Suddenly, I feel Reid's hand leave my waist, and before I can protest, he steps in front of me, a protective barrier against their verbal onslaught.

Anthony raises a brow, amusement clear in his voice. "Awe, is the white boy going to defend you now, Amelia?"

"Leave Amelia alone and get the hell out of here," Reid asserts, his voice steady.

Anthony's smile fades into a frown, and he takes a threatening step towards Reid.

Before things can escalate any further, Jada speaks. "Come on, guys. You're supposed to be picking me up early."

She throws an appreciative look at Reid, a look that makes me want to punch her in her smug face. "It's been fun messing with the slut, but we have to go."

Her words hang in the air, an ugly reminder of how vicious they can be. As luck would have it, Jada's suggestion seems to do the trick, and with a final sneer, they turn and leave. I turn to Reid, my heartbeat finally beginning to slow down.

"Thank you for stepping in, but you didn't have to do that," I tell him, my voice filled with gratitude.

He looks down at me, a softness overcoming the previous hardness in his eyes. "You're my girlfriend, Amelia. Nobody gets to disrespect you. Not while I'm around."

His cheeks redden slightly as he confesses, "Honestly, I've never been in a fight before." He lets out a laugh, breaking the intense atmosphere. "But something inside me just wanted to protect you. I was ready to punch that guy in the face," he adds, the corner of his mouth pulling up into a lopsided grin.

I can't help but laugh at that, the familiar, comforting sound echoing through the now almost empty hallway. Standing on my tiptoes, I pull him into a soft kiss, my heart fluttering at the contact. Pulling back, I look up into his warm eyes.

"Thanks again, Reid," I say as I squeeze his hand reassuringly.

With one final shared smile, we part ways to head to our respective classes. The next class passes as slowly as always. The monotonous drone of the teacher's voice, the squeak of chalk against the blackboard, and the occasional whispered conversations form a symphony of regular school life. Relief washes over me when the bell finally rings, signaling the end of the period. I gather my books and rush to my next class, finding Hazel already sitting in her usual seat by the window. I slip into the seat next to her and turn to face her.

"Hazel, you wouldn't believe what just happened," I blurt out, not waiting for her to ask.

She turns to me, her eyebrows raised in surprise. "What's up, Ames?" she asks, using her nickname for me. I take a deep breath, setting the stage for my tale.

"I ran into Jada, Kendra, and Anthony in the hallway," I say, my voice dropping to a whisper.

Her eyes widen at the mention of their names. I recount the confrontation, my words spilling out in a rush. I tell her about the snide comments, the hurtful words, and the sheer audacity of Kendra and Anthony.

"But you know what?" I say, a small smile creeping onto my face. "Reid was there, and he was so protective. He stepped in and defended me. It was... it was amazing."

Hazel blinks, taking it all in. Then she let out a snort.

"I wish I was there because I would have punched Jada and Kendra and kicked Anthony square in the balls," she declares, her eyes flashing with anger. I can't help but laugh at her fiery spirit.

"They were picking up Jada, that's why they were at the school," I explain.

Hazel nods, processing the information. Then, a mischievous grin lights up her face.

"So, Reid was your white knight, huh?" she teases, wiggling her eyebrows suggestively. "You two are so in love. He protected you because he loves you. Admit it, Ames."

I feel my cheeks heat as I sit back in my seat, my heart pounding in my chest. I realize I might be falling in love with Reid. And that thought... it scares me.

"In the tempest of intense romantic feelings, we navigate the stormy seas of passion, charting a course through the unpredictable waves of desire, and discovering that, sometimes, it's in the chaos that the most beautiful connections are found."

Finally, lunchtime has arrived, and I have put the morning confrontation behind me. Yet, somehow, Hazel's words are still bouncing around in my head, like a song I can't shake off. As I absentmindedly munch on my sandwich, I can't help but wonder if maybe Reid is falling in love with me, too. It's something that's been quietly whispering at the back of my mind, but now it's louder than ever. Hazel's voice abruptly shattered my reverie.

"Amelia, Benjamin is throwing a party at his house tonight, and we're going," she stated matter-of-factly.

I blink, taken aback. "What?" I ask, my mind still trying to shift gears.

"You heard me," Hazel replies, a smirk playing on her lips. "I'll pick you up around ten and wear something cute. You don't want to scare Reid away with your unflattering Amish dresses."

I let out a laugh, the sheer audacity of Hazel's words lighting a spark of excitement within me. As Hazel rambles about her outfit plan for tonight, I can't help but get caught up in her infectious excitement. She's talking about this sequin mini dress she'd bought last week and how it's the perfect time to debut it. We are so engrossed in our conversation that we didn't notice the time fly by. The bell piercing through the cafeteria noise breaks our chatter, signaling the end of the lunch break.

Hazel and I say our goodbyes, promising to text each other about any more party details before we split up for our respective classes. As I was walking towards physics, I can't help but feel a rush of anticipation. A smile creep onto my face as I enter the room, spotting Reid's familiar figure seated at our usual spot. As I walk towards our usual spot, our eyes meet, and we smile at each other. Just as I'm about to take my seat, Reid leans in, and our lips meet in a sweet, familiar kiss. Suddenly, a voice rings through the room, shattering the comfortable bubble we had created around us.

"Well, would you look at that!" Mrs. Allen says loudly, her voice resonating through the room, interrupting our embrace. "Their kiss is like a perfect balance of forces, demonstrating the conservation of momentum. Just like in physics, every action has an equal and passionate reaction."

She points at us with a knowing smile, making a playful reference to our kiss. A blush creeps up my cheeks as I stammer an awkward apology, Reid wearing a similar expression next to me. The classroom burst into a chorus of giggles, filling the room with a contagious energy that's hard to resist. I can't help but join in and laugh.

Leaning closer to Reid, I lower my voice to a whisper. "Are you going to Benjamin's party tonight?" I ask, my gaze locked onto his.

He hesitates, his eyes flickering with uncertainty before he finally spoke. "I've been thinking about it," he admits. "I don't usually go to parties." A small smile tugs at the corners of his lips. "But I'll go if you're going."

His words, casual yet sincere, make my heart skip a beat.

"Then I guess I'll go too," I say with a smile that matches his.

School seems to fly by, a blur of facts and equations, my mind constantly wandering back to the party. As soon as I step inside the house, a wave of relief washes over me. Mom had given me the green light for Benjamin's party.

"It's late on a school night, I know," she'd says with a knowing wink. "But I was young once too."

Mom's smirk widens into a knowing grin, her eyes twinkling with mischief as she leans in. "And I remember what goes on at these parties too, Amelia. Keep your cup close. Don't let anyone bring you a drink. Get your own." Her voice drops to a whisper, her hands gesturing for emphasis as she delivers her last piece of advice. "And most importantly, keep those legs closed."

I let out a breathy laugh, feeling the blush creep up my cheeks. I can always count on Mom for her blunt yet sound advice.

I stand in my room, staring at the reflection in the mirror. I'd tried on so many outfits, they're now strewn all over the room. Each discarded dress seems to mock me, a manifestation of my indecisiveness. There's the blue one with the cute frills that Hazel had given me for my birthday. There is also the black lace number that I'd bought on a whim but never mustered the courage to wear. Then there is the red dress, simple yet classy. I hold it against my body, examining myself in the mirror. I'd never been one for fashion, but tonight, I was desperate to get it right, so I let the dress fall to the floor before letting out a sigh of frustration. Now, panic is setting in and I'm running out of time, and I still haven't decided what to wear.

I rummage through my closet one more time, my eyes landing on the safe choice, my favorite pair of jeans and a pretty top. Tonight isn't supposed to be about playing it safe, is it? I shake my head, going back to square one, staring at the mountain of clothes that sit before me. Destiny and Iris are in my room, laughing at my frantic state. My floor is a chaotic mix of discarded clothes, outfits being tossed aside as I try to find the perfect one.

"Amelia, I swear you have no sense of style," Destiny teases, her eyes twinkling with mirth as she rummages through my closet. "It's a good thing I'm here. You need all the fashion advice you can get."

I stick my tongue out at her, laughing as she holds up a hideous skirt with a dramatic gasp. Iris is making a game out of the discarded pile of clothes on the floor, twirling around in a too-big jacket and mismatched shoes.

Destiny disappears into the abyss of my closet, the sounds of hangers scraping and fabric rustling filling the room. After what feels like an eternity, she emerges, holding a garment in each hand with a triumphant smile. She's holding a pair of high-waisted jeans and a cropped floral blouse. The jeans hug my small curves perfectly, while the blouse adds a touch of femininity with its vibrant print. Destiny completes the look with a pair of ankle boots.

The outfit, once overlooked, now exudes confidence and charm, making it impossible to resist. She pairs it with a delicate silver chain necklace with a tiny moon pendant, hinting at a touch of whimsy. It's an outfit I had overlooked countless times, yet in Destiny's hands, it feels like it has been transformed, imbued with an air of confidence and charm that's irresistible.

Destiny, with her expert touch, gently applies a hint of makeup to my face. Just a dusting of eyeshadow to complement my skin tone and a dab of gloss on my lips to give them a subtle sheen. As she put on the finishing touches, she styled my hair in a way that highlights my natural black girl curls in a blend of charm and simplicity. Suddenly, the sound of a horn blared outside, pulls me out of my thoughts.

"Hazel's here!" My mom's voice echoes from downstairs.

I quickly thank Destiny in a whirlwind of gratitude and excitement, as I grab my bag and race towards the door.

"And Amelia," I hear Mom call out just as I'm about to step outside, "Tell Hazel to come in and say hi next time."

I nod, shooting her a quick smile before closing the front door behind me. As I slide into the passenger seat of Hazel's car, she turns to me with a wide grin.

"Girl, you look amazing!" she says, as her eyes sparkle with excitement.

I can't help but return her compliment. "You look great too, Hazel!"

Her outfit is a perfect blend of edgy and chic, perfectly reflecting her vibrant personality. The air between us crackles with anticipation and excitement as she revs up the engine. The familiar sound of our favorite song blares through the speakers, drowning out any room for nervousness. We sing along, our voices intertwining in a harmony of friendship and joy as we make our way to Benjamin's house. The city lights whizz past us in a blur, heightening our excitement for the evening ahead.

As Hazel pulls up to Benjamin's house, my heart skips a beat. Cars line the street, a clear testament to the popularity of the event. We end up parking a little down the street in the closest spot we could find. As we step out of the car, the pulsating rhythm of the music reaches our ears, a mix of thumping bass and catchy tunes that make me want to dance. We can hear the sounds of laughter and chatter, punctuated by the occasional cheer. As we walk towards the house, we can see students outside, their bodies swaying to the music, their faces lighting up with excitement.

Stepping inside, we're met with a scene straight out of a

movie. The house is packed, a sea of familiar faces laughing, chatting, and dancing. The energy is infectious as the music seems louder, and it fills the room with an unspoken camaraderie. Some students huddle in groups, some dance in the middle of the room, and others catching up over drinks. The atmosphere is electrifying, a perfect blend of chaos and joy.

As the sounds of the party thrummed through the room, a nudge at my side pulled me out of the cacophonous haze. Turning my head, I follow Hazel's pointed gaze towards a corner of the room. It's there I see Reid standing in an awkward stance and scanning the room. As his gaze locks with mine, an unexpected shiver runs down my spine. There is something in his stare, an intensity that seems to seep into my soul, and I'm sure he even realizes the effect his gaze has on me.

Before I can process the rush of emotions, Hazel's voice cuts through my thoughts. "I see Benjamin. I'll catch up with you later."

She gives my shoulder a reassuring squeeze before disappearing into the crowd. I take a deep breath, feeling my heart pound against my rib cage as I make my way to Reid. With each step, the awareness of eyes on us grows, turning the room into a stage where we were the main actors. As I reach him, I feel a pull towards him in a way words cannot explain. Without thinking, I stand on my toes, close the tiny distance between us, and plant a kiss on his lips.

Pulling back, I feel his lips curl into a bemused smile. His eyes twinkle in a way that invites me to divulge my deepest secrets and desires. Soon, we find ourselves lost in a whirlwind of conversation, words spilling over each other to bridge the gap no wider than a breath between us. Yet, our intimate bubble is periodically burst by the intrusive stares from fellow students. It's as if Reid and I are some sort of spectacle in a zoo, an exotic breed on show for their amusement.

Fed up, I lace my fingers through Reid's, pulling him out of his spot. Ignoring the surprised look on his face, I led him through the crowd towards Hazel and Benjamin. Trusting me, Reid follows, our determined strides only interrupted by the occasional classmate who steps out of our way.

"Benjamin?" I ask, my voice hard, but with a clear plea in my eyes. "Is there somewhere quiet we can go? People can't stop staring at us like we're freaks of nature." My words were met with a bark of laughter from Benjamin, while Hazel's lips twitch in amusement.

"Sure, Amelia," Benjamin replies, still chuckling. "You can head upstairs. There's a spare bedroom, first door on the left."

With a nod, a sigh of relief escapes my lips as I tug Reid along, eager to escape the prying eyes. I guide Reid through the chaotic scene, a silent plea in my eyes that he trusts me. I just want to enjoy his company without feeling everyone's eyes on us. As we ascend the stairs, the noise from the party seems to fade, replaced by the rhythmic thumping of our hearts. I turn the handle of the spare bedroom, pushing the door open to reveal a quiet, dimly lit space. As the door closes behind us, the hushed silence falls like a warm blanket, wrapping us in a cocoon of solitude.

Suddenly, the intimacy of the situation hits me like a ton of bricks. It's just Reid and me, alone in a bedroom. I hadn't given it a second thought when I was trying to escape the curious stares downstairs, but now the reality of the situation is glaringly apparent. I can feel a blush creeping onto my cheeks as I glance at Reid, his expression unreadable in the soft light.

I walk over to the bed, trying to appear nonchalant despite the butterflies in my stomach. Throwing a casual glance over my shoulder at Reid, I pat the spot next to me. I grin, a little amusement playing in my eyes as a faint blush colors his cheeks. The sight is endearing, to say the least. After a moment's hesitation, he moves to sit next to me and the bed dips slightly under his weight. Determined to keep the atmosphere relaxed and friendly, I pick up the thread of our conversation from downstairs.

The whole time we're talking, I can't stop staring into his blazing green eyes. He looks at me as if I'm going to disappear if he blinks. The intensity of his stare causes me to stop talking. We stare at each other for a few more seconds before his lips descend on mine. I close my eyes and get lost in the kiss. I can't stop the slight moan that escapes my lips. Soon, the kiss deepens, and I open my eyes to see Reid's eyes closed, enjoying the kiss.

He pushes into me more, and I lie back as he climbs on top of me. I can feel how much he's enjoying this as soon as his body presses into mine. He feels long and solid beneath his pants. I run my hands along his back and wrap my legs around his waist. He pushes into me, rubbing himself against my center. We both moan, as it feels so good. Both of us are trying to ease the ache we've created in each other.

Something between us shifts, and we rub against each other in earnest. I pull back from the kiss and smile up at him. His cheeks are flushed, and he moans as he rubs against me faster. I move my hips up and down, increasing the friction between us.

"Oh, god," he says as his hardness twitches between my legs.

We resume kissing, and he moves his hands to my sides and holds me firmly. The kiss turns sloppy. Our tongues battle, our breaths heavy, and our moaning becomes louder. Thankfully, the music is blaring downstairs, or else everyone will hear us.

"Reid," I moan as I feel my body winding tighter.

We're panting with desire, lost in the pleasure we're giving each other. He starts to move faster, and I moan louder. He grunts deep and pulls my ass up to press harder into me as he gets lost in the moment. I gasp and shake as my orgasm hits, wave after wave of pleasure coursing through me. I've never felt this sensation before, even with Anthony. Reid grinds a few more times before he stops, and his head falls to my shoulder as he shakes.

I feel him pulsating between me as he comes. He kisses my shoulder as he holds me tight. He slowly rocks his hips again, riding it out until the very end. Eventually, we both still and catch our breaths. Everything gets quiet, and he lifts his head from my shoulder. He looks at me and cups my cheek. He places a gentle kiss on my lips before moving off me. I sit up and straighten my clothes.

"Um, I was not expecting that," I say with a small smile.

Reid's neck and face flames in embarrassment as he rubs the back of his neck. "Um, yeah. That got intense."

"Reid," I say as I grab his hand. "I'm not sorry that happened."

He smiles at me. "I'm not sorry either."

"But we have a problem," I tell him, and he frowns at me. "We don't have a change of clothes. I don't know about you, but I'm pretty sticky right now."

That gets him to laugh. Luckily, there's an ensuite bathroom, and we take turns going in and cleaning up as best we can. After we finish fixing our appearance, I tell Reid we should head back downstairs. It's getting late, and I have to head home before my mom kicks my ass for missing curfew.

When we make it downstairs, I find Hazel still hanging out with Benjamin. I tell her I have to get home, and she tells Benjamin bye. Reid and I look at each other with secretive smiles before I kiss him goodbye. The entire ride home, I couldn't keep the smile off my face.

"In the garden of cute young love, every day is a new petal, unfolding in the tender sunlight of shared smiles and laughter. As we navigate this floral journey hand in hand, our love grows with each sunrise, a delicate bloom that flourishes and brightens, painting the canvas of our story with hues of joy and discovery."

IMPENDING TIME APART

Ever since Benjamin's party, things have changed between Reid and me. It's like we crossed a line, not all the way, but we've been more... intimate. His touch is no longer just friendly. It's tinged with an electricity that wasn't there before. A lingering hand on my back, a soft brush of fingers against my hand, simple gestures that now send a shiver down my spine. There's a tension between us that's palpable, a silent conversation that's louder than any words. It's terrifying and exhilarating, and I can't help but wonder where this will lead.

Every day that rolls by, Reid becomes more and more etched into my thoughts, his actions and words playing like a favorite song in the back of my mind. The warmth in his eyes seems to be for me alone. I see it, in the way he looks at me, in the way he speaks to me, in the way he's always there, right when I need him. And it's not just me — I can see he feels the same way. His smiles are brighter, his jokes are funnier, and there's an eagerness about him, a sparkle in his eyes that I've never seen before.

School has been a blur, like a movie playing on fast-forward. The start of school at the end of August and getting lost between classes all seem like eons ago. It was September when I met Reid and formed a connection that I'd never felt before. Then came October, filled with Spirit Week's crazy costumes and homecoming's whirlwind of excitement. Now, we're on the cusp of Thanksgiving break. I blinked, and the end of August turned into November. It's hard to believe how much has changed in such a short time, how much I've changed.

For the first time since Reid and I became... whatever we are now, we're about to be separated for an extended period. The upcoming Thanksgiving break looms ahead, a yawning gap of time that I'd usually look forward to, but this year, it's different. This year, I've got Reid.

We've spent practically every waking moment together for weeks now, our lives intertwining in a way that feels both exciting and terrifyingly intimate. The thought of not seeing him for an entire week, of not seeing his smile... it's a strange knot of anticipation and dread in the pit of my stomach. That's how it is with Reid. He's become a part of my everyday life, a constant presence that brings warmth, laughter, and a sense of belonging I didn't know I was missing.

Hazel and I are tucked into the back corner of the classroom, the monotonous drone of the teacher fading into the background. We're supposed to be working on a group project, but our minds are miles away from the subject. Hazel leans over to get my attention.

"So, I'm being dragged to see my grandmother over break," she says, sounding as dramatic as she always does. "And she does this thing, Amelia. You won't believe it. She takes out her false teeth and soaks them in a glass overnight. Right there on her bedside table!"

Hazel makes a face, and I can't help but laugh. The image

is so vivid and, honestly, a bit gross. This is classic Hazel, always finding humor in the weirdest places.

"Oh, Hazel, it's not that bad. It's just grandma things," I say, still chuckling. "My family is coming over for the holiday. I'm actually quite excited about it."

Hazel wiggles her eyebrows at me, a mischievous glint in her eyes. "Ooooh, does this mean Reid gets to meet the fam?" she asks, her grin teasing.

My cheeks immediately heat, and I shake my head quickly.

"No, no," I stutter out, "I don't... I don't think that would be... ideal. Especially since my mom hasn't met him yet."

Our conversation is suddenly cut short as the teacher calls out to us. "Amelia, Hazel, this isn't social hour."

It's clear we've been talking too loudly. I cast an apologetic glance towards the teacher and nod, promising to get back to work. My thoughts drift away from the school project. With the upcoming break, my mind shifts towards the final volleyball game.

We're up against the team we lost to earlier in the season. It's a grudge match of sorts, and the anticipation in my veins is palpable. I've replayed the last game in my head over and over. Each missed serve and failed block a stubborn reminder of our defeat. This time it's different. There's an air of electric excitement surrounding me, a buzz of potential victory that's more potent than any previous game we've played.

The thought of our team, united and strong, facing off against our rivals is enough to make my heart pound in my chest with a mix of nerves and exhilaration. The prospect of turning the tables on them, of showing them how much we've improved, has me positively giddy with anticipation. It's all I can think about, even as I try to focus on the task at hand. The classroom fades into the background, replaced by the vision of a roaring crowd and a volleyball court. The break may be getting closer, but that game is all I can see.

Before I know it, the day is a whirlwind of lessons and laughter, passing in a blink of an eye. The bell rings, signaling the end of my last period - Economics. The numbers and theories from class still swirl in my mind as I pack up my things and leave the room. As I trudge out of the classroom, thoughts of supply and demand giving way to thoughts of Reid, I am greeted by a sight that instantly warms my heart and brightens my day. There he is, leaning casually against a locker, an alluring mix of charm and boyish good looks.

I approach him, and just as I'm close enough, he pushes off the locker and opens his arms wide. As if drawn by an invisible force, I walk straight into his embrace, his arms wrapping around me in a comfortable, familiar hug. The tension from the day melts away, replaced by the comforting hum of Reid's presence. His smell, a blend of fresh laundry and that unique Reid-scent that I can't quite pin down, envelops me.

I allow myself a moment to just breathe him in, to let the soothing rhythm of his heart under my ear anchor me back to reality. Then I pull back slightly, my hands resting on his chest as I look up at him. There's a warmth there, a softness in his eyes that makes my heart flutter. A slow smile creeps onto my face, a mirror of the one that's playing on his lips. I stretch up on my tiptoes, closing the distance between us until my lips meet his in a sweet, simple kiss that sends a shiver of warmth through me, a whisper of promise for the days to come.

We break the kiss, and he looks at me with an expression I can't quite decipher. "Amelia," he begins, and immediately, I sense there's something amiss. His voice is serious, almost apologetic. "I... I won't be able to make your volleyball game," he confesses, his fingers tracing circles on my back in a soothing manner. "My dad needs help with something after school."

A pang of disappointment hits me, and I try to mask it with a gentle smile. "Oh," is all I manage.

We had been discussing the match for weeks, and the thought of him not there, in the stands, cheering me on, is suddenly disheartening. But I understand. His family has been through a lot lately, and he's been stepping up to help his dad in any way he can.

"So... I wanted to see you now." He continues, "I wanted to wish you good luck."

The sincerity in his eyes warms my heart. It's just like Reid to make sure he gets to see me before I play a big game. Despite my disappointment, I appreciate his effort and his honesty. A part of me knows I would have been more upset if he had made promises he couldn't keep.

"Thanks, Reid," I murmur, leaning in to give him a quick kiss on the cheek.

He gives me a little squeeze, reassuring me without words. I pull away and give him a smile, a promise of understanding and acceptance. Off to the side, Hazel makes a gagging sound, breaking the moment.

"You guys are so cute it makes me sick," she says, a teasing grin across her face. She throws an arm around my shoulder, pulling me into her side.

Turning to Reid, she gives him a mock-serious look. "Don't you worry one bit, Reid," she declares. "I'll be there cheering enough for the both of us."

The humor in her voice and the twinkle in her eye bring a much-needed light to the moment, and I can't help but laugh.

Reid gives a nod, a soft smile playing on his lips as he lets me go. "Kick some ass," he murmurs, his voice full of pride.

I nod, taking a step back and offering him one last smile before turning to join Hazel. We walk away, arm in arm, the sight of Reid slowly shrinking in the distance. Soon enough, we're in the locker room, a whirlwind of nerves and excitement as we prepare for the game.

Stepping onto the court, a wave of adrenaline washes over me. The crowd roars, a sea of faces blurring together under the harsh gymnasium lights. Yet, there's one absence I feel acutely. Reid. The sight of his empty seat in the bleachers stings, but I push it aside. This is our moment, our chance to show what we're capable of. My teammates surround me, a solid wall of camaraderie and shared determination.

The smell of the court, the feel of the volleyball in my hands, the pulsating energy of the crowd, it all comes together, grounding me in the moment. Then, the whistle blows. It's game time, and I'm in the zone. The world fades away until all that's left are my teammates, our opponents, and the game. A game we're ready to win.

The intensity of the game is palpable. Each serve is a thunderbolt, each dig a daring dance with gravity, each spike a declaration of war. The ball ricochets around the court like a pinball, a blur of white against the polished wood and overhead lights. Our opponents are formidable, matching us point for point, pushing us to play harder, faster, smarter. We move as one, a synchronized machine fine-tuned over countless practices and games. Sweat glistens on foreheads, drips down necks, and stains jerseys as we give it our all. Shouts of encouragement from the bench and the crowd form a symphony of support that fuels our determination. It's a dizzying, electrifying, relentless tempo from whistle to whistle. The tension ratchets up with each point scored, each mistake made, each opportunity seized or squandered.

The ball soars towards me, a white blur against the bright lights of the gymnasium. My heart is pounding in my chest, my senses heightened. I plant my feet, my arms extended, ready to receive the serve. The moment the ball touches my palms, I direct it upward, setting it perfectly for Hazel's attack. The gym echoes with the thunderous sound of Hazel's spike, a satisfying thwack that sends the ball rocketing over the net and onto the opposing court.

I can hear the collective gasp of the crowd, the adrenaline surging through my veins like a live wire. Sweat trickles down my forehead, but I hardly notice. My gaze is fixed on the ball, my mind calculating angles and trajectories. The ball bounces back, a shot fast and low. I dive, the world tilting as I stretch my arm out, the volleyball grazing my fingers at the last possible second.

A roar of approval erupts from the crowd. I can feel a grin stretching across my face, the satisfaction of a job well done. The cheers from our bench are deafening, the high fives from my teammates grounding me in the energy of the moment. The sting in my palms only serves to amplify the thrill, a testament to the intensity of the game. My pulse thunders in my ears, a steady rhythm that matches the pounding of my sneakers on the court.

I look towards the bleachers, imagining Reid's face. I know he'd be on his feet, cheering at the top of his lungs. But I don't let his absence dampen my spirits. Instead, I channel it into my game, playing hard. The final whistle blows, and as our victory is confirmed, a wave of euphoria sweeps over me. We did it. We won. The cheers are deafening, but in this moment, everything feels just right. I look at my teammates, their faces flushed with victory and smile.

As I step out of the locker room, changed and refreshed, I see Hazel leaning against the wall, her arms crossed. She looks up as I approach, a smile tugging at the corner of her mouth.

"Took you long enough," she quips, pushing off from the wall.

I roll my eyes, a grin spreading across my face. "Well, not all of us can shower at lightning speed."

Hazel laughs, throwing an arm around my shoulders as we walk towards the exit. "Anyway, great game today, Amelia," she says.

I feel warmth spreading through me at her words, "Thanks, Hazel."

The ride home is a blur of singing and laughter. Hazel has control of the music, and we belt out the lyrics to our favorite songs, joy and triumph fueling our off-key renditions. The stars twinkle above us as we navigate the familiar streets, the world outside a quiet contrast to the euphoria inside the car. The night is ours, a celebration of our victory, and we revel in it.

As I arrive home, my excitement bubbles over as I recount the game to my mom and sisters. It filled the living room with animated gestures and reenacted plays, their faces mirroring my excitement at every twist and turn of the story. Their cheers and laughter mirror the energy of the crowd, a familiar symphony that I carry with me even as I retreat to the sanctuary of my room.

Just as I'm about to switch off my bedside lamp, my phone buzzes. It's a message from Reid.

"Goodnight, Amelia," it reads. "I'm going to miss you over break."

A warmth floods through me, a soft echo of the adrenaline rush from the game.

I feel a smile tug at my lips as I text back, "Goodnight, Reid. I'll miss you too."

As I settle into my bed, the events of the day replay in my mind - the thrill of the game, the joy of our victory, and the comfort of Reid's message. I fall asleep with a smile on my face, my dreams filled with the echoes of cheering crowds and the promise of many more victories to come.

"IN THE HEARTFUL ALBUM OF FAMILY, LOVE IS THE MELODY THAT PLAYS THROUGH EVERY SHARED LAUGH AND EVERY WARM EMBRACE. TOGETHER, WE COMPOSE A SYMPHONY OF JOY, WHERE FUN IS THE RHYTHM THAT DANCES THROUGH THE NOTES OF OUR LIVES, CREATING A HARMONIOUS MASTERPIECE THAT LASTS A LIFETIME."

The first couple of days of break is a whirlwind. The family arrives, and the festivities start. It's all laughter, tales, and catching up on life. Amidst all this, my phone buzzes constantly with texts from Reid. He, too, is having a similar experience with his visiting family. We've been swapping stories back and forth – the fun, the insanity, and the inevitable family quirks that surface during these gatherings. It's been a flurry of activity, but I wouldn't have it any other way.

I'm driving around with my mother, running errands as we embark on our mission, hopping from one store to another, gathering everything we need to keep the festivities going smoothly. We filled the backseat of the car with fresh produce and food, transforming it into a makeshift storage unit.

As we pull into yet another store's parking lot, I can't help but let out a dramatic sigh. "Mom, are we done yet? How many more stores do we need to visit?"

My voice is a playful whine, the familiar dance of a parent and child during holiday errand chaos.

Laughing, she glances at me, her eyes shining with pure amusement. "Oh, stop being so melodramatic, Amelia! Just one more, I promise. We're almost done."

True to her word, we make it through the last store in record time, despite my faux protests, and we head back home. As we pull into the driveway, our car looks like a traveling farmer's market. As if under some unspoken agreement, family members filter out of the house, lining up to grab bags from the car and carry them inside. It's a jumble of chatter and laughter, punctuated by the occasional shout of surprise as someone discovers the weight of a heavy bag. Soon, the kitchen is buzzing like a beehive.

The countertops are filled with fresh produce, flour packages, and cans of all sorts. Everyone, from my youngest cousin to my great aunt, is engaged in some sort of task - peeling, chopping, stirring, or just passing things around. There's a sense of camaraderie and unity that only a shared kitchen duty can bring. As I survey the scene, I can't help but feel a swell of love and gratitude for this crazy, noisy, wonderful clan of mine. And despite the chaos, the thought of the mouthwatering meal that we're prepping for tomorrow makes it all worth it.

As the sun sets, I nestle into the cozy living room alongside my family. It's movie time. A long-standing tradition, we've always gathered to watch "A Charlie Brown Thanksgiving". Even though I've watched it so many times that I could probably recite the dialogue by heart, the charm never fades. As the familiar theme music begins, a wave of nostalgia washes over me. I lean back into the plush cushions of the couch, a content smile playing on my lips. Each scene is a childhood memory, each line a shared joke between us.

I glance around the room at the faces lit by the flickering TV light, everyone entranced by the timeless classic. I might know every beat of this movie, but every time feels like the first. Wrapped up in the warmth of the moment, I can't help but feel thankful. This is what it's all about—family, tradition, and love. As crazy as the past few days have been, I wouldn't trade these moments for anything.

Finally, I find a moment of peace as the movie ends. I decide to grab a glass of water from the kitchen. Just as I'm about to reach for the refrigerator handle, I hear my phone ringing from the other room. The screen lights up, and I see Reid's name flashing. My heart skips a bit. I change direction and head to the quiet of my room.

Picking up the phone, I take a deep breath before answering. "Hey, Reid."

"Hey, you," comes Reid's warm voice from the other end of the line.

"How are you? We just finished watching a movie as we're all prepped for tomorrow's dinner," I tell Reid, my voice bubbling over with excitement. "I can't wait for all the soul food we're going to have."

"Soul food?" Reid asks, his voice laced with curiosity.

I can't help but laugh at his confusion. "Yes, Reid, soul food. You know, food that fills not just your belly but your spirit, too? We're going to have sweet potato pie, greens, fried chicken, cornbread, and my mom's famous mac and cheese. Trust me, it's going to be a feast!"

There's a pause before Reid responds, a hint of envy in his voice. "That sounds amazing, Amelia. Honestly, compared to that, what I'm going to be eating sounds pretty boring and bland."

We both burst into laughter, sharing in the humor of our different Thanksgiving traditions. As our laughter fades into a comfortable silence, Reid's tone turns serious.

"Amelia, I miss you," he confesses, his voice just above a whisper.

A warm smile spreads across my face, knowing that he's there on the other end of the line, feeling the same way I do.

"I miss you too, Reid," I respond, my voice soft yet full of affection.

There's another moment of silence, but it's the comfortable kind that only comes with close friendships.

"I just wanted to hear your voice," he finally admits, breaking the silence. "I'll let you get back to your family now, and I can't wait to see you after the break."

"I look forward to it, Reid," I assure him, a sense of excitement building within me.

After exchanging a few more words, we end the call, and I return to the living room, back to the warmth of my family, but with the comforting thought of seeing Reid soon.

As dawn breaks, Thanksgiving Day arrives in all its glory. The house awakens to a symphony of chatter, laughter, and the clatter of kitchen utensils. It's like a well-orchestrated melody, each sounds perfectly in tune with the holiday spirit. The aroma of mom's famous mac and cheese baking in the oven, the sweet scent of the pie crusts as they turn golden, and the mouthwatering smell of the turkey roasting — all mingle together, creating a tantalizing fragrance that permeates the house.

As I make my way back to the living room, my cousin Destiny walks through the front door with a stranger following behind her. She's all smiles, her arms gesturing animatedly as she talks.

"Everyone, this is Jason," she announces, stressing the word 'friend'.

Jason walks over to us, a shy smile plastered on his face as he shakes hands with everyone, but I can't help but notice a hint of apprehension in his eyes.

As Jason steps into the light, I have time to study him

more closely. He has a rich, dark complexion that stands out against his white shirt, a contrast that only serves to amplify his handsome looks. His hair is cropped short and neat, revealing a clear, thoughtful forehead. His eyes are a warm, dark brown as if holding a story waiting to be told, and despite a hint of nervousness, they hold an undeniable spark of kindness. The sharp angles of his jawline give way to a strong chin, and he carries himself with quiet confidence, his tall frame exuding an air of calm composure. He definitely seems like Destiny's type.

Before he can even settle down, my uncles Ryan and Charles swoop in, their eyebrows raised suggestively.

"So, Jason. Destiny tells us you're a 'friend'," Uncle Ryan begins, the word friend wrapped in air quotes.

Uncle Charles chimes in. "Yeah, a 'friend'. So tell us, do you like our Destiny?"

Jason's face turns a shade of red, almost matching the cranberry sauce on the counter.

"Well, sure, Destiny is a great friend," Jason stammers, his eyes darting nervously toward Destiny.

"But do you like her?" Uncle Ryan asks again, a mischievous twinkle in his eyes.

"I mean, yeah, I like her as a friend." Jason's voice is shaky, the word 'friend' emphasized, just as Destiny had done earlier.

My uncles exchange glances before Uncle Charles asks, "And what are your intentions with Destiny?"

"My intentions?" Jason repeats, his face a mask of bewilderment. "Well... I intend to help her eat all that mac and cheese she's been talking about."

The room erupts into laughter, and I can't help but join in.

As we all gather around the beautifully set table, I can't

help but feel a wave of contentment wash over me. The vibrant orange hues of the festive tablecloth, the sparkling silverware, and the golden glow of the candles create a warm and inviting atmosphere. We all sit down, Reid's voice still lingering in my mind, adding to the happiness that's bubbling up inside me.

Mom brings the golden-brown turkey to the table, its mouthwatering aroma wafting around the room. The mac and cheese, greens, and cornbread soon follow, filling the table with colorful, tantalizing dishes. The room fills with appreciative 'oohs' and 'ah's' as everyone eyes the feast before us.

Dad says a heartfelt prayer, thanking the Lord for our family, our health, and the love that binds us. Following tradition, we all hold hands, our eyes closed, as we listen to his words. We fill the room with a profound sense of gratitude and the inherent magic of Thanksgiving enveloping us all.

As we open our eyes, the feasting begins. The room comes alive with the sounds of cutlery clinking, laughter ringing, and lively conversations filling the air. The food is delicious, every bite brimming with flavors that are as comforting as they are delectable. I take a moment to savor the sweetness of the sweet potato pie, the creamy goodness of mom's famous mac and cheese, and the crispiness of the fried chicken. Each dish is a testament to Mom's culinary skills and the love she pours into her cooking.

As we share stories, jokes, and personal updates, the bond that ties us together feels stronger than ever. There's Destiny, blushing each time Jason compliments her cooking. Uncles Ryan and Charles are engaged in a friendly debate, their banter adding to the lively atmosphere.

As the night progresses, I feel a sense of completeness. Sitting here, surrounded by my loved ones, indulging in soul food that's equally nourishing and comforting, I can't help but think, this is what Thanksgiving is all about — love, gratitude, and togetherness. It's a moment of peace amidst the chaos of life, a testament to the enduring spirit of our traditions and the ties that bind us. And as I look around the table, I can't help but feel thankful for the warmth of my family and the promise of seeing Reid soon.

"IN THE REALM OF DESIRE, LOVE BECOMES A RELENTLESS FORCE, A DESPERATION THAT WHISPERS IN THE SHADOWS OF THE HEART, MAKING IT HARD TO DENY THE NEED FOR A CONNECTION THAT TRANSCENDS THE BOUNDARIES OF REASON. IT'S A HUNGER THAT ONLY THE TOUCH OF YOUR PRESENCE CAN SATISFY—A CRAVING THAT LINGERS, UNDENIABLE AND INTOXICATING."

UNEXPECTED ENCOUNTER

As I take another bite out of my sandwich, Hazel looks at me with a smirk. "So, how are things with Reid?"

Swallowing, I can't help but smile. "It's going well. Great, actually."

Her brows wiggle suggestively, and I roll my eyes, a blush creeping to my cheeks. "Don't even start, Hazel."

But of course, she doesn't listen. "So, have you two...you know?"

I let out a sigh, shaking my head. "No, Hazel. We haven't. But we've...you know...fooled around a bit during the times we've snuck off together."

Hazel's reaction is predictable, a shriek of glee erupting from her as she yells. "My best friend is getting some creamer in her coffee!"

I laugh in response, shaking my head at her choice of euphemism. As we continue our lunch, Hazel drops another bombshell, informing me she and Benjamin were now an item. I tell her I'm happy for her. In true Hazel style, she doesn't miss a beat.

"We should double date some time!" she suggests, much to my amusement.

I rolled my eyes at her, but didn't shoot down the idea entirely. We finish our lunch, and I stand up, hoisting my tray with the remnants of our meal. Hazel mirrored my actions, and we walked side-by-side towards the bins to dump our trays. The clattering sound of empty trays and the buzzing noise of the lunchroom conversations fade as I turn back to Haze to tell her I'd see her later. Hazel gives me a nod, her eyes twinkling with a mix of mischief and excitement at our shared secrets. She grins and waves me off as I turn to go, leaving her to finish her day as I head to my class.

As I'm navigating the bustling corridor to get to my next period, an unexpected tug on my arm yanks me off my path, pulling me into an empty classroom. I whirl around, my mind prepared to unload a barrage of words onto the culprit, but my frustration melts away when I catch sight of him. There, grinning back at me, is Reid. The sight of him immediately lights up my face, my lips curling upward into a bright smile.

He pulls me close and puts his hand on the back of my neck before pulling my face to his. His lips meet mine, firm but soft, and the slow, sensual kiss sends a powerful need surging through my body. I press my lips harder against his, and our kiss becomes urgent. Our mouths open with his tongue stroking mine. Wetness pulls between my legs, and I squirm to relieve the pressure.

I can feel him growing hard beneath me, and I moan in his mouth. He steps closer, pushing into me more. His hardness twitches against me, and his hands move to my sides, holding me as he rubs himself against me. We haven't had sex yet, and I'm quite sure he's a virgin. I've had sex once before with my shitty ex-boyfriend, but now that I'm with Reid, I wish I hadn't.

Suddenly, Reid pulls me, and we walk with our mouths

fused together until he falls into a chair with me straddling him. He grunts, and I groan as his hardness hits my center. We move together. I'm pressing down on him, rubbing myself as he slams himself upwards against me. We moan in unison, both of us feeling the intensity of the moment. Despite us having our clothes on, the feeling is fantastic.

"Reid," I say as I pull my mouth away from his. "We could get caught."

"I know, baby," he says, rubbing himself against me more.

I moan and kiss him again, lost to the sensations because he called me baby. He's never done that before, and I love it. He moans in my mouth, feeling it too. Reid is solid against me, rubbing just the right way to relieve my swollen ache. Our movements turn frantic, and he moans louder each time he pushes his hips up, over and over again.

"God, baby," he says as his hands grab me everywhere now.

Our bodies move in a steady rhythm. My breath is coming faster, and I press harder down on him, seeking more friction. I'm so wet, and it feels so good. I rub against him once more and still as I come so hard that I'm moaning loudly, but Reid shields it by slamming his lips against mine. He stills, and I feel him pulse against me. He moans against my mouth as he comes too. When we're finished, we're panting and kissing each other softly.

Reid pulls back and smirks at me. "That was not supposed to happen."

"Well, it did," I say with a laugh. "And now we've missed class, and we need to change clothes."

He gazes at me, and I can't help but avert my gaze. He cups my cheek.

"I'm not sorry it happened. I've never felt this way before, Amelia," he says. "Sometimes I don't know what to do with all these emotions. I find myself doing things I never thought I'd do. I can't seem to help myself when it comes to you."

I lean down and kiss him with everything in me. He returns it with equal passion. Just then, a bell rings, startling us both, and we break the kiss. We wait for the halls to clear and head towards the locker rooms to change clothes.

As I change my clothes, Reid's words echo in my mind, making my heart flutter uncontrollably. The afternoon's unexpected encounter was a whirlwind of emotions that left me breathless and yet clamoring for more. Reid's raw honesty had taken me aback, but it had also filled me with a warmth that was indescribable. There was an unexpected vulnerability in his confession that made him even more endearing.

It's clear that our connection is growing deeper and crossing boundaries we had not expected. As I step out of the locker room, feeling the coolness of the hallway against my flushed skin, I can't help but feel a sense of exhilaration at the thought of what lay ahead for Reid and me.

We move towards our respective classes, the lingering sensation of our encounter making it impossible to concentrate on the lessons. Time slips by in a blur, and before I know it, the last bell echoes through the school's hallways, indicating the end of classes for the day. I can't help but feel a rush of adrenaline as I prepare for my volleyball game against Smithson High. As I change into my team's colors, I can feel the buzz of anticipation coursing through me.

The gym is already beginning to fill up by the time I arrive. I can see the faces of students, teachers, and parents in the crowd, their voices merging into a low hum. My heart flutters as I spot familiar faces. My mom and my sisters had made it. There they were, waving their handmade signs and cheering. A surge of warmth spreads in my chest as I see their smiles. Their presence, their support, means the world to me.

The whistle pierces through the clamor, signaling the start

of the game. The gym had taken on a life of its own, the echo of the bouncing ball punctuated by the stomp of shoes on the polished floor and periodic roars from the crowd. I can feel the electricity in the air, as palpable as the ball in my hands. I tune out the noise, focusing on the net that stretches before me, the faces on the other side blurred into insignificance.

As the setter, I'm the team's strategist, the director of the orchestra. I launch the ball into the air, my hand making contact with a satisfying smack. The ball sails over the net, landing squarely in the opponent's court. My team erupts in cheers, their jubilation ringing in my ears. I can't help but join in, my heart pounding in rhythm with the applause that fills the gymnasium.

The rest of the game is a flurry of serves, digs, and spikes. Each successful play is a symphony of precision and team-work, my pulse syncing with the rhythm of the game. I dive and leap, my body responding instinctively to the ball's trajec-tory. My hands sting from the repeated impact, but it's a pain I relish, a testament to the commitment we have all made.

Scoring a point felt like conquering a mountain. The ball slams against the opponent's court, followed by the thun-derous applause from our supporters. For a moment, the world seems to slow down, as all eyes are on us, the victorious underdogs.

I glance towards the crowd, catching sight of my family through the vibrant energy that fills the gymnasium. The sounds of their cheering reach my ears and I can't help but smile, my heart swelling with warmth. Their handmade signs with words of encouragement seem brighter than all the lights illuminating the room. Suddenly, a familiar voice slices through the clamor, strong and distinct. Reid. My smile widens as I turn to see him standing there, a vision among the sea of faces. His presence, his support, brings a comforting calmness that radiates through me.

Our eyes meet and his smile mirrors mine. The intensity of his gaze sends a thrill of exhilaration through me, stirring a blush that quickly spreads across my cheeks. The connection between us remains unbroken, even in this crowded room. His presence adds a whole new level of motivation, making me want to play better, push harder, and win not just for my team, but for him.

Through it all, the atmosphere is electric. The crowd is a sea of emotion, their cheers and jeers fueling our determination. The taste of victory is sweet, but the journey, the battle on the court, is even more exhilarating. As the final whistle blows, I know we had left more than just sweat on that court. We had poured our heart and soul into the game, and the echo of our triumph would resonate long after they turned the lights off.

Stepping off the court, I can still feel the lingering adrenaline coursing through my veins, buoyed by the triumphant cheers of the crowd. I make my way over to my mom and sisters, their faces light up with joy and pride. Hugs and excited chatter envelopes me as I revel in their warmth and love. Out of the corner of my eye, I notice Reid standing off to the side, engrossed in conversation with his friends. He looks up and our eyes lock for a moment. He raises his hand, signaling he'd call me later. I nod, acknowledging his unspoken promise.

I'm grateful that Reid hadn't made his way over to us. There is a part of me that's eager for him to meet my family, just as much as I wanted to meet his. Yet, I knew that this bustling gymnasium, fresh off the euphoria of victory, isn't the ideal setting. I longed for a quieter, more intimate atmosphere. A place where we could all sit down, share a meal, converse, and genuinely get to know each other. The mere thought of it fills me with a sense of anticipation, painting a hopeful picture of what lay ahead for Reid and me.

Hazel, her blonde hair tied back in a high ponytail, comes bounding over to us, her face radiating with an irrepressible grin.

"Great job, Amelia!" she yells, her voice nearly drowned by the loudness of the gymnasium, yet somehow reaching my ears, crystal clear.

She turns to greet my family with a familiarity that only comes from years of friendship.

"Hey D, squirt, and Ms. Campbell," she says, her tone light and teasing.

My mom and sisters greet her back in unison, their faces lighting up at her arrival. Hazel has always been like another member of our family, and their warmth for her confirms this sentiment.

"Thanks, Hazel," I reply, trying to match her infectious energy.

We chat a little about the game, about my excellent spikes, and our upcoming championship match.

After a few minutes, I excuse myself. "We've got to head home. Mom has a victory dinner waiting for us."

"Sounds great. See you tomorrow, Amelia," Hazel shouts over her shoulder before disappearing into the throng of people.

Getting into the car with my mom and sisters, I can feel the excitement from the game still coursing through me. We chat and laugh, swapping stories from the game and the reactions of the crowd. Suddenly, mom glances at me in the rearview mirror, her eyes dancing with a mischievous twinkle.

"Catching a blush on the court, were we, Amelia?" she asks, her voice playfully teasing.

The question catches me off guard. "What do you mean?" I ask, my cheeks heating.

"That smile on your face... it was glowing, even from the

stands. Who's the boy who's got my girl grinning like that?" she says, her gaze not leaving mine in the mirror.

A knowing smile plays on her lips as she waits for my answer.

As my mother's teasing question hangs in the air, Destiny chimes in from the seat next to me.

"I saw her smiling at a group of boys, but I couldn't really tell who it was," she says, her voice a mix of curiosity and innocent confusion. "They were all looking in her direction."

Before I can respond, Iris joins the conversation. "It's the tall boy with the piercing brown eyes, isn't it?" she asks, her voice holding the unfettered certainty that only a nine-year-old can possess.

I can almost see her triumphant grin as she waits for my reaction.

Rolling my eyes at Iris's guess, I give my sisters a playful nudge. "Oh, you mean Benjamin? He's dating Hazel, you know," I clarify, trying to keep my voice casual.

I can't help but feel a twinge of satisfaction at seeing their slightly crestfallen expressions. Intrigue replaces the curiosity in their eyes as I add, "There is a boy, though. And I promise I'll bring him home for you all to meet."

With that, I lean back in my seat with a secretive smile playing on my lips and the image of Reid's warm gaze still fresh in my mind.

"In the gallery of my days, your face is the masterpiece that brightens every canvas, a sunbeam that sweeps away the shadows. In your smile, I find the brushstrokes of joy, and in the sparkle of your eyes, everything feels not just okay but beautifully illuminated."

GETTING SICK

Waking up this morning is a battle. I feel like a truck had hit me, every limb aching and my head spinning. I can hardly muster the strength to even open my eyes. The exhaustion is so overwhelming that I drift back into unconsciousness, my mind slipping into a fog of fatigue. Then I feel a gentle tap on my shoulder, stirring me from my sleep. I turn to find my mom standing there, concern etched across her face.

"I'm not feeling well," I mumble, my words barely more than a whisper.

She immediately springs into action, thermometer in hand, asking a flurry of questions to gauge my symptoms. After a few minutes of checking and cross-checking, she determines I have a fever. It's a relief to know that the fatigue wasn't just mental.

"You're staying home today, sweetheart," she says, her voice filled with a touch of motherly worry. "I'll call the doctor and see if we can get you in tomorrow. For now, just get some rest."

I drift in and out of sleep throughout the day, the world around me a blur of colors and shapes. Whenever I open my

eyes, I find a plate of food or a glass of water waiting by my bedside. Even the sight of food makes my stomach churn, so I ignore it most of the time. My phone buzzes occasionally, messages from Reid and Hazel popping up on the screen. When I didn't show up at school, they'd checked in on me, their worry seeping through the lines of text. I sent a few responses, letting them know I was at home, sick.

Despite my lack of energy to engage in conversation, they continued to text throughout the day, their messages a comforting reminder of their presence. Responding is another battle altogether, a task that seems to require more energy than I have in reserve. I appreciate their concern, but at the same time, I want nothing more than to sink into the depths of sleep, away from the discomfort of my ailing body.

The day seems to flicker by in disjointed segments, each moment a mere flash before it's replaced by the next. Mom brings me a bowl of homemade soup, the rich aroma wafting up from the steaming broth. She tells me the doctor can see me tomorrow. Her face is a mirror of relief and worry. I take a few spoonfuls of the soup, but my appetite is practically nonexistent.

As comforting as the warmth is, I can hardly taste anything. Exhaustion tugs at me, pulling me back into the welcoming embrace of sleep. Just as I'm about to surrender, my phone buzzes on the bedside table. It's a text from Reid, his words simple but sincere, "Get better soon, Amelia." A small smile tugs at my lips before I succumb to sleep once more, his words echoing in my dream-filled slumber.

The blinding white walls of the doctor's office seem to close in around me as I perch on the edge of the examination table. Dr. Patel, who I've known since I was a kid, bustles about, his stethoscope draped around his neck. He did the typical checks. Listened to my heart and lungs, checked my pulse, looked into my ears and down my throat. He asked about my symptoms, making notes on his clipboard as I answered. Next, he ordered a couple of tests. The nurse taking my blood sample and another one that I was too tired to understand or remember.

After what feels like forever, Dr. Patel walks back in, the results of the tests in his hands. He wears a neutral expression as he speaks.

"Amelia, you have a bacterial infection. The medical term for it is...."

He continues on, but whatever he says just sounds like gibberish to me. My mom and I exchange glances, her eyes mirroring my confusion. Dr. Patel chuckles at our baffled faces and reassures us.

"Don't be scared by the terminology. It's a common infection, especially during the winter months when everyone's adjusting to the cold. Infections like these tend to spread more during these months. It's nothing life-threatening, so don't worry," he says.

With a reassuring smile, Dr. Patel writes me a prescription for antibiotics, jots down a list of over-the-counter medications my mom can pick up to treat the symptoms, and wishes me a swift recovery. We leave the doctor's office, our next stop being the pharmacy to collect my medication, and then a quick run to the supermarket for a few additional supplies. Finally, we make it back home, the day's errands leaving me completely drained. Without missing a beat, Mom has me take the first dose of antibiotics as soon as we got back.

She also hands me a pain reliever, her eyes soft but stern as she reminds me. "You need to take this on time, Amelia. No skipping doses."

I just nod, too tired to protest. After that, I trudge back upstairs to my room, my body aching and craving the comfort of my bed. I crawl under the covers, letting out a sigh as the soft fabric envelopes me. The day has been long, and all I want is to sink into sleep, hoping that tomorrow will bring some relief.

The following days are a blur of medications, rest, and intermittent visits from Hazel. She'd pop in, always armed with a bag full of treats and a burst of energy that I could only wish to match. Her visits were a welcome change from the monotony of my sick days, bringing with her stories from school and the outside world. She'd flit around my room, tidying up, chattering away about everything and nothing. She never stayed too long, understanding that I needed rest. But her presence, brief as it was, always lifted my spirits a bit.

Reid's concern was palpable, even through the text. He offered to come by a few times, his messages laced with worry. I appreciated his gestures, but I couldn't bear the thought of him seeing me in such a state. I'd always envisioned our first meeting in my home to be a pleasant one. One where I could introduce him to my mom and sisters without looking like a complete train wreck. Each time he offered, I'd find a reason to decline, promising to call him once I was feeling better.

As the days passed, I noticed a slow but steady improvement in my health. I'd regained my energy, my appetite was slowly returning, and most importantly, the constant ache in my body was subsiding. The medication, although bitter, seemed to do its job. I wasn't back to my normal self yet, but I was getting there. Each day was a step towards recovery, and I was looking forward to the day when I could step out into the world again, healthy and re-energized.

It's Friday, finally, and for the first time in what feels like forever, I feel better. Good enough to go to school, even. I can't deny the role the antibiotics and the rest of the medication played in this recovery. Despite my initial distaste, I admit, they worked wonders. As I go through the motions of my morning routine, I can't help but remember Dr. Patel's parting words. That even if I think I'm fine, I should finish the course of antibiotics in its entirety.

So, as much as I want to be done with it, I resolve to stick it out. Sitting on the edge of the sink, I pop the cap off the antibiotic bottle, take out a pill, and swallow it down with a swig of water. I can't help but breathe a sigh of relief as I look into the bottle, seeing only one left. With that minor victory under my belt, I head downstairs, ready to face the day.

Stepping into the kitchen, I'm met with the rich aroma of freshly brewed coffee and the familiar clatter of pots and pans. Mom turns to me, her eyes scanning my face as if looking for any sign of lingering illness.

"Are you sure you're feeling well enough to go to school, Amelia?" she asks, her voice filled with concern.

I nod in assurance, shooting her a small but confident smile. "Yes, mom. I'll be fine."

Just as we're exchanging smiles, a loud honk echoes from outside.

A split second later, Hazel's voice rings out. "Amelia! Let's go!"

Her voice is filled with its usual boisterous energy. It's the best sound I've heard in a while.

Mom shakes her head with a smirk and sends me off with a warm, "Have a great day at school."

I grab my bag and head out, the cool morning air making me feel even more alive. As I approach Hazel's car, she greets me with a wide, infectious grin.

"I'm so glad you're back. Reid has been walking around like a lost lovesick puppy," she laughs, and I can't help but join in, a bubble of laughter escaping my lips.

Walking into school, Hazel and I are lost in conversation, catching up on all the little things I'd missed. As we head to our lockers, I suddenly feel a familiar sensation, like I'm being watched. Turning around, my eyes meet Reid's. His eyes sparkle with relief as he approaches me, his pace quickening. I greet him with a bright smile.

As soon as he's close enough, he bends down, planting a soft kiss on my cheek before asking, "How are you feeling today, Amelia?"

His concern is genuine, and it warms my heart.

"I'm feeling much better, Reid," I reassure him, my voice steady.

"That's good to hear," he says, a sigh of relief escaping his lips before leaning in to share a deep, passionate kiss that leaves my toes curling.

During our intimate moment, Hazel clears her throat. "Hey, no tongue wrestling in the school hallway!"

Pulling back, Reid and I burst into laughter at her comment.

Hazel playfully elbows me. "See? I told you. A lovesick puppy."

We share another round of laughter before heading off to class. The day unfolds beautifully, and it feels so good to be back. The school is buzzing with the usual chatter and energy, a stark contrast to the last few days spent in the solitude of my room. My friends greet me with warm smiles, the teachers compassionate and understanding as I catch up on the missed work. Reid's presence makes it even more special. He'd occasionally sneak glances at me during class, his soft smiles radiating nothing but warmth and care.

Lunch is delightful, spent in the company of friends, full of laughter, lots of catching up, and even some good-natured teasing. Hazel and Reid keep the atmosphere light, their banter entertaining everyone around us. In those moments, I can't help but appreciate how everything feels normal again, how the humdrum of my daily life had resumed its rhythm.

As the sun set, painting the sky in hues of orange and

purple, I reflect on the past few months with Reid. Our relationship had taken a beautiful course, evolving from playful flirting to something much deeper, much more intimate. Each shared moment, each whispered word, each lingering touch only deepened our bond. The past few days of illness had proven just how much we cared for each other.

His concern, his patience, his unwavering support, it all painted a picture of a relationship that was maturing, that was becoming a stronghold in my life. As I lay in bed that night, I realized with a heart full of warmth just how much Reid had become a part of my life, an integral part of my very being.

"On our first date, butterflies pirouetted in the theater of my stomach, their delicate wings whispering the sweet anticipation of something extraordinary. Little did I know, as the night unfolded, those butterflies would evolve into a symphony, and with each note, I fell deeper in love—a melody that continues to play in the harmonious journey of our shared hearts."

THE FIRST OFFICIAL DATE

I'm lounging comfortably on my sofa, the dull hum of the television providing a soothing backdrop to the quiet Saturday morning. Suddenly, my phone comes to life, shattering the tranquility with its insistent buzz. I glance over, and a smile immediately graces my face. It's Reid.

"Hey, Reid," I answer, my voice soft and laced with affection.

"Hey, Amelia. I hope I didn't interrupt your Saturday morning relaxation binge," he teases, his voice warm even through the phone.

"Nah, you're good company, Reid. What's up?" I ask, my smile growing wider even though he can't see it.

"Just wanted to check up on you. How did you sleep?" he asks, genuine concern seeping into his tone.

"I slept well, thank you. I guess it's taking a little longer to get back to one-hundred percent," I reply, chuckling softly.

His laughter echoes mine, creating a harmonious symphony over the call. Then, he asks the question that sends butterflies fluttering in my stomach, "Would you like to go out with me tonight, Amelia?"

A happiness swells within me, spreading warmth through my veins.

"I would love to, Reid." I answer with a voice full of joy.

As soon as I hang up the phone, a bubble of exhilaration forms within me, urging me to my feet. Without a second thought, I rush down the hallway to Destiny's room, bursting through the door with a force that would stir even the heaviest of sleepers.

"Destiny!" I say, barely able to contain my excitement. "Reid just asked me out on a date. Help me get ready!"

The words tumble out in haste, my heart pounding against my ribcage. Destiny, still rubbing the sleep from her eyes, jolts upright in her bed, her eyes widening in surprise. For a moment, she just stares at me, processing my frantic announcement. Then, a shriek of pure joy escapes her, filling the room with contagious excitement.

"Oh my god, Amelia! Finally!" she exclaims, leaping from her bed to engulf me in a bear hug. "I'm so excited for you. Of course, I'll help you get ready!" she declares, her voice filled with a determination that reassures me.

Barely containing my excitement, I let Destiny lead me toward my vanity, my heart pounding with anticipation. As she rifles through my wardrobe, I watch my reflection in the mirror. I'm a bundle of nerves, a heady mix of anticipation, elation, and a smidgen of anxiety. I want to look perfect for Reid.

A triumphant "Aha!" from Destiny breaks me out of my thoughts. I turn to see her holding up a beautiful dress. It's a shade of emerald green that makes my heart flutter with delicate lacework on the bodice that gracefully flows into a chiffon skirt. It's simple yet stunning, just the thing I'd love to wear.

I run my fingers over the soft fabric, a smile etching onto my face. Destiny hands me a pair of low heels, a perfect match for the dress. They're elegant, adorned with a subtle glitter that catches the light beautifully but doesn't distract from the dress.

Just as I slip on the second heel, the door creaks open, and my mom enters the room. Her hands hold a small velvet box, and her eyes sparkle with a gentle warmth as she approaches me. Opening the box, she reveals a delicate pair of diamond studs and a matching necklace, simple yet elegant. My heart swells at the sight, and I can't help but reach out to touch the cool metal.

"These were your grandmother's," she tells me softly, her voice full of emotion. "I never thought Anthony was right for you, but seeing you like this with Reid made me bring them to you, as I can see this night is special to you."

As she gently fastens the necklace around my neck and places the earrings in my ears, her hands are steady.

"You look beautiful, Amelia," she whispers, pulling me into a heartfelt hug.

Looking at my reflection once more, I see a girl transformed, radiant, and ready for her date, brimming with anticipation. At that moment, I'm truly ready for the night to unfold. My phone buzzes again. It's Reid.

"Hey, Amelia," he begins, his voice unexpectedly somber, and my heart sinks. "My dad had a work emergency. He had to take the car, and I...I don't think I'll be able to pick you up. I guess...we'll have to cancel our date."

His voice trails off into an uncomfortable silence. I'm hit with a wave of disappointment that leaves me speechless. All the excitement and anticipation drain away, replaced by an overwhelming sense of deflation. Destiny looks at me, her eyes reflecting my disappointment.

"Can't Reid get a ride from someone else?" Destiny asks.

Her question hangs in the air as I relay it to Reid. He

ponders the idea, and then his voice lightens up a bit. "I can call Benjamin and see if he can take me."

As Destiny and I climb into her car, we hash out the details with Reid. The evening might not be what we'd all pictured, but it's something. As Destiny starts the engine, I can't help but feel a spark of the anticipation I'd felt before. Regardless of how we get there, we're going on our date, and I can't wait to see what the night has in store.

As we pull up to the restaurant, the soft glow from its interior lighting casts a comforting warmth against the growing darkness of the evening. My hand reaches for the door handle, and just as I'm about to swing it open, I catch sight of Destiny doing the same.

"Hold on, Destiny," I say, a playful sternness underlining my tone.

"What? I'm just stretching my legs," she replies, a mischievous glint in her eyes. "And maybe trying to see the mystery guy who's got my sister grinning like a fool." Her words are laced with a teasing humor that sends ripples of laughter through me.

"You're staying right here, Destiny," I counter, still chuckling. "I don't want you freaking him out with your big sister interrogation mode."

"But Amelia..." Destiny whines, pulling her best puppy dog face to sway my decision.

"Nope! Not going to work, D." I say before she can launch into a full-blown tirade. "I promise to invite Reid over for dinner and a formal introduction, but tonight, it's just him and me. Okay?"

With a resigned sigh and a roll of her eyes, Destiny concedes. "Fine, have it your way, but don't think you're off the hook that easily, Missy!"

With one last shared laugh, I step out of the car, my heart

filled with a renewed sense of anticipation for what the evening might hold.

Stepping through the doors of the restaurant, I'm instantly enveloped by a warm, welcoming ambiance. The subtle hum of chatter and the gentle clinking of cutlery create a symphony of normalcy that feels strangely comforting. My gaze quickly scans the room, instinctively seeking that familiar face. There he is. Reid. It's as if my body always knows where he is, like a compass always pointing north. Almost immediately, our eyes meet across the crowded room, and the corners of his mouth curve up into a smile that makes my heart skip a beat.

I make my way towards him, the click-clack of my heels against the polished floor echoing my anticipation. Reid gets up as I approach, his warm smile as inviting as the cozy restaurant around us. He leans in, planting a soft kiss on each of my cheeks, a gesture so simple, yet overflowing with sincerity. My cheeks flush at the contact, more from the sweetness of the gesture than the physical touch.

As he pulls out the chair for me to sit down, I can't help but admire the gallantry of his actions. His smile lingers as he retakes his seat, his eyes never leaving mine. The disappointment from earlier has all but evaporated, replaced by a comforting sense of rightness. I know we're exactly where we're supposed to be.

Reid's gaze roams over me, and his eyes widen just slightly. "Amelia," he breathes out, "you look absolutely beautiful." His words warm my heart, and I grin at him.

"Thank you, Reid. You look quite handsome yourself," I reply, not hesitating to return the compliment.

His face breaks out in a modest smile, and I can't help but laugh lightly at his obvious bashfulness. My eyes wander, taking in the tastefully decorated interior of the restaurant.

"This place is really nice, Reid." Pausing for a moment to

expertly articulate my concerns without appearing too direct, I continue, "I mean, it seems quite... upscale."

His laughter fills the air, a heartening sound that eases any lingering tension. He reaches across the table, enveloping my hand in his own. With a gentle squeeze, he maintains eye contact, his gaze earnest.

"Amelia," he begins, the corners of his mouth lifting into a soft smile, "for the last couple of weeks, I've been working odd jobs for my dad just to take you out to a place like this for our first romantic date."

His admission surprises me, but the affection in his eyes is unmistakable. "I wanted to make it special."

His words hang in the air, wrapping the moment in a tender warmth that leaves me speechless.

"Reid," I say, gazing into his earnest eyes. "Everything we do is special. You're special to me. You know I don't care about how much money you spend. It's time that matters to me."

His eyes soften at my words, and his smile deepens, a testament to his understanding and acceptance. He leans in, pressing a quick, affectionate kiss to my lips, and a blush heats my cheeks. His actions speak louder than words, a silent promise of the care and respect he holds for me. Before he can respond verbally, a waiter approaches our table.

He tactfully waits for the moment between us to pass before asking, "Good evening. Are you ready to order?"

Reid's eyes skim over the menu, his brow furrowing in concentration. He clears his throat, turns to the waiter, and says, "I'll have the salad."

My eyebrows shoot up in surprise, my mouth opening to voice my confusion. However, before I can articulate a single word, Reid's cheeks flush a vibrant shade of red.

"I- I meant the steak," he corrects himself hurriedly, his eyes darting away in embarrassment.

The waiter nods understandingly, jots down our orders, and quietly retreats. After a moment of silence, Reid turns to me, his eyes avoiding mine.

In a barely audible whisper, he confesses, "I'm nervous, Amelia."

It's an endearing admission, one that pulls at my heartstrings. I reach across the table, placing my hand atop his in a gesture of reassurance.

"Reid," I say, my voice soft yet firm, "that was the most charming mistake I've ever seen."

He laughs and relaxes. Our meal arrives, and the conversation flows naturally. It's as if we're in our own little world, oblivious to the world buzzing around us. The food is exquisite, each bite a symphony of flavors that sets my taste buds aflame.

After clearing our main course, we indulge in desserts. Of course, Reid insists on trying every item on the menu. We lose ourselves in the sweetness, the shared tastes further strengthening our bond.

As our evening draws to a close, Reid escorts me outside, the cool night air a stark contrast to the warm atmosphere we're leaving behind. As we step into the dimly lit parking lot, I spot Benjamin waiting patiently to drive him home. Destiny had texted me she'll be late by a few minutes.

"Go on, Benjamin's waiting. I'll call you when I get home." I reassure him.

His reluctance is palpable, but he nods, respecting my decision. Before climbing into the car, Reid pulls me close. He leans down, pressing a scorching kiss onto my lips, leaving me breathless.

"Good night, Amelia," he murmurs against my lips, his voice low and warm.

As he pulls away, my heart aches with the sudden absence

of his touch. I'm still grinning like a fool when Destiny pulls up, her cheerful yell breaking my reverie.

"Amelia, get in the car!" she hollers, her voice echoing in the quiet night.

Her eyes twinkle with unasked questions, but she holds her tongue, for now. As we pull away, I can't help but glance back at the restaurant, the memory of the evening still fresh, my heart beating in rhythm with the memory of Reid's kiss. When we arrive home, I head straight to my room to shower and change clothes.

As I step out of the shower, the scent of my lavender body wash following me like a gentle cloud, I pull on my pajamas and wrap a towel around my freshly washed hair. Exiting the bathroom, I almost walk into my room without noticing anything unusual. But then I see them. Destiny and Mom are sitting on my bed, their faces exhibiting a level of expectancy that instantly makes me blush.

"Well?" Destiny prods, her eyes curious, expectant, and a little mischievous.

"Well, what?" I respond coyly, barely able to suppress the grin spreading across my face.

"Amelia, don't tease us! How was your date?" Mom chimes in, her smile as bright as mine.

I can't help but laugh at their excitement. I sink onto the bed beside them, my heart overflowing with joy as I recall the night's events.

"It was wonderful," I start, my voice bubbling with happiness. "Reid was a perfect gentleman. The restaurant was exquisite, and the food... oh, the food was divine."

I continue, sharing the charming parts of our first date, from Reid's adorable mix-up with the menu to the shared laughter that flowed freely between us. The room fills with my laughter and theirs, an echo of the happiness that is still fresh in my heart.

As I finally wind down, Destiny hugs me tightly, her grin mirroring my own. "I'm so happy for you, Amelia," she whispers, her happiness for me clear in every word.

Mom hugs me next, her eyes twinkling with joy. "We're both so happy for you, sweetie. Reid sounds like a wonderful young man."

"He is," I reply, unable to hold back my smile.

As Mom stands to leave, she turns back; her gaze thoughtful.

"Amelia, it's time for us to meet the young man who's putting stars in your eyes," she says gently, her words hanging in the air.

I nod, feeling a flutter of excitement at the prospect of introducing Reid to my family. It feels like a significant step, a new chapter in this blossoming relationship.

"I'll talk to him," I promise.

With that, Mom leaves the room, her excitement clear in her departing smile. I move to lie down, the softness of my bed enveloping me like a comforting embrace. As exhaustion seeps into my bones, I close my eyes, the memories of the evening playing like a sweet melody in my mind.

I can still taste the lingering sweetness of dessert on my lips, still feel the warmth of Reid's hand in mine, still hear the tender lilt of his laughter. As the memories continue to replay, a contented sigh escapes my lips. I fall asleep, my dreams painted with the tender hues of our first date.

"In the quiet spaces where vulnerability meets trust, taking a significant step becomes the brushstroke that paints our love in richer hues. It's an intimate exploration, a shared secret between two hearts, as we venture into a realm where connection deepens, and the tapestry of our love becomes woven with threads of profound closeness."

THE NEXT LEVEL

Students at school are still whispering about me and Reid. It's getting pretty old and is irritating me. We're not some circus act for people to gawk at. Often, our friends lovingly label us the "odd couple", the lively, vivacious volleyball player paired with the quiet, gentle basketball player. They jest about our contrasting temperaments and how we navigate our relationship despite them. Well, they're not entirely wrong. Reid and I, we're like two sides of the same coin, different yet seamlessly connected.

His tranquility tames my wild spirit, and my liveliness injects a spark into his serene world. Our differences are the chords that, when strung together, create a harmonious melody. Yes, we are opposites, but together, we've discovered a beautiful harmony that only stresses our bond.

Reid has a way of surprising me that softens the edges of even the gloomiest days. I'll open my locker to find a handwritten note tucked between my textbooks, its words woven with the care and thoughtfulness that is so uniquely Reid. The chicken-scratch handwriting, complete with crossed-out words and random doodles, brings an instant smile to my face. He'd leave little messages like "Your smile is my favorite work of art" or "You are the light of my life, brightening every day."

They're simple words, but they carry a warmth that reminds me of his presence even when he's not physically around. And then there are the snacks. Somehow, he always knows when I've had a challenging day and needs a little pick-me-up. It's not uncommon to find my favorite chocolate bar or a bag of those pretzels I love so much waiting for me. These small, thoughtful gestures, as inconspicuous as they may seem, are Reid's own special way of saying, "I'm here for you," and they mean more to me than he'll ever know.

As each day passes, I fall deeper into the labyrinth of love, the center of which is Reid. His every gesture, every word, every smile, they all stir something profound within me—a feeling so intense that I can't help but be swept into its current. I yearn for his company, for his gentle laughter that tickles the silence between us, for his steady gaze that holds a world of understanding. The beat of my heart syncs with the mere mention of his name, the rhythm echoing the melody of love that my heart plays for him.

In the midst of this whirlwind of emotions, a question hovers over my mind, casting a long shadow of doubt—does he feel the same way? Does his heart skip a beat when he sees me, like mine does for him? Does my absence leave a void that only my presence can fill? I yearn to know, yet I fear the answer. For now, I am content to dwell in this sweet uncertainty, cocooned in the warmth of his company, awaiting the day when our feelings are spoken aloud.

It's finally the weekend, and I'm a bundle of nerves. Reid's coming over. He's never been to my house before, and today he'll meet my mom and my sisters for the first time. I feel a knot in my stomach as I try to imagine what could go wrong.

My sister Destiny walks in, her eyes catching mine in the mirror. She sees right through me, as sisters usually do.

With a playful smirk, she teases, "You're nervous, aren't you?" I roll my eyes at her, but she just giggles in response.

Suddenly, Iris joins in. She's never been one to miss out on an opportunity to tease me.

"Amelia, you must really like the boy," she observes, her voice laced with a teasing tone.

I feel my cheeks heat, and I can't help but smile. Yes, I do like Reid. I like him more than I've ever liked anyone before and today, he'll be stepping into my world, meeting the women who've shaped me. Today, our worlds will intertwine a little more, and I'm both excited and terrified. But knowing that he'll be here soon, well, that's enough to calm my nerves. For now, at least.

The doorbell rings, breaking the silence that had settled in the room. I jump at the sound, my heart pounding like a drum in my chest. This is it. Swallowing my nerves, I rush to the door, taking a moment to steady myself before pulling it open.

"Hey, Reid," I blurt out, trying to sound casual despite my racing heart.

He's standing in front of me, looking as handsome as ever, his soft eyes twinkling with warmth.

"Hey," he responds, his voice carrying a soothing melody that quells my anxiety.

He steps forward, enveloping me in a comforting hug that feels just like the safe haven I associate with him.

As I step back, I take in his calm demeanor, contrasting starkly with my frenetic energy.

"Are you ready to meet my crazy family?" I ask, wringing my hands nervously.

He laughs, the sound echoing around us, light and sincere. His laughter ignites a spark of hope within me, reassuring me that no matter how the evening goes, our bond will remain unscathed.

"Yes," he confirms, his voice steady, his eyes never leaving mine.

A surge of relief washes over me as we step inside, ready to face the chaos together. Taking Reid's hand, I lead him further into the house. The comforting and familiar chatter of my family progressively grows louder as we approach the living room. As we round the corner, my mom and sisters come into view.

"Mom, Destiny, Iris, this is Reid," I introduce, my voice wavering slightly.

The chatter ceases, their eyes widen in shock, and the room falls silent, the air now heavy with anticipation. I can practically hear my heart thudding in the quiet.

Breaking the silence, Reid steps forward, his hand outstretched confidently.

"Nice to meet you, Ms. Campbell," he says, his voice resonating through the tense air.

My mom, taken aback, finally breaks into a warm smile, reaching out to shake his hand. Shifting his gaze to Destiny and Iris, Reid extends his hand to them as well.

"Nice to meet you too," he asserts, his charm unfurling in those five words, effectively breaking the ice.

Destiny's the first to recover from the shock. She blinks a few times before shooting me a knowing glance.

"Nice to meet you, Reid. I must say, you are not what I was expecting," she says.

Her words hang in the air, heavy and filled with an unspoken curiosity. Iris, true to her nature, brings her own brand of uncensored honesty to the table.

"Yeah, I never thought it was a white boy," she quirks a brow, her lips curling into a mischievous grin. "So, you got jungle fever huh?" I can almost feel my cheeks burning as I shoot her a wide-eyed glare.

Before I can even formulate a response, Mom interjects. With a swift smack to the back of Iris's head, she admonishes, "Iris, behave yourself before I beat your ass."

"Ow," she whines. "I heard that on a TV show. I thought it was a compliment."

The room fills with a stunned silence once more, only to be broken by Reid's hearty laughter. Despite the awkwardness of the moment, there's a warmth in his laugh that somehow makes everything okay.

As the evening unfolds, the atmosphere in the room becomes more relaxed and fun-filled. Reid fits right in, seamlessly blending into the chaotic yet loving rhythm of my family. We share food, hearty laughter, and engaging conversations, the air around us humming with the warm vibes of camaraderie. I can sense Reid growing more comfortable by the second; his laughter is genuine, his eyes sparkle with joy, and his presence feels as natural as one of us. In the middle of our lively discussion, Mom spins the conversation towards a more serious topic, her gaze fixed on Reid.

"So, Reid," she begins, her tone shifting from light-hearted to more earnest. "What are your intentions with my daughter?"

The room grows quiet in anticipation of his response.

Reid's eyes meet mine before he turns back to my mom, his expression sincere. "I want to date Amelia," he confesses, his voice steady and resolute. He looks back at me. "We've grown incredibly close over the past few months, and I really like her."

His words hang in the air, a testament to the unspoken bond between us. A surge of happiness swells within me, echoing the rhythm of my beating heart.

Reid continues, his eyes never leaving mine. "In fact," he

adds, a hint of nervousness creeping into his steady voice, "I'd like to take Amelia out on another date tonight if she'll let me."

I blink, surprise washing over me. Mom nods her approval and rises from her seat.

"Alright, you two better get on with your date. The girls and I have things to do today, anyway." She turns to Destiny and Iris, who remain seated. "Leave Amelia and Reid alone. They need their privacy," she instructs.

With a sly grin, Destiny turns to Reid. "Treat my sister right, and I won't have to kick your ass," she warns.

Iris, mischievous as ever, throws up a fist. "I've got a knuckle sandwich waiting for you, so behave yourself."

Ignoring their comments, Mom ushers them out of the room. She then turns back to me, her voice serious.

"Remember what I said. Wrappin' before the tappin'," she advises, making me blush furiously.

Reid gives me a puzzled look, and I can only hope that my face isn't as red as it feels. Our date is a simple yet incredibly memorable affair. Reid takes me to a small, family-owned Italian restaurant nestled within the heart of the city. As we walk in, I can feel the intimacy of the place. The interior is quaint, softly lit, emanating a sense of warmth and comfort. It was as if we're enclosed in our own world, away from the hustle and bustle of the city outside.

We're guided to a corner table, away from the prying eyes of other patrons. The ambiance is perfect; the soft jazz music playing in the background set a soothing rhythm, and the faint chatter of other customers add to the authenticity of the experience.

Reid, being the gentleman he is, pulls out my chair for me. As I sit down, he gently grasps my hand, looking into my eyes with an unwavering intensity. His gaze is filled with a promise, a commitment that our relationship is just on the cusp of something extraordinary.

Our conversation flows effortlessly throughout the evening. We talk about everything, from our deepest fears to our wildest dreams. Laughter punctuates our conversation, each shared joke and story bringing us closer.

The food is exquisite. We savor a wide range of delicious Italian culinary delights, the explosion of flavors tantalizing our taste buds. We end our meal with a heavenly tiramisu, its flavors lingering on our tongues as we bask in the sweet remnants of our date.

As the evening came to a close, Reid walk me to my doorstep, his arm wrapped protectively around me. He leans in, his eyes twinkling under the soft glow of the porch light. As our lips meet in a gentle kiss, I can feel an undeniable spark, a chemistry that felt like the most natural thing in the world.

As we stand there, on the threshold of my family's home, I fumble for the keys, eventually finding them in the small pocket of my purse. Turning the key in the lock, I push the door open, revealing the silent, empty house.

"It's strange," I murmur. "They're should be home by now." Glancing back at Reid, I smile. "Do you want to come in?"

He gives me a small smile before nodding his head. "I'd love to."

Stepping inside, I can feel the quiet tranquility of the house wash over me. It's a stark contrast to the lively chaos we had left behind, yet strangely comforting. As I slip off my shoes, Reid follows suit, stepping further into the house.

The silence felt almost palpable, bouncing off the walls and echoing back to us. I glance at Reid, who seems as captivated by the tranquil environment as I was.

"I'm not really ready for the night to end," I confessed,

my gaze meeting his. His eyes lit up at my words, and he gives me a warm smile.

"Me neither," he agrees. "Why don't we watch a movie or something?"

I nod, leading him up to my room. As we settle on my bed, I power up my laptop and scrolled through our movie options.

After scrolling past drama, comedy, and romance, we finally settle on an action flick. A bold choice, but the adrenaline rush promises to keep the night interesting. Reid's hand rest on my back, his fingers lightly tracing a rhythm that unknowingly echoes the pounding of my heart. His touch is light, soothing, yet filled with an electric charge that sparks goosebumps on my skin.

Before long, our shared laughter and soft whispers drown out the action sequences on screen out. I turn to face him, my eyes meeting his. The teasing twinkle in his eyes is replaced with a more serious, intense gaze. With our faces inches apart, we both lean in. The kiss is slow and sweet, filled with the promise of more.

One thing leads to another, and the action movie is long forgotten, replaced by the real-life passion unfolding between us. We decide, almost wordlessly, that it's time to take our relationship to the next level. It feels right and comfortable. As if we'd crossed an unspoken boundary, stepping into a more intimate world.

Our kiss became an all-consuming, fiery passion. The kiss becomes aggressive, and I yank his shirt up, touching his muscles. I pull some more, yanking it over his head because I want/ to see his beautifully sculpted body. I can feel his erection through his pants, and I reach down to undo the button before sliding my hand inside. He moans at the contact and thrusts upward.

I gasp at the feel of him because he's bigger than I

thought. We keep exploring each other, stripping our clothes off piece by piece until we're naked and panting from the intensity of our passion. He reaches over to his wallet and pulls out a condom. I raise an eyebrow at him, and he shrugs sheepishly. He rolls the condom on and positions himself on top of me.

He pushes in slowly, and I widen my legs to give him more access. I wince a little because he's big. Bigger than my ex, and it's not like I've been having sex, so it stings a little. He moans as he pulls back and thrusts back in. Then he's moving fast, as if he can't control himself. He's thrusting in and out, moaning loudly as he picks up his pace. His movements are short and jerky. I moan from the sensations, but it's not enough to get me there. Reid pushes in one last time and moans into my neck. I feel his cock jerking inside me as he fills the condom.

He pulls out and rips the condom off before tossing it in the trash can by my bed. He lays back on top of me, gazing down into my eyes as a blush covers his cheeks.

"Amelia, that was my first time," he confesses.

Surprise covers my face, not by his admission, but by the vulnerability in his voice. I look down at him, his face radiating a mix of excitement and nervousness that mirrors my own emotions. I'd had one boyfriend before Reid, but this feels different, more meaningful. It's only the second time for me. I pull him into a comforting embrace, a smile playing on my lips.

"You have nothing to worry about, Reid," I whisper, our heartbeats syncing in the room's silence. "It was special for me, and I hope it was special for you, too."

He moves up and kisses me. He kisses me with such force that the breath is knocked out of my lungs. The kiss turns passionate once again, and soon, he's thick between my legs. He moves to line himself up and thrusts in. I moan at the sensation as I run my fingers through his hair. He's thrusting in and out at a steady pace, going deeper each time. His thrusts are less jerky than the first time, and he's looking at me with an assessing gaze.

I pull his face back to mine and kiss him to let him know how good he's making me feel. His pace picks up, and soon he's thrusting into me in hard, steady strokes. He tightened his grip on me and ground in deeper.

"Fuck," I moan.

"You feel so good, baby, I'm not going to last must longer," he says against my lips.

He grunts and rocks deeper, and I shutter as my orgasm rips through me. My orgasm sets him off, and soon, he's jerking inside me, moaning about how good it feels. He kisses me slowly as his hips return to their unhurried rhythm. Eventually, he stops moving, and I smile up at him. He pulls out, and I feel wetness leaking down my leg.

He looks back up at me in horror as he realizes he didn't put on a condom the second time. Reid started spluttering apologies, panic clear in his eyes. He's visibly shaken, as his eyes dart from mine to the discarded condom in the trash. I can tell he is on the verge of a full-blown freakout, but I won't let him. I reach out, cupping his face and forcing him to meet my gaze.

"Reid, look at me, focus on me," I say, my voice calm and steady. Once I have his undivided attention, I offer him a reassuring smile. "I'm on birth control, okay? We're safe. Everything will be okay," I reassure him, the edges of my words soft with understanding.

The panic in his eyes gradually subsides, replaced by a flicker of relief, and I snuggle closer to him. As he holds me close, I feel his chest rising and falling against me in deep, steady breaths. I glance up at him, only to find his gaze already on me, his eyes a rich mixture of emotions that leave me pleasantly surprised. The intensity of his stare, the raw vulnerability etched on his face, it's as if I'm seeing this side of him for the first time. His eyes are filled with a profound emotion that I'm scared to name.

A soft smile tugs at Reid's lips as he runs his fingers through his tousled hair. He then looks into my eyes and takes a deep breath.

"Amelia," he begins with a certain tenderness in his voice. "These past few months with you have been... incredible. I'm not sure when it happened or how, but somewhere along the line, I... I fell in love with you."

I feel the corners of my mouth pulling up into a wide smile at his confession. My heart is thudding wildly in my chest. I reach out and gently caress his cheek.

"Reid," I respond, my voice just above a whisper. "I love you too."

His words wash over me, like a soothing balm to my racing heart. We both lay there, enveloped in each other, lost in a world of our creation. Outside, the world goes on, but inside, it's just us. Two bodies, two hearts, intertwined in a dance as old as time itself. I hold him closer, my fingers tracing lazy patterns on his back.

"I love you too, Reid," I whisper again.

The look of pure joy that lights up his face is worth more than a thousand words. He nestles his face in the crook of my neck, his warm breath fanning my skin, sending shivers down my spine. We are silent as our hearts speak volumes in the tranquility of the moment.

"Love is the timeless melody that resonates through the symphony of our lives, weaving together the harmonies of joy, the crescendos of shared dreams, and the tender notes of enduring connection. It's a masterpiece written on the parchment of the heart, a language spoken in the whispers of understanding, and a journey where every step is a dance in the rhythm of affection."

Ever since that night, Reid and I can't keep our hands off each other. It's like our need for each other can't be fulfilled. We find every opportunity to get each other naked, and it's never felt better. Hazel won't be at school today, so I head toward my locker to grab my books. As I'm bent over, digging around inside, I feel a presence behind me and hands on my hips. I yelp in surprise and straighten to look behind me. A smile creeps up when I see Reid looking at me with that look he gets before we sneak off somewhere.

Reid pulls me back flush against his body, his hands curving around my waist protectively. The familiar warmth of him radiates through me, making my heart race as if it's the first time. He reaches past me, his chest pressing into my back, to close the locker door in one fluid motion.

His actions are smoothly practiced, as if he's always meant to be here, with his arms around me. The scent of him, the feel of him, it's intoxicating. I lean back into his embrace, my body instinctively seeking the comfort of his. The world outside our little bubble seems to fade away as I lose myself in the feel of Reid against me. He leans in, his breath warm against my ear, sending a shivery thrill down my spine.

"Come with me," he murmurs in that low, husky voice that never fails to ignite a spark within me.

Before I can formulate any coherent response, he's pulling me along with him. His pull is insistent, yet there's a playfulness in his quick pace that has me laughing, a sound that echoes brightly down the hall. I find myself caught up in the whirlwind that is Reid, my heart pounding in an exhilarating rhythm with our swift footfalls.

Reid turns left down an empty hallway and shoves open the door to an empty classroom. He closed the door behind us and pushes me up against the door. I love that he's moved on from the shy, virginal boy I first met and into a more confident, take-charge boy I've grown to love. He looks at me with a gleam in his eyes and flips the lock on the door.

He leans in and gives me a kiss that curls my toes. He moves closer, and I can feel his arousal against my stomach. His hand moves to the button on my jeans and undoes it. My hands move to the front of his pants, and I rub him, eliciting a sexy groan from him. In one quick and impressive move, Reid has my pants down my legs, and me turned around facing the door with my ass sticking out. I gasped at the sudden change in position.

"I need you, baby," Reid says in my ear.

I laugh at how insatiable he's become. I hear him unzip his pants, and he moves my underwear to the side. He pushes inside me, and my head falls back to his shoulder as I moan. He moans low in his throat and kisses my neck as he starts thrusting. Reid moves at a hard, steady pace that sends shivers through my entire body. I push back against him, and he lets out a low, guttural sound before shoving me hard against the door.

Then he's driving into me hard, and the door shakes. I

gasp in surprise because that will draw attention. He pulls me back and moves me to bend over a desk, all without pulling out. His thrust becomes urgent, and I tremble as I feel my orgasm approaching. He puts his hand over my mouth as my moans become louder.

He's grunting and moaning and when he says my name, I come all over him. The wetness that seeps between my legs allows him to glide in and out much smoother. I spasm around him and he curses before pushing in deep. His cock throbs as he jerks inside me, filling me with his come.

He finally stops jerking and kisses my neck before pulling out. I feel the evidence of what we just did leaking down my legs. I send Reid a faux glare as I show the mess we made.

"I'm sorry, baby," he says, though he doesn't sound sorry at all. "I can't help myself around you."

I try hard to stop the smile that wants to break free. We fix our clothes before Reid peeks out the door to make sure the halls are clear. He motions for me to follow him, and we leave quickly. We're late for first period, and I rush back to my locker to grab my things. The moment we step into the classroom, we're met with a hostile glare from Ms. Clark.

"Amelia and Reid, so glad you could finally join us," she drawls, her sarcasm as sharp as a blade.

The entire class turns to look at us, and I can feel my cheeks turning red. Reid squeezes my hand in reassurance as we make our way to our seats at the back of the room.

Immediately, Ms. Clark resumes her demonstration. "Now, as I was saying, sculpting hands can be quite challenging. They are delicate and complex, requiring careful attention to detail," she begins, her hands molding the clay with practiced ease.

I lean forward, trying to shut out the embarrassment of our late entrance and focus on the intricacies of the lesson.

Out of nowhere, Reid leans over and whispers into my ear, his warm breath sending tingles down my spine.

"What to hang out at Benjamin's after school?" he asks, his voice light and casual.

A pang of disappointment hits me. I wish I could say yes, but I shake my head slowly.

"I can't, Reid," I reply. "I have a volleyball game today. It's the game that will decide if we make it to the State Championship."

I wait for a flicker of disappointment to cross his face, but his eyes light up in a way that takes me by surprise.

A corner of his mouth lifts in a grin, his dimples deepening as he promises. "I'll be there, cheering you on, baby."

Classes pass by in a blur. Before I know it, I'm in the gym, stretching my limbs and mentally preparing for the game. The cacophony of bouncing balls, squeaking shoes, and the chatter of my teammates fills the room.

My mom couldn't make it. She's stuck at work again. Iris is tied up with her own after-school activities, but Destiny is here, her infectious enthusiasm cutting through the pre-game tension like a ray of sunshine, especially the one in our trio who can always be counted on.

I catch sight of Reid, standing off to the side, his gaze locked on me. I can't help but give him a small wave, my heart fluttering at the intensity in his eyes. He smiles back, that cheeky grin that always makes my stomach flip, and returns the wave.

Suddenly, Coach Thompson calls us in, her booming voice drowning out the surrounding noise. We gather around her as she gives us a last-minute pep talk. Her words, full of belief and encouragement, invigorate us all. Across the court, the opposing team begins their warm-ups, their unified movements a stark contrast against the excited chatter of our own team. Despite the rising anxiety, I can't help but feel a rush of adrenaline.

The shrill of the referee's whistle pierces the air, and all at once, it's as if time stands still. I can hear the pounding of my heart, the rush of blood in my ears. Then, the moment breaks, and we're off. The game is a blur of motion, a kaleidoscope of diving saves, and powerful spikes. I feel my muscles stretch and strain as I jump, hit, and dive. The volleyball seems to have a life of its own, zipping back and forth above the net, an elusive prey that both teams are desperate to conquer.

Our opponents are relentless, their serves harsh and fierce, their defense sturdy and unwavering. But we fight back with equal fervor. Every point won is a minor victory, a step towards the goal. Sweat trickles down my brow, stinging my eyes, but I barely notice. My entire world has narrowed down to the court and the game. The crowd fades into the background, their cheers muffled and distant. I glimpse Reid from the corner of my eye. He's on his feet, his face a mask of tension and excitement.

Suddenly, the ball comes hurtling towards me. It seems to hang in the air for a moment, suspended by some invisible force, before I spring into action. I take a leap, my fingers grazing the rough texture of the ball as I strike it with force, sending it soaring over the net. There is a collective gasp from the audience, a moment of suspense as the ball descends on the other side.

It hits the ground with a satisfying smack. The opposing team is too stunned to react in time. Immediately, the gymnasium erupts in cheers, the sound washing over me in a wave of exhilaration. I can't help the triumphant smile that spreads across my face as I turn to see Reid. His face lights up with pride and disbelief. That point is for him. That point is for us.

The intensity of the game only escalates as we continue to

battle it out on the court. Each volley, each serve, each spike, it's like a dance, a contest of strength and agility, of strategy and willpower. But as the game goes on, I can feel the scales tipping, not in our favor. The opposing team is formidable, their teamwork impeccable, their determination unwavering. Our energy wanes, our movements become sluggish, and our hope flickers. Then, the final whistle blows.

They display the score for all to see: we have lost. It's like a cold splash of water extinguishing the last burning embers of hope. The gymnasium falls eerily silent, the cacophony of cheers replaced by the deafening silence of defeat. I look around at my teammates, their faces a mirror of my disappointment. This is the end of our season, the end of this journey we started together. I glance towards Reid, expecting to see disappointment. Instead, I see a comforting smile and pride in his eyes.

I glance over towards Destiny, standing on the sidelines. Through the sting of defeat, her smile is like a balm, warm and encouraging. She gives me a thumbs up and then mimes steering a car, signaling that she's going to bring around our beat-up old station wagon. As we line up to shake hands under the net, a sign of sportsmanship and mutual respect, my heart is heavy, but I hold my head high.

We trudge to the locker room, our heads bowed, our spirits slightly dampened. Coach Thompson, however, never one to let us wallow in defeat, immediately spoke. Her voice echoes off the locker room walls, filling the silence. She talks about how proud she is of us, how much we've grown this season, and how she knows we'll go even further next year. Her speech, always full of passion and sincerity, slowly reignites the flame of hope within us.

Once the speech is over, I head to the showers. The warm water washes away the sweat and grime, washing away the stress and tension of the game. I change into fresh clothes, feeling lighter already. As I step out of the locker room, the hallway is mostly empty as the crowds have dispersed. Then, I see him. Reid is leaning against the wall, waiting for me. His eyes light up when he sees me, the same cheeky grin on his face.

I walk through the emptying hallway and approach Reid, every step echoing in the suddenly too-quiet school. His arms open wide as I reach him, and he pulls me into a comforting hug. As he leans back, his hand cradles the back of my head, and gently, he places a kiss on my forehead.

His voice is low and soothing as he whispers, "You guys played a good game, Amelia. I'm really proud of you."

I feel a warmth spread through me at his words, a sense of appreciation that dulls the edge of defeat.

I manage a small smile, whispering a "Thank you, Reid."

Arm in arm, we walk out of the school and into the night. The parking lot is awash with the glare of headlights, a line of cars snaking their way out of the grounds. The low hum of engines and the murmur of departing spectators fill the air.

Turning to Reid, our eyes meet, and I lean in to give him a quick kiss.

"Good night, Reid," I say, our breaths visible in the chill of the evening.

I then pull away and start walking down the road, heading towards Destiny's old station wagon, still parked a little way off under a streetlight.

Once in the car, the scent of the worn leather seats and the familiarity of Destiny's music playlist playing quietly in the background provide a comforting reprieve. Destiny steals a glance at me, her eyes reflecting the glow of the dashboard lights.

In her own special way of comfort, she says, "You played well tonight, Amelia. It doesn't matter that we didn't make it to state. You should be proud of how far you've made it."

Her words, sincere and encouraging, seep into me, slowly replacing the sting of defeat with a sense of accomplishment. I nod in response to Destiny's kind words, but say little else. I'm silent for the rest of the ride home, save for the soft hum of the car's engine and the occasional quiet tune drifting from the car radio. As I stare out the window, the passing street-lights cast a rhythmic pattern of light and shadow across the car's interior, matching the fluctuating thoughts in my mind. I replay the game in my head, analyzing each serve, each spike, each missed opportunity. But amid the disappointment and regret, there is also a sense of resolve.

We put up a fight, and even though we didn't come out on top, we made it a battle to remember. Reid's words echo in my mind, a soothing balm on my bruised ego. I sigh, a small smile playing on my lips as I lean my head against the car window, the cool glass a welcome counterpart to my heated thoughts. As we pull into the driveway, I shake off the lingering images of the game and the night.

Mom gets home a little later, her usual bright smile slightly dimmed from a long day at work. Destiny, with her knack for breaking the silence, tells her about the game. I watch as her eyes flicker towards me, a hint of sympathy in her gaze.

"It's okay, Amelia," she says, her voice steady and comforting.

We all gather around the dinner table, the aroma of Mom's cooking temporarily pushing away the bitter taste of defeat. We exchange stories and laughter, the energy in the room pulling me out of my introspection. As the evening wears on, I excuse myself from the dinner table, fatigue from the day's events finally catching up to me. Padding up the stairs, I find solace in the familiar comfort of my room. With a last glance at the night outside, I switch off my bedside lamp and slide under the covers, allowing sleep to claim me.

"In the language of love, every carefully chosen gift becomes a whispered sonnet, expressing sentiments too profound for words. Each wrapped token is a chapter in the story of affection, a tangible reminder that in the art of giving, we bestow not just presents but pieces of our hearts, weaving a tapestry of love that transcends the material and resonates with the melody of heartfelt connection."

The countdown to Christmas break is on, and Hazel and I find ourselves in the throes of the holiday shopping rush at the mall. We're on a mission to find the perfect gifts for Benjamin and Reid.

It's an absolute whirlwind here at the mall. The atmosphere is buzzing with energy as countless shoppers hustle from store to store, their hands laden with bags heavy with gifts. Everyone seems to be on a time-sensitive mission, just like us. The hustle and bustle of the crowd, the holiday music echoing through the halls, the festive decorations, it all blends into a Christmas carousel spinning at full tilt. The scent of cinnamon and pine fills the air from the candle shop nearby, adding to the festive sense of urgency. You can almost feel the Christmas spirit tangibly swirling around us in amongst the sea of shoppers.

"I'm thinking something gadgety for Reid. He loves all that tech stuff," I suggest, perusing through a store filled with shiny new electronics. "And maybe a book for Benjamin? He mentioned something about wanting to read more."

Hazel shakes her head. "Nah, too predictable. How about this? Let's get Benjamin a nice cologne. Remember that one we smelled in the store last time?" She grins, a twinkle in her eye. "I swear he will smell divine with it on. I'll just eat him up!"

I burst out laughing. "You and your love for good-smelling men, Hazel. Okay, cologne for Benjamin, it is. As for Reid," I pause for a moment, an idea forming in my mind. "I saw this sleek watch in a store the other day. I think he'd really like that."

Hazel guides me towards one of the fancy fragrance stores, her step purposeful as she beelines for the cologne section. She grabs the one she had spoken of, Benjamin's soon-to-be cologne, and waves it under my nose for approval. I nod, the scent already making me anticipate Benjamin's reaction, and we secure that purchase.

Next, it's off to the watch store, my eyes immediately finding the sleek piece I'd eyed for Reid. It's even more impressive up close, a perfect blend of elegance and technology that is entirely Reid. With the watch safely tucked away in our shopping haul, we turn our attention to the rest of our list.

The rest of the day is a blur of bright store lights, laughter, and the rustle of shopping bags. We tick off items on our list, presents for our parents, siblings, and family, each chosen with a great deal of thought and love. By the time we leave the last store, hands full and heart's content, we're brimming with the joy that only a successful Christmas shopping spree can bring.

As our shopping marathon draws to a close, Hazel and I decide to refuel at the food court, indulging in our favorite greasy treats. Midway through our fries, Hazel's phone buzzes, her eyes flicking to the screen. She looks up at me, a sly smile playing at the corners of her lips.

"Hey, want to come over to my place after this?" she asks.

"Sure, sounds like a fun way to unwind after shopping," I respond, polishing off the last of my burger.

After we finish eating, we make our way to Hazel's house, the car ride filled with chatter and leftover excitement from the day. The moment we pull up to her house, my eyes catch sight of Benjamin and Reid waiting on the porch.

A surprised laugh escapes my lips as I turn to Hazel. "Why didn't you tell me they were going to be here?"

Hazel just shrugs, her grin growing even wider and I can't help but return her cheeky smile.

As we pull into Hazel's driveway, we decide to leave the guys' presents in the car so they can't see what we got them. The chilly evening air nips at our faces as we tumble out of the car and head for the front door. Hazel's parents are out for the night, making the house feel extra cozy and inviting. Reid and Benjamin share a look as they hold the door open for us, their curiosity piqued, but we're not about to cave. We'd reveal the gifts when the time is right.

We make our way into the living room, flinging ourselves onto the plush sofas. I sink into the cushions, my tired legs thanking me. The room is warm and inviting. Hazel's mom always has a knack for making any space feel like home. Around us, the house is quiet but for the soft hum of the heater.

Hazel grabs the remote and flicks on the TV, passing around a bowl of popcorn she'd apparently prepared earlier. The scent of buttery popcorn fills the room, adding to the homey atmosphere. We nestle into the comfortable furniture, our shopping endeavors momentarily forgotten as we lose ourselves in a world of sitcoms and laughter. The room fills with the comforting sound of our shared amusement, the twinkling Christmas lights adding a magical touch to the scene.

As we're engrossed in the TV show, out of the corner of my eye, I see Benjamin lean in close to Hazel. He whispers something in her ear, to which she responds with a bright smile. They share a quick look before standing up, excusing themselves from the room without a word. The click of Hazel's bedroom door echoes through the otherwise quiet house, and Reid and I exchange glances before breaking into quiet laughter. I know I can guess what they're about to do.

As Hazel and Benjamin disappeared into her room, Reid and I share another glance before turning our attention back to the TV. Even as the laughter from the sitcom fills the room, the atmosphere feels different. It's charged, electric. A sudden awareness of Reid's presence next to me on the couch sends a jolt through my body. The light from the TV illuminates his face, casting a soft glow that highlights the sharp lines of his jaw and the intense focus in his eyes as he watches the screen.

My heart races in my chest, pounding like a drum, and I can't tell if it's from the sudden silence or the proximity of Reid. He glances at me, his gaze meeting mine, and in that moment, the rest of the world seems to fade away. The sound of the TV becomes a muted background noise, drowned out by the sound of my heartbeat. I've known Reid for months, but at this moment, it feels like I'm seeing him in a completely new light. I can feel the tension between us, thick and palpable. It's as if an invisible force is pulling us together, an undeniable magnetism that neither of us can ignore.

He swallows hard, breaking the silence. "So, what do you think Hazel and Benjamin are up to?" he asks, his voice shaky but casual, trying to dissipate the tension that's wound itself around us.

I chuckle, a low, seductive sound. "Probably the same thing we should be doing. I've got something I want to try. Will you let me?" I ask him.

His gaze intensifies as he nods his head. I slide off the couch and get on my knees in front of him. My hands travel up his muscular thighs to the button of his pants.

"Baby, what are you doing?" he asks as I unzip his pants.

"I want to give you a blowjob," I tell him with a smirk.

I send him a seductive look as my hand reaches inside his pants. He's long and hard as my hand closes around him. Reid sucks in a breath, and his cock jumps in my hand. Nervousness takes over because I've never done this before, but I want to do it with him. I don't know what I'm doing, but I'm hoping to make him feel good. I let go of his dick and move to slide his pants down. He lifts a little to make it easier, and I smile at him once his pants fall to his ankles.

I lean forward and kiss the tip, watching as he shudders a little at the contact. The blazing look in Reid's eyes emboldens me to continue, and I run my tongue along the bottom up to the tip before taking the head in my mouth and sucking.

"Damn, baby," Reid says as he leans his head back and closes his eyes. "That feels good."

His cock jumps when I do it again. I move to take him fully inside my mouth, and he pushes up, unable to help himself. He's filling my mouth so completely that I gag a little as he reaches the back of my throat. I bob my head up and down a few times, and the sounds he makes are like music to my ears. I pull back and wrap my fingers around his base before stroking him. My hand moves up and down slowly, feeling every vein. Stroking him while looking at the emotions filter across his face makes me smile.

As I take him in my mouth again, I look up to see him staring down at me. The look in his eyes sets my body on fire, and I feel myself growing wet. I reach over and grab his hand, putting it on top of my head. I can tell he likes this, but I don't want him to be afraid of getting into it like I am. He takes the hint and grabs my hair. His grip is not hard, but full of need and want. He must see something in my eyes because he moves my head.

My lips stretch wider as he grows harder in my mouth. With his grip firmly in my hair, he thrust his hip up as I bob my head down. We set a steady pace while I suck him hard. Reid's breathing turns heavy, and he moans. Suddenly, I'm pushed back and am fully on my knees, as Reid is now in a standing position while I suck him. He moves faster, fucking my throat as he need drives his movements. His other hand grips my head and he really gets into it, pushing deeper into my throat. His movements turn jerky.

"Baby," is all he manages to say through the heavy breathing.

Reid tries to pull back, but I grip his hips to hold him in place and bob my head faster. His hands tighten in my hair a second before he comes. He moans loud as his cock jerks in my mouth. Wave after wave flows into my mouth and I swallow it all because I think that's what you're supposed to do. Reid jerks for a long time, pouring down my throat while moaning uncontrollably.

When he finishes, I lean back on my knees and smile at his state. He looks so much more relaxed as he looks at me.

"So, I hope you liked it," I tell him nervously. "That was, uh...I've never done that before."

"That was incredible," he breathes out. "I've never done that before, either." He turns red and rubs the back of his neck. "Are you okay? I really got into it."

"I'm more than okay, Reid," I say. "I'm glad we got to experience that together."

He cradles my cheek and looks at me lovingly. "I love you, baby."

"I love you too, Reid," I tell him.

Before we can say more, we hear a door opening. Reid

scrambles to pull up his pants and buckle them. Just as we get situated on the couch again, Hazel and Benjamin return to the room. They can't keep the smiles off their faces. Reid and I look at each other with a knowing smile before we continue watching TV as if nothing happened.

"Discovering love is like stumbling upon a hidden treasure in the vast landscape of life. It's the thrill of finding something precious, a feeling that transforms the ordinary into the extraordinary. In the symphony of emotions, the crescendo of love is the sweetest melody, making the journey through life truly extraordinary."

Reid and I continue to grow closer with each passing day, our bond strengthening in ways that surprise me. He's always there, a steady presence in a flurry of teenage drama and schoolwork. We spend hours talking on the phone, sharing dreams and fears, secrets and laughter. He listens with patience, his soft words of comfort or advice warming my heart and making me feel seen and understood. He's become my confidant, my rock. Either with each shared glance or quiet conversation.

As the snowflakes begin to fall, my heart feels as heavy as the dark winter clouds above. Volleyball season is over, as we didn't make it to the championship. Monday, I'll be heading off with my family for our annual winter retreat. Normally, I would be excited, but this year, it's different. Reid won't be coming along. His family is visiting, and he needs to spend time with them. I understand, of course, but it doesn't seem to make the parting any easier. It's going to be a long winter break without Reid.

Ever since that transformative night in my bedroom, an undeniable spark has ignited between Reid and me. We find ourselves swept up, seeking opportunities to be alone together every chance we get. I can't help but let out a contented sigh as I reminisce about the intimacy we've shared.

The connection, the closeness, the undeniable friction between us—it's beyond anything I could have ever imagined. As I sit here, a dreamy smile plays on my lips. It's like I'm wrapped up in a romantic whirlwind, and I wouldn't have it any other way. Though the winter break may be long without him, the memories of our stolen moments keep me warm.

Suddenly, Hazel's voice slices through my thoughts, snapping me out of my comfortable reverie. The anger pulsating from her words is palpable, and without even meaning to, my ears perk up. She blurts out that she and Benjamin broke up. Taken aback, I ask her what happened.

In a flurry, she tells me she saw Jada with Benjamin, laughing, touching... and she didn't like it one bit. She had told Jada to move her skank ass and to go flirt with someone else's boyfriend. But the shocker came when Benjamin didn't back her up. Instead, he told Hazel to leave Jada alone.

Once Jada was out of earshot, Hazel had lost it on Benjamin. She couldn't believe he was defending someone like Jada, a person who never hesitated to throw her bitchy attitude around. And to top it off, Benjamin never spoke up, especially when Jada crossed the line with his best friend's girlfriend. The argument escalated, the tension spiraled out of control, and Hazel ended up breaking things off with Benjamin, convinced he had more-than-friendly feelings for Jada.

"I'm really sorry to hear about you and Benjamin, Hazel," I say, reaching out to squeeze her hand gently. "Breakups are always tough, but you know how things go. It's possible that this is all just a big misunderstanding and you two will patch things up soon."

Hazel doesn't reply, just sits there, her gaze fixed on somewhere far away. I take a deep breath and continue. "Speaking of relationships... I'm meeting Reid's family this weekend." I can feel the butterflies in my stomach as I say it out loud. "I'm really nervous..."

"Why?" She finally turns to look at me, her expression softening a bit. "You two are practically inseparable. I'm sure his family will love you."

I give a weak smile. "I hope so. My family doesn't mind that Reid's white, but when I mentioned where he lived... Mom wasn't too happy. She thinks people in that area might not be kind to people like me."

Hazel squeezes my hand back. "You'll never know until you try, right?" she says, "And no matter what, we've got your back, Amelia."

I feel my heart warm at her words, and I nod, grateful for her support. The shrill sound of the lunch bell breaks through our conversation, a signal that our fleeting moment of solace in the busy school day has ended. Together, Hazel and I dump our trays and begin navigating our way out of the bustling cafeteria. As we make our way through the crowd, the clamor of the lunchroom fades. Suddenly, familiar arms encircle me from behind, pulling me close. That familiar scent of sandalwood and peppermint fills my senses, a scent so intrinsically linked to him that my heart flutters in anticipation. An involuntary smile blooms on my face before I even hear his voice.

"Hey, baby," Reid murmurs into my ear, his voice a low rumble that sends shivers of delight down my spine.

Even in this chaotic school hallway, his presence brings a sense of calm, a moment of joy in an ordinary day.

Turning in his arms, I look up to meet Reid's gaze. His eyes gleam with a mixture of mischief and affection that sends my heart racing. A moment later, he leans down, his breath tickling my cheek before his lips finally find mine. It's a sweet and intoxicating kiss, one that renders us completely oblivious to the world around us. It's like we're lost in our own little bubble, away from the chaos of the lunchroom and the bustling corridors.

Suddenly, we hear a throat clear, an unmistakable sound that instantly breaks our bubble. We pull apart to find Ms. Peters standing there with a stern expression on her face.

"School is for learning, not sucking faces," she admonishes, a hint of a smile tugging at the corners of her mouth. "Get to class."

Reid and I exchange an amused glance before bursting into laughter. The sternness of Ms. Peters' words contrasted with the amused twinkle in her eyes is just too comical. Still chuckling, we break away from each other and start heading toward our next class.

As we stride into chemistry class, Reid and I find our usual lab table and take our seats next to each other. Mrs. Ramires, a petite woman with wisps of gray hair escaping her bun, starts the lesson with her usual energy. Amidst the monotone hum of her lecture, Reid subtly catches my hand, sending a wave of warmth spiraling up my arm. He places a gentle kiss on the back of my hand, his eyes never leaving mine. The flutters in my stomach intensify, threatening to make me giddy.

"Ready to meet my family tomorrow?" he asks, his voice barely more than a whisper.

I can tell he's nervous, which makes me nervous. But I pull off a confident smile and nod.

"Yes, I am," I tell him, hoping that my voice sounds more certain than I feel.

However, there's a niggle of unease that I can't shake off, a fear that's been haunting me ever since we planned this meeting. I know I need to share my fears with Reid. I take a deep breath, squeezing his hand lightly before I speak.

"Reid, I'm a little worried," I confess, my voice quivering slightly. "I'm worried about... about how they'll react to us being in a relationship." I quickly add, "I don't mean to speak ill of them, not at all. It's just... these are my worries."

I watch him closely, gauging his reaction, hoping he understands my apprehension. Reid's eyes soften as he takes in my confession. He brings his other hand up to cup my face, his thumb brushing away a strand of hair that's fallen across my eyes. The tenderness in his touch is enough to momentarily still my fears.

"Amelia," he starts, his voice a soothing balm to my frayed nerves. "I want you to know something." He takes a deep breath, his ocean-blue eyes never leaving mine. "I love you. Like, I really, really love you."

His words hang in the air between us, a sweet declaration that sends my heart into a joyous somersault.

"I love you with every beat of my heart, every breath I take," he continues, his voice barely more than a whisper, but the sincerity of his words rings loud and clear. "I love you with the kind of love that transcends boundaries, breaks barriers... the kind of love that is all-consuming, yet leaves you yearning for more. The love I have for you is like the northern star in the vast expanse of the night, unwavering, constant, and guiding me through the darkest times. It's a love that doesn't see color or race, but only the beautiful soul that you are. And I feel it, Amelia, deep in my bones every day."

I can see the depth of his feelings mirrored in his eyes, the raw emotion that resonates in every word. It's overwhelming, it's terrifying, but it's also so utterly beautiful that it leaves me breathless. Reid's eyes are earnest, his words sincere.

"Amelia," he says, as if he's holding something incredibly precious. "My family will love you because I love you."

The gravity of his words sends shivers down my spine, but also a warmth that spreads through me like a healing balm. He continues, his voice barely more than a whisper now.

"They will see the amazing girl I fell in love with. The girl who is strong, kind, and beautiful inside and out. They'll see the girl who brings a smile to my face every day, the girl who fills my world with magic and colors. Believe me, baby, you have absolutely nothing to worry about."

His words, like a promise, hover between us, filling me with hope, and slowly, the knot of anxiety in my stomach unfurls.

The words are there, sitting on the tip of my tongue, ready to be poured out into the world.

"Reid, I love you too." I say, my voice barely a whisper, yet carrying a weight that feels as significant as the moment itself. "Your love is like sunshine after a storm. It's warm, comforting, and it makes everything else seem insignificant in its radiant glow. Your love makes me feel cherished, like I'm the most important person in the world to you. And that feeling, Reid, it's incredibly intoxicating."

I pause for a moment, my heart beating wildly against my ribcage. "Your love makes me feel like I can conquer anything, like I'm not alone in this big world. It gives me strength, hope, and a sense of belonging I've never experienced before."

I draw in a shaky breath, my eyes locked onto his, hoping he can see the sincerity and depth of my feelings mirrored back at him. "And for that, Reid, I am eternally grateful. I love you more than words can express."

The rest of the school day flies by, with Reid's reassuring words echoing in my mind. I can still feel the warmth of his hand on my cheek, the intensity in his eyes as he professed his love. It's a profound, transcendent love that sends my heart into a frenzy whenever I think about it.

Soon, Hazel and I are on our way home, passing familiar sights in the neighborhood. As we step inside, the comforting aroma of mom's homemade cookies fills the air, creating a cozy atmosphere of warmth and love. My sisters, Destiny and Iris, are already seated at the kitchen table, their eyes filled with anticipation as Mom takes another batch of cookies out of the oven. Laughter and conversation fill the air as I join them, our family routine wrapping around me like a comforting blanket.

I lean back in my chair, a contented smile on my lips as I soak in the warmth of the moment. Despite my earlier worries, I can't help but feel optimistic. Meeting Reid's family might not be as daunting as I thought. If Reid's love for me is any indication, his family is bound to be just as loving and accepting.

"Amelia, you're glowing!" Hazel says, her eyes dancing with amusement.

I roll my eyes at her, trying to hide the blush creeping up my cheeks. Iris hops over from her chair, her eyes wide with curiosity.

"Are you in love, Amelia?" she asks, tilting her head to the side. Iris, always the more sensitive one, gives me a knowing smile. "It's Reid, isn't it?" she teases, and I can't help but smile back.

I suppose love is hard to hide when it fills you up to the brim and makes your heart feel like it's about to burst.

"Alright, alright," I finally give in, raising my hands in surrender. "Yes, it's Reid. And yes, I'm in love."

At this, the room erupts in cheers and giggles. It's embarrassing but also heartwarming. Amidst the teasing, there's a shared sense of happiness, a joy that resonates within our family bond.

Sitting across from Mom, I watch as she gently stirs her tea, her eyes filled with a tender mix of concern and joy.

"Amelia," she begins, her voice soft yet firm, "I'm incredibly happy for you. Seeing you in love, it's beautiful. But, sweetheart, you must be careful."

She pauses, her gaze dropping to the steaming mug in her hands. "Remember when you and your ex-boyfriend broke up? You were so sad, honey. It broke my heart to see you like that."

She lifts her gaze to meet mine, her eyes filled with wisdom that comes only with experience. "You thought you were in love then, and perhaps you were, in some way. But it's nothing compared to what I see in you now, with Reid," she says, her voice barely more than a whisper, but her words echo loudly in the silence that follows.

"If things don't work out between you two, it's going to devastate you, Amelia. I see it in your eyes. I see how much he means to you," she continues. "So please, be careful with your heart because love..." she sighs, a distant look in her eyes. "Love has an immense power, Amelia. It can either make you or break you."

Her words, though spoken softly, carry an impact that hits me like a freight train, leaving me with a sense of trepidation. But amidst the fear, there is also an understanding, a bittersweet realization of the truth in her words. Love can indeed be a double-edged sword, capable of bringing both immense joy and pain.

Almost immediately, Hazel jumps in, her eyes sparkling with amusement. "No way, Amelia. Reid and you, you've got the forever kind of love." She grins, her gaze fixed on me. "I can see it, loud and clear. And when I'm giving my speech at your wedding," she winks dramatically, "I'm going to tell everyone how I single-handedly brought the two of you together."

Her words break the seriousness of the moment, and the room erupts with laughter. I can't help but join in, the warm sound wrapping around me, driving away any lingering doubts and fears.

The rest of the evening unfolds in a whirl of food, games, and fun. Our family's laughter is the perfect accompaniment to the delicious smell of Mom's cookies wafting through the house, creating an atmosphere of joy and love. Hazel's infectious enthusiasm pulls everyone into a game of charades, and even Mom, usually the observer, joins in, her laughter ringing out in the room.

Amidst the laughs and the playful banter, I find my heart swelling with a sense of happiness, a feeling of home. As the evening winds down, Hazel finally heads home, leaving behind an echo of laughter and a night of cherished memories.

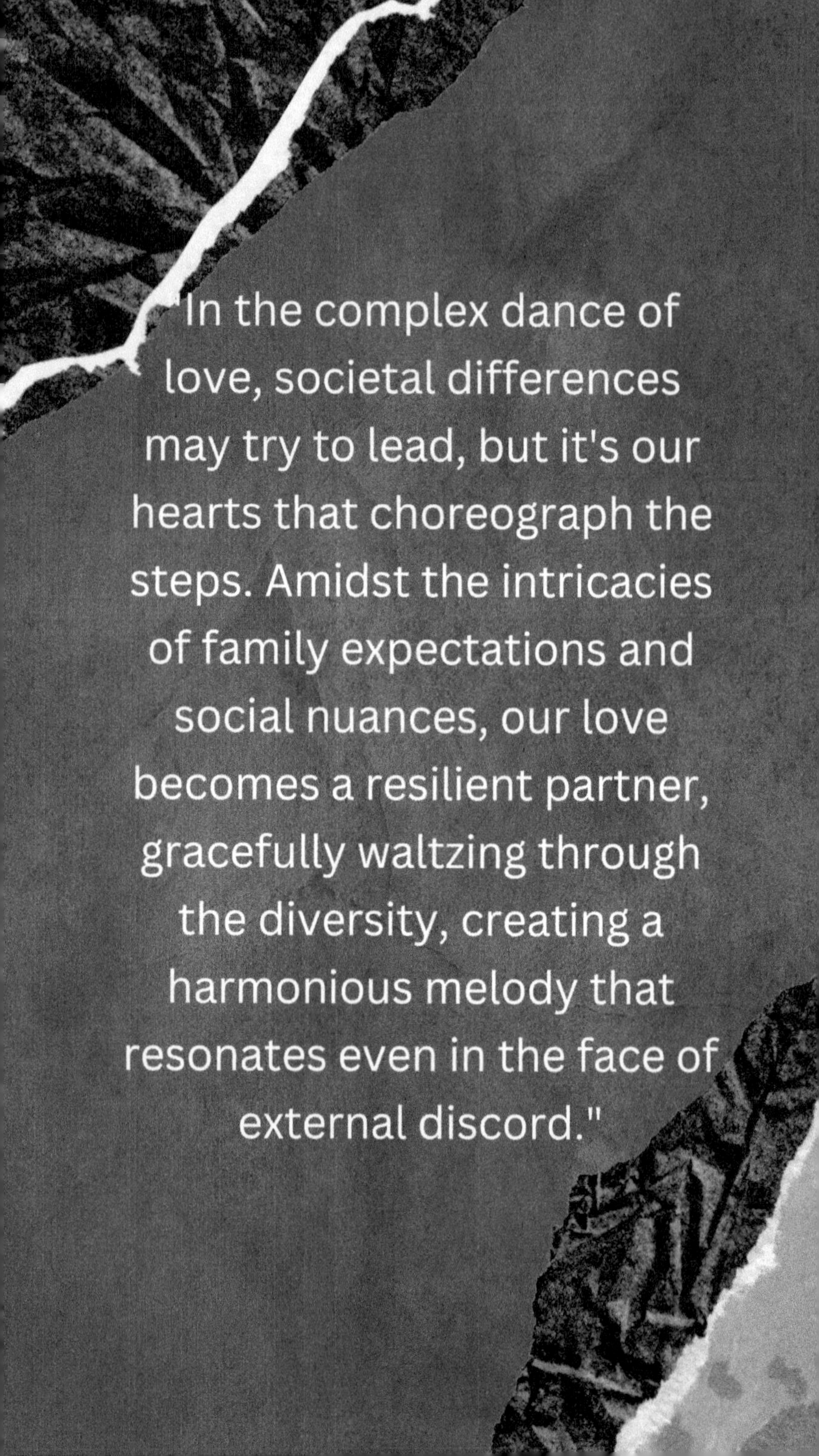

"In the complex dance of love, societal differences may try to lead, but it's our hearts that choreograph the steps. Amidst the intricacies of family expectations and social nuances, our love becomes a resilient partner, gracefully waltzing through the diversity, creating a harmonious melody that resonates even in the face of external discord."

THAT DIDN'T GO AS PLANNED

Today's the day. The day I meet Reid's family. I've been standing in front of my mirror for what seems like hours, changing outfits like a maniac. Is this dress too casual? Is that one too formal? I'm overthinking everything. Destiny's sitting on my bed, watching me spiral into a fashion crisis. She's got this look on her face - part amusement, part concern.

Suddenly, she breaks the silence. "Amelia," she says, "it really doesn't matter what you wear. You're not trying to win a fashion contest. You're just meeting Reid's family. They should like you for you, not for your clothes. And if they don't..." her voice hardens, "then screw them. They don't deserve to be part of your love story with Reid, anyway."

Destiny's right. I know she's right. But it's easier said than done. As I look in the mirror one last time, my reflection seems to echo her words back at me. I'm not trying to win a fashion contest. I'm just meeting Reid's family. They should like me for me. I let out a deep breath, finally settling on my favorite sundress and a pair of comfortable flats. I tame my wild mane of hair into a casual bun, a few loose curls framing my face.

Just as I'm done, my mom's voice calls from downstairs, "Amelia, it's time to leave!"

I grab my purse, give Destiny a grateful smile, and head out the door.

As I slide into the passenger seat of my mom's car, my heart pounds like a drum in my chest. My mom takes one look at me and gives me a comforting smile. "You've got this, Amelia," she assures me, turning the ignition. "Everything will be fine. Just be yourself." Her words wash over me like a soothing balm. I nod and send a quick text to Reid, letting him know that we're on our way.

The drive to Reid's parents' house feels like the longest journey of my life. Each passing minute is a ticking time bomb, filling me with anticipation. Before I know it, we're pulling up to a beautiful two-story house. Reid is there, waiting outside. He's wearing a blue shirt that matches his eyes, and my heart skips a beat.

"Call me when you're ready to be picked up," my mom says, leaning over the console and giving me a reassuring squeeze on the shoulder. I can do this. I swing the door open, step out into the sunshine, and start my walk towards Reid.

As I approach, Reid's eyes light up in a familiar way that always warms my heart. He strides towards me, his casual gait somehow still managing to look elegant.

"Hey, baby," he whispers into my ear as he pulls me into a hug, his voice a soothing melody that seems to quiet my racing heart.

His arms wrap around me and I melt into his embrace, the outside world momentarily forgotten. He pulls back slightly, looking into my eyes for a moment before he places a gentle kiss on my lips. A soft blush creeps onto my cheeks and I can't help but smile. This is Reid - my Reid. And no matter how nervous I am about today with him, I feel safe. He takes my hand, interlacing our fingers, and leads me towards the house. As I take a final glance back at my mom's car before stepping inside, I feel a fresh wave of resolve. I can do this.

As Reid opens the door, a wave of warmth and the scent of home-cooked food envelops us. The house is filled with the soft hum of conversation, punctuated by bursts of hearty laughter. Family photos adorn the walls, telling stories of shared memories. Reid's parents, a couple of striking resemblance to him, greet us with welcoming smiles. His mother's genuine warmth radiates throughout the room as she ushers us into the heart of their home - a cozy, lived-in kitchen.

A large oak table is set with mismatched plates and an assortment of food that makes my mouth water. Reid's family is larger than I expected - siblings, grandparents, aunts, uncles, and cousins, all gathered together. Despite the crowd, there's an intimacy in the air, a sense of love and camaraderie that makes the house feel like a home. I take a deep breath, squeezing Reid's hand, feeling a little of my anxiety melt away.

As we enter the living room, a hush falls over the room and all eyes turn towards us. The lively chatter that filled the house moments ago suddenly dies down. It feels like the room has been vacuumed of sound, and I can hear my heart pounding in my ears. Reid squeezes my hand reassuringly, and I return his squeeze, grateful for the solidity of him beside me.

Reid is the first to break the silence. His voice is steady, a touch of pride ringing clear. "Mom, Dad, this is my girlfriend, Amelia," he introduces me. The room remains silent, the tension palpable. Unfazed, Reid continues, "Amelia, this is my mom and dad. These are my brothers, Logan and Nathan..."

He goes on, introducing me to each member of his family. I try to keep track of all the names, knowing how important this is to Reid. As I meet each pair of eyes, my nerves settle, replaced by a quiet resolve. This is Reid's family, the people who made him the man he is today. And I now have the privilege of being part of this family.

I lift my hand, my fingers fluttering in a shy wave towards everyone in the room. The silence stretches for what feels like an eternity until finally, it's broken by Reid's mother.

"Hello, Amelia," she says, her voice filled with warmth and sincerity, washing away the awkwardness that had momentarily filled the room. "Welcome, and it's so nice to meet you."

The person who stands out most to me from that day is Reid's grandmother, Nana Rose. A picture of elegance and grace. Her age-defying energy fills the room as she moves about, her smile radiant and welcoming. She approaches me, her eyes twinkling with curiosity and kindness.

"So, you're the lovely Amelia that our Reid can't stop talking about," she says, her voice a soft melody.

I blush at her words, and she laughs, a sound that's like wind chimes on a breezy day. She takes my hand into her own, her skin soft and warm.

"You have a beautiful aura, dear," she tells me. "I can see why Reid is so smitten." I feel my heart swell at her words. In that moment, I felt accepted and embraced, not just by Nana Rose, but by Reid's whole family.

The evening wears on and I find myself wholly engrossed in the familial atmosphere. We all sit around the dinner table, plates clattering, laughter echoing through the house. Reid's mom regales me with tales of his childhood, each story more embarrassing than the last. I can't help but laugh as she recounts a tale of a young Reid trying to skateboard down the house stairs, resulting in a broken arm and a dent in the wall.

Logan, more reserved and stoic, remains aloof from the conversations. Each time I attempt to engage him in conversation, he meets my words with a just a grunt and an impassive stare. Nathan's warmth and approachability balanced his chilly demeanor. Nathan's remarks, however, are more candid than I expected. He jokes about how Reid spends hours in the bathroom, insinuating he's been jerking off to pictures of me.

The table bursts into laughter while Reid, blushing fiercely, quickly retorts, "Shut up, that's not true!"

His cheeks flush in embarrassment, but he's grinning all the same. The room filled with laughter and good-natured teasing.

Excusing myself from the table, I make my way to the restroom. The small space is nicely decorated, filled with family photos and little trinkets that hold stories of their own. After taking care of my needs, I wash my hands under the warm water, looking at my reflection in the mirror. My cheeks are flushed, my eyes sparkling, and there's an indefinable glow about me. I can't help but smile. Despite the initial nerves, the evening is going better than I could have ever imagined. Reid's family - they're warm, welcoming, and they feel like home. I feel a swell of happiness at the thought of being part of their family, of Reid's life.

Just as I step out of the bathroom, I bump into Logan. He stares at me for a moment, his eyes scrutinizing my every move.

"I can tell my brother loves you," he finally says, breaking the silence. His voice is low, almost a whisper. "He may not have told us, but it's apparent in everything he does. He's never had a girlfriend before. Never been in love before. Girls like you... you're too much for him. He needs a nice, quiet girl, not some rowdy hood chick."

I reel back in shock, his words piercing my elated bubble. My heart pounds in my chest, a bitter taste rising in my mouth.

"You don't know me, asshole," I shoot back, my voice trembling slightly.

He simply nods, a smirk playing on his lips. "No, but I know girls like you. He can't handle it. If you break my brother's heart, I'll ruin you."

With that, he turns on his heels and walks away, leaving me standing there - stunned, shaken, and questioning everything.

The icy words from Logan still echo in my ears as I collect myself, shake off the encounter, and head back to where everyone's gathered. Suddenly, I find myself cornered by Reid's uncle, James. A smug smile plastered on his face, he looked me up and down.

"What is my nephew doing dating a girl like you?" he sneered, his words dripping with disdain. "We don't do that sort of thing in this family. You need to run along back to the gutter you came from. I won't have him dirty himself with a black girl."

His words hit me like a blow to the stomach, taking the wind out of me. I swallow hard, my mind reeling, my heart pounding with fear, with anger, with disbelief.

"Color has nothing to do with love," I say, my voice trembling but steady.

"I'll be damned if I sit back and watch my nephew date a filthy black whore."

The venom in his voice shocks me to my core, but before I can respond, a new voice slices through the air. Strong, resolute, protective.

"Say something like that again, and I will end you," he yells at his uncle.

Reid. His voice rings loud and clear across the room, a whip-crack of raw emotion. I turn to see him standing at the entrance of the room, his face set with an icy resolve.

The hum of conversation in the other room comes to an

abrupt halt, replaced by a stunned silence. One by one, the family gathers, drawn by the escalating tension. Reid marches towards his uncle, his body radiating with anger.

"Apologize to Amelia right now," he demands, his voice as hard as steel.

His uncle's face remains unmoved; a stone wall, refusing to budge. "No, Reid. You're better than this. I'm protecting you. Being with a black girl is not right."

The words hang in the air, a palpable force of prejudice. A gasp escapes Reid's mother, her expression one of shock and disbelief.

"James," she begins, her voice shaky, "We will not treat Amelia like that."

Reid's response is swift and decisive. He shoves his uncle, the sudden movement causing a collective intake of breath from the onlookers.

"See!" his uncle bellows, pointing an accusing finger in my direction, "She's changing him. He would never have acted like this if it weren't for her. She's turning him against his family."

I feel a lump in my throat and a knot in my stomach. The room spins around me as I try to process what's happening. "I... I think I should go," I croak, my voice barely audible.

As I move to grab my things, my hand shakes, reaching for my purse, my coat, anything to provide a semblance of escape. My fingers fumble for my phone, ready to dial my mom's comforting number. Before I can make the call, a firm hand closes around mine, halting my movement. Reid. His eyes are a storm of emotion, his grip tight. Without uttering a word, he pulls me away from the crowd, leading me upstairs to his room.

He closes the door behind us, shutting out the chaos that still reigned downstairs. It's quieter here, the silence offering a momentary respite from the tension. In one swift movement, he pushes me up against the door, his body closing the space between us. His lips crash into mine, the kiss long, hard, and desperate. It feels like a promise, an apology, a plea.

Reid pulls back from our kiss, but remains close, so close that our foreheads touch lightly. His breath, uneven and hot, fans across my face as he looks into my eyes. The intensity of his gaze sends a shiver down my spine.

"You are everything to me," he whispers, his voice filled with conviction.

A flurry of emotions whirls within me, a tempest stirred by his words. Before I can reply, his lips are back on mine, his kiss deep, exploratory, and all-consuming, resonating through me, all the way down to my toes. His hands weave into my hair, securing me to him as he kisses me with a fervor that steals my breath and sets my heart pounding like a drum. It's a moment etched in raw honesty and profound emotion, and in that instant, I realize I am completely, irrevocably in love with him.

Even as the muffled sounds of heated arguments punctuate the silence from the floor below, I lose focus on anything but Reid. His breath mingles with mine and my world narrows down to just the two of us. The urgency of our kiss escalates, a raw desire that's as poignant as it is potent.

As if magnetized, our bodies move in an unspoken consensus towards the bed, shedding the barriers of clothing that separate us, each piece that falls away, increasing the intimacy of the moment. His body hovers over mine, his skin against mine in a tactile symphony of sensation that sends a wave of anticipation shivering through me. His eyes meet mine, a silent question hanging in the air between us.

I nod my head. "Take it all away. I want it to just be you and me. At this moment. No one else between us," I tell Reid.

"You are precious, baby," he says as he pushes my legs open. "And so fucking beautiful."

He positions himself between my legs and rubs his erection back and forth over my wet slit. My breath hitches, and a shudder runs through my body. I rub my fingers through his hair as his eyes lock with mine. My fingers tighten in his hair as I rub myself against him.

"I love you so much," he says with a sexy smile.

He thrusts inside me as he fuses his mouth with mine. He kisses me deeply before peppering kisses across my cheek and down my throat as he thrusts against me. I moan breathlessly as he thrusts inside me again. His fingers dig into my sides to hold me in place. He picks up his pace and starts thrusting into me hard. I know we shouldn't be doing this with his family downstairs, but we need this moment. We need to be close, to convey our love, to reassure each other that nothing would come between us.

As the sensations roll through my body, I can only gasp as I try to keep my moans down. I bring my mouth to his and kiss him as my orgasm hits. Reid moans and thrusts harder, prolonging my orgasm. My body shakes and convulses from the force of it. When I come down, Reid pulls out, and I see the evidence of my arousal glistening on his dick. He turns me over and props my ass in the air before thrusting back inside. I love that Reid has grown from being timid his first time to taking what he wants and how he wants it.

His hands grip my cheeks and pull me back as he thrusts forward. He fucks me so hard, I can't think straight, I can't do anything but moan into the bed. The only sound in the room is our hips slapping together, but his family is too busy arguing downstairs to hear what's going on in his room. My hips move as I push myself back on my own, meeting his hard thrusts.

"That's it, baby," he says.

Waves of extract roll through me, and I clamp tight around him as I come, moaning into the bed once more. He gives a few more hard thrusts and seats himself deep inside me. His cock jerks as he comes over and lets out the sexiest moan I've ever heard. He pulls out, and the evidence of our lovemaking runs down my legs as I lay back on the bed. Our breaths return to normal as the pleasure fades.

I feel Reid's warm body curled around mine, fitting together like two pieces of a puzzle. His muscular arm wraps securely around my waist, and he pulls me closer until I'm flush against him. His breath tickles the nape of my neck as he whispers soothing words.

"Don't let my uncle's words bother you, Amelia. It's just noise." His voice is soft and steady, a comforting balm to my raw emotions.

His words seep into my consciousness, chasing away the remnants of my distress. I cover his hand with mine, intertwining our fingers, a silent affirmation of our bond.

"It's just you and me, Amelia. That's all that matters. Together, Always and Forever," he continues, his voice resolute, his grip firm.

Those words, so simple yet powerful, reaffirm our connection and fortify the foundation of our relationship. The world may be chaotic outside, but within Reid's embrace, I find a sanctuary brimming with love and reassurance.

"In the season of twinkling lights and festive mirth, our love becomes the warm glow that illuminates the winter nights. Like a cherished ornament on the tree of joy, it sparkles with the magic of togetherness, turning every moment into a gift wrapped in the ribbon of shared affection. In the dance of snowflakes and the carol of hearts, our love is the most beautiful melody of Christmas joy."

CHRISTMAS RETREAT/CABIN

Reid's mother offered a genuine apology after that unfortunate incident, which helped me a little. She seemed as surprised as me about his behavior, making it clear she didn't condone it. I wrestled with whether or not to tell my family about what had happened, but in the end, I decided it was important to be honest. My sisters were livid. Destiny, in all her fiery passion, threatened absurd retaliations against Reid's brother Logan and Uncle James. Iris contemplated more subtle forms of revenge.

It was my mother's words that stayed with me. She warned me that being in an interracial relationship wouldn't be easy and that it would present challenges I'd have to be ready to face. She reminded me of my youth, at just eighteen, and questioned if I could truly understand the depth of the forever love I believed I felt. Her advice is to enjoy the relationship while it lasts, subtly hinting at the fleeting nature of teenage love.

As I lock the front door, I can't help but feel a flutter of excitement. Mom is already in the driver's seat, map in hand, while Destiny and Iris are squabbling in the back over who got window privileges. Our bags, packed full of all the necessities for our retreat, are stashed safely in the trunk.

"Ready, ladies?" Mom called out, peering at us over her sunglasses.

I take one last look at our home as we'll be away for a week, and with a nod, I reply, "Let's hit the road!"

The entire drive is filled with the soft chimes of my phone, each one a message from Reid.

"Miss you already," he texts, making my heart flutter despite the miles between us.

"Miss you too," I reply, staring at the familiar road stretching out before us.

His next message brings a slight frown to my face. It's his apology for his uncle's behavior, a constant dull ache in our conversations.

"Let's just leave it in the past," I text back, trying to reassure him. Then, a change of topic.

"Do you like your gift?" he asks.

My hand instinctively goes to the heart-shaped necklace he'd given me, its cool metal offering a strange comfort.

"Yes :-)" I texted back, my fingers brushing the delicate pendant. "And do you like yours?" I ask, remembering the watch I had chosen for him.

The response is almost immediate. A picture of him proudly sporting the watch on his wrist. It looks good on him.

"Yes :-)" he responds, and I can't help but smile.

Just as I'm about to reply to another of Reid's messages, Iris' teasing voice breaks through my little bubble of happiness.

"Aww, look at our Amelia, all smitten and starry-eyed! Haven't seen you stop smiling since Reid started blowing up your phone."

She giggles, poking fun at my newfound euphoria. I can feel my cheeks heating, a blush creeping up my face.

"Oh, hush, Iris!" I retort, attempting to sound annoyed despite the grin that I can't wipe off my face.

Pulling up to the cabin, I can't help but feel a rush of warmth despite the chilly winter air. Seeing Grandma waiting on the front porch, her face beaming with joy, and my aunts and uncles waving enthusiastically from the windows, I feel my heart swell with happiness.

As soon as the car came to a stop, I practically leaped out, my boots crunching on the snow-covered driveway. With the cold air nipping at my cheeks, I throw my arms around Grandma, her warm embrace feeling like home. I then move onto my aunts and uncles, each hug filled with laughter and the promise of good times.

"Amelia, Destiny, Iris," Mom's voice rings out, pulling me out of my thoughts. "Time to grab the bags."

Dutifully, we scurry to the trunk, each of us picking up our designated luggage. Watching Mom follow the rest of the adults inside, I can't suppress the excitement bubbling up inside me. The holiday retreat has officially begun.

Dutifully following Mom's instructions, we picked up the bags from the trunk and began making our way towards the door. Suddenly, I feel an impact on my back and spin around, dropping my bags just in time to duck as a second ball of snow flies right over my head, where I'd been standing just a moment before.

A wave of cold spread down my back, soaking through my coat, but I barely notice it, the sound of Iris' laughter catching my attention ringing out from behind a nearby tree. With a gleam in my eye, I bend down and scoop up a handful of the sparkling, powdery snow on the ground, quickly shaping it into a rough ball.

"All's fair in love and snowball fights, Iris!" I call out,

mischief tinging my voice, as I hurl my snowy retaliation in her direction.

I watch as Iris' eyes widen in surprise when she realizes her attacker is no longer defenseless. She tries to dodge my attack, her laughter echoing in the quiet forest, but my aim is true. The snowball hit its mark, and Iris squeals as the cold snow meets her warm coat. In retaliation, a handful of hastily scooped-up snow came flying my way. The cold hits me like a slap in the face, but I'm too caught up in the adrenaline to care. Destiny joins the fun, armed with her own barrage of snowballs, and soon our laughter fills the air and the soft thud of snowballs hitting their targets.

After what felt like hours, our snowball fight comes to a halt when we hear Mom's voice calling us from the porch.

"Girls! Time to come in before you catch a cold," she calls sternly, her hands on her hips.

We're breathless, flushed from the cold and the running around, but the joy on our faces is clear. We step into the warm house, our clothes soaked and clinging to us, leaving a trail of melting snow in our wake.

"Goodness, you girls are soaked!" Mom says when we pile into the foyer.

She looks us over, shaking her head, but there's an amused sparkle in her eyes. "Off you go. Get out of those wet clothes and into the shower before you freeze to death!"

She shoos us upstairs, laughter ringing through the house once more. The warmth of the cabin wraps around us, melting away the chill in our bones as we change out of our wet clothes, the remnants of our impromptu snowball fight but a memory.

Warm and changed into dry clothes, we descend the staircase to the cozy, familiar sight of the living room. The soft glow of the Christmas lights twinkling against the rustic log wall, everyone engrossed in a holiday movie. The low hum of the television and the occasional laughter fill the room.

As soon as the credits roll, Grandma rises from her chair, announcing, "Cookie time!"

We all follow her into the kitchen, our childhood tradition still intact. It doesn't matter how old we get, baking cookies with Grandma is a ritual we cherish. Iris and Destiny take to their usual roles, measuring out the flour and sugar while I help Grandma with the mixing. We fill the entire house with chatter, the sweet aroma of baking cookies mingling with the sound of laughter and conversation.

In between the cookie batches, amidst all the hubbubs, I overhear snippets of our plans. We have fun-filled days ahead: sledding down the hill behind the cabin, ice skating on the frozen pond, and tubing along the snow-covered trails. The holiday cheer is infectious, the anticipation for the next day's adventures adding to the festive atmosphere. The holiday retreat is off to an unforgettable start.

The next morning, I wake up to the mouthwatering smell of freshly brewed coffee and pancakes wafting up from the kitchen. I follow the comforting aroma downstairs, where everyone is already gathered around the breakfast table, their faces bright and eager for the day ahead.

After filling our bellies with Grandma's delicious pancakes and gulping down coffee and hot chocolate, we bundle up for the day's adventure. Layer by layer, we put on our winter gear, wool socks, thermal under layers, snug sweaters, thick pants, snow boots, gloves, scarves, and finally, our puffy coats. Each piece of clothing serving as a shield against the biting cold.

Once we step outside, the world has transformed into a magical winter wonderland. The sunlight sparkles off the pristine white snow, blanketing everything in sight. The cabin stands majestically against the snow-covered scenery, with the sleds leaning against its sides like silent promises of the day's fun.

Lugging our sleds, we trudge through the knee-high snow to the hill behind the cabin. It's just steep enough to make the climb a mild challenge and the descent a thrill worth every effort. As we line up at the top, our sleds gleaming under the morning sun, I can feel my heart fluttering with anticipation.

One by one, we take turns sliding down the hill. The sleds cutting a path through the snow as we scream and laugh, the cold air rushing past. Iris was the first to go, her laughter fading as she zoomed down the hill. Destiny followed, whooping in delight. Finally, it was my turn.

As I push off, the world blurs around me. The wind whips my face, the sled shakes beneath me, and I can hear nothing but the roar of my own exhilaration. The descent is exhilarating, a mixture of adrenaline, laughter, and the occasional yelp as the sled takes an unexpected turn.

Just like that, our day passes in a blur of snowball fights, snow angels, and countless sled rides down the hill. As the sun sets, painting the sky with hues of pink and orange, we make our way back to the cabin, our bodies tired but our spirits high. The holiday retreat has gifted us another unforgettable day.

As the day's exhaustion finally settles in, I sink into my bed, the warmth of the heavy quilt a stark contrast to the chilly night outside. In the quiet solitude of my room, I pick up my phone from the bedside table, scrolling through the contacts until I find Reid's name. The dial tone rings a few times before he picks up.

"Hey, baby," his voice, familiar and comforting, echoes on the other end of the line.

"Hey," I murmur in response, a contented smile playing on my lips.

"How's your trip going?" he asks, genuine curiosity seeping into his words.

We talked for a while as I narrate the day's events. The snowball fights, the sled rides, and grandma's irresistible cookies. Reid shares his day too, his words painting a vivid picture in my mind, as if I were there with him. As the conversation wears on, my eyelids feel heavy, the day's fun finally catching up.

"You should get some rest, babe. We'll talk tomorrow," Reid gently suggests, as if he senses my fatigue.

"I love you," he whispers, the words warming me from within.

"I love you too," I reply, my voice barely above a whisper.

Hanging up the phone, I surrender to the inviting pull of sleep, with my heart filled with the comfort of our conversation. The last thought that crosses my mind before sleep claims me is the sound of Reid's voice, and I can't help but drift into dreams with a smile on my face.

The rest of the week at the cabin is a whirlwind of activity, each day brimming with laughter, adventure, and the unrivaled joy of family. We skate on the frozen pond, our bodies swaying to the rhythm of the icy wind. We zipped through the snow-covered trails on tubes, our cheers breaking the silence of the winter landscape. Also, we even took a sleigh ride. The rhythmic jingle of sleigh bells in sync with the horses' trot creating a magical symphony. Throughout the day, Reid and I kept in touch, our texts buzzing on our phones, and our nightly phone conversations filled with shared laughter and soothing comfort.

Christmas day dawns, the air filled with the unmistakable scent of hearty breakfast and piping hot coffee. I rouse myself from the coziness of my bed, the Christmas spirit pushing away any remnants of sleep. I make my way to Destiny's room, nudging her awake. She swats me away in her usual manner, grumbling for me to leave her alone. I can't resist teasing her and give her a gentle push that sends her tumbling out of bed. The thump of her hitting the floor was immediately followed by her glare. However, all anger deflates at the sight of my unabashed laughter, and she can't help joining in.

Next, we go to Iris's room, only to find it empty. Figuring she must already be downstairs, we follow suit. As we appear from the staircase, a chorus of "Merry Christmas!" greets us, the room filled with broad smiles, twinkling eyes, and the undeniable warmth of family. The holiday spirit is truly alive and well, and this Christmas is shaping up to be one of the best in memory.

As I step into the bustling kitchen, the aroma of cinnamon, fresh coffee, and baking pastries assaults me, instantly enveloping me in warmth. The Christmas tree in the corner of the room is adorned with twinkling lights and handmade ornaments, each one a memento from Christmases past. Underneath the tree, a sea of brightly wrapped presents eagerly await their turn to spread delight. The fireplace is aglow, casting dancing shadows across the cozy room, while outside, snowflakes fall gently, adding to the white blanket that covers our world.

Laughter and casual chatter echo around me, and I can see my family members moving about, their faces lighting up with a joy that comes only with the Christmas spirit. The atmosphere is one of pure love, happiness, and anticipation. It's as if we were in a bubble, insulated from the rest of the world and its worries. It's Christmas, one of the most cherished times of the year, and I can't help but feel a swell of affection for this moment, this place, and the people I am lucky enough to call family.

The exchanging of gifts is always a special moment in our family's holiday tradition. As I kneel by the tree, its lights casting a warm glow on the colorful array of presents beneath, a feeling of gratitude fills me. With each name read aloud, there's a pause, a held breath as we carefully unwrap the tokens of love chosen with thought and care. I received a beautifully bound book from Iris, knowing she remembered my love for reading.

Destiny, ever the practical one, gifts me a warm scarf, perfect for the frosty days outside. Laughter echoes around as each present unveiled surprises us, delights us, or makes us giggle. We fill the room with a sense of happiness, and looking around at the excited faces of my family, my heart swells. This is what Christmas is all about. Love, laughter, surprises, and the joy of being together.

As the day gradually came to a close, we sit down for a heartwarming Christmas dinner. We cover the table with mouth-watering dishes, each one holding a memory of Christmases past. We eat, laugh, share stories, and raise our glasses in toasts of love and thankfulness. After the dinner plates are cleared, we gather in the living room, a Christmas movie playing softly on the television as we bask in the glow of the tree lights.

As the movie ends, yawns became more frequent, and our eyelids droop with tiredness. One by one, we retreat to our rooms, bidding each other goodnight. As I snuggle into my bed, I pick up my phone and dial Reid's number.

"Merry Christmas, Reid," I speak softly when he answers.

There's a pause, and then his voice came through. "Merry Christmas, Amelia."

The words feel like a warm hug, and I feel my heart fill with happiness. "I'll see you when you get back," he adds, and I smile, already looking forward to our reunion.

With a final goodnight, I hang up the phone and close my eyes, the sound of Reid's voice lulling me to sleep. It had been an incredible day, filled with love, laughter, and the magic of

Christmas, and I drift off to sleep with a contented sigh and a smile on my lips.

The day after Christmas dawns, and with it came the bittersweet task of packing our bags and saying our goodbyes. Mom has to return to work, so we're leaving a day early. We hug everyone tight, promising to visit soon, and with that, we hop into the car and embark on the journey back home.

The entire drive, our car reverberates with the sound of Christmas melodies. We sing along, our voices blending, creating our own unique harmony. Despite the joyous atmosphere, sleepiness creeps over me. My eyelids droop, and soon, I'm lulled into a deep slumber by the hum of the car and the soft melodies.

A gentle nudge from Mom wakes me as we pull into our driveway. I groggily help with the bags, with my muscles protesting the early wake-up. We walk into our house, and a familiar sense of comfort washes over me as I step onto the familiar grounds of home. Mom has work later and promptly disappears upstairs for a quick nap.

After unpacking my suitcase, I join Destiny and Iris on the couch for a movie—a comforting routine to get back to normalcy. The evening is still young when Mom wakes up and heads out for work, reminding us to eat dinner. I can feel my eyelids getting heavy as the events of the past few days catch up with me. So, I bid my sisters goodnight and retreat to the solitude of my room, surrendering to the inviting allure of my bed.

A sudden, unexpected knock on my window jolts me from sleep. Blinking away the remnants of slumber, I turn to see a familiar figure smiling at me from the other side of the frosted glass. Reid. His unexpected visit sends a jolt of surprise through me, but also a rush of happiness. Scrambling from the coziness of my bed, I walk over and slide open the window. A burst of cold air rushes in, but the warmth of

Reid's presence soon replaces it as he climbs through the opening and into my room. I promptly close the window, blocking out the winter chill.

No sooner had I turned to face him than Reid engulfed me in his arms, his lips finding mine in a fervent kiss. Surprised, I gasp in surprise, but soon melt into the kiss, returning it with equal intensity. His arms are firm around me, guiding me backwards until the back of my knees hit the bed. We fall together onto the soft mattress, our bodies entwined and lips still locked in a passionate kiss. We exchanged no words as our clothes come off and our bodies come together. The overpowering sensation of Reid's touch, the taste of his lips, and the intoxicating scent of his cologne replaces every thought. This unexpected visit, this stolen moment, is like a dream, and I have no intention of waking up anytime soon.

"As Cupid strings his bow and the world is draped in shades of love, our hearts become a symphony, playing the sweetest notes of affection. Valentine's Day is not just a date on the calendar; it's a canvas where our love paints a masterpiece of shared dreams, whispered promises, and the timeless romance that beats in the rhythm of our entwined hearts."

CELEBRATING VALENTINES DAY

The Christmas break and New Year's flew by in a blink of an eye. Reid and I snuck out on New Year's Eve. Slipping into our warmest jackets, Reid and I tiptoed out of the house, the quiet crunch of snow under our boots the only sound in the frosty night. It's the annual New Year's Eve gathering in the park. The twinkling fairy lights, the laughter echoing in the chilly night air, and the anticipation of a brand new year made it even more magical.

As the clock struck midnight, Reid and I, under the shimmering stars and the bustling energy of the city, exchanged our New Year's resolutions. We promised to be each other's safe harbor amidst life's storms, to love and cherish each other with every sunrise, and to always find a reason to smile, even on the rainiest of days. Holding his hand, gazing into his eyes, our resolutions weren't merely promises but the beginning of a new chapter, written in the ink of love, commitment, and endless possibilities.

As the last vestiges of the holiday season faded away, we got back to the hustle and bustle of school. Getting back to classes was a bittersweet experience. Gone were the late mornings and lazy afternoons of the Christmas break, and in came the early alarm chimes and the frenzied rush to make it to the first class on time.

Seeing familiar faces and a few new ones in the hallways brought a sense of normalcy, a comforting rhythm to life that was missing during the holidays. Even the smell of textbooks and the sight of a chalkboard filled with equations had its own nostalgic charm. Yes, there were homework assignments to complete and tests to study for because school is a mountain of academic responsibilities that seemed to grow with each passing day.

As Hazel and I meander through the bustling, echo-filled corridors on our way to lunch, an unexpected pair of arms encircles me. Before I can react, I am lifted into the air, spinning around in a heady whirl of laughter. I feel my feet losing contact with the ground, my world blurring as I revolve. My laughter echoes around the hall. Suddenly, the familiar, comforting scent of Reid washes over me, a mixture of fresh pine and musk. I close my eyes, letting the scent wrap around me like a warm blanket. Gently, he sets me down, my feet sinking into the cool tile floor.

"Hey babe," he murmurs softly in my ear, his voice a melodious hum that sends shivers down my spine.

"Hey, handsome," I reply as I turn around.

I look at Reid, and my eyes fall upon a single radiant red rose cradled gently in his hands.

He steps closer, and with a boyish grin playing on his lips, he presents me with the rose, saying, "A rose for a beautiful girl."

The sincerity in his eyes makes my heart flutter. I take the rose from him, the soft petals brushing against my palm.

"Thank you," I murmur, my voice barely above a whisper as I am overwhelmed by the simplicity yet depth of his gesture.

I bring the rose closer to my face, the delicate aroma of the flower filling my senses. The scent is intoxicating, but it's his loving gaze that truly takes my breath away.

An unexpected warmth envelops my hand, causing me to look down. Reid has intertwined his fingers with mine, the heat from his hand spreading a comforting warmth up my arm. I look up into his eyes, mirrors of warmth and affection, as he gives my hand a gentle squeeze.

"Happy Valentine's Day, Amelia," he says, a soft smile lighting up his face. His voice is the sweetest melody, igniting a flutter in my heart.

The world seems to fade away as I get lost in his gaze, the noise of the bustling corridor replaced by the sound of my heartbeat in my ears. I can't help but return his smile, my heart overflowing with happiness.

"Happy Valentine's Day, Reid," I respond, squeezing his hand back.

The simplicity of the moment, standing here hand in hand, wishing each other on this day of love, feels more significant and beautiful than any grand gesture could ever be.

Reid's gaze lingers on me as he asks, "Amelia, would you like to go out with me on a date for Valentine's Day?"

The question hangs in the air between us, his eyes glinting with hopeful anticipation. I find myself unable to voice my excitement, my vocal chords betraying my racing heart. I nod my head eagerly instead, an infectious grin spreading across my face. As if on cue, Reid's smile broadens, mirroring my own.

Before either of us can say another word, the harsh sound of the bell cuts through our moment, ushering us back to reality. It's time to get to class. Hazel, ever the pragmatic one, grabs my arm, her grip firm yet gentle.

"Come on," she says, pulling me away from Reid. "You guys can smooch and bump uglies later."

Turning towards Hazel, I notice a shadow pass over her usually bright eyes. "Are things still bad with Benjamin?" I ask, my voice sincere, laced with concern.

Hazel's response is quick, her words harsh. "Benjamin's an ass, and he can eat a dick."

Her words hang heavy in the air, a stark contrast to the blissful bubble that Reid and I had been in just moments ago. As Hazel and I reluctantly part ways with Reid and head towards our first class, I can't help but feel a sense of anticipation building up inside me. The day ahead looms large, stretching out like an endless desert highway with no end in sight. Each tick of the clock seems to echo through the classroom, a constant reminder of the painfully slow passage of time. The teacher's voice drones on in the background, a dull monotone that is almost hypnotic in its monotony.

Each glance at the clock seems to only confirms that time has decided to crawl today, each minute stretching out into an eternity. The lessons seem to drag on and on, the words in the textbook blurring into a meaningless jumble of letters. Even lunch, which is usually a welcome break, brings no relief. The conversation around me fades into a dull buzz, my mind already racing ahead to the evening.

With each passing hour, the anticipation for my date with Reid grows stronger, pulsating through my veins like a living, breathing entity. I can barely focus on anything else. His face constantly appearing in my mind's eye, the sound of his laughter echoing in my ears. The thought of spending Valentine's Day with him sends butterflies fluttering in my stomach, a sweet, intoxicating sensation that fills me with an undeniable sense of joy.

As the end of the day slowly but surely approaches, I can hardly contain my excitement. Every fiber of my being is buzzing with anticipation, a thrilling undercurrent of energy that makes it nearly impossible to sit still. When the last bell finally rings, it's as if a dam has burst inside me. The prospect of finally being with Reid sends a ripple of elation through me, turning the dreary day into a distant memory. As I gather my things and head towards the exit, I can't help but smile.

Just as I'm about to dash out the door, caught in the whirlwind of my excitement, Hazel hooks her arm through mine, guiding me in the opposite direction. Surprised, I look at her, confusion clear in my eyes.

"Hazel, what's going on? Where are we going?" I ask, my heart pounding in my chest.

With a mysterious smile, Hazel responds. "I'm driving you home, Amelia. I've actually texted Benjamin to tell Reid that he's not allowed to see you until he picks you up for your date tonight."

I stare at Hazel with my mind racing. First, I'm stunned that she communicated with Benjamin, whom she's mad at, and second, I'm baffled about why Reid and I can't see each other.

"Is there any particular reason we can't see each other?" I ask, my brow furrowed in confusion.

Hazel quirks an eyebrow at me and chuckles. "Amelia, you are not being left alone to pick an outfit for your date tonight. Your taste in fashion is horrendous. As your best friend, I refuse to let you go out looking like a rainbow-colored Picasso painting that's been through a blender."

Thankfully, the drive to my house is quick and Hazel gets out of the car quickly, determination in her eyes. She storms into the house with me hot on her heels.

"You're being ridiculous, Hazel," I say as I continue to follow her.

With a dramatic roll of her eyes, Hazel forges her way into my room, making a beeline for my closet. She scrutinizes each item of clothing with a critical eye, pulling out various pieces with a flourish before discarding them carelessly on my bed.

"Hazel, be careful!" I scold as I see a favorite sweater of mine crumpled up among the discarded pile.

She doesn't seem to hear me, already engrossed in the haphazard mix of colors and patterns that make up my wardrobe.

"Sweetie, we really need to go shopping," she sighs, sounding more like a disappointed mother than my best friend.

I can't help but laugh at her dramatics, though a part of me also feels a twinge of anxiety. I've never been one for fashion, always choosing comfort over style. But Hazel, with her knack for pulling together outfits that are both stylish and practical, has always been my go-to fashion guru. Finally, after what seems like an eternity of rummaging, Hazel pulls out a simple black dress with a wide smile.

"This is perfect!" she yells, holding it up against me.

I can't help but mirror her grin. Leave it to Hazel to find a gem amongst the chaos of my wardrobe. The dress is simple yet elegant, something I can feel comfortable yet confident in. It's perfect.

"Thank you, Hazel," I tell her sincerely, a rush of gratitude washing over me.

She just winks in response, her eyes sparkling with mischief. "Well, what are best friends for, if not to save you from fashion disasters?"

As Hazel moves on from my closet, she heads straight for my vanity, her eyes glinting with a familiar, excited spark. She proceeds with a clear vision, selecting makeup products with swift precision. I take a seat on the stool, pulling my thick, curly hair off my face to give her a clean canvas. Hazel applies my makeup with the steady hand of an artist, blending shades on my eyelids and defining my lips with a soft, natural color.

"Now for the hair," she declares, grabbing a bottle of leave-in conditioner and a wide-toothed comb from the drawers.

She works the product into my hair, untangling knots and defining curls with the comb. It's a process that requires patience and care, and Hazel does it with ease, her hands moving in gentle motions.

Once she's done, Hazel hands me a mirror, and I take a good look at myself. My curls fall around my face in soft waves, framing my makeup-enhanced features perfectly. I look beautiful, and the smile that spreads across my face is genuine and full of joy.

Before I can say anything, my mom's voice echoes up the stairs. "Amelia! Reid's here."

My heart leaps in my chest, and I look over at Hazel, her own smile matching mine perfectly.

She gives me a final once-over. "You're ready, Amelia. Knock him dead."

With a last nod of approval from Hazel, I rise from the stool and make my way towards the stairs. My heart pounds in my chest like a drum, its rhythm faster with each step I take. As I round the corner, I catch sight of Reid leaning casually against the front door, his hands shoved in the pockets of his jeans.

His eyes dart up at the sound of my footsteps, and his breath hitches, eyes widening as they take me in. The corners of his mouth twitch into a soft smile.

"Beautiful," he whispers, almost as if he's in awe.

His voice barely reaches my ears, but it sends a jolt through my body, leaving a warm flush in its wake. I can't help but smile, my cheeks burning with a blush that I can't control.

My mom, who's been watching our exchange from the

doorway of the kitchen, speaks up then, her voice laced with amusement.

"You two go ahead and get on out of here," she says, waving us towards the door. "Don't want to be late."

I give her a quick nod, my smile never leaving my face, before turning back to Reid. With a deep breath, I step forward, ready to embark on what's sure to be an unforgettable night.

As Reid opens the door of the borrowed car, a wave of chivalry washes over me. I can't help but smile as I slide into the buttery leather seats. The car roars to life under Reid's hands, the purr of the engine blending seamlessly with the soft jazz playing on the radio, setting the tone for the evening.

The car pulls up to a stunningly lit building, the soft glow of the lights casting a romantic atmosphere over the cobblestone pathway.

"Wow, Reid, this place is beautiful," I breathe out in awe.

He just smiles at me, parking the car and making his way to my side to open the door. He offers me his hand, which I take, my heart fluttering at the contact.

As we step inside, I'm immediately taken by the restaurant's charm. The place is enchanting, a vintage chandelier, flickering candlelight on every table casting warm shadows, the soft clinking of cutlery blending with the gentle murmur of conversations and the occasional laughter. The aromas wafting from the kitchen make my mouth water, and I can't help but think that this is every bit as romantic as I've ever dreamt it would be.

Reid pulls out the chair for me like a gentleman and I thank him, our eyes meeting for a moment that feels like an eternity. We settle into a comfortable silence, the ambiance of the restaurant enveloping us.

"You look stunning tonight, Amelia," Reid says, his eyes warm and sincere.

I feel my cheeks blush at his words, my heart pounding fiercely against my chest.

"Thank you, Reid," I say, my voice barely above a whisper.

His smile in response is everything, lighting up his face and making my heart do flips.

The dinner progresses with easy conversation and shared laughter, the atmosphere feeling dream-like. As the night falls deeper, we find ourselves lost in the moment, the world outside the restaurant seeming to fade away. The candlelight flickers across Reid's face, casting shadows that make him look even more handsome. I get lost in his eyes, the soft glow reflecting in them making my heart skip a beat.

In the midst of our conversation, Reid reaches across the table, his hand covering mine. His touch sends a jolt up my spine, leaving a warm trail in its wake.

"Amelia," he says, his voice low and filled with emotion. "I can't imagine being here with anyone else. This night feels perfect because you're here with me."

His words leave me breathless, my heart pounding in my chest as I squeeze his hand in response.

"Reid, I feel the same way," I reply, my voice soft but steady.

The look in his eyes makes me feel cherished, loved, and I know in that moment that this is just the beginning of an unforgettable journey for us. I know we're young, but that doesn't mean our love is imaginary. Our age doesn't make our love any less real than someone twice our age.

The night gradually comes to a close, the stars in the sky serving as a gentle reminder of the time that's passed. Reid pulls up to my house, the engine humming to a stop. He turns to me, his eyes sparkling under the dim light of the dashboard.

"I had a great time tonight, baby," he says, his voice sincere.

I feel a warmth spread through me at his words, my smile genuine as I reply, "Me too, Reid."

Our faces draw closer, a magnetic pull between us that's impossible to ignore. Our lips meet in a leisurely kiss, the world outside fading into insignificance. Pulling back slightly, he whispers "I love you" against my lips. The words hang in the air, filling it with an indescribable warmth and causing my heart to flutter uncontrollably. He pulls away then, giving me one last look before stepping out of the car and into the night.

I enter the house, the sound of the closing door echoing through the silence of the night. My mother is there, her smile bright as she stares at me.

"You two are so cute together," she quips, her eyes shimmering with a reminiscent glaze. "Reminds me of when I was young."

Her words bring a smile to my face, the sincerity of her sentiment touching a chord within me. I thank her before heading up the stairs, my mind filled with the memories of the night. As I reach the top of the stairs, I hear my mother's voice call after me.

"Amelia," she says, her tone tender yet tinged with concern. "You have to be careful. I see how you're getting more and more wrapped up in Reid. He's a wonderful boy, but I don't want to see you heartbroken because you've become so consumed by him."

I pause at the top of the stairs as her words sink in. I turn back to look at her, her eyes filled with a mix of love and worry.

"Mom," I begin, my voice steady, "I understand your concern, but things between Reid and me... they are just perfect. You have no idea how happy he makes me."

She's about to interject, but I raise my hand to stop her. "I promise I'll be careful, and I won't let my guard down completely. I also won't let the fear of getting hurt stop me from experiencing this... this love, this happiness."

I give her a reassuring smile, hoping to ease the worry lines that have formed on her forehead. I turn around then, continuing my way up the stairs, my heart still filled with the warmth of the night, but my mind alert to my mother's words of caution.

Once in my room, I prepare for bed, my thoughts consumed by the events of the evening. As I slip into my bed, I can still feel the lingering warmth of Reid's words, their sincerity echoing in the silence of my room. The smile on my face doesn't fade as I drift off into sleep, the memory of the night creating a pleasant lullaby that guides me into a peaceful slumber.

"In the tapestry of teenage milestones, love is the vibrant thread that stitches together moments of innocence and discovery. Each shared glance, every whispered promise, becomes a cherished chapter in the novel of youth, leaving an indelible mark on the pages of our hearts—a sweet reminder that amidst the tumultuous journey of adolescence, love remains the most enduring and magical milestone of all."

Our relationship seems to be wrapped in a protective bubble, shielded from the realities that my mother had warned me about. The weeks blur into one another, each day filled with stolen kisses, shared laughter, and endless conversations. I am deeply, utterly, blissfully in love. The kind of love that makes you forget about everything else, the kind that makes you believe in forever. I am eighteen and in love, and for the time being, this is my world.

Hazel and I stand by our lockers, deep in conversation about our upcoming group project, when I feel a familiar presence approaching. I turn to see Reid with his hair tousled just the way I liked it. With a quick glance at Hazel, he leans in and presses a swift, sweet kiss to my lips. His eyes lock onto mine, filled with a warmth that sends shivers down my spine.

"Amelia," he begins, the corners of his mouth lifting into that sexy smirk I find irresistible. "Will you go to prom with me?"

My heart flutters in my chest, a grin spreading across my face.

"Yes, Reid," I say, the words tumbling out in a happy rush.

I wrap my arms around his neck, pulling him in for a hug, feeling his arms tighten around me in response. His scent, a mix of sandalwood and a hint of the outdoors, envelopes me, making this moment feel nothing short of perfection.

Hazel burst into laughter. "As if there was any doubt that you were going with her, Reid," she teases, her eyes twinkling with amusement.

Reid just chuckles, his eyes never leaving mine. "Even so," he replies, his voice low and warm. "She deserves to be asked properly."

Hazel readily launches into a tirade about how we had only three months to plan everything because May is around the corner. From picking out dresses and shoes to figuring out hair and make-up, her list is endless. Reid laughs, ruffling his hair in that adorable way he does when he's amused.

"I'm going to head to class and let you ladies get on with your 'girl talk'," he says, still grinning.

I giggle, reaching up to give him a quick peck goodbye. As he walks away, Hazel and I stand there, wrapped up in the delightful chaos that promises to be our prom preparation.

Hazel and I barely take a few steps toward our class when the school's intercom crackles to life. A list of names stream from the speakers, the counselor's voice as familiar as the hum of the hallways. As our names; Hazel, Amelia, Reid, Benjamin, and others echo in the corridor, a ripple of uncertainty runs through me. We exchange quick, puzzled glances before rerouting towards the counselor's office.

Upon our arrival, the counselor greets us with a broad smile, an infectious sense of excitement radiating from her.

"The college letters have started arriving," she announces, her voice filled with a blend of pride and anticipation.

I feel an adrenaline rush at her words, my heart pounding like a drum against my ribcage. Some colleges, she says, sent their acceptance letters to the schools rather than the applicants' homes.

Hazel spots Benjamin across the room and calls out to him, her voice sharp with an undercurrent of irritation. Unfazed, Benjamin greets her with a nod, not attempting to challenge the coolness in her voice or return a harsh word in kind. The tension between them is palpable, but they quickly turn their attention to the envelopes in their hands, stepping aside to give each other space.

I tear open the first of my letters, my heart pounding with a mix of excitement and dread. The logos of Aurora University, Evergreen College, and Blue Ridge University decorate the top of the letters, their names proudly emblazoned on high-quality paper. I allow myself a slight moment of triumph before my eyes flick over to Reid.

He holds letters of his own, the shining seals of Horizon University, Cascade Institute of Technology, and Radiant Sciences Institute catching my eye. An odd sensation creeps over me as I realize the truth. None of these schools are in-state... and none of them match my own. I blink, the realization hitting me like a punch to the gut. In our blissful cocoon of teenage love, we'd somehow overlooked this crucial detail in our plans for the future. We hadn't applied to any of the same schools.

I reach out, gently touching Reid's arm to get his attention. He turns to look at me, his eyes wide and questioning.

"Did you apply to any school in the state?" I ask, my voice barely above a whisper. Reid shakes his head, a bewildered look crossing his features.

"No," he says, his voice steady. Then he mirrors my question. "Did you apply to any schools out of state?"

I shake my head, biting my lip, "No, I always planned to stay in state. I wanted to be close to my family."

The words hang in the air between us, drawing an obvious line of distinction in our visions of the future.

Reid is quiet for a moment before he breaks the silence. "I always intended to go away to college. I wanted to go to a good school for technology." His voice is firm, resolute.

A knot forms in my stomach, the enormity of our situation sinking in. I take a deep breath, steadying my nerves. "Maybe there are still schools accepting applications. You can apply to an in-state school."

Reid looks taken shocked by my suggestion, his eyebrows furrowing. "And you can apply out of state," he counters.

"But Reid," I protest. "My family has always been here. My whole life is here."

"And my dreams, Amelia, are elsewhere," Reid counters, his voice hardening. "Technology isn't just a hobby, it's my future."

"What about us?" I ask, my voice shaking. "Is there a place for us in your future?"

"Of course, Amelia," he says, searching my face. "But I can't just give up my dreams."

"I'm not asking you to," I snap, the hurt swelling up inside me. "But it seems you're asking me to give up mine."

"I didn't say that, Amelia," he responds defensively. "I just suggested you could also consider other options."

"And what if I don't want to?" I shot back, my eyes welling up with tears. "What happens to us, then?"

"I... I don't know, Amelia," Reid admits, his voice barely a whisper. "We can have a long-distance relationship."

The silence that follows is deafening. Our words, once filled with laughter and shared dreams, had turned into a battleground of unspoken fears and stubborn stances. The weight of the future hangs heavy between us, like a cloak we're both unable to bear. The realization that our paths might diverge creates a rift, an insurmountable barrier that neither of us had expected.

A cascade of emotions surges within me. Confusion, disappointment, fear, and a deep sense of loss. The corridors echo with the heart-wrenching sound of our dreams clashing, the once harmonious symphony of our togetherness now a cacophony of discord and uncertainty.

The dream of our shared future, once as vivid as the aurora, now seems as elusive as a mirage. The letters in my hand feel like weights, pulling me and Reid in opposite directions. I feel despair like a bitter chill, seeping into our bones and freezing the warmth that once flowed freely between us. The very foundation of our relationship quakes under the onslaught of this unexpected revelation, leaving us both shaken and disoriented.

As the remnants of our first real argument hang heavy in the air, I feel a profound wave of sadness wash over me. But life, as I'd learn, doesn't stop for heartache. With a deep breath, I push our disagreement to the back of my mind while clinging to the faint glimmer of hope.

There are still a few more college letters due to arrive, and who knows? Fate might yet play its hand; we could end up at the same school or distractions, offering a brief reprieve from the storm that was brewing just beneath the surface. Close enough to keep our relationship alive.

Reid and I move on amidst the turmoil, our shared silence speaking volumes. We act like nothing has happened, a facade to keep our world from falling apart. The school days roll by in a blur, each one bringing us closer to the end, the palpable thrill of graduation making the air hum with excitement.

As Hazel maneuvers the car through the city streets, I scroll through my phone, consciously avoiding her gaze. She has always been the more observant one, quick to pick up on subtle changes in my demeanor. I glance up as she parks the car, her eyes catching mine in a steely gaze.

"Alright, spill it," she states more than asks. "How are things with you and Reid? You guys seem off lately. Is it about college?" Her blunt question hangs in the air, slicing through my practiced facade.

I turn to meet her gaze, swallowing hard before nodding in affirmation. The words seem to get stuck in my throat, but I push through, determined to sound more confident than I felt.

"Yes, it's about college," I admit, my voice wavering. "But we'll be fine. It's just a minor challenge that we have to overcome. We'll get through it." I force a smile, hoping to reassure both Hazel and myself.

As Hazel turns up the volume of the radio, a soft melody fills the car, providing a welcome distraction. We allow the music to envelop us, a soothing balm for the tension that had built up. Each lyric, each note, carries a semblance of normalcy that feels both foreign and comforting. We drive the rest of the way in silence, save for the soft whispers of the radio, our thoughts lost in the rhythm of the music.

Pulling up to the mall, a wave of excitement washes over me as the anticipation of finding the perfect prom dress eclipses, if only for a moment, the concerns that had burdened my mind. We walk into the mall and the air buzzes with chatter and laughter, the vibrant atmosphere a stark contrast to the harsh reality we're temporarily escaping from. Our steps lead us to a dress shop, filled with a dazzling array of colors and styles.

The very sight of the beautiful dresses, the thought of the impending prom night, sparks a flicker of excitement within me. This is a moment I had been looking forward to, a heartening interlude amidst the turbulent waves of change. As we enter the shop, I can't help but hope to find a dress as resplendent as my dreams.

The store is an explosion of colors, from deep royal blues to vibrant pinks, each dress more glamorous than the last. My fingers trail over the silken fabric of a deep burgundy gown, the intricate beading catching the light. A sense of anticipation fills the air. Every customer in the store chasing the same dream, to find that one dress, the perfect dress.

Hazel walks over, a handful of dresses draped over her arm. "What do you think?" she asks, holding up a strapless emerald gown.

I shake my head. "It's too glitzy for me, I think. But it would look stunning on you."

She grins, disappearing behind a dressing curtain. Moments later, she emerges in a dress that fits her like a dream.

"You were right, it's perfect!" she declares. I laugh, my heart lifting at the sight of her radiant smile.

I pick up a champagne-colored dress, the soft, flowy fabric appealing to my simpler taste. Slipping into it, I feel like a princess. It's the perfect blend of elegance and simplicity, the color complementing my skin tone.

Hazel gave a nod of approval. "That's the one, Amelia. You look gorgeous."

I blush, twirling in front of the mirror, the dress billowing around me. We continue this process for a while, trying on dresses, vetoing some, and setting others aside for consideration. Despite our different tastes, Hazel gravitating toward bolder, more glamorous styles and me preferring subtle elegance, we respect each other's opinions.

After we finalize our dress choices, Hazel in her stunning emerald gown and me in my elegant champagne dress, the next step is finding the perfect pair of shoes. Hazel chose a pair of golden stilettos, the intricate strappy design glinting in the store lights. The gold creates a dazzling contrast against the emerald of her dress, enhancing its beauty. She looks like a queen, every bit as radiant as I know she will be on prom night.

For my champagne dress, I pick a pair of cream-colored heels. They are simple yet elegantly designed, the heel not too high, perfect for a night of dancing. Delicate lace detailing covers the shoes, adding a touch of sophistication that matches my dress perfectly. Trying them on, I feel a rush of excitement. The shoes are not just beautiful, but they are comfortable too, a balance that's hard to find.

With our shopping bags in hand, we make our way to the food court. The aroma of different cuisines wafts through the bustling space, making my stomach grumble in anticipation. However, just as we are deciding where to eat, a wave of nausea washes over me. I feel hot, my head spins, and a sudden feeling of faintness causes my knees to buckle. Hazel notices immediately and with a worried look, guides me to a nearby bench.

"Don't worry, Amelia," she says, her voice steady and calming. "There's a restaurant here that serves soups. I'll get you some. Just stay here and take deep breaths."

As Hazel rushes off, I close my eyes, focusing on my breathing. I can hear the distant murmur of chatter around me, the noise blending into a single hum. After what feels like an eternity, Hazel returns with a bowl of warm, fragrant soup and some food for herself.

"Here," she tells me, handing me the soup. "This should help."

I manage a weak smile, my heart filled with gratitude for her unwavering support.

"Thank you, Hazel," I whisper, the aroma of the soup already helping to ease my nausea.

As I slowly sip on the soup, and Hazel ate her food, I feel

my strength returning. The soup is soothing and comforting, providing the much-needed warmth and nourishment that I need. After a while, I feel well enough to stand, and with Hazel's help, we slowly make our way out of the mall and head home.

As soon as we arrive home, I hold my breath, stepping into the house cradling the dress and the shoes I'd bought. The excitement is palpable as I unveil the champagne dress and cream heels to my mom and sisters. Their faces light up at the sight of the dress, the delicate fabric flowing like liquid gold in the soft light of our living room. They gush over how beautiful I will look, their eyes sparkling with excitement.

"Amelia, you're going to look absolutely stunning!" my mom shrieks, her hands gently caressing the soft fabric of the dress.

Despite the warm words and the joy that fills the room, I find it hard to muster a genuine smile. I'm not feeling well. The earlier wave of dizziness and nausea had not completely faded. I chalk it up to a cold coming on, not wanting to worry them further.

"I think I'm coming down with a cold," I say, hugging the dress closer. "I just need to lie down for a while."

Their smiles falter, replaced by looks of concern, but they understand, helping me to my room and leaving me to rest.

As the door creaks open, I open my eyes to see Mom enter, carrying a tray with a bowl of steaming soup and a bottle of medicine.

"I made chicken soup, Amelia. It's always good for colds," she whispers, placing the tray on my bedside table. She opens the medicine bottle and pours out two tablets. "And don't forget to take this medicine," she reminds me, her eyes filling with concern.

"Thanks, Mom," I mumble, my throat raw. Her face

softens at that. Her hand reaches out to brush away a loose strand of hair from my face.

"Feel better, okay? You need to be in top shape for the prom," she tells me, her voice carrying a note of cheerfulness that I know is meant to lift my spirits.

She stands up, her hands smoothing out the creases in the blanket. With a final comforting squeeze on my shoulder, she turns to leave.

"Get some rest, Amelia," she calls over her shoulder before the door closes behind her. Alone in the room once again, I look at the tray with my heart swelling with gratitude for my mother's care. I reach out to take the soup, its warmth spreading through me.

"In the tapestry of life, challenges are the unexpected threads that, once woven, alter the very fabric of our existence. They are the pivots that redirect our journey, demanding resilience and courage. Embracing these challenges isn't merely a course correction but an opportunity to weave a story of strength and transformation —a narrative where the unexpected becomes the catalyst for a new and profound chapter in our lives."

LIFE CHANGING REVELATION

Staying home while everyone else was at school for the first three days this week was a real bummer. The sickness hit me like a freight train, leaving me weak and nauseous, with bouts of vomiting that felt never-ending. Among this gloom, Reid was my beacon of hope. He came over every day, arms laden with food and medicine, his mere presence banishing the gloominess that had enveloped me. His acts of care were small but significant, easing not just my physical ailment, but also lifting my spirits.

As I walk out the door, I can't help but smile at the sight of Hazel dancing crazily in her car. Her infectious energy is exactly what I've missed these past few days. Getting into the car, Hazel turns to me, her eyes sparkling with happiness.

"I'm so glad you're coming to school today, Amelia. It's been so boring without you," she tells me.

Her words make me laugh, and before I know it, we're both engaged in some silly dance as we head to school. Upon arrival, we head to our lockers to grab our books, the familiar routine grounding me after days of illness. Suddenly, I feel a pair of arms wrapping around me from behind. I don't need to turn around to know it's Reid.

"Hey baby, I'm glad you're feeling better," he whispers in my ear, his voice warm and comforting.

I close my eyes for a moment, taking in the comfort of his embrace and the normalcy of this school day. It's good to be back. Twisting around to face Reid, I give him a bright smile.

"Hi," I say simply before standing on tiptoe to brush my lips against his.

The world seems to narrow down to just the two of us as the kiss deepens, our bodies instinctively leaning into each other as if seeking more. A loud throat-clearing cuts through the bubble we're in.

"You two should save the X-rated stuff for the bedroom," Hazel chides us, her tone teasing.

Reid and I break apart, laughter bubbling up from both of us.

Still fanning herself dramatically, Hazel jokes, "Seriously, I might have just gotten pregnant from that passionate kiss Reid just gave you."

All humor drains from my face as Hazel's words sink in. I can't remember when my last period was. The laughter in the corridor fades into background noise as my mind races. Suddenly, the world around me feels unreal, as if I'm watching it from a distant place. Reid looks at me, confusion etching his features, but I can't bring myself to say anything more. The reality of the situation slowly dawns on me, the implications sending shivers down my spine. I feel as if the ground beneath me is crumbling, leaving me floating in a state of uncertainty and fear.

The word 'pregnant' echoes in my mind, amplifying my fear with each repetition. My heart hammers in my chest, pumping out a rhythm of terror that drowns out everything else. A wave of nausea rolls over me, but it's different this time, not like when I was sick. It's a feeling of dread, a fear of the unknown. I've always been careful, always used birth control.

The thought that it might have failed me is terrifying. The world around me blurs as panic takes a hold of me, its icy grip squeezing my heart. My mind is a whirlpool of fear and confusion. I'm not ready for this. I can't be pregnant. Not now. The possibility threatens to consume me, leaving me feeling helpless and lost. I need to get things clear. I need to know for sure.

Reid's face is etched with concern. "Amelia, are you okay?"

I muster a small smile, doing my best to keep my voice steady as I reply, "Yeah, I'm fine, Reid."

I can see the disbelief in his eyes, but he doesn't push. Instead, he simply nods, waiting for me to continue.

"Hazel needs me to go with her to the counselor's office for something," I quickly add, glancing at Hazel.

She looks equally confused, but at the sight of my expression, she doesn't question it. Instead, she nods, playing along.

"I'll see you in class, okay?" I tell Reid, hoping he won't probe further.

Relief washes over me as he nods, allowing me to leave without further questioning. Grabbing Hazel's arm, I guide us to walk down the hallway. We keep a fast pace and I don't dare look back, afraid Reid might see the worry written all over my face. Once I'm sure we're far enough away, Hazel turns to me, her eyes narrowed in confusion.

"Okay, what the hell is going on, Amelia?" she asks, concern etched into her features.

I take a deep breath, my heart hammering in my chest. "Hazel, I don't think I just had a cold... I think I'm pregnant," I blurt out, the words raw and piercing.

Hazel is stunned into silence, her eyes wide as she stares at me. I can't hold back the tears anymore and they flow freely down my cheeks. Hazel reacts quickly, wrapping her arms around me in a comforting hug. She tries to soothe me, her voice soft as she whispers reassurances into my ear.

"Amelia," she says, pulling back to look at me. "Let's not jump to conclusions. After school, we'll run to the store and buy a test. You can take it at my house to find out for sure, okay?"

I nod at Hazel's suggestion, wiping away the tears before managing a shaky, "Okay."

As we part ways to head to our respective classes, I take a deep breath and put on a brave face. All throughout the day, I try my best to act normal despite the turmoil churning inside me. The impending test hangs like a dark cloud in the back of my mind, casting a shadow over everything. Reid senses that something's off, but he attributes it to the after-effects of my recent sickness. I don't correct him. I make it through the day, each class dragging like a nightmare.

When the final bell rings, I tell Reid I'll call him later, that I have something to do with Hazel after school. He looks a bit puzzled, but he doesn't question me further and gives me a quick kiss before we part ways. His touch is comforting, but it also brings a pang of guilt. If I am pregnant, how will he react? Shaking off the thought, I head out of the school with Hazel by my side, both of us bracing for the uncertainty of what's coming.

Sitting in Hazel's car, I can feel my heart pounding. It reverberates through my whole body, a constant reminder of the reality I'm potentially facing. Hazel is silent, focusing on the road as she drives us to a pharmacy in a part of town where no one knows us. The anonymity is a slight comfort in a sea of uncertainty.

Hazel dashes into the pharmacy, leaving me alone in the

car. I try to steady my breathing, but the silence only amplifies my anxiety. Moments later, she's back, a small bag held tightly in her hand. I don't need to see its contents to know what it is. The ride to Hazel's house is silent, each passing moment adding to the tension.

Hazel's house is empty when we arrive. Her parents are still at work. I'm grateful for the privacy. Hazel barely gives me a moment to breathe before she pulls me to the bathroom, thrusting the bag into my hands.

"Just take the test, Amelia," she says, her voice soft yet firm.

I nod, unable to form words. I'm about to find out if my life is about to change forever. As I step into the bathroom, the feeling of cold tiles under my feet sends a chill up my spine. I glance at my reflection in the mirror, barely recognizing the girl staring back. I hold the small bag in my trembling hands, the weight of its contents far heavier than it should be. Slowly, I open the bag, pulling out the pregnancy test. It's a simple object, a white plastic stick no longer than my hand, but its implications are life-altering.

I scan the instructions, printed in a simple, impersonal font on the tiny leaflet. Even as I read, my mind is a hurricane of worry and fear. I follow the steps methodically, as instructed. Pee on the stick, cap it, and lay it flat. The simplicity of the action is a stark contrast to the storm of emotions whirling inside me.

The instructions then say to wait two minutes. Two long, tortuous minutes that might as well be an eternity. I glance at my phone and set a timer, each beep echoing my racing heartbeat. I put the phone down and pace the limited space of the bathroom, my heart pounding in an anxious rhythm in my chest.

Each step is heavy, weighed down by the gravity of the unknown. My mind races through the myriad possibilities, each one more terrifying than the last. My hands clench and unclench in a futile attempt to shake off the anxiety. I feel the fear gripping my throat, making it hard to breathe. The silent bathroom seems to close in on me, every ticking second a reminder of the impending reality.

My knees feel weak, and my body is heavy with dread. The helplessness of waiting, of not knowing, gnaws at my soul. I glance at the phone, each passing second on the screen a cruel mistress of time, drawing out the suspense. The fear, the anxiety, the anticipation, all merged into one torturous emotion, a desperate plea for the two minutes to be over.

The piercing sound of the alarm jolts me out of my thoughts, forcing me back to the cold tiles and the stark reality of the bathroom. My body is rigid with tension as I reach for the stick that holds my fate. My breath hitching in my throat, I pick it up, my eyes scanning the result window. A gasp escapes my lips as I see it, the undeniable evidence. Two pink lines. My heart drops at the sight, my worst fear is confirmed.

The world seems to tilt, my breath coming in quick, shallow gasps. I'm pregnant. The words echo in my mind, the gravity of the situation settling in. My hand instinctively goes to my flat belly, the reality of the tiny life inside me both terrifying and surreal. As the shock gradually gives way to a wave of emotions, I am left reeling, the pregnancy test still clutched in my hand. A knock echoes throughout the cold, sterile room, ripping me from my thoughts.

"Amelia? You've been in there for ten minutes," Hazel's voice, muffled by the door, breaks through the silence.

I don't answer. I can't. My sobs hitch in my throat, choking on any words that might have come out. Hazel doesn't wait for a response. The door creaks open, revealing Hazel's worried face. Her eyes quickly take in the scene. Me, huddled on the floor, the used test clutched tightly in my hand, my tear-streaked face a clear sign of the result. Hazel's eyes soften, her immediate reaction not one of judgment but of concern, of compassion. She moves closer, her steps cautious, as if she's afraid any sudden movement might break me further.

"Oh Amelia," she murmurs, her voice barely more than a whisper as she comes to sit beside me. "It's going to be okay."

Her words are soothing, a gentle balm to my raw emotions. Yet, they feel so far from the truth. My mind whirls, the positive result on the test clashing brutally against the plans I had for my life. College, a career, freedom, they all seem distant, their allure tarnished by the reality of the two pink lines.

I'd imagined a different life, one filled with late-night study sessions, graduation caps, and the thrill of landing my first job. But now, it all feels like a collapsing house of cards, torn apart by the growing life within me. Fear grips me, the uncertainty of the future is daunting.

I'm just a teenager, barely ready for the responsibilities of adulthood, let alone motherhood. The path I've meticulously planned is now overshadowed by an alternative path, one I didn't choose but must now travel. The fear is paralyzing; it's all-consuming, yet I know I have to face it. For the tiny life inside me and for myself, I have to find a way to reconcile my plans with this new reality.

Hazel's car purrs softly as we pull out of her driveway, the hum of the engine providing a stark contrast to the deafening silence. The entire ride home, I'm lost in my thoughts, a million fears, doubts, and questions running through my mind. Each passing streetlight casts fleeting shadows on Hazel's focused expression, her grip on the steering wheel steady, despite the turmoil of emotions I know she's navigating.

When we pull up to my house, I barely register the

familiar sight of my childhood home. Its comforting familiarity now seems estranged, tainted by the secret I'm carrying. Wordlessly, I unbuckle my seatbelt and step out of the car, my legs surprisingly steady. Hazel watches me, her gentle concern visible in her eyes, but she says nothing. She doesn't have to. We both know that words are inconsequential in the face of what's happening.

My house is eerily quiet when I step inside, my mom and sisters still away. I'm grateful for the solitude, for the silence that matches the storm inside me. Without a word, I trudge up the stairs to my room, the weight of the world resting on my shoulders.

As the night blankets the world outside, I lay on my bed, my mind a whirlpool of thoughts. The phone on my nightstand lights up with a call coming through. It's Reid. I ignore it, the sound of the ringtone echoing my racing heartbeat. He texts, but I don't bother reading the message. I can't. Not when my world is crumbling around me. All I can do is stare blankly at the ceiling while the magnitude of what's happened sinks in.

Our lives, mine, Reid's, even the tiny life inside me. Everything has changed and there's no going back. The reality of it is overwhelming, the knowledge that nothing will ever be the same again. I'm not just a teenager anymore. I'm a teenager who's going to be a mother. That thought consumes me, the shadows of the night merging with the darkness of my fears. As the world outside falls into a peaceful slumber, I lie awake, the silence of my room a stark reminder of the journey I have ahead.

The abrupt knock on my bedroom window jolts me from my restless thoughts, sending a shiver down my spine. I startle, shaking off the enveloping shadows to peer towards the sound. Silhouetted in the dim glow of the moonlight is Reid, his figure unmistakable even through the veil of darkness. A wave of emotions floods over me; relief, fear, confusion. Swallowing hard, I push myself off the bed and rush to the window, quickly unlatching it and helping him climb inside.

"Reid," I whisper, my voice barely audible, "What are you doing here?"

My heart pounds in my chest, the rapid beats echoing my fear of getting caught. Reid isn't supposed to be here, not at this hour, not with the world oblivious to the turmoil we're facing.

As quietly as I can, I rush to my bedroom door, pressing my ear against the cool wood to listen for any signs of stirring from my mom or sisters. The house is silent, their peaceful slumber untouched by the secrets seeping into the darkness. Heart still racing, I lock the door and turn back to Reid, his presence in my room a stark reminder of the path that lies ahead, a path that I never foresaw yet now am compelled to tread.

"You didn't answer my calls or my texts. I came to check on you," Reid responds. His words are wrapped in concern, his eyes searching mine. I summon a small smile, pushing away the cascade of emotions threatening to spill over.

"I'm sorry I didn't answer, Reid," I murmur, cradling my burgeoning secret close. "I'm fine, really. You need to leave. I'll see you at school tomorrow."

I try to keep my voice steady and my facade convincing. Reid moves closer, his hands enveloping mine, his touch igniting a spark that seems out of place in the pool of my fears. His lips find mine in a kiss filled with so much passion it leaves me breathless.

"If something is wrong, you know you can tell me. I'm here for you," he whispers, his voice lingering even as he pulls away.

My smile is my only response, a silent promise that I'll see him at school. As Reid slips back out the window, he casts one last look my way, a look that entwines a promise and a question. Alone once again, I crawl into bed, the silence of my room amplifying the sound of my sobs. As I cry myself to sleep, I am consumed by a chilling fear. A fear of the unknown. A fear of the future.

"In the crossroads of life, some decisions stand as daunting as mountains, their shadows casting uncertainty over our path. To choose is to embark on a journey where the echoes of that decision resonate through time, leaving an indelible mark on our existence. Not every path leads to sunshine, for some decisions, once made, become the sculptors of our destiny, molding our lives with consequences that, at times, alter the landscape in ways we never imagined—sometimes not for the best."

MAKING A DECISION

I'm roused from my sleep this morning by Destiny, an unusual occurrence that instantly has me feeling a sense of confusion.

I look at her, my brow furrowing in confusion. "What's wrong?"

"I sense something's off with you. If you need to talk, I'm here to listen," she says.

Overwhelmed, I can't hold back the tears anymore. They fall freely, a dam bursting open, releasing pent-up emotions. It's so sudden, I'm surprised by how quickly it happens. It's a testament to how overwhelmed I feel by the situation.

"Destiny," I stammer, voice choking with emotion, "I'm pregnant, and I'm scared." The tears keep coming no matter how much or fast I wipe them away. "I keep imagining what Reid would think." I try to explain, my voice barely a whisper now. "What if we break up? What if we can't make it? Will our dreams just remain dreams?"

I feel a knot in my stomach as I let out the fears that have been haunting me, the worries that keep me awake at night.

Destiny looks at me, her eyes softening as she takes my hands in hers.

"Amelia," she says, her voice steady. "You have options."

Something about the way she says it makes me feel like I can breathe again, if only a little.

"You can keep it," she begins. "If you believe you're ready for the responsibility that comes with parenthood." Then she continues. "Or you can put it up for adoption. There are so many loving families out there that can provide a wonderful home." She doesn't flinch as she gives the last option. "And if neither of those feels right, you can choose to not go through with the pregnancy. This is your life, Amelia, and the decision is yours."

I find myself lost in a whirlwind of thoughts, each option presenting a new, uncharted path. If I keep it, my life would forever be intertwined with a child. I imagine small hands reaching out for me, the sound of soft giggles filling the silence of my apartment. Reid's smile mirrored on a face much smaller than ours. But what if he isn't there? What if he leaves and I'm left alone, a single mother with a child who is nothing more than a reminder of the love that once was?

The thought of adoption brings a different pain, the pain of letting go. I see myself going through the months of pregnancy, feeling every kick, every heartbeat, only to say goodbye at the end. I imagine the child growing up, wondering why their mother gave them away. Would they find a loving home, parents who would cherish them as their own? Or would they fall prey to the horror stories I've heard, living a life they didn't deserve?

Then there's the last option, the one that I can't even bring myself to think about. It feels so wrong, so unnatural. But it would end the uncertainty, the fear. It would be as if nothing happened at all. However, as I sit here, my hand instinctively moves to my stomach. A surge of protectiveness washes over me. This baby, my baby, is part of me. A Part of Reid. It wasn't planned, but maybe it doesn't need to be. We made this baby together. It's a part of him just as much as me. Maybe he would want to stay, to be a father. Or maybe he would leave, and that's a risk I would have to take.

Finally, after what feels like an eternity, I look up, my decision clear. "I'm going to have it, Destiny," I say, my voice steady. "Whatever happens, happens. I can do this. I have to believe that."

Destiny gives me a firm nod, her face solemn. "If that's what you want, Amelia," she says, her voice steady, "I'm here for you, always." She pauses then, her face takes on a serious expression. "But you know you have to tell Mom. This isn't something you can hide, at least not for long."

The mention of Mom sends a jolt through me. The thought of facing her, of breaking the news to her; It's terrifying. Destiny is right. I can't hide this forever. I give a small nod with my heart heavy. Yet, before I think about telling Mom, there's someone else who needs to know.

"I have to tell Reid first," I tell Destiny, my voice barely above a whisper.

I arrive at school the next day with my stomach in knots. I try my best to avoid Reid, darting through the crowded hallways and slipping into classrooms at the last possible moment. It's not that I don't want to see him. In fact, it's quite the opposite. Every fiber of my being aches to tell him. To share this burden that has suddenly been placed on my shoulders. I just can't bring myself to say the words yet. To turn our world upside down. Hazel does her best to distract him, creating a buffer between us as we navigate from one class to the next.

She's a godsend, always there when I need her. However, Reid is impossible to avoid in the classes we have together. We usually sit together, sharing notes and inside jokes, a small island of familiarity in the sea of faces. Ignoring him now isn't an option, but I can't bear to meet his gaze either.

I keep my eyes trained on the blackboard, taking excessive notes to keep my hands busy and my mind focused. Every so often, I can feel his gaze on me, heavy and questioning, but I simply can't muster the courage to return it.

As the day drags on, a gnawing anxiety builds within me, a constant humming reminder of the secret I'm clutching close. I find my hand unconsciously drifting towards my stomach, a protective gesture that only heightens my nervousness. I have to remind myself repeatedly to keep my hands busy, to keep them away from the telltale sign of my secret. Each passing minute feels like an eternity, the ticking of the clock echoing my heartbeat in a cruel symphony of time.

When the final bell rings, a wave of relief washes over me. I hastily gather my things, not caring about the books and papers that go flying in my haste. Hazel is right behind me, her worried eyes mirroring my own. I barely manage to catch my breath when I hear it.

"Amelia!" The familiar voice sends a chill down my spine.

I turn around to find Reid, his face a mix of concern and confusion. I can't help but look into his eyes, those beautiful eyes that I've fallen for time and time again. But this time, they hold a different meaning for me. I blink back the tears threatening to spill, offering him a sad smile before quickly averting my gaze. Without another word, I turn on my heel and leave, leaving him standing in the middle of the deserted hallway. We get into Hazel's car and as soon as the engine starts, her phone starts to ding and ring in a continuous loop.

"Benjamin again," she mutters, her thumb pressing down on the ignore button with more force than necessary.

She looks at me, her eyes softening. "Reid is worried sick, Amelia."

I stay silent, my gaze fixed on the passing scenery outside

the window. Hazel sighs heavily, running a hand through her hair before continuing,

"You need to tell him, Amelia. Worrying him like this, it's not fair. It's... it's wrong." She pauses, her grip tightening on the steering wheel. "Look, I hate to be the one to say this, but you're handling this all wrong. You're shocked, I get that, but treating him like this because you're going through something...it's bullshit, Amelia."

I can tell Hazel is trying to get through to me, her words harsh but necessary. But right now, every word feels like a blade slicing through my already fragile state.

We pull up to my house, and I bolt from the car, not even waiting for Hazel to park. I run straight to my room, slamming the door behind me and sinking onto the bed with my body shaking. I bury my face in my hands, my mind a whirlwind of thoughts and I'm so lost in my own world that I don't notice the door opening until Destiny walks in, a plate of food in her hands.

"I told Mom you weren't feeling well," she says, setting the plate down on my bedside table. "So I brought you food before she could do it."

I manage a weak smile, mumbling a thank you as I reach out to take the plate. I pick at the food, forcing myself to eat despite the nausea rising in my throat. Suddenly, the room spins, and I shove the plate back at Destiny, rushing to the bathroom just in time. I fall to my knees, emptying the contents of my stomach into the toilet. Tears prick at my eyes as the nausea subsides, replaced by a dull ache. I feel a hand on my back, gently rubbing circles and offering soothing words. Destiny is always there for me, despite it all.

"You're going to be okay, Amelia," she whispers as I lean heavily against her, my body shaking. "We're going to figure this out together."

I rise unsteadily to my feet, the taste in my mouth sour

and unpleasant. My legs are wobbly, but I make it to the sink, where I hastily brush my teeth and rinse out my mouth. Destiny is there, a steady presence by my side as she helps me back to bed. The walk seems longer than usual, the events of the day having taken a toll on me. I settle into the sheets, my body achy and exhausted.

"Amelia, you need to tell Mom," Destiny says, her voice gentle but firm, "If she finds out on her own, she will not be pleased."

I wince at the thought, the imagined disappointment in Mom's eyes enough to send a fresh wave of nausea through me. She picks up the untouched plate, her expression unreadable as she sets it back on the table.

"Goodnight, Amelia," she says, stepping out of the room and leaving me alone with my thoughts.

I lay there in the dark; the silence deafening. I feel so alone, so lost, and I want to rewind time to go back to a simpler time when my biggest worry was what to wear to school. But life doesn't work that way, does it? I curl up into a ball, my knees pressed against my chest as the tears fall.

I let them, not bothering to wipe them away. Crying is all I can do right now, the only way I know how to express the turmoil inside me. As sleep finally finds me, my last conscious thought is a prayer, a desperate plea for strength, for courage. For tomorrow, I have to face another day, another battle.

"IN THE REALM OF REVELATION, WORDS BECOME THE ARCHITECTS OF OUR RELATIONSHIP— CONSTRUCTING BRIDGES OF UNDERSTANDING OR WALLS OF CHANGE. THE NEWS WE SHARE HOLDS THE POWER TO SCULPT THE CONTOURS OF OUR CONNECTION, BE IT IN THE GENTLE GLOW OF JOY OR THE SOBERING SHADOWS OF TRANSFORMATION."

TELLING REID

I wake up feeling like a hot mess. My eyes are puffy and heavy, as if I had been crying all night. Slowly, I get dressed, feeling each fabric against my skin like a thousand tiny needles. As I walk downstairs, Destiny and Iris are already there, exchanging morning pleasantries. Destiny catches my reflection and, misinterpreting my bedraggled state for a rough night's sleep, jokes.

"Looks like sleep whooped you good, huh?" She burst out laughing, but I can't find the humor this time.

Iris, more perceptive, notices my silence. "You okay, Amelia?"

I shrug it off with a weak excuse. Something about a late-night movie marathon. Grabbing a bagel from the kitchen counter, I make a beeline for the front door, hoping to escape further inquiries.

As I arrive at school, Hazel meets me with a sympathetic smile, silently acknowledging my uncharacteristic quietness. Reid is waiting by my locker as he always does, his familiar grin somehow out-of-place today. He plants a soft kiss on my lips, then pulls back, studying my face with a puzzled look. I don't have the energy to explain or pretend, so I simply take his hand and lead him towards our first class.

The day moves in a daze, a blur of lessons and chatter that feels distant and muffled. I barely speak and my responses are limited to nods and half-smiles. I'm lost in a sea of thoughts, as my mind is a whirlpool of confusion and emotions. Reid is perceptive, his eyes never leaving me, as if trying to read the unsaid words written all over my face.

Finally, as the day is nearing its end, he finally corners me. "What's wrong, Amelia?" He asks with worry, but I find myself unable to articulate my feelings.

Shaking my head weakly, I avoid his gaze. "Nothing, I'm just tired," I mumble.

He frowns, but he refuses to accept my evasion. "Bullshit, Amelia," Reid retorts, his voice firm. "Tell me the truth. Did I do something? Did I say something that upset you?"

He pleads, his eyes mirroring his concern. I want to reassure him, to erase the worry lines etched on his forehead, but the words choke in my throat. The dam of emotions that I'd been holding back finally breaks, and I find myself crying, tears streaming down my face. Reid looks shocked because he hadn't expected this reaction. I pull away from Reid, wiping my tears hastily. Taking a deep, shaky breath, I look up at him. His eyes are filled with confusion and concern.

"Reid," I start, my voice barely above a whisper. "I'm pregnant."

The words hang in the air between us, a stark revelation that will undoubtedly change our lives forever. For a moment, Reid is stunned into silence, his eyes wide and his mouth agape. I can't decipher his expression, and I feel a wave of panic washing over me. It feels like hours had passed in those few seconds of silence. Afraid of his reaction and assuming the worst, I turn away, intending to escape the situation.

Before I could take even a single step, Reid reaches out

and pulls me back. His grip is firm yet gentle. He wraps his arms around me in a hug, holding me close to his chest. The tension slowly seeps out of my body as I lean into his embrace.

"Amelia," he whispers into my ear, his voice filled with warmth. "Baby, everything is going to be alright."

His words, though simple, fill me with a sense of relief and comfort. In his embrace, I find my haven.

As Reid holds me close, I can hear his heart beating steadily against my ear, a comforting rhythm during my turmoil. He takes a deep breath, as if gathering his thoughts, before breaking the silence.

"Amelia," he says, his voice softer than I'd ever heard. "I love you. More than I could ever put into words." His words echoes in the quiet space between us, wrapped in a sincerity that makes my heart flutter. "And this," he pauses, placing his hand on my stomach gently, "This changes nothing."

Reid pulls away slightly, just enough to look into my eyes. His gaze is intense, filled with an emotion I can't quite name, but it's comforting.

"We'll get through this. Together," he says, a determined edge to his voice. His fingers trace patterns on my back, a subconscious action that somehow eases my anxiety.

"And no matter what happens," he adds, his voice barely above a whisper. "It's you and me. Always has been, always will be."

His words, though simple, resonate within me. They serve as a promise, a vow that he will be there by my side, through the good and the bad, every step of the way. I find solace in his words, my fears gradually subsiding. In that moment, I knew we'd face whatever the future held together.

As the days rolls into a week, a sense of relief washes over me. Finally, the secret I had been carrying was shared with Reid, and he took it far better than I could have ever imagined. His support, his words, his actions; everything he did was to assure me we were in this together.

Each day, he makes sure I'm comfortable, often bringing me little treats or just sitting with me when the fatigue becomes too much. Somehow, Reid's relentless optimism is infectious, his confidence in our ability to face this together giving me strength.

It feels like we're in a bubble, just the two of us, dealing with what's coming. Hazel and Benjamin are the only ones who know about our situation. Their support and understanding means the world to us. Hazel is a rock, her encouragement and advice helping me navigate the waves of morning sickness and fatigue. Benjamin, too, is unexpectedly supportive, offering to help in any way he can.

Amidst all this, there's one person who I've yet to tell. My mother. Every day, as I hide the bouts of morning sickness and the overwhelming fatigue, I wonder how to break the news to her. The idea of revealing the predicament I had landed in fills me with trepidation. The fear of her disappointment, of the potential clash of our worlds, haunts me. As each day passes, it becomes clear that I can't hide this forever.

As I walk into the house, I find my mother sitting in the living room, her brows knitted in worry. The moment she sees me, she breaks the silence.

"Amelia," she starts, her voice gentle yet firm. "I know something's up. You've been distant, hiding things. And if I have to guess," she pauses, looking me straight in the eyes. "Are you pregnant?"

Her words hang in the air like a harsh verdict. I feel my heart pounding in my chest, my worst fear coming to life. Tears well up in my eyes, blurring my vision. My mother has always been astute, noticing the slightest change in my behavior, but I hadn't expected her to guess the truth so accurately.

My voice chokes in my throat as I struggle to respond, to confirm her suspicion. The room seems to close in on me; the walls echoing my mother's words.

"I... I am, mom," I whisper, the words tearing through the heavy silence.

The tears I'd been holding back finally break free, streaming down my face. I brace myself for her reaction, for an outburst, for disappointment. Yet, all I get is silence. It's daunting, making me feel more vulnerable than ever. The fear of her reaction, of the impending collision of our worlds, is overwhelming, shaking me to my core.

"How did you know?" I ask.

"I am your mother," she responds, her voice softer than I expected. "I know my children, and I know when something is different about them. Though, I may not say something all the time, but that doesn't mean I don't know things. When I see a change that makes me worry, that's when I step in."

Her words, so simple yet filled with such profound wisdom, make my heart ache. I feel a strange mixture of relief and guilt wash over me. I'm relieved that my secret is out, but the guilt of not telling her myself, of making her worry, was overwhelming.

Tears flow freely down my face, each droplet carrying a piece of the fear and guilt I'd been harboring. My heart is heavy with regret, and I choke on my tears as I try to speak.

"I'm so sorry, Mom," I choke out between sobs.

The words echo around the room, a stark confession that I hope will somehow ease the tension. Yet, among the tears and the guilt, there's a glimmer of hope. For in my mother's words, I hear not disappointment but understanding.

After a lingering silence, my mom finally speaks. "Amelia," she starts, her voice calm, "I had a feeling this would be the scenario." Her words wrap around me like a warm blanket, easing the tension slightly. It isn't the hostility I was bracing myself for. Instead, there was a strange understanding in her voice. A mother's intuition, perhaps.

"No school for you tomorrow," she continues. "I've set up an appointment with the doctor."

The sudden decisiveness in her voice catches me off guard, but the motherly concern that fueled it is all too familiar. Despite the unexpected circumstances, my mom is stepping up in ways I hadn't even begun to comprehend, her actions speaking louder than any words of consolation. In her own quiet way, she is telling me I'm alone in this.

I dial Reid's number, my heart pounding in my chest as I wait for him to pick up. When I hear his voice on the other end of the line, a wave of relief washes over me.

"Reid," I begin, my voice shaky. "My mom... she knows. She knows I'm pregnant." I pause, letting the words sink in. "She set up a doctor's appointment for me tomorrow."

With a pause on the other end of the line, I can almost feel the surprise hanging in the air between us. When Reid finally speaks, his voice is steady, but his concern is palpable.

"Should I go with you?" he asks, his words echoing my own thoughts.

I hesitate, considering his offer. Part of me yearns for his support, for the comfort of his presence. Yet, I know this is something I need to face with my mother.

"No, Reid," I respond, my voice stronger than I feel. "Let me... let me give her some time to wrap her head around this."

His silence on the other end tells me he understands. We are in this together, but for now, I need to navigate this path with my mother. The dawn of the next day brings with it a sense of reality. As I climb into the car with my mother, the gravity of the situation finally hits me. Our journey to the doctor's office is quiet, the silence punctuated only by the rhythmic hum of the car engine. The tension is thick, yet there is an underlying understanding, a shared anticipation of the imminent confirmation.

At the doctor's office, the nurse calls me in, and they pull my blood to run a pregnancy test. We wait around for the result, and it confirms what I already knew. They tell me to wait while they set up the room to do an ultrasound. She comes back out and tells me to follow her to an exam room. I lie on the table and lift my shirt like she tells me to. She places a glob of cold gel on my stomach and places the want on my belly. As soon as the nurse turns the screen my way, a small form pops into view.

"There's your baby," she says, pointing at the fuzzy image.

A wave of emotion wells up inside me as I gaze at the tiny life forming inside me. The nurse scrunches her brows in concentration as she moves the wand across my belly, pausing occasionally to take a few measurements. I watch the screen, mesmerized by the sight of my child, a little being that's part of Reid and part of me. After what feels like an eternity, she breaks the silence.

"According to the measurements," she begins, her voice steady and professional. "You're approximately three months along. That puts your due date around August 7th."

The words reverberate through the room, filling the air with a new sense of reality. Three months. I am three months pregnant. This is no longer a secret, no longer an abstract concept. It is real. It is happening, and it is tangible in the form of the little life fluttering inside me.

The words echo in my head, a surreal affirmation of the life growing within me. Watching the black-and-white images on the screen, I can see the baby moving around in my stomach. It's an odd feeling, as if gas bubbles are floating around in my stomach, but this is so much more, another life making its presence known in such a gentle way.

The sight on the screen is fascinating, almost alien, yet

filled with a warmth that slowly seeps into my heart. It's more real than anything I'd ever experienced, a tangible proof of the tiny life that was a part of me, of Reid, of us.

After the appointment, my mother surprises me by suggesting we grab lunch. We find a quiet spot in a nearby cafe, the hustle and bustle of the lunchtime crowd providing a soothing background noise. As we sit here, sipping on our drinks, my mom looks at me with a strange mixture of concern and determination.

"Your life has changed, Amelia," she says, her voice steady yet filled with an undercurrent of emotion. "You're going to be a teenage mother, and it will not be easy. But I want you to know that you're not alone. We'll get through this together."

Her words, simple and direct, hit me like a punch in the gut. They are a stark reminder of the reality I'm facing, a reality that's becoming a more real with each passing day.

She then asks me the question that I'd been dreading. "Does Reid know about the baby?"

I nod, managing a small smile. "Yes, he knows. He's been supportive."

Her brow furrow slightly at my answer, and a moment later, she asks the next logical question. "Does Reid's family know?"

I shake my head, suddenly feeling like a little girl caught in a lie. "No, he hasn't told them yet."

Her reaction is immediate and clear. "He needs to tell them, Amelia," she replies, her voice firm. "You will not be put in a situation where you're the only one shouldering this responsibility. His family needs to be involved, too."

Looking into her eyes, I can see the fierce determination that's a part of her, a part that she's passing onto me. My life has changed, yes, but I'm alone. I have my mom, and I have Reid. Now, we just need to let Reid's family in on our little secret.

The words rang in my ears, an echo of my mother's clear, firm command. "Call Reid, Amelia. Tell him we're coming over and make sure his parents are there."

I hold my phone tightly, apprehension knotting my stomach as I dial his number. Pressing the call button feels like making a pact with fate, a leap into the unknown.

"Yes, Reid," I stammer when he answers, my voice barely above a whisper, "We... we're coming over. Please make sure your parents are home."

My heart pounds against my chest as we make our way to Reid's, anxiety gnawing at me with each passing minute. As we pull up to the house, Reid is waiting for us, the anxiety etched across his face, mirroring my own.

"Hello, Ms. Campbell," he greets my mother as I climb out of the car, his voice barely hiding the tension that hangs in the air.

"Hello, Reid. Are your parents' home?" my mother asks, straight to the point, wasting no time on pleasantries.

Reid nod yes, and we head inside, ready to face whatever was waiting for us. Walking through the front door, it hits me like a wave of cold water. This is the first time our parents are meeting. And they're not meeting for a birthday party, or a graduation, or dinner. They're meeting because Reid and I have life-changing news to share. I let out a sigh. This has to be the worst way I could have even imagined our parents meeting.

Reid takes the lead, introducing his parents to my mom. "Mom, Dad, this is Ms. Campbell, Amelia's mother," he says, his voice strained under the weight of the impending news.

We all take seats in the living room, the normalcy of the situation making the reality of our news seem even more outlandish.

Reid's mother, a petite woman with gentle eyes, turns to

us, a smile playing on her lips. "So, what is it you want to discuss?" she asks, oblivious to the storm that's about to hit.

Reid turns towards his parents, takes a deep breath and, dropping his gaze, lets the words fall out.

"Amelia is pregnant," he says, his voice barely more than a whisper.

The room goes silent, the weight of his words hanging heavily in the air.

"In the embrace of love, obstacles become stepping stones, and difficulties transform into opportunities for growth. Together, we navigate the complexities of life, hand in hand, our love illuminating the path with a reassuring light."

MAKING IT WORK

Reid's parents didn't seem overjoyed, but they didn't look distressed, either. As I observed their reactions, I realized they were taking it all in stride, accepting the situation as one of life's many unpredictable moments. Their calm demeanor conveyed a sense of understanding, as if to say, "these things happen."

Unfortunately, things took a turn when Reid's mother broached the subject of marriage. My heart pounded in my chest as she suggested, rather insistently, that Reid and I should get married. To my surprise, my mother intervened.

"Look, this isn't the old days," she tells them, her tone firm yet composed. "They made a mistake, yes. But we can't force them into a marriage just because Amelia is pregnant." I look over at Reid, who seems as shocked as I am. "They're not even opposed to the idea, but they're just too young. We need to think this through carefully."

"I understand your concerns," Reid's mom counters, her voice carrying an edge of desperation. "But I've seen too many instances where the father walks away, leaving the mother to raise the child alone. We can't let that happen here. They need to marry."

My mom is quick to respond. "That won't ensure anything, and your statement speaks ill of your son. I'm sure that's not your intent." Reid's mom tries to speak, but my mom cuts her off. "We all want what's best for them, but rushing them into a marriage isn't necessarily the answer."

As my mom cut through the tension-filled air with her last statement, I can feel the room becoming suddenly quiet. Reid and I sit here, enveloped in an uncomfortable silence as our parents' debate came to an abrupt halt. The echoes of their heated words reverberate in the room. The minutes passing feels like an eternity, the air heavy with unsaid words and unbidden feelings. Suddenly, my mom rises from her seat, her face a mask of determination.

"Amelia is not getting married, and that's final," she declares, her voice ringing clear and resolute in the room.

Her gaze then softens as she looks at Reid's parents. "It was nice meeting you, and I wish we met under different circumstances. Hopefully, going forward, we can have more civil conversations."

She then turns to me. "Let's go, Amelia."

Her words, as well as the underlying strength in her voice, offers me a comforting assurance that no matter what, I'm alone in this. She is firmly standing in my corner.

As the door shuts behind us, casting a last look on the evening's drama, I feel a whirlwind of emotions. I'm overwhelmed, caught between relief and a sense of unease. Relief washes over me, knowing my mother is firmly on my side, ready to face the world for my sake. Yet, a feeling of unease settles within me, brought about by the thought of the consequences of bringing a child into the world under such circumstances.

There is fear, too. Fear of the unknown and fear of the

future. Beneath it all, there is an undeniable feeling of grati-tude. I am grateful for my mother's unwavering support, her stern resilience, and the love that shows clearly in her eyes. She is my rock in the tumultuous sea of uncertainty, and for that, I will always be grateful.

Life returns to normal after that turbulent meeting with Reid's parents. Reid, bless his heart, is doting on me like never before. He'd always check if I'm okay, ask if I need anything, or simply just be there, his presence a constant source of comfort. Surprisingly, every time I visit Reid's house, his mom always greets me with a smile.

She seems genuinely excited about the baby, often mentioning how much she loves the name Samantha and how she wishes the baby is a girl, so we can name her that. And I, well, I am growing, both in size and in the attention I was attracting. My belly is showing more, and our situation had become the talk of the school.

Standing at my locker, caught in a conversation with Hazel, my eyebrows up as she talks.

"You're getting bigger by the day, Amelia," I can't help but laugh, the humor in her statement disarming the self-consciousness that had been gnawing at me.

"Yes," I reply, placing a hand on my growing belly. "I'm going to have to find another prom dress to fit into because I'll be as big as a whale."

We both erupt into laughter, the sound ringing through the hallway filled with students rushing between classes. Just then, Reid and Benjamin walk up, catching the tail end of our laughter. Reid, with his signature warm smile, wraps his arm around my waist, drawing me close and planting a light kiss on my temple.

"Hey, babe, how are you feeling?" he asks, his eyes reflecting concern. It warms me to know that despite every-thing, he is here, standing by my side.

"I'm fine," I assure him, my gaze meeting Hazel's as we close our lockers and walk toward class.

As I wobble down the hallway, I notice a figure approaching us. It's Jada, with her signature evil smirk, that screams trouble.

"So, you went and got yourself knocked up, huh?" she snarls, a nasty glint in her eyes. "You did it on purpose. You trapped Reid."

The accusation hangs heavy in the air, a painful punch to an already bruised situation. Hazel is quick to react, getting up in Jada's face.

"Watch what you say, Jada, before I punch your teeth out," she snaps, protective as always. Though Jada just laughs, her gaze never leaving mine. It's as if she's trying to burrow into my soul with her hurtful words. Benjamin, until now a silent spectator, suddenly steps forward, his face steeled with determination.

"Shut up, Jada," he interjects, his voice louder than I'd ever heard it before. "Quit stirring up shit. You're just mad because you had a crush on Reid and never made a move. You're mad that he's with Amelia."

Jada's smirk fades into an expression of surprise, and a ripple of whispers spread through the crowd. I can see the truth hit her. Benjamin had called her out on her feelings for Reid, feelings she'd never been brave enough to act on. Reid, who is still looking at me, squeezes my hand reassuringly and pulls me away from the brewing storm.

"Don't listen to her, babe," he says, his voice firm yet comforting. "She's wrong. I don't feel trapped. She's trying to create problems that don't exist. Don't let her words come between us."

His words feel like a warm blanket, reassuring me amidst the cold accusations being flung my way. Jada's accusations are like a rock thrown into the calm waters of my life, creating ripples that ultimately threaten to morph into a storm. The impact of her words is far-reaching, causing me to question my decisions and my relationship with Reid. Despite his reassurances, I can't help but feel a gnawing unease, wondering if there is any truth in Jada's spiteful claims.

The rest of the day drags on, each hour feeling like an eternity as I try to focus on my classes. Finally, school ends, and we're on our way home, Reid by my side. As we walk into his house, his parents greet us warmly. After exchanging pleasantries, we trudge upstairs to his room, a familiar haven where I can forget about my worries, even if just for a little while. We spread our books out on his bed, ready to dive into our homework, but my concentration is interrupted by the rumbling of my stomach. Reid looks at me, his eyes sparkling with amusement.

"Time to feed my woman," he declares, making me burst into laughter.

He quickly disappears downstairs, returning shortly with a bowl of pasta. The enticing aroma of his mom's cooking makes my stomach growl louder. I heartily dig into the food, savoring every bite. Once my hunger is sated, we return to our study session. Eventually, my eyelids grow heavy, and I surrender to sleep. When I wake up, I find Reid sleeping peacefully next to me, a comforting presence in my chaotic life.

As I lay here on Reid's bed, I find myself studying his face, the soft rise and fall of his chest with each breath, the curve of his lips, the handsome line of his jaw. I wonder what features our child will inherit. Will they have his eyes and my nose? The curiosity tingles, and it brings a small smile to my face.

"I can feel those beautiful eyes staring at me," Reid

murmurs, his eyes still closed and a playful smirk tugging at his lips.

I chuckle, leaning in to place a soft peck on his cheek. "I'm just wondering who our baby will look like more. You or me," I admit, my own eyes gleaming with anticipation and wonder.

Reid's hand tenderly cradles my belly, his soft eyes meeting mine with a loving gaze. His voice is low, filled with conviction as he speaks.

"Our baby is going to be beautiful, just like their mother." His fingers trace a gentle path over my stomach as a thoughtful look crossing his face. "If it's a girl," he continues, his gaze dipping to my belly, then back to my eyes. "She'll have your beautiful big brown eyes and a smile that will light up the entire room, just like yours." His words are a caress, his love for me and our unborn child clear in every syllable.

He chuckles lightly, his other hand brushing through his hair teasingly. "And if it's a boy, he'll have his father's boyish charm and killer looks," he winks playfully, but there is sincerity in his eyes. "And most importantly," he adds, his hand covering mine on my belly. "They will be loved. No matter what."

I look deeply into Reid's eyes, my heart fluttering at the love and acceptance I find in them.

"Are you sure you don't feel trapped?" I ask, my voice barely more than a whisper.

The vulnerability in my tone is raw, stripped down to the bare truth of my fears. I take a deep breath, my gaze never leaving his.

"It's not like I set out to get pregnant on purpose, Reid," I confess, my words rushing out in a torrent of honesty. "I honestly didn't mean for this to happen. I was on birth control."

Reid rolls on top of me and kisses me deeply. I moan at

the feel of him, feeling safe and warm and like nothing in the world can tear us apart. He reaches down and pulls my shirt over my head, leaving me in just my bra and pants. He kisses my neck and moves down between my breasts. While he's busy kissing to tops of my breasts, he reaches behind me and unclasps my bra. My full breast spills out, and he takes the nipple of one in his mouth while his hand caresses the other.

He continues to kiss me and moves down to my stomach. His hands encase my growing belling and he peppers it with kisses. He moves down to unbutton my pants and slides them off. He sits back and looks at me with those piercing green eyes that I love so much.

"When I look at you, Amelia, pregnant with my baby, I don't feel trapped." Reid's voice is firm and sincere, his gaze never leaving mine.

"In fact, I feel the opposite. I feel... grateful. Grateful to have you in my life, grateful to have the privilege of being a part of this journey with you." His thumb gently traces the curve of my cheek as he speaks, the tenderness in his touch mirroring the emotion in his voice.

"Seeing you with our child, it's nothing short of a miracle. You're glowing, babe. There's this beautiful, radiant aura around you that I can't help but be drawn to." His hand moves from my cheek to rest on my belly, his eyes fill with awe as if he were touching something precious.

"I love you, Amelia. I love everything about you. Your strength, your courage, your resilience. And I can't wait to meet our baby. To hold him or her in my arms, to see a part of you and a part of me brought to life. I feel excited, overjoyed even." His voice was a mere whisper now, filled with emotion.

"I want to be there for every step of this journey, Amelia. To be there for you, for our baby. I'm not going anywhere, I promise." His gaze holds mine, a silent vow passing between us. I feel a tear slip down my cheek, but I'm smiling, feeling more loved and cherished than ever before.

A smile tugs at the corners of my mouth as I look at Reid as my heart swells with a love so profound it leaves me a little breathless.

"Yeah, we may be young, but we're still adults. We're eighteen, and we can handle this," he adds, the determination in his voice a mirror of the resolve in my eyes.

Reid moves back then, his clothes hitting the floor in quick succession. A shiver of anticipation runs through me as he gently turns me onto my side and positions himself behind me. The warmth of his body radiates against my back, a familiar comfort as we continue our journey into uncharted territory together.

He slides inside me, and his forehead touches the back of my neck as he exhales. "Do you feel that, Amelia? Do you feel the way I feel?"

I moan as he slides in and out of me. I have no words to describe what I feel. It's always good between us. His hand moves around me to cup my belly as he slides back inside. We both moan in unison as he fills me, slamming in deep. Then he brings his hand up and cups my chin, turning my face toward his. He kisses me hard as he drives into me from behind. My body shudders as he slows his pace, giving me long, slow strokes. I groan as his dick throbs inside of me.

"Damn, baby, you feel so fucking good," he whispers in my ear.

He reaches up and palms my breast, using it as leverage to pull my body back against his as he strokes in deep. A ripple moves through my body as I clench around him. The intensity between us grows, and soon we're moving at a frantic pace again. I push my hips back into him, encouraging him to speed up. He sinks in further, and I moan.

"Oh, fuck," I cry out as he surges into me over and over again.

The ache between my legs builds until I go crashing over the edge. I buck against him as I ride out my orgasm, convulsing against him. His hips snap faster, and he's moaning and breathing harder in my ear.

"Fuck, baby," he moans as he seats himself deep inside of me and comes.

His dick jerks uncontrollably, and he continues small thrusts to ride out his orgasm. We lay there as our breathing slows down. I feel him pull out and turn me onto my back. He gazes down at me with his eyes full of love.

Before Reid can muster a word, a sudden gasp escapes my lips. My eyes widen in surprise, and an unexpected giggle bubbles up from the pit of my stomach.

"Reid, I just felt the baby kick," I tell him, my voice filled with wonderment and excitement.

I guide Reid's hand to the swell of my stomach and watch as his face lights up with joy when he feels the tiny movement. The sensation of the baby's movement sends a thrill of joy through my body, a tangible reminder of the life growing inside me. It feels like a gentle flutter, almost as if a tiny butterfly had taken flight in my belly. Each kick, each shift, is a sweet, intimate secret shared between me and our baby. This is a joyous affirmation of life, a celebration of the bond between mother, father, and child developing even before birth.

Reid's expression of awe is priceless. It's as if he's looking at a miracle unfolding right beneath his touch. The tender smile on his face speaks volumes about his love, not just for me, but for the life we created together. His fingers pressed gently against my stomach, cherishing the feel of our baby's tiny movements. His eyes are filled with an emotion so profound, so raw, it takes my breath away. It's a mixture of awe, joy, love, and just a hint of worry. The worry of a soon-to-be-father who wants nothing but the best for his child.

The reality of our impending parenthood, the overwhelming surge of love we feel for our unborn child, and the anticipation of the journey ahead, it all swells within us, binding us closer together. The baby's movement is not just a physical sensation. It's an emotional journey. A beautiful, intimate beacon of the life we are about to welcome into our world.

"IN THE MIDST OF LIFE'S UPHEAVALS, WE FIND STRENGTH IN ACCEPTING OUR NEW REALITY. LOVE BECOMES THE RESILIENT MELODY, PLAYING ON DESPITE THE DISCORD, WEAVING JOY INTO THE TAPESTRY OF OUR EXISTENCE. IN THE ACCEPTANCE OF CHANGE, OUR HEARTS DISCOVER A STEADFAST RHYTHM, EMBRACING THE HARMONY THAT PERSISTS, PROMISING BRIGHTER MOMENTS EVEN IN THE MIDST OF TURMOIL."

GOING SHOPPING

It's the weekend, and Reid's mother has just pulled up in her silver sedan to whisk me away. She's here to take me shopping for baby things, a task that feels far more monumental than I had expected. Reid told me yesterday about his mom's plan. At first, I was hesitant, but his words of encouragement echoed in my mind, nudging me into accepting her offer.

"It'll be good for you, babe," he had said. "You need this."

As I slide into the car, I feel a sense of apprehension mingle with excitement.

Reid's mom starts the car and chats as she maneuvers through the traffic. "How's everything, Amelia?" she asks, her voice radiating warmth.

I manage a small smile, holding onto the seat handle slightly tighter. "Everything's good, Mrs. Carter. Just a bit... overwhelming, I suppose."

Her laughter rings out, bright and cheery. "Oh, just you wait, dear. This is only the beginning! But don't you worry, you'll be a wonderful mother."

Her words instill a sense of comfort, yet a nudge of uncertainty still lingers. I nod, gazing out of the car window at the passing scenery. "Thank you, Mrs. Carter. I hope I can live up to those expectations."

The drive to the mall is surprisingly short, as the usually congested roads are clear of any major traffic. Mrs. Carter skillfully maneuvers the car into a parking spot conveniently located close to the main entrance. The irony's not lost on me. Today promises plenty of walking, yet Mrs. Carter is so thoughtful to minimize my distance from the car to the mall. I can't help but appreciate the gesture despite its triviality in the grand scheme of things.

We exit the car, the cold fresh air washing over me, carrying with it a newfound energy and anticipation. As we stride towards the entrance, the bustling sounds of the mall greet us, an atmosphere that somehow feels oddly soothing. I take a moment, breathing in the familiar scent of the mall before we embark on our shopping expedition.

The mall is abuzz with shoppers, echoing with chatter and the soft clatter of shopping carts. The air is a blend of enticing scents, the aroma of fresh coffee and baked goods wafting from the nearby café. We step into a baby store, its entrance decorated with pastel hues and soft toys. Mrs. Carter's face lights up, her eyes sparkling with delight as she beholds the array of baby items.

Despite my initial apprehension, I find myself drawn into the charm of the store. My eyes wander over the aisles, filled with a myriad of baby items in soft, muted tones. There are baby clothes, cribs, diapers, strollers, and so much more. Each item is a testament to the impending arrival of our baby.

Mrs. Carter, in her element, confidently strides through the store, her hands reaching out to touch the soft fabrics of the baby clothes. There's a consistent theme to her choices, gender-neutral colors. Shades of greens, yellows, whites, and grays fill our cart, a beautiful palette that doesn't conform to the traditional pink or blue.

"Isn't this delightful, Amelia?" She asks, holding up a tiny onesie. Her mirth is contagious, and I find myself smiling and nodding in approval despite the twinge of guilt creeping up on me.

Her enthusiasm is overwhelming, yet I can't shake off the discomfort that gnaws at me. "Mrs. Carter," I murmur hesitantly, "This is too much. We can't let you pay for all this."

She waves my concerns away; her face beaming with joy. "Nonsense, dear. It's my pleasure. Besides, every grandchild of mine deserves the best."

The day unfolds with an array of purchases, each one carefully selected with love and consideration. The overwhelming apprehension I initially felt gradually fades, replaced by a sense of gratitude and warmth towards Mrs. Carter.

As we exit the baby store, Mrs. Carter guides me to another store. This one, however, caters to expectant mothers. I halt, puzzled for a moment, until she turns to me with a mischievous glint in her eyes.

"Well, Amelia, you're only going to get bigger, and you need clothes to compensate for that." She laughs heartily at her own joke, and I stand there, taken aback.

I immediately shake my head, protests forming on my tongue, but she takes my hand, her gaze softening.

"You're part of our family now, Amelia, and I want to do this for you," she tells me.

A wave of gratitude washes over me, and I smile, following her into the store. I roam around, my fingers brushing over the luxurious fabrics. I finally settle on a few pieces I like, but when I glance at the price tags, I gasp in disbelief.

Mrs. Carter chuckles, shaking her head. "Maternity

clothing should be cheaper, considering it's only worn for a short while."

With that, she purchases the clothes, completely dismissing my protests. Feeling spent from the shopping, we agree to grab a bite at the food court.

We collect our food, I with my hearty burger, crispy fries, and thick chocolate shake, while Mrs. Carter opts for a vibrant plate of Chinese cuisine. We navigate our way through the busy food court, selecting a nearby table for our culinary pit-stop, our shopping bags at our feet. As we sink into the familiar routine of unwrapping and arranging our food, a comfortable silence descends upon us.

We take the first few bites without conversation, the hum of the mall and the clatter of trays and cutlery around us providing a soothing white noise. Mrs. Carter seems just as content as I am to enjoy our meal in companionable quiet, each lost in our own thoughts as we refuel for the rest of the day. Finally, Mrs. Carter breaks our comfortable silence. Her voice is soft, yet her words carry a weight I haven't felt before.

"Amelia, I want to be honest with you," she begins, her eyes meeting mine. "When I found out that my son is going to be a father at such a young age... well, I wasn't happy. Before he met you, he had dreams and aspirations, you see, and they're going to be a challenge to achieve now. Because of the baby."

Her words ensnare my heart in a vice-like grip. I feel a surge of defensiveness and indigence. The pleasant aura that was surrounding us seems to have vanished, replaced by a palpable tension. I take a moment, letting my emotions settle before I respond.

"Mrs. Carter," I begin, my voice steady. "This wasn't on purpose, and I don't appreciate it sounding like you're blaming me for creating an obstacle in your son's life."

I pause, taking a deep breath. "What about my life, Mrs. Carter? This baby affects me just as much, if not more. And the last time I checked, it takes two to make a baby. Your son was a willing participant in all of this."

I can't help but feel a certain satisfaction in standing up for myself. This isn't just about him, it's about us. Both of us.

Mrs. Carter reels back, clearly unprepared for my defensive response. "Amelia," she starts, her voice softer. "I don't blame you. But you must understand, Reid's father, he's... well, he's even more upset about this situation."

I open my mouth to interrupt, but she raises her hand. "Please, Amelia, just see it through our eyes for a moment. As parents, how could we be thrilled that our eighteen-year-old son is expecting a baby? This impacts everyone around you. That's not to say that it's not good news or joyful news. A baby is a blessing, a miracle, and inherently a good thing. It's just the circumstances, the timing of it all..."

I sit quietly, taking in her words, processing them, feeling their weight. I can see where she's coming from. She's thrilled to become a grandmother, but upset that it's happening so soon, at such a crucial stage in our lives. Reid and I haven't even had a chance to explore the world, to truly live and grow into adults.

As her words sink in, a realization dawns upon me. Reid's mom is subtly hinting that we, in becoming biological parents, have unintentionally thrust her and my mother into parenthood again because the truth is, we're going to need heavily need their help. Leaning back in my chair, I look at Mrs. Carter, wrestling with my words.

"I'm sorry, Mrs. Carter," I say, my voice steady but heavy. "I'm sorry that my relationship with Reid has disrupted your life. Is that what this is about? Are you asking me to break up with him so that he can achieve his dreams?"

She looks taken aback. "No," she says, and her smile is

genuine. "No, Amelia, that's not it at all. I can see how much you and Reid love each other. I would never want to inflict that kind of pain on my son."

She reaches across the table, her hand covering mine. "I like you, Amelia, and I think you're good for Reid. You've gotten him out of his shell. You've shown him a side of life he wouldn't have otherwise seen."

I feel a swirling mix of relief and gratitude. I hadn't realized how much I needed to hear her say those words.

"I believe in honesty, in speaking our minds," she continues. "I didn't want our relationship, our potential friendship, to start based on uncertainties. This is just me wanting to clear the air, to state my stance, so that we can move on from this point and happily welcome this baby into our loving families."

"Mrs. Carter," I begin, feeling a lump forming in my throat. "I appreciate your honesty. I guess I was so focused on how this was affecting Reid and me, I didn't consider how it would impact your lives."

I observe her, searching her face for any hint of resentment or blame, but all I see is understanding and, surprisingly, relief. She smiles at me then, an inviting warmth radiating from her.

"Now that we're done eating, why don't we continue shopping for my new grandbaby?" she suggests, her excitement genuine.

A wave of relief crashes over me, my heart pounding in my chest. I'm glad that Reid's mom wanted to clear the air. It's important we understand each other, with no uncertainties or hidden resentment lurking between us. Now, we can focus on welcoming this baby into our lives with love and acceptance. This is a new beginning, not just for Reid and me, but for our families as well.

As we move past the uneasiness of our conversation, Mrs.

Carter and I spend the rest of the day wandering through the mall, exploring baby sections of various stores. We marvel at the tiny outfits, the soft, plush toys, and the intricate designs of baby furniture. We share excited laughter over the cutest onesies and a mutual sigh of wonder at the delicate cribs. The tension from our earlier conversation seems to have dissipated, replaced by a sense of family and anticipation.

Our arms grow heavy with bags, but our spirits are lightened with every item we check off the baby checklist. It's a strange feeling, this mix of anxiety and excitement. I'm about to step into a whole new world, and with Mrs. Carter's support, it somehow feels a little less daunting.

The ride home is comfortable, filled with soft chatter about the baby's potential room decor at her house and cute baby giggles. As we pull up outside my house, Mrs. Carter turns off the engine and turns to me. Her eyes are warm and welcoming.

"Amelia," she says, leaning towards me. "You're part of this family now. Don't hesitate to reach out if you need anything or if you need help."

Her words, genuine and heartfelt, stir something within me. I feel a sense of belonging, a sense of acceptance in Reid's family I hadn't realized I was seeking. A tender smile stretches across my face as I clasp her hand.

"Thank you, Mrs. Carter," I say, my voice thick with gratitude. With a last glance, I exit the car.

As I enter the house, the familiar scent of home greets me. My mom, who's been waiting for my return, looks up from the book she's reading.

"How did shopping go, Amelia?" she asks, her eyes brimming with curiosity.

I set the shopping bags down and turn towards her.

"It went well, Mom," I reply, a soft smile gracing my lips. "I had a heart-to-heart with Reid's mom."

Before she can respond, I stride towards her, catching her off guard with an unexpected embrace. I feel her stiffen for a moment before she relaxes into the hug, her arms wrapping around me in return.

"I'm sorry, Mom," I murmur into her shoulder. "I'm sorry that this baby will impact your life."

I feel her pull back slightly, her hands holding onto my shoulders as she studies my face.

"Amelia," she starts softly, a tender smile on her face. "No matter what you might think, this baby is a blessing and will be loved deeply. Don't worry about how things will change. Just focus on how everything will be alright."

Her words, filled with reassurance and warmth, envelop me like a comforting blanket, giving me the strength I need to face the journey ahead. I sink into the couch beside my mom, a few shopping bags forming a small mountain on the coffee table in front of us.

"Now, show me what you got today," Mom says.

"Well, let's see," I start off, my hands picking around the edges of the first bag. "Mrs. Carter got the cutest little onesies, you know, the ones with the bunny prints?"

I pull out the tiny outfit, unfolding it to reveal the adorable print, and my mom's eyes light up with delight. We go through the rest of the bags, my voice dipping and rising as I narrate the story of each item Mrs. Carter had picked out. From the soft, plush baby blankets to the pastel-colored mobile with little birds.

"And you won't believe this," I say, a chuckle escaping my lips. "She's already planning to renovate one of their spare rooms into a nursery. She's talking about painting murals, hanging stars from the ceiling, even getting one of those smart cribs that rock the baby to sleep."

My mom laughs, her eyes twinkling with amusement and

joy. "Oh my, this baby is going to be so spoiled by both grand-mothers," she says, shaking her head in disbelief.

Heading to my room, I lay down on the bed and breathe a sigh of relief because my feet hurt. An hour passes in a blur of contemplation when my phone suddenly lights up, Reid's name flashing on the screen. A smile dances on my lips as I answer.

"Hey, Reid," I greet him, a soft sigh escaping me.

"Hey, Babe. How did shopping with Mom go?" he asks, his voice filled with curiosity.

A chuckle escapes me. "It was... interesting. She was so excited, Reid. We even had a heart-to-heart," I confess, a smile lingering on my lips as I recount the day's events.

The conversation takes a turn when I my voice turns seri-ous. "Are you sure you're okay with all of this?"

There's a pause, and I rush to fill the silence. "I mean, I can't help but feel that everything between us is going to change, and not for the better."

Reid laughs for a moment before saying, "Amelia, that's just your hormones talking and making you sensitive."

I join in his laughter. "No, it's not," I say, the laughter dying down.

Then he turns serious. "Amelia," he says, his voice steady and filled with sincerity. "I love you. This is something that would've happened somewhere down the line in our relation-ship anyway, so it's just a bit earlier than expected."

His words fill me with a warmth that spreads throughout my being. "Do you really believe that?" I ask, my voice barely above a whisper.

"Yes," he says firmly. "Because our love is the kind of love that will last forever. And when the time is right, we'll have more kids. A house full of little Carters running around."

We share a moment of laughter, the image of our future blossoming vividly in my mind.

"I love you," I say, my voice filling with emotion.

"I love you too," he replies, his words wrapping around me like a warm hug before we hang up.

The room falls silent as I stare at the phone in my hand, Reid's words echoing in my ears. Our love is the kind of love that will last forever. With a smile playing on my lips, I gently place the phone on my nightstand, Reid's assurance a soothing balm for my whirling thoughts.

"In the labyrinth of life's challenges, love presents the complex choice between what the heart desires and what is deemed best. Navigating this intricate balance, love teaches us that sometimes, what's best is a path that diverts from the truest desires of the heart."

PICKING NAMES

As the weeks flow by, I grow, not just in physical size, but in apprehension and anticipation. The mirror reflects a different version of me. Every day I'm bigger, and it can feel uncomfortable sometimes. But I'm not alone on this journey. I've worked everything out with the school for the home learning program. It's a recent venture for me, exciting and nerve-wracking in equal measure, but next week, I'll dive in head-first and start schooling from home.

As for the Prom, it's just around the corner. The thought of missing out on such a milestone initially saddened me, but then Mom, my pillar of strength, came home with a beautiful maternity gown. Pulling the dress over my head, I step out to show Mom and my sisters. Mom's eyes instantly well up with tears as she tells me how beautiful I look.

"Just wait 'til you go into labor in the middle of the dance floor!" Iris chimes in.

I can't help but laugh at the absurdity of the image she's painted.

"Well, at least we can skip the 'safe sex' talk for prom night!" Destiny adds.

Even in this situation, we all burst into laughter, only to be silenced by a stern look from Mom. The room falls quiet as she turns to me, a mix of love and sadness in her eyes.

"My baby is having a baby," she murmurs. "This isn't what I wanted for you, Amelia."

I avert my eyes, a lump forming in my throat. I don't know what to say, and the silence is stifling.

To change the subject and lighten the mood, I flash a smile and tell them, "I received three more letters in the mail today."

Standing, I smooth down the dress and add, "I'm going to change my clothes, and I'll be right back so we can open them together."

I return to the living room, the letters tightly clutched in my hand, and we all move to the familiarity of the kitchen table. My heart pounding in my chest, I carefully open the first letter. Eyes scanning the words, I let out a cry. It's an acceptance letter to their education program, coupled with a scholarship offer.

My mom and sisters, unable to hold back their excitement, flood me with congratulations and cheers. The joy is infectious, and I find myself laughing along with them, a genuine smile lighting up my face.

I open the next letters, still riding the wave of euphoria. Two more acceptance letters, although without the allure of scholarships. Yet, the acceptance alone feels like a victory, a testament to my hard work and determination. My smile stubbornly sticks around, and I can't help but feel a sense of pride.

Just as I'm basking in the moment, my mother's voice cuts through the celebration. "Will you and Reid be attending the same school?"

The question hangs in the air, turning the moment sober.

My smile falters slightly as I reply. "I have to talk to him. I don't know yet if he applied to these schools."

I meet my mother's gaze, her eyes reflecting a sadness that echoes my own unspoken fears. She says nothing more, but her silence often reveals more than her words. This college situation it's more than just about me now, and I can't help but feel the weight of it all.

With my acceptance letters bundled safely in my bag, I make a beeline for Reid's house as Destiny drives me over there. I can't help but feel a bubble of excitement in my chest as I think of sharing this news with him. Seeing his house come into view, a wave of nerves crashes over me, but I push that aside, focusing on the hope that these letters signify. I ring the doorbell and my heart pounds in sync with the chime. As the door swings open and Reid's face comes into view, his eyes lighting up at the sight of me, I can hardly contain my excitement.

"Reid," I blurt out, unable to help myself. "I got accepted! I got into three more schools!"

"That's great, baby," he says as he pulls me in for a hug.

Stepping into Reid's house, the familiar scent of home-cooked food wafts through the air, a testament to Reid's culinary exploits.

"Were you cooking?" I ask, curious.

He grins, nodding towards the half-chopped vegetables on the kitchen counter. We fall into an easy conversation, the tension from earlier dissolving into the comfort of our shared banter. Yet, a question burns at the back of my mind, its weight growing heavier with each passing moment.

"So, Reid," I begin, mustering the courage to address the elephant in the room. "Have you thought about your college plans? Are you considering any schools in-state, or maybe not too far away?"

I try to keep my voice casual, but the undercurrent of my

emotions betrays a hint of my underlying concern. Reid freezes as my question hangs in the air, the cheerful banter from moments ago seeming to fade into the background. An agonizing silence follows, stretching out and filling the space between us. He then slowly turns around to face me, his piercing green eyes looking rather subdued. I can almost feel my heart stop as I wait for an answer.

"I got accepted..." he starts, his voice barely a whisper. He swallows, visibly gathering his thoughts before he continues. "I got accepted to Crestview University."

Crestview? A prestigious institution, two thousand miles away from our little hometown. I feel my heart drop, my mind racing as I try to process the implications of what he's just revealed.

He doesn't stop though, pushing on as if he's afraid he won't be able to say it all if he doesn't get it out now. "It's an excellent school, Amelia. And they have a great program for what I want to study... I was thinking, you know, if I get a good education there, it could lead to a well-paying job... And I could really support us... our family."

His words hang in the air between us. A well-paying job. Support for our family. I can't help but recognize the noble intention behind his decision. But right now, all I can think of is the vast distance that threatens to come between us.

"I understand Reid," I interject, my voice shaking as I grapple with my swirling emotions. "But don't you see? We are a family now. And family should stick together."

Reid sighs, running a hand through his hair. "Babe, I am doing this for us. I thought you, of all people, would under-stand," he says, a note of frustration creeping into his voice.

"But you moving two thousand miles away does not feel like 'us,' Reid," I retort, my heart pounding in my chest. "It feels like you're choosing your future over our present."

He looks at me, hurt flashing in his eyes. "That's not fair,

Amelia," he says quietly. "I am not choosing my future over us. I am choosing us, our future family, over everything else."

Unable to hold back my tears, I feel them fall, one by one. "But Reid, your choice might mean the end of us," I whisper, the cruel reality of our situation finally sinking in.

"Amelia, listen to me," Reid says urgently, reaching out to take my hands in his. His eyes are filled with a rare intensity that I've seen only a handful of times before. "This won't be the end of us. We're stronger than that."

"Reid, I..." I begin, but he cuts me off.

"No, let me finish," he insists, squeezing my hands gently. "I know it's a huge distance. I get that. But if you think that two thousand miles is enough to ruin what we have, then maybe... maybe you don't love me as much as I thought you did. Maybe you don't believe in us as much as I do." His voice trembles slightly as he finishes, the hurt clear in his eyes.

I reel back as if someone has slapped me, the sting of his words hitting me harder than I expected. "Reid, that's not fair..." I whisper, but he's not done.

"No, Amelia," he interrupts, his voice firmer now. "It's not about being fair. It's about what's real. And what's real is that I love you. What's real is that I believe in us. I believe in us enough to believe that we can make it work, no matter the distance. And if you don't... then maybe our love isn't as strong as I thought it was." His voice drops to a whisper as he adds. "Maybe it's not as real as I thought it was."

For a moment, I stand there. Stunned. His words reverberate in my ears, stinging like a harsh winter wind. I had always believed in our love, in its strength and endurance. Yet now, confronted with Reid's harsh ultimatum, I question everything. I cast my mind back to our shared dreams. Dreams of a home, of children, of a life spent side by side.

Those dreams still live in my heart, as vivid as ever, but now they seem to clash with Reid's vision of his own future. A future that he sees at Crestview University, two thousand miles away. I'm left standing here, caught in the crossfire of our conflicting aspirations. As the silence stretches on, I wrestle with the painful reality that we want the same things, but our paths to them are diverging.

"That's not fair, Reid. It's two thousand miles away and four years of our lives. How can you be so cavalier about this decision?" I ask him.

I look up at him, his green eyes searching mine for any sign of an answer. And in that moment, I realize the truth. Our love may have brought us together, but it might also be what tears us apart. Because sometimes, even the strongest love can't conquer everything. Not when our paths are leading us in different directions. As much as I want to believe in our love, I can't ignore the growing realization that perhaps it just isn't enough. Then, as if sensing my inner turmoil, Reid gently wipes away my tears and pulls me close.

"I'm sorry, Amelia," he whispers against my hair. "I know this is hard for you, too."

I give Reid a small push, putting some distance between us. "Maybe you're right, Reid," I say, my voice barely a whisper.

His grip tightens reflexively at my words.

"No, I'm not right. I'm sorry I said that," he stammers out, a rare note of vulnerability in his voice. I try to pull away again, but his grip only tightens.

"Everything is so complicated now," I confess, my voice thick with unshed tears. "I... I think I need to head home."

As I move to leave, Reid grasps my hand, his green eyes locking onto mine with desperate earnestness. "We're going to be alright, baby. Just believe me. Believe in us, okay?"

I nod, not trusting myself to speak. Without another word, I turn and leave the house with the door closing behind me with a soft click. As I walk away, I can't help but replay

Reid's words in my mind, the desperate hope in his voice etched into my memory. I want to believe him. I want to believe in us. But right now, all I can feel is a heavy knot of uncertainty, the future we once dreamed of together seeming more elusive than ever.

The week passes in a blur, and the weight of the unspoken words between Reid and me hangs heavy in the air. We tiptoe around the argument that had taken place in his house, a silent agreement to bury the disagreement deep beneath the surface. As the days pass, I look forward to the end of the week, if only because it brings with it an ultrasound appointment. An opportunity to see our baby once again.

Finally, the day of the appointment arrives. I send a message to Reid, telling him the time of the ultrasound. His response comes quickly, a single line expressing his excitement at getting another glimpse of our child. I manage a smile at his enthusiasm, a bitter-sweet smile that feels forced and yet comforting at the same time. I tell him the time and place to meet me there. There's a pause, and then a frown crosses his face, a slight crease in his forehead that reveals his confusion.

Perhaps he had assumed that we would go to the appointment together, but I removed myself from that expectation. However, he doesn't voice his thoughts, and I can't help but feel a vague sense of relief. The silence between us continues, the unspoken words building an invisible wall that we both are too afraid to break down.

The doors of the doctor's office swing open before me, revealing a lobby filled with the familiar hum of hushed conversations and rustling magazine pages. My heart leaps at the sight of Reid waiting patiently among the sea of patients. He rises to his feet immediately upon spotting me, a smile softening his features.

"Hey, babe, how are you feeling?" he greets, his voice filled with palpable concern.

I manage a small smile, a wave of relief washing over me.

"I'm fine," I reply, just as the receptionist calls my name, her voice slicing through the muted sounds of the waiting room.

Despite the simple exchange, the weight of our recent argument, still unspoken, still unresolved, hangs heavy in the air, its presence an uninvited guest during our reunion.

The ultrasound room is bathed in a soft, blue light, creating an atmosphere of calm and tranquillity. As we lay our eyes on the ultrasound screen, a sense of anticipation permeates the air, thick and palpable. Holding Reid's hand, I can feel the steady thump of his pulse, a tangible mirror of our shared anxiety and excitement.

The nurse, a woman with a comforting smile and calming presence, moves the wand across my belly, her experienced eyes focused on the screen.

"Would you like to know the sex of your baby?" she finally asks, her voice gentle and unhurried.

We exchange a glance, a silent conversation passing between us. Reid gives my hand a reassuring squeeze, his green eyes sparkling with excitement and trepidation.

"Yes, we'd like to know," I respond, my voice barely more than a whisper.

The nurse nods, her gaze returning to the screen. After a moment, she looks up, a smile tugging at the corners of her lips. "Congratulations, it's a boy!" she announces, her voice warm and filled with genuine happiness.

The news lands in the room like a soft sigh, hitting us with an impact that leaves us breathless. A boy. Our son. The reality of it settles in, turning our dream into something tangible and real.

We share a look of pure joy, our eyes speaking volumes about the love we have for each other and our unborn son. Tears well up in our eyes, turning the world into a blurry kaleidoscope of overlapping emotions. Happiness, relief, excitement, all intermingling and cascading over us. The weight of our argument seems to lift, replaced by the shared joy of this beautiful discovery of our son. Our future. Our love personified.

As we leave the appointment together, my hand instinctively moves to my stomach, a gesture of protective love for our unborn son. I can't help but smile as I glance at my phone, the screen lighting up with a flurry of notifications. I had sent a text to my mom and sisters, sharing our joyous news. Their responses were instantaneous, a series of elated emojis punctuating the message thread. I can practically hear their excited squeals through the screen.

Reid, meanwhile, just got off the phone with his mother. She's thrilled too, though I detect a touch of wistfulness in her voice. She'd quietly hoped for a granddaughter, but the joy of a grandson is no less, and her happiness is evident in her every word.

Reid turns to me, a question in his eyes. "Amelia?" he begins, "Would you like to come over?"

I agree, welcoming the opportunity to share more moments together as I don't know how many more we'll get. Soon, we arrive at his place. As fatigue creeps in, I find myself lying in his bed, lulled by the comforting scent of him on the sheets.

Reid's hand travels over my swollen stomach, his fingers tracing the contours of our unborn child within me. His face is illuminated with a tender smile, his thoughts seemingly miles away. Then his gaze meets mine, a newfound curiosity in his eyes.

"Now that we know it's a boy, what names are you

thinking of?" he asks, his voice pulling me back from my own silent thoughts.

I smile while placing my hand atop my rounded belly, feeling the faint fluttering movement beneath.

"I was thinking of a few. Maybe Daniel, Liam, or Noah. What do you think?" I ask, curious to hear his thoughts.

A grin spreads across Reid's face, his excitement palpable. "I was just thinking of Brian, Mason, and Liam."

At that, I laugh, the sound echoing in the quiet room. "No way we are thinking of the same name!"

Reid gazes into my eyes, his own shining with amusement and tenderness. "We know each other so well, baby. It's no wonder we thought of the same name."

"So, we're going with Liam Carter?" he questioned, testing the name in the air between us.

"I like that," I tell him. "I also like Mason, too."

Reid nods, a confident decision in his eyes as he answers. "Liam Mason Carter."

I smile at hearing the name we're going to name our baby boy.

"In the echo of shared laughter and the warmth of intertwined hands, our love stands as a fortress, unyielding against the tests of time. Through every challenge and triumph, we reaffirm the strength of our bond—a love that refuses to be dimmed, a flame that only grows brighter with every heartbeat shared."

TIME FOR PROM

I've been doing school from home, and I'm glad because it's gotten harder to move around. From my viewpoint, schooling from home has been quite a unique experience. At first, it was tough to adapt to the confined space, missing the hustle and bustle of school hallways.

Yet, not having to commute every day has added precious minutes to my sleep schedule. Now, there's an air of anticipation at home. The prom has arrived. The thought of dressing up and dancing, being a normal teenager, brings a smile to my face.

As Hazel arrives, I can't help but chuckle. She's staggering under the weight of the myriad bags she lugs along. Hazel has always been known for her over packing, but this is next level even for her. I watch her as she huffs, puffs, and finally stumbles through the doorway, desperately trying to keep her balance. It's a comical sight, but it's quintessentially Hazel, and I wouldn't have it any other way.

"Hey Hazel, need a hand there?" I ask, trying to suppress my laughter.

She glares at me from under the pile of bags, her cheeks flushed with exertion.

"Very funny, Amelia," she grumbles, dropping her bags onto the floor with a loud thud. "I just thought we could use some options for the pictures."

"Options? Hazel, it looks like you've packed half your wardrobe," I tease, eyeing the bags curiously. "Are you planning a fashion show?"

Hazel rolls her eyes. "I'm just being prepared. You know how important tonight is going to be. We need to look our best, not that you would know anything about that!"

I laugh, lightly rubbing my belly. "I've only got one option, and that's the maternity dress mom bought," I say, a smirk playing on my lips.

The swell of my stomach under my palm is a constant reminder of the changes in my life. Hazel's eyes flicker to my bump, and we share a moment of laughter, caught in the absurdity and beauty of the situation. This prom night is going to be unforgettable, a blend of typical teenage fun and the surprising twist life has thrown at me.

Suddenly, the sound of laughter echoes from the hallway, and my mom walks into the room. She stops in her tracks, eyes widening as she takes in the mountain of bags Hazel has brought.

"Well, it looks like we're hosting a pop-up boutique here," she jokes, her smile lighting up the room.

The laughter in her voice makes my heart swell with warmth.

Looking at Hazel, she shakes her head in mock disbelief before her gaze softens. "Come along, girls. Let's get you two upstairs and start getting ready."

As she ushers us towards the stairs, I can't help but grin at the sight of us. A pregnant teenager and her over packing best friend, gearing up for a prom night that promises to be anything but ordinary.

We head up to my room and the process of getting ready begins. Hazel, true to form, has brought a spectacular array of dresses, each more glamorous than the last. She tries them on, one by one, twirling in front of the mirror, scrutinizing every detail. I sit on my bed and watch the fashion show unfold, with Hazel fluffing, tucking, and adjusting, each dress billowing around her as she moves.

As Hazel progresses through her pile of options, Mom works on our hair. She's always had a deft touch, transforming even the most unruly strands into a work of art. I watch Hazel's hair transform from a mass of curls into a sleek and sophisticated updo. My hair, typically unruly, is turned into soft waves cascading down my shoulders.

Just as Hazel decides on her dress, the emerald one that we'd picked out together on our shopping trip, Destiny shuffles in with her makeup kit in tow. She's the Picasso of the family, wielding her brushes like a maestro. With a flourish of blush here, a swipe of mascara there, and a perfectly drawn eyeliner flick, she masterfully brings our best features to the forefront.

As we're getting ready, a burst of energy comes bounding into the room in the form of my little sister, Iris. She darts around us, singing off-key and occasionally tripping over Hazel's discarded dresses. She's a whirlwind, a bundle of exuberance, and while her antics are a bit of a nuisance, they also fill the room with a certain infectious joy.

The air in the room is thick with a blend of laughter, perfume, and the unmistakable buzz of anticipation. Even though the circumstances are far from ordinary, this is exactly the kind of prom night chaos I had envisioned. It's imperfect, hectic, and absolutely perfect.

After a flurry of last-minute adjustments, an hour that feels both like a whirlwind and an eternity, we're finally ready. Hazel, in her emerald dress, looks breathtaking, with a glow that can rival the stars. And I, in my maternity dress, feel beautiful in a way I never thought I could. Standing side by side, we're a peculiar, perfect vision of prom night dreams with a twist.

"Girls! Can you come downstairs, please?" Mom's voice echoes through the house, pulling us from our thoughts.

The sound of our heels clicking on the wooden floor signals the start of the photo session that's become a family tradition.

"Let's get some pictures while we wait for the boys," Mom adds, the excitement in her voice matching the butterflies in our stomachs.

Hazel and I strike a pose, our smiles beaming into the camera as Mom captures the moment. The light in her eyes mirrors the shared excitement between Hazel and me. No sooner had we finished posing than the doorbell rings, sending my heart into a flutter. My mind is swimming with the thought of Reid's reaction to when he sees me. I pace quietly, trying to calm myself, while Iris, ever the helpful little sister, dashes off to open the door.

To my surprise, Benjamin walks in alongside Reid. I glance at Hazel, my eyes silently questioning why she hadn't mentioned he was her date. She simply shrugs nonchalantly, her usual way of saying 'don't ask me, I don't know'. I turn back, ready to greet them, but the sight of Reid stops me in my tracks.

Reid, in his classic black suit, stands tall and handsome. His deep-set eyes, the color of vibrant emeralds, sparkle with an irresistible charm. His hair, usually wild and untamed, has been styled with a handsome, rakish air. The suit clings to his athletic frame, accentuating the broadness of his shoulders and the strength in his arms. The sight of him sends shivers down my spine, stirring a warm thrill that courses through my veins. He's the embodiment of masculine elegance, the epitome of all my teenage dreams.

The sight of his lips curving into a smile when he sees me strikes a chord in my heart, a symphony of emotions that leaves me breathless. His smoldering gaze meets mine, and in that moment, I'm convinced he's the most beautiful sight I've ever beheld. His presence is like a gravitational pull, drawing me in, making my heart flutter with anticipation. The magnetic appeal goes beyond his physical attributes. It's his spirit, his soul, that makes him irresistibly attractive.

As Reid's gaze locks onto mine, a softness overtakes his features. His eyes seem to cradle me, enveloping me in a sensation so warm and comforting that it feels like the world is melting away. His look speaks volumes, saying everything without uttering a single word. It's a look of absolute awe and adoration, a look that suggests that he sees nothing else but me.

This gaze, so intense and unmasked, it makes my heart beat faster. I feel my cheeks flush and a warm, fuzzy feeling spreads throughout my body. His gaze is undeniably magnetic, pulling at me in a way that goes beyond the physical. I am his center of attention, his entire universe, in this one precious moment. His unwavering stare makes me feel cherished, important, and, most importantly, loved. It's a feeling so warm and empowering, so beautiful that it almost makes me weak in the knees.

Breaking our moment, Mom's voice slices through the heavy silence in the room. "Alright, you two. Enough with the lovey-dovey eyes. Reid, Benjamin, come over here. It's time for pictures before you boys escort these lovely ladies out."

The room fills with laughter, the spellbinding moment dissipating, replaced by the familiar hustle and bustle. It's a pleasant chaos, filled with flashing cameras, laughter, and the comfortable buzz of our family's unique brand of love.

As we take our pictures and say our goodbyes, we soon find ourselves in Benjamin's car on our way to the prom. Hazel, ever the social butterfly, nestles in the passenger seat, already engrossed in conversation with Benjamin. In the back seat, Reid and I are tucked into our own little world.

He leans in, his breath tickling my ear, his voice a velvety murmur. "You look beautiful, baby."

His compliment brings a smile to my lips. "And you look sexy in that suit," I respond, my eyes drinking in his handsome profile.

His hand lifts to palm my cheek, a gentle touch that sets my skin tingling. Slowly, he leans in, his lips finding mine in a tender kiss that sends a delightful shudder through me. We lose ourselves in the kiss, a symphony of shared breaths and softly echoed moans.

Suddenly, Benjamin's laughter cuts through the intimate silence. "Hey, you're not having sex in the backseat of my car on the way to prom!"

His joking comment breaks the spell, and our kiss abruptly ends. Reid chuckles, his gaze meeting Benjamin's in the rearview mirror. We fill the air in the car with laughter and light-hearted banter, a perfect prelude to our drive to the prom.

As Benjamin's car pulls up to the entrance of the grand, twinkling venue, my heart skips a beat. The prom location, an opulent hotel ballroom, is enchanting in its extravagance. They bathed the exterior in a kaleidoscope of vibrant colors, with beams of light dancing off the façade, creating a spectacle that leaves us awe-struck. We step out of the car onto a plush red carpet that leads to the entrance. The air is electric with anticipation and excitement, filled with the chatter and laughter of our friends and peers.

The grand entrance opens up to a magnificent hall, shimmering with thousands of fairy lights. The hall glows in a soft, iridescent glow, enhancing the already stunning décor. Its atmosphere is intoxicating, the music pulsates through us, and the energy of the crowd is palpable. As we navigate through the throng of elegantly dressed students, the reality of the evening sets in. This is our prom, a night we've been dreaming of, and it's more magical than we could have ever imagined.

As we settle into the vibrant ambiance, I feel the weight of curious glances cast our way. I straighten my posture, holding my head high and my hands cradling my baby bump. Their stares no longer faze me. Yes, I'm pregnant. Yes, I'm at prom. Their incredulous expressions and whispered speculations can't touch me anymore. I'm beyond their petty judgments, wrapped in the warmth of my contentment. They can gawk all they want. It won't change a thing. After all, staring isn't going to make my baby bump vanish.

We find an empty table near the edge of the dance floor, a perfect spot to dump our belongings. The sleek, glass-top table is soon cluttered with our handbags, boutonnieres, and corsages. Anchored by the comfort of our claimed space, we're ready to join the lively throng on the dance floor.

Hand-in-hand, Reid and I lead the way, Hazel and Benjamin trailing behind us. The music swells around us, an infectious rhythm that seeps into our bodies and guides our movements. We merge into the crowd, our bodies swaying to the beat.

As we dance, the shimmery lights that dangle from the ceiling twinkle like stars against the darkened room, casting a surreal glow around us. I lose myself in Reid's arms, the rhythm of the music melding with the beat of my heart. The rest of the world seems to fade into insignificance as we lose ourselves in our own little universe. The whispers and stares are like white noise, barely noticeable against the symphony that is Reid and me.

Despite the baby bump that I carry, we move in sync, our bodies swaying to the rhythm of the music. Every once in a while, Reid would lean down, whispering sweet nothings into my ear, his warm breath sending delightful shivers down my spine. With his hand placed gently over my bump, we dance the night away, a perfect picture of young, undeniable love.

The DJ's tune changes to a gentle, slow melody. Reid's grip on my hand tightens slightly, pulling me closer. His other arm wraps protectively around me, his hand resting gently against our unborn child. We sway in time with the music, lost in a world of our own.

His lips brush against my ear as he leans down. "I love you, Amelia." His voice is a soft whisper, filled with emotion. "You and our baby... you're my world. You've filled my life with so much love and happiness, more than I ever thought possible. We're about to start a new chapter in our lives, sweetheart. A chapter filled with sleepless nights and baby coos, with first steps and first words... and I can't wait to experience every single moment with you."

His words strike a chord deep within me, bringing tears to my eyes. I pull back to look into his sincere, loving eyes, a smile playing on my lips.

"Reid," I begin, my voice soft and filled with warmth. "I love you too. We are, and will always be, a perfect team."

I lean in to kiss him gently, pouring all my love and gratitude into this tender moment. The rest of the night, we danced, we laughed, we simply let ourselves be young and in love. My feet tapped to the beat of the music, my heart throbbed in sync with Reid's. The rhythm was intoxicating, each song pulling us further into the merry chaos of prom night.

Laughter bubbled from my lips as Reid twirled me

around, his grin as infectious as the energy in the room. The spotlight wasn't on my baby bump anymore. It was just us basking in the glow of our happiness.

Prom night was everything I'd thought it would be and more. I had dreamed of the sparkly dresses, the romantic slow dances, the giggles shared with friends. But the reality was so much more magical. It was the warmth of Reid's hand in mine, the loving smiles shared between Hazel and Benjamin, and the solidarity and acceptance we experienced as young parents-to-be.

It was the promise of a future together, a beautiful affirmation of our love. As the night grew darker and the stars shone brighter, I knew that this was a night I would remember.

"In the crucible of adversity, even the strongest love faces the tempest, where challenges cast shadows that obscure the path forward. It's in these moments of struggle that the resilience of love is truly tested, and though the journey may seem arduous, it's the unwavering flame within that persists, fighting against the darkness, determined to illuminate the path to a triumphant dawn."

The days after prom seem to merge into one another, a whirlwind of homework, finals, and the hustle of closing out senior year. At this point, my weekly checkups have become a routine part of my schedule, the anticipation of my baby's arrival growing with every visit to the doctor. Amidst it all, graduation is just a blink away, and there's so much to do.

From collecting my cap and gown to returning the stack of library books I've spent the last school year buried in, I'm ticking off one task at a time. It feels like I'm standing on the precipice of a whole new chapter, caught between the thrill of what's coming and the bittersweet farewell to my school days.

As soon as I set foot in the familiar school hallway, a broad grin spreads across my face. I make my way to my locker, ready to undertake the somewhat sentimental task of clearing it out. The last two weeks for us seniors are pretty laid back.

With finals already out of the way, there aren't any classes to attend, just opportunities to soak up these last moments. My stride is light and easy as I saunter down the hall. Out of the corner of my eye, I notice Reid in an animated conversation with Jada. As I edge closer, their voices become clearer, their conversation more distinct.

"Reid, I'm sorry that you're saddled with a child right out of high school. You won't have time to experience college, to really live before you settle down," Jada tells him in a voice tinged with sympathy.

"Thanks, Jada," Reid responds, a forced smile on his face. "I didn't plan this, but I will do what's right."

Jada nod and puts her hand on his arm. "And that's admirable, Reid. But is this really what you want?"

Reid hesitates, his smile faltering. "Jada..." he starts, but stops.

There's an uncomfortable silence before Jada asks him again. "Is this what you want, Reid? Aren't you feeling trapped? Do you really believe that she was on birth control?"

It feels as though time stands still before he finally replies. "It doesn't matter what I want, Jada. This is my life now."

I gasp at his reply. The sound echoes loud enough in the hallway to draw their attention. Reid's shocked eyes meet mine and Jada smirks as they turn to see me gaping at them.

Without a moment's hesitation, I close the distance between us, the fury clear in each taut line of my body. Jada needs to stay the hell out of my business.

"Reid, you have no business discussing our situation with Jada," I snap, my voice echoing off the lockers.

"Baby, I..." Reid starts, but I cut him off with a wave of my hand.

"From the sounds of it, you don't seem too enthusiastic about becoming a father," I accuse, the hurt surfacing in my voice.

Jada, not one to back down, interjects. "Are you delusional, Amelia? Why should he be thrilled about being a dad at eighteen?"

I round on her, my icy glare fixing her in place. "Shut your fucking mouth, Jada, before I do something I might regret," I warn, my fists clenching at my sides.

My eyes whip back to Reid, a livid look on my face. "Is this how you really feel, Reid? Because you sure as hell sounded resigned to the idea of being a parent."

Reid blinks at me, apparently taken aback by my outburst. "Amelia, that's not what I meant," he stammers. "Jada's question caught me off guard."

I cross my arms over my chest, raising an eyebrow skeptically at him. "Bullshit, Reid," I bit out. "If you really wanted our baby, if you were really excited about this, your answer would have been immediate."

I can feel my heart pounding in my chest, my anger and hurt mixing in a bitter cocktail of emotion. I knew he felt trapped. Regardless that this pregnancy was a mistake, we're making the best of it. We're happy even though things have changed significantly for us. I thought Reid was on the same page, but I guess not.

"And all those things you said on prom night, were they all bullshit, too?" I challenge, my voice trembling.

Reid opened his mouth to speak, but I didn't give him the chance.

"I suggest you go home and really think about whether you're up for this, Reid. Think long and hard about whether you want to be a part of this. To be a part of our baby's life," I tell him, my voice quivering with barely suppressed fury. "Because I won't accept anything less than one hundred percent."

Without waiting for a response, I turn on my heel and storm away, the sound of my heeled boots echoing ominously in the now silent hallway. I leave my locker as it is, the forgotten task of cleaning it out a trivial concern in the grand scheme of things.

Arriving home, I'm surprised to find my mom in the

kitchen, taking advantage of a rare lunch break at home. The moment she sees me, her warm hazel eyes fill with concern. Without saying a word, she opened her arms wide. That was all it takes.

The tears I had been fighting back came rushing forward, and I hastily stumble into her comforting embrace. We stand there, her arms wrapped tightly around me as I sob into her shoulder. She doesn't ask questions, doesn't demand any explanations. She just holds me, whispering soothing words and gently rubbing my back, letting me cry out the hurt and disappointment.

When my tears finally subside, she nuzzles me back, her hands holding my face as she looked at me.

"Amelia," she says softly. "You don't have to tell me anything right now. Whenever you're ready, I'll be here to listen."

After planting a kiss on my forehead, she lets me go, and I make my way to the sanctuary of my room. Throughout the day, my phone buzzes relentlessly with calls and texts from Reid. I didn't answer, instead choosing to drown myself in reruns of my favorite shows, a welcome distraction from the storm of emotions roiling inside me. Hours roll by, the room growing dimmer, the sounds from the TV quietly filling the silence.

That's when I heard it. A soft, persisting knock against my window. Turning towards it, I see Reid standing outside, his hand still raised in a knock, his eyes pleading. I stare at him through the glass, my emotions a tangle of hurt, anger, and confusion. After a long moment, I release a sigh, push off from the bed, and slowly make my way towards the window.

I unlatch the window, allowing Reid to clamber into my room. His gaze sweeps over me, an unspoken question lurking in his eyes. I watch him wordlessly as he starts to pace, the silence in the room growing heavy.

"Amelia," he starts, but his voice falters, and he resumes his restless pacing.

He runs a hand through his hair, his jaw clenching tightly. His usual laid back composure had given way to a visible tension. His eyes, usually filled with warmth when he looks at me, are now clouded with uncertainty. I remained silent, waiting for him to gather his thoughts while my heart pounds anxiously in my chest.

Reid moves towards me, and the tension in the room is thick. Gently, he guides me to sit on the edge of my bed. He lowers himself to a squat before me, taking my hand in his. His gaze is intense, his eyes searching mine as he starts to speak.

"Amelia," he starts, his voice low and steady. "What I said earlier... it didn't come out right." He pauses momentarily, as if gathering his thoughts. "When Jada asked me if this was what I wanted, I hesitated. Not because I didn't want this, but because I was reflecting on us."

His thumb traces small circles on the back of my hand, his touch soothing despite the whirlwind of emotions I was feeling.

"I never pictured having something so... perfect, Amelia," he admits, a hint of vulnerability creeping into his voice. "I always thought I knew what I wanted in my life, but then I met you, and everything I thought I wanted pales in comparison to what I have with you."

He gives my hand a gentle squeeze, holding my gaze firmly. "When I said it doesn't matter what I want, I don't mean it in the way you think. I meant that what I thought I wanted doesn't compare to what I have now."

His words hang in the air between us, his honesty piercing through the wall of hurt I had built up. The anger and confusion I had been feeling dissipates, replaced by a sense of relief and a glimmer of hope.

Reid swallows audibly. His grip on my hand tightens, and he continues. "Baby, do you remember our first date?" His eyes flickers with a hint of nostalgia. "I was so nervous that I accidentally ordered a salad instead of steak for dinner. You laughed and said that it was the most charming mistake you'd ever seen." He pauses, a soft chuckle escaping his lips. "That moment, I knew I was falling hard for you. Not because of your breathtaking beauty or your infectious laugh, but because you found charm in my blunders."

His gaze locks onto mine, his thumb still tracing idle patterns on my hand. "You're like the first rays of sunshine breaking through a cloudy dawn, the calm after a storm, Amelia," Reid's voice drops to a whisper. His eyes, so full of sincerity, bore into mine, reinforcing every word he said. "You make me want to be a better version of myself. You make me want to face the unknown, the challenges, because with you, I know I can endure it all."

He leans closer, his voice dropping even lower, his breath warm against my skin. "Amelia, you mean more to me than you'll ever know. You've filled a void I didn't even know existed. You're my missing puzzle piece, my perfect melody in a chaotic symphony. I love you, Amelia. More than words can express, more than the stars in the night sky, more than the waves love the shore."

He pauses. "I want this, Amelia. I want you, I want us, I want our baby. Because it's a part of you, and I love every part of you, without hesitation, without doubt."

His declaration leaves a resounding silence in the room, a testament to the power and depth of his words. By the time Reid finishes speaking, tears had slid down my face. They are a testament to the overwhelming surge of emotions his words had triggered. Reid rises from his position, pulling me into his arms in a comforting hug. His voice is a soothing whisper in my ear, a balm to my frazzled nerves.

"Everything will be okay, Amelia," he says, and I believe him.

We're interrupted by my mother's voice, her tone carrying a hint of amusement. "If you're done making up, Reid can go home. I let it slide the last two times, but next time, use the door to enter my house, Reid!"

There is a pause before both Reid and I burst into laughter. The tension that had hung so thickly in the air dissipates, replaced by a sense of relief. As I walk Reid back to the window, our unofficial entrance and exit, he grabs my face with both hands, his touch gentle yet firm. He leans his forehead against mine, our gazes locked in a silent conversation.

"Together, now and always," he murmurs, the promise in his words reverberating through me.

I echo back. "Together, now and always," my voice barely a whisper, but the conviction in it is unshakeable. We exchange a quick and sweet before he climbs out of the window.

Today a heavy rain beats against the glass of my window. It echoes the turmoil in my heart. The thunder mimicking the tension building up inside me. Graduation is just around the corner, a milestone I had looked forward to, but now it looms ominously before us, a ticking time bomb threatening to shatter the delicate truce between Reid and me.

Our last argument still hangs in the air, a specter haunting our every interaction. The impending reality of a long-distance separation overshadowed the excitement of walking across that stage, of throwing our caps into the air. Our paths are diverging. While Reid is headed for a prestigious college across the country, I'd chosen to stay here, to pursue my dreams.

The smiles we share seem forced, the laughter hollow. Each day brings us closer to the end of an era... our era. Will our love survive the miles between us? Or will it crumble, a beautiful castle built on the sands of time, swept away by waves of changes and challenges?

I can't shake the nagging doubt that keeps creeping in. The uncertainty is a constant companion, and the tension between us, a tangible force. I miss the harmony we once had, the ease of being with Reid. Now, every moment is a struggle, every word a potential landmine.

The nights grow longer, or at least they seemed to. As I lay awake, staring at the ceiling, my mind is in a turmoil, wrestling with fears that refuse to subside. I wonder if Reid truly wanted this life we are embarking on. A life filled with responsibilities, sacrifice, and compromise.

The fear that I might have cornered him into a future he didn't desire gnaws at me, casting a shadow over our shared moments of joy. I yearn to believe his assurances, his declarations of love, but the nagging doubt remains, whispering discord into my moments of peace.

Then there is the impending distance. The thought of being miles apart from Reid sends a shiver down my spine. Can our love stand the test of distance, or will it crumble under the pressure, fading slowly until it was nothing but a distant memory? The love we share is special. I know that.

We have weathered stormy seas, overcome immense hurdles, but this... this was different. The uncertainty of the future is a phantom that looms over us, its presence felt in every stolen glance, every forced smile, every strained conversation. I miss the easiness, the laughter, the shared dreams. Now, with every ticking second, we inch closer to the crossroads, where love will be put to the ultimate test.

Every time I bring up the subject of Reid going away to Crestview, an icy chill seems to settle between us, freezing our warmth and ease. An invisible wall. His eyes harden and I can see him erecting defenses, preparing for the inevitable argument.

"It's for us, for our future, Amelia," he'd insist, his tone firm.

But I can see the steel in his eyes. He is too focused on providing for our family, too engrossed in his vision of a secure future, to understand the damage his absence could cause. The sacrifices he's making are noble, yes, but they are also causing cracks in the foundation of our relationship.

Crestview University is his ticket to better job opportunities, a step on the ladder to a comfortable life. But at what cost? He is absent, physically and emotionally, too caught up in his dreams of success to realize what he is leaving behind. Our shared dreams are slowly turning into his ambitions, our mutual decisions into his choices. It's as if he's determined to carry the weight of the world on his shoulders, forgetting that we were supposed to be a team, that we're in this together.

The more he pulls away, the more I feel the sting of isolation. I'm proud of him, yes, but I also miss him, his presence, his family involvement. The echo of his laughter around my room, the reassuring feel of his hand in mine, his comforting hugs on a bad day. I missed all of it. I fear for Liam, who is growing up fast, too fast.

I want to make Reid understand, to help him see that his absence will cause more harm than good. That we need him here, now, not later. But every time I try, it ends in a futile argument, both of us nursing our hurts in silence. It's a tug of war, a battle of wills. I wish with all my heart for a compromise, a middle ground where we can meet, where our dreams and sacrifices wouldn't stand at odds with each other.

Reid argues that I'm too focused on us being a family. That I'm leaving all my hopes and dreams behind because I'm having a baby. He says the baby is just a curve ball that we have to navigate to get to where we want to be and I'm losing sight of that. That he's the only one with a level head and the sight to see what needs to be done for us to succeed. I argue that family is important to me, but he doesn't see it my way. He says making the hard decisions now and making the necessary sacrifices is about family. That if he has to go away and visit periodically and if I have to count on his mom or my mom to babysit while I attend school, then he'll make the same decision every damn time if it mean he'll be able to successful for us.

Our disagreements seem to have a life of their own, springing up between us like thorny vines that we can neither ignore nor tear away. Each argument leaves us more frustrated, more doubtful. Are we really so different? I can't help but wonder. Reid is as passionate about our future as I am, maybe even more. But it is his definition of 'our future' that leaves me bewildered.

His version involves a world revolving around his dreams, his ambitions, with little room for us. My heart aches, for even in his passion, I see the boy fell in love with, the boy who cared for me, loved me with a fierceness that took my breath away. How can this loving boy be so blind to the turmoil our relationship is going through?

As we navigate the last weeks of high school, our relationship seems to hang by a thread, a thin, fragile thread that can snap at any moment. Every night, as I lay down to sleep, I find myself asking the same question over and over again. Are we strong enough to withstand this storm? The love we have for each other is potent, beautiful, but can it weather the onslaught of our conflicting dreams?

I don't have the answers, and that scares me. Will the love that had brought us so far also guide us through this? Or will our differences pull us apart, leaving behind nothing but fragments of a shared past and a dream of what could have been? I don't know, and the uncertainty is tearing me apart.

"Amelia, you're a fucking idiot," Hazel says as she barges into my room.

"Well hello to you too," I say sarcastically.

She walks over and sits on my bed. "I spoke to Reid, and he sounded like shit. He doesn't know how to fix this rift that's between you two."

"I didn't create this rift," I tell her.

"You need to pull your head out of your ass," she snaps." Not everything is about you, Amelia."

My eyes widen in shock. "I'm not making anything about me. This is about me, Reid, and Liam. Reid doesn't want to be here, and I have a right to be upset."

Hazel looks at me like I've grown two heads. "I'm going to give it to you straight. Yes, you have a right to be upset. However, Reid has a right to be upset, too. You're mad that he doesn't want to give up on his hopes and dreams to become the family man you want."

I go to speak, but she puts a hand up to stop me. "He's upset that you're ready to give up your hopes and dreams for your family."

"That's not it at all," I snap.

"Ever since you found out that neither of you applied to the same school, you've been upset that he won't change schools, meanwhile you refuse to change your school," she continues as if I hadn't spoken. "Now, with the baby, you're using it as an excuse to get him to do what you want. You're trying to guilt trip him by implying that it's not okay for him to miss Liam's milestones while he's away."

"You're taking his side," I snap at Hazel.

She shakes her head sadly. "No, I'm not. I'm trying to make you see clearly. Sacrifices come with parenting. You better understand that now. Get the hard shit out of the way now. Liam won't even remember Reid's time away. Hell, Amelia. You haven't talked about school since you found out you were pregnant. It's like you pushed all your dreams away as if you can't focus on that with a baby."

Her words sting, and I look away. "I don't want to talk about this anymore, Hazel. I just want to concentrate on graduating and preparing for Liam's arrival."

She shakes her head at me and storms out of the room. I see mom standing in my doorway. I can tell she wants to say something, but she, too, shakes her head and walks away, leaving me alone with my thoughts.

"As we turn the pages of life and venture into the next chapter, our love story evolves from the innocence of youth to the depth of maturity. Growing up becomes a beautifully written narrative, each moment a sentence that binds us closer, and with every page turned, our love story continues to unfold, a testament to the beautiful journey of maturing hearts."

I't's graduation day. The excitement running through my veins is like an electric current. I maneuver into this adorable maternity outfit, perfect for underneath my graduation gown. It's difficult to put on clothes with this belly, but hey, I manage. As I wobble down the stairs, I can hear the familiar sounds of mom in the kitchen. It's like she has this unending energy. As soon as she spots me, she insistently tells me to sit down and fuel up with some breakfast. It's going to be a long, exciting day.

With a satisfied stomach, I hug Iris affectionately as we prepare to leave. Our beloved family car hums to life as Mom, Destiny, and I settle down, buckling up for the journey. I can't help but admire the familiar sights through the window as we make our way to the graduation venue. The hustle and bustle of the city somehow seems even more vibrant today.

Once we find a parking spot, which seems like a victory in itself, we begin our trek towards the venue. The anticipation bubbles inside me, adding a spring to my steps. The grand facade of the building comes into view, and I can't help but marvel at the sight. With Mom and Destiny by my side, we collectively take a deep breath and make our way inside.

As we enter the venue, there's an immediate surge of energy. It's like stepping into a hub of youthful exhilaration, every corner buzzing with anticipation. The venue itself is breathtaking. Tall, elegant drapes hang from the ceiling, their royal blue hue matching our school colors perfectly. The stage is a grand spectacle, resplendent with flowers and banners, the podium standing there like a beacon, waiting for us to cross the threshold into the next chapter of our lives.

There's an infectious murmur of chatter echoing through the hall, a blend of nervous students, proud parents, and excited teachers. Laughter and mixed languages fill the air, creating a symphony of sounds that will remain etched in my heart forever. I lock eyes with a few familiar faces, their smiles mimicking my own.

Out of the corner of my eye, I spot Reid. He's with his family, his parents beaming with pride and his younger brother trying to tame his excitement. As our eyes meet, Reid flashes me a warm smile, his eyes twinkling in that unmistakable way that always leaves me slightly breathless. Instantly, my nerves settle, replaced by an inexplicable calmness that only Reid's presence can bring. With his family trailing behind him, Reid heads our way.

Mom looks up, and recognizing Reid, flashes him one of her welcoming smiles. They exchange casual and pleasant greetings between them, despite their last meeting.

Suddenly, an announcement over the intercom instructs everyone to find their seats. Mom, Destiny, and Reid's family make their way toward the designated section for families while Reid and I filter in with the other students. The seating arrangements are in alphabetical order, so I end up a few seats away from Reid. We exchange a last reassuring smile before we separate, weaving our way through the sea of blue gowns and colorful tassels.

Each chair becomes occupied, and the tension in the air is thick, but there's also an undercurrent of excitement, of joy for this memorable milestone. As the last whispers die down and everyone gets comfortable in their seats, the ceremony begins. The room falls into a hush as the principal walks up to the podium.

He carries an air of authority. His graying hair, glasses, and the slight stoop in his shoulders are all familiar. He speaks, his voice echoing through the room, commanding attention. His speech is an inspiring one, reflecting on our years spent in the institution, the friendships forged, and the knowledge we've gained.

He talks about the future, the uncertainty it holds, and assures us we're prepared, not just with academic knowledge, but with values and virtues that the school has instilled in us. His words are not just for us, the graduates, but also for the proud parents, the dedicated teachers, and everyone who has played a part in shaping us. As the principal concludes his speech with hearty congratulations, there's a sudden eruption of applause.

The principal gracefully steps down from the podium, making way for Ms. Peters. She confidently strides up to the mic and announces the commencement of the diploma ceremony. One by one, my fellow graduates are called to the stage. They walk up, their names resonating in the hall, take their diplomas, pose for a picture, shake hands, and descend the steps. The procession continues, a rhythm of names and applause, of pride and accomplishment.

Suddenly, my name echoes through the speakers. "Amelia Campbell."

A rush of adrenaline hits me as I stand. Like a reflex, Reid swiftly rises to help me. I look up at him, our eyes meeting, and I can't help but beam. He returns my smile, his eyes filled with pride and excitement. I take his offered hand and, with his support, I manage to get up from my seat. I turn around and start my journey down the aisle, a wobbly yet determined walk towards the stage.

As I climb the stairs, a wave of emotions hits me. This is it, the moment I've been waiting for. I walk across the stage, every step a testament to my journey. I take my diploma from Ms. Peters, our hands shaking in a moment of mutual respect. We pose for a picture, the flash momentarily blinding me. We exchange a few words before I walk off the stage, diploma in hand, my heart full of pride and joy.

As I gingerly make my way back to my seat, Reid once again comes to my aid, rising from his seat. He gently helps me sit down, his hand steady on my back. A couple of students later, it's Reid's turn. His name rings out and he makes his way to the stage. He repeats the same ritual, his face glowing with pride as he accepts his diploma. Once his ceremony is over, he returns to his seat, our smiles meeting again.

My gaze snaps toward the stage when I hear Hazel's name, and I clap and cheer with everyone in the room. Hazel arrived late to the ceremony, but I'm glad she got to walk across the stage. She was helping her parents' pack. Despite our disagreement yesterday, she called me last night in tears when she found out that they were taking a summer trip and would miss her graduation. I told her to talk to her parents and convince them that this only happens one time and she doesn't want to miss it.

Ultimately, they apologized for not realizing how important this was for her and said they'd go so she could walk across, and then they'd leave afterward. Hazel glances at me as she leaves the stage and puts her hand up, showing that she'd call me. I nod my head and give her a wavy goodbye.

As the last name is called, Ms. Peters retreats from the podium, replaced by Mr. Martin, our beloved math teacher. He steps up, clearing his throat, and the entire hall falls silent in anticipation.

"Ladies and gentlemen, esteemed colleagues, proud parents, and most importantly, the class of 2007," he starts, his voice steady and commanding respect.

"Setting goals is not merely about outlining your dreams on a piece of paper. It's about giving yourself a roadmap, a compass for the journey that lies ahead," he continues, his words ringing with the authenticity of the experience. Something about his words stirs within me, reaching parts of my heart I didn't realize were waiting to be touched.

"Each of us is bestowed with a unique journey, a unique set of challenges. But remember, there's immense power in overcoming those challenges, in proving to yourself that you're stronger than you ever thought possible." I feel my heart hitch at his words - it's as if he's speaking directly to me, assuaging my anxieties and fears about the future.

"Remember, the choices you make today will paint the canvas of your life tomorrow. Choose wisely, make informed decisions, and always, always listen to your heart." His words, so simple yet profound, resonate with me. It's almost as if he's echoing the thoughts that have been swirling in my mind, providing some clarity amidst the whirlpool of uncertainty.

"Life is like navigating a ship in the vast ocean. There will be storms, there will be calm, and there will be detours. But keep your compass handy, your goals clear, and you'll reach your desired destination." His closing remark rings out, echoing through the hall and etching itself into my heart.

"You may move your tassels," he says, and we move them to the other side. "I give you the class of 2007!" he yells out when we finish.

The room instantly erupts in cheers, a cascade of caps

flying through the air, the graduating class expressing their joy and relief in this symbolic act. The moment is surreal, a blur of smiles and cheers, of hugs and laughter. Amidst the excitement, movement catches the corner of my eye. I turn to find Reid weaving his way through the crowd, his gaze fixed on me.

In the blink of an eye, he's there, standing in front of me. He reaches out, pulling me into him. Before I can react, his lips are on mine, sealing our own private celebration in a deep, passionate kiss. The world around us fades away, the cheers and applause becoming a distant echo.

All I'm aware of is Reid, his strong arms holding me close, his heart beating against mine. I lose myself in the moment, in the sweetness of his kiss, in the promise it holds. As we pull away, breathless and grinning, the world comes rushing back, the joyous celebrations of our classmates surrounding us.

Reid and I weave our way through the sea of people, looking for our families. They're huddled together in a corner of the lobby, their faces lighting up as they see us approaching. I can't help but smile at their expressions, a mix of pride and joy. Just as we're about to reach them, a sudden twinge in my back stops me in my tracks. It's sharp and fleeting, but enough to make me wince. I reach back to rub the spot, trying to soothe the sudden pain. Concerned, Reid turns to me, his eyebrows knitted together.

"Are you okay?" he asks, his voice filled with worry.

"Yeah, I'm fine," I assure him, waving off his concern.

It's probably just a strain from all the excitement. We continue our journey towards our waiting families, my arm hooked through Reid's, a slight grimace still lingering on my face.

Our families, bursting with pride, smother us in well-deserved congratulations and warm hugs. Amidst the chatter and laughter, we all agree on the perfect way to commemorate our big day - a grand feast at our favorite Italian restaurant in town. Everyone seems excited about the decision, and we plan to meet at the restaurant to celebrate our graduation and the bright futures that lie ahead of us.

As we bid each other temporary farewells, the nagging discomfort from earlier makes itself known again. I shake it off, attributing it to the stress and excitement of the day. I'm determined not to let anything ruin this special moment for Reid, our families, and me.

Upon reaching the restaurant, the air buzzes with chatter and laughter, the atmosphere light and jovial. We share stories, each of us recounting our own unique experiences and memories from the school year. As I look around, I can't help but notice that Reid's parents and my mom, despite their previous disagreements, are chatting and laughing together. A wave of relief washes over me - tonight, we are just one big, happy family.

Later, as I lie in bed, the quiet of the night seems to amplify my thoughts. I reflect on the rollercoaster ride that the school year has been, the highs and lows, and the graduation that marked the end of an era. A sigh of contentment escapes me. I'm finally done with high school.

A gentle flutter in my belly brings a smile to my face. Becoming pregnant wasn't part of the plan, but now, it's a reality I wouldn't change for the world. The fluttering reminds me of the little life growing inside me, our baby. I place a hand on my belly, excitement for this new chapter in mine and Reid's life making my heart race.

As I drift off to sleep, I can't help but feel a profound sense of gratitude for the unexpected turns life has taken. We have a journey ahead of us, a journey of parenthood, and I'm eager to embrace what's to come.

"Love is an enigmatic journey, a relentless pursuit that tests the limits of our patience and resilience. It's a paradoxical blend of bliss and struggle, where the beauty lies in the difficulty, and the strength of love is measured by its ability to weather the storms. In the labyrinth of emotions, love is undeniably hard, yet it's this very challenge that unveils the depth and authenticity of our connection."

I've been feeling a mix of emotions these past few weeks. There's a part of me that's buzzing with excitement, but to be honest, it's the misery that's been mostly keeping me company. Currently, I'm in a state that can best be described as 'miserably expectant'. My body is no longer my own. It's a hotel for this little person who seems insistent on practicing gymnastics at the most inconvenient times.

Every ten minutes, like clockwork, I'm running to the bathroom. I'm always hungry, like a ravenous beast that can't be satiated. My emotions are all over the place. I march downstairs looking like something the cat dragged in.

I look at Mom, and all I can say is, "I want this baby out now!"

"Amelia, honey," mom says, her voice laced with an infectious chuckle I just couldn't help but mirror. "I know you're having a tough time with the baby kicking and all, but always remember that pregnancy is a bit of an oxymoron."

She has this quirky smile on her face, the kind that told me she was about to drop a classic 'mom joke'. "It's the most wonderfully miserable experience a woman can ever have."

Well, I can't argue with that. Pregnancy really is a wonderfully miserable journey. I waddle over to the refrigerator, and my eyes instantly fall on a container of strawberries. My mouth water at the sight. I grab the container and head to the kitchen table, plop down with a sigh of relief.

As mom moves around the kitchen, preparing for her day at work, we chat about everything and nothing at all. We talk about the baby's room, the name Reid and I picked, and how she will probably spoil this kid rotten. Amidst all the talking and laughing, I mindlessly reach into the container, plucking out one strawberry after another. It's only when I hit the bottom of the container that I realize I'd eaten all of them. I look down, shocked and a bit embarrassed.

"Well," I say, glancing at my mom and laughing. "I guess the baby likes strawberries."

I watch as Mom laughs, her eyes crinkling at the corners as she leans down to plant a loving kiss on my cheek. "Take care, darling. Enjoy your 'me' time," she murmurs, her voice warm and comforting, before stepping out of the house and leaving me alone.

With Destiny at work and Iris at school, I suddenly relish the quiet, the house filled only with the soft hum of the refrigerator and the occasional ticking of the clock. Deciding to make the most of this peaceful interlude, I shuffle my way into the living room, sinking into the plush couch and flicking on the TV.

An hour or so must have drifted by, a haze of daytime TV and my idle thoughts, when the doorbell rings. Pulling myself up from the comfy embrace of the couch, I waddle over to the door, curiosity stirring within me. I swing open the door to find Reid standing there. His face lights up with a warm smile that reaches his eyes. A bright beam spread across my face, mirroring his.

"What are you doing here, Reid?" I ask in surprise.

"I just thought I'd stop by, see how you're doing," he replies, his smile never leaving his face. As he lifts the bags he's carrying, he adds, "And I brought snacks."

I can't help but laugh, shaking my head at his thoughtfulness as I stepped aside to let him in. We settle onto the couch with the television providing a soft, comforting background noise as we sink into the cushions. Reid opens up one bag, and we both help ourselves to the assortment of snacks. As we munch away and watch some mindless daytime TV, the casual nature of it all makes me feel a sense of normalcy that I hadn't felt in a while.

Before long, Reid shifts, settling himself onto the floor at my feet. He gently lifts one of my swollen feet and starts massaging it. I lean back against the couch, closing my eyes and letting out a moan of pure relief. His hands work magic, kneading the aching muscles and soothing the tightness that had built up.

I can feel the tension leaving my body, and I murmur a soft, "That feels so good, Reid."

"I want you to feel good, babe," he says.

Reid rubs my feet for a while until I feel his hands drifting up between my legs. I look down to see the sexy and intense gaze staring back at me. Luckily, I have on a maternity dress because being pregnant in the middle of the summer is not fun, and I hate having on too many clothes. His hands continue to move upward until he lifts my dress. He gradually stands and pulls my dress over my head and pulls my underwear down.

He leans down and kisses me. Our tongues duel with each other as we moan. His hands cup my larger breasts and tweak the nipples. I jerk at the sensation and moan again, louder this time. Reid pulls away from the kiss and strips out of his clothes. I watch as his rock hard body comes into view with each piece that he takes off.

The effect he has over me never ceases to amaze me. He stalks toward me and moves to lie on top of me, keeping himself elevated by his arms so he doesn't crush my large belly. We resume kissing and running our hands over each other's bodies. I feel his dick rub against my wet slit and tilt my hips up, trying to create more friction.

Reid gives me what I'm looking for, because he turns me on my side and positions himself behind me. His chest against my back with his hand cradling my belly, Reid thrusts inside me. His lips are near my ear, and I can hear his deep breathing as he thrusts in and out of me.

He kisses my neck and reaches up to grab a breast to pull me back against him. I move back every time he thrusts forward, taking him deeper every time. Soon, we're moving faster and moaning as we chase our orgasms. I let out a long moan as my body explodes. I shake violently, and Reid gives a few more pumps before groaning loudly in my ear.

His dick jerks as he comes inside me. We're breathing heavily, and he pulls my face to his for a kiss. He pulls out, and we clean up before getting dressed again. Just as we're settling back on the couch to resume eating our snacks and watching TV, Destiny comes home with Iris running in behind her.

Their voices echo through the hallway as they greet us. "Hey Amelia, hey Reid," Destiny calls out, her tone light and airy.

Iris, following behind her, gives us a quick nod of acknowledgment, her focus already on her school bag.

"Iris, go up to your room and start on your homework," Destiny instructs her, her voice shifting from friendly to authoritative in an instant.

As Iris scampers off, Destiny turns her attention back to Reid and me with a mischievous glint in her eyes.

"You two can't fool me," she says, her voice dropping to a

conspiratorial whisper. "I've got this spider sense, you know." She waggled her eyebrows suggestively. "Reid's Tab A was in Amelia's Slot B before we came home, wasn't it? You both look thoroughly... satiated."

The corners of her mouth twitch upwards, her eyes sparkling with amusement at our shocked expressions. With a victorious chuckle, she saunters off down the hallway, leaving a flustered Reid and me in her wake. We watch TV for a little longer, the comforting hum of the background noise serving as an anchor for my scattered thoughts.

My heart is thrumming in my chest, a rhythmic beat that seems to echo the question I'd been wanting to ask Reid for the past couple of weeks. As a commercial for some hair product blares from the television, I decide to take the plunge.

Gathering my courage, I turn to Reid, my eyes searching his. "Reid," I start, my voice sounding smaller than I expected. "Have you... have you decided to go to a closer school so you can be near me and Liam?"

The question hangs in the air between us, heavy and pregnant with possibilities. Reid looks at me, his eyes searching mine, before he hesitates. I can see the internal struggle playing out in his gaze, the warmth in his eyes dimming as he faces me.

"Amelia," he starts, his voice steady yet laced with a tinge of regret. "I... I haven't changed my mind." His words hang heavily in the air, a tangible reminder of the impending separation. "I'm still going away."

His admission feels like a punch to my gut, the reality of his departure suddenly looming ominously. I blink back the tears that wells up in my eyes, nodding silently as I process his words. We still aren't on the same page. He is leaving. I protest against his decision and he argues back.

The argument escalates, our voices raising in pitch and

volume as we stubbornly cling to our respective stances. I'm pleading, urging him to reconsider, to understand the implications of his decision on our little family. He, on the other hand, is adamant, his words thick with frustration and the familiar stubbornness I'd come to associate with him. Suddenly, Destiny burst into the room.

"Will you two just shut the hell up?! This is not the time nor the place for this kind of argument!" she chastises, her voice laden with authority.

We both fall silent, startled by her interruption. Reid shakes his head, a bitter laugh escaping his lips. He turns to me, his gaze hard and unyielding.

"I'm leaving, Amelia," he announces.

Without a backward glance, he stomps towards the door and slams it shut behind him, leaving a stunned me and Destiny in a room that suddenly felt too big and too quiet.

Tears well up in my eyes, spilling over and running down my cheeks uncontrollably. Destiny swiftly moves towards me, wrapping her arms around me in a comforting embrace. Her soothing words are a gentle whisper, a balm to my raw emotions.

"Go have a lie-down, Amelia," she suggests, her voice soft yet firm. "I'll bring you some tea."

Nodding silently, I trudge towards my room, my body heavy with the weight of my broken heart. Lying in bed, I stare blankly at the ceiling, my thoughts a whirl of confusion and hurt.

The warmth from Destiny's tea cup seeps into my hands as I mumbled a soft. "Thanks." Left alone, I slip into a state of numbness.

Time seems to lose its meaning as I lay there, my gaze fixed on a spot on the ceiling, my mind lost in the maze of my emotions. However, the sound of the door creaking open snaps me back to reality. My mother walks in, her expression a mask of concern. Destiny, it seems, had filled her in on the fight with Reid.

My mother takes a seat on the edge of the bed, reaching out to cradle my hand. "Amelia, Destiny told me about your argument with Reid," she begins, her voice calm and steady. "I'm sorry that you're going through this, but I want you to think about something."

I look over at her, my curiosity piqued despite the turmoil of emotions within me. She takes a deep breath, her gaze meeting mine. "You and Reid are at a crossroads in your lives. Both of you have different career aspirations and different schools beckoning you. You're growing, Amelia, and so is he. And growth often means change, sometimes in directions we don't expect."

A lump forms in my throat as I listen to her words. She continues. "You both have different paths you want to tread, aspirations you want to achieve. It's only natural that these paths may not always align. And that's okay."

I can feel my heart pounding in my chest as she speaks.

"And then there's Liam," she adds softly. "He's a blessing, yes, but he shouldn't be the only reason you and Reid try to stick together. You cannot build a solely on the responsibility of a child."

Her words hang in the air, a stark reminder of the reality Reid and I are trying to navigate. I take a deep breath, my mind buzzing with the implications of her advice. It is a harsh truth, but one that I need to confront. Maybe it's time that Reid and I have an honest conversation about our future, not just for us, but for Liam as well.

My mother gets up from the edge of the bed and kisses my forehead, her gaze full of understanding and compassion. She exits the room, leaving me to mull over her words, her advice ringing in my ears. I feel a storm of emotions raging within me. Confusion, sadness, anger, and a sense of loss. I think deeply about what she said, the reality of Reid and me at crossroads, navigating a precipice of change that neither of us had expected.

On the other hand, I wonder if I'm amplifying the situation. I am acutely aware of the love Reid and I share, a love that had been tested time and again. We are young, yes, but the depth of our feelings is not reflective of our age. I know in my heart that we love each other, and the sheer intensity of that love gives me hope. Can it not be the glue to hold us together, to navigate this tumultuous phase?

With these thoughts echoing in my mind, I slip under the covers, my body craving the comfort of sleep. I close my eyes, the darkness a canvas for my swirling thoughts. I allow myself to revisit our shared memories, the love, the laughter, the heartbreak, and the countless beautiful moments we'd carved together.

As sleep envelopes me, my last conscious thought is of Reid, his smile, his touch, his love. With a silent prayer for our shared future, I surrender myself to the oblivion of sleep.

"In the garden of young love, where hearts are tender and dreams are bold, the joy of producing life is a testament to the resilience of love. Despite the circumstances, the arrival of new life becomes a celebration—an affirmation that, in the tapestry of youth, even amidst challenges, love prevails, painting the world with the hues of joy."

I wake up with a gasp of pain, the intensity of it catching me off guard. Sitting upright in bed, I hunch forward as another spasm of sharp pain shoots through me, doubling me over. My eyes widen as the realization dawns on me. This could be it. I could be in labor.

As I swing my legs over the side of the bed to stand, a wave of pain so intense hits me, I double over, clutching my belly. Taking a tentative step forward, a sudden wetness between my legs startles me. I gasp in a mixture of shock and anticipation. I think my water just broke.

I stagger my way to my mother's room, each step a shaky, uncertain dance with the pain that's seizing me. My jaws are clenching so tightly, I'm half afraid I might crack a tooth, but it's the only way I can manage not to scream. Halfway there, a cramp cuts through me like a knife, forcing me to stop and lean against the wall. I suck in breaths through tightly gritted teeth, trying to ride out the pain without collapsing.

When I finally reach my mother's room, my hand trembles as I push the door open. "Mom," I gasp out, but it's more of a groan than a word.

She's awake instantly, sitting up in bed and squinting at me in the darkness. It doesn't take her more than a second to understand.

"Oh, Amelia," she murmurs, and even in my pain-filled haze, I can hear the excitement and worry in her voice. "It's time, isn't it?"

As my mother, swift and deft despite her age, assists me into fresh clothes, my legs buckle under the pain. I'm leaning heavily on her, unable to stand on my own. After I'm dressed, she guides me to the kitchen table, her arm a comforting, solid presence around my waist.

"Just sit here for a minute, love," she instructs, helping me into a chair. "I'll go grab the hospital bag and call Reid... and his parents."

I nod, my breath coming in short, fast pants. The pain is a constant now, an all-consuming force that leaves me no room to think or feel anything else. I watch, nearly detached, as my mother moves around, handling everything with a calmness I can't fathom. I can hear her voice in the background, murmuring into the phone, but I can't make out the words. She appears back in the kitchen with a determined look on her face.

"Reid and his parents will meet us at the hospital," she tells me, her hand squeezing mine. "And don't worry about Iris. Destiny's already been briefed, and she'll keep an eye on her."

Despite the pain, I manage a small nod. I'm grateful, so incredibly grateful, for my mother's calm efficiency. She helps me up again, whispering soothing words in my ear as we stumble towards the car. The pain is so intense now it's all I can do to put one foot in front of the other.

We somehow make it to the car, and as I sink into the seat, the relief is almost palpable. My mother's behind the wheel in seconds, and we're off, racing through the quiet pre-dawn streets to the hospital.

As the car jolts to a stop, I squint through the windshield at the hospital entrance. There's Reid, pacing anxiously back and forth like a caged animal, his eyes scanning the incoming traffic. The sight of him fills me with a strange mix of relief, annoyance, and a pang of love. As Mom's old car comes to a halt, he's by my side in an instant.

"I'm here, baby," he stammers, hands trembling as he helps me out of the car. He's trying to keep his voice steady, but his fear is almost palpable. "I'm so sorry about our argument earlier, and I didn't mean to upset you. I—"

"Reid?" I cut him off, gripping his arm to steady myself as another wave of pain hits me. I can feel the sweat trickling down my forehead as I grit my teeth. "Shut the hell up and help me. We can talk about that later."

The moment we step into the hospital, my mother takes on the role of a general leading her troops. With a firm determination in her voice, she talks to the first nurse in sight, explaining the situation. Before I know it, I'm being ushered into a private room that can accommodate everyone during the birth.

I barely have time to process what's happening as nurses move around with swift precision, getting me hooked up to machines and comfortable in bed. The sterile smell of the hospital, the icy touch of the medical equipment, everything seems to blur into a whirlwind of activity around me.

Mom tells the nurse that I need medication for the pain, and the nurse nods before leaving the room. Then the doctor walks in. His face is a calm mask of professionalism. He and his team conduct their checks, and then he delivers the news.

"I'm sorry, Amelia," he says. "You've progressed too quickly for an epidural."

I stare at him as the words sink in slowly, shock washing over me. The realization that I have to endure this searing pain until the end hits me like a punch in the gut. I have no other choice but to brace myself for what's about to come. The pain, raw and unfiltered, is my reality now. Until the moment I'll hold my baby in my arms, there's nothing to do but endure.

As the contractions intensify, they take on a rhythm of their own, a cruel symphony of pain that ebbs and flows with a terrifying predictability. Each wave starts as a dull ache in my lower back, spreading and intensifying until it feels like a vice is squeezing my abdomen. My breaths become sharp and rapid as I fight through each wave, my knuckles white as I grip the bedsheets.

"Squeeze my hand, Amelia," Reid offers, and I take him up on it, my grip almost bone-crushing.

He winces but doesn't pull away. I take comfort in his presence, his hand in mine, his voice whispering words of encouragement.

A nurse bustles in, checking the monitor and my dilation. "You're doing great, Amelia," she assures me.

Her words do little to ease the waves of pain that wash over me. Every muscle in my body tenses as I brace for the next contraction, and just as I think I can't take it anymore, it eases off, leaving me trembling and gasping.

The doctor reappears periodically, checking on my progress. His voice is a calm presence amid the storm of pain. Around me, the room fills with a tense anticipation. Mom, Reid, and his parents linger at the edges of my vision, their faces a mix of worry and excitement.

Despite progressing quickly, things have seemed to slow down. I haven't dilated past seven centimeters. Hours stretch into an eternity, the room thinning and thickening with each wave of pain. I can hear my voice, hoarse and strained, filling the room as each contraction hits.

Suddenly, Reid lies on the bed next to me, his arm snaking around my waist. I can't help but sob, the pain mingling with a wave of emotion that overwhelms me. He pulls me closer, his voice soft in my ear.

"Amelia, love, I've been reading... a lot," he begins, his voice shaky but determined. "I've read about how to hold a baby, how to support their head and neck. And I've practiced changing a diaper on a teddy bear...it was messier than you'd think."

I manage a chuckle through my tears, surprised by his confession. He continues, "I've also learned about bathing a baby, how to cleanse those small, delicate parts without hurting the little one. And about breastfeeding, the positions, latching... and different formulas, in case breastfeeding doesn't work out."

His words wash over me, a warm comfort amid the ice-cold waves of pain. I'm shocked, but it's a pleasant surprise.

"Reid..." I gasp, not quite believing it.

He's been putting in time, preparing himself to become a father. He's been involved from the very beginning. Just as the joy bubbles up inside me, another contraction hits. It's a blinding, all-consuming pain that tears through my body. My hand instinctively finds Reid's, squeezing his fingers with all the strength I can muster.

He doesn't pull away, his hand a steadying presence through the pain. As the contraction subsides, I let out a shaky breath, the shock and joy of Reid's revelation a soothing balm. The door swings open and the doctor steps in, his face more serious than before.

"Amelia," he starts, his tone grave. "You've been in labor too long. Each contraction is putting unnecessary stress on the baby. We need to perform an emergency C-section."

I feel my heart drop as his words sink in, and I instinctively turn to Reid, my eyes wide with fear. A C-section was never part of the plan. As if reading my thoughts, Reid squeezes my hand in reassurance.

A nurse hands him a set of scrubs, telling him. "You need to change into these. You can stay with Amelia during the procedure."

Reid simply nods, taking the clothes and stepping out of the room. The whirlwind of activity picks up again as I'm prepared for the surgery - my bed moves, instruments clatter, and conversation becomes hushed murmurs.

Soon, I'm wheeled into the operating room, the bright lights overhead blinding me. The anesthetist calmly explains the procedure before administering the anesthesia. I feel a strange sensation, a creeping numbness that slowly takes over. My heartbeat echoes in my ears, and as the numbness reaches my chest, the echo fades into a dull throb.

"Can you feel this?" the doctor asks, prodding my stomach.

I shake my head. It's an odd sensation, knowing there's contact but not being able to feel it. Reid's back by my side, his familiar presence comforting amidst the chaos. He takes my hand, giving it a gentle squeeze, as if to say, 'I'm here. We're in this together.' Surrounded by medical professionals, under the harsh clinical lights, the surgery begins, and through it all, Reid remains by my side.

As the procedure begins, I feel an odd sensation. No pain, but a distinct pressure, a pushing and pulling that's entirely alien. It's as if I'm disconnected from the lower half of my body, a spectator observing my surgery from a distance. Reid's voice breaks through the clinical sterility, his words a soothing contrast to the cool, detached voices of the doctors.

"Amelia," he whispers, his voice filled with raw emotion.

"You're doing wonderfully. You're so strong, love. I'm so proud of you."

His words wash over me, anchoring me amidst the surreal experience. His hand, warm and steady, never leaves mine.

"I love you, Amelia," he continues, his voice barely above a whisper, filled with a depth of emotion that leaves me breathless. "You, me, and our baby, we're going to be the best team. I can't wait to start this new chapter with you."

The doctor's voice slices through the moment. "We're almost done. Are you ready to meet your baby?"

More odd tugs and pulls ensue, an eerie detachment as they manipulate my body beyond my sight. Then, an incredible moment. A piercing cry fills the room, a sound so raw and real that it cuts through the numbness. They're placing a writhing, crying bundle on my chest. There are tears streaming down my face as I meet the gaze of a tiny, perfect face.

"Hi, Liam," I whisper, my voice fill with awe and wonder. "I'm your mom."

Reid leans in close, his eyes mirroring my tears, brimming with unshed emotion. "And I'm your dad."

He looks at me, a look of pure adoration on his face. "He's perfect..." he murmurs, his voice choked with emotion.

At that moment, I knew our lives had changed forever. For the better. As soon as the nurse gently takes Liam from my chest to clean him and carry out their checks, the doctors start to close me up. The room buzzes with a new energy.

The doctor turns to Reid. "You can leave now and spread the good news. We'll wheel her out when we're finished."

Reid nods, but there's an uncertainty in his eyes as he asks, "Are you sure she'll be alright?"

The doctor lets out a hearty laugh and reassures him, "Yes, of course."

He comments on our childish love with a shake of his head before returning his concentration to the task at hand.

Reid leans over, his lips brushing my forehead in a tender kiss. "I'll be waiting for you," he whispers.

Then, he's gone, leaving me in this bright, sterile room, with the anticipation of seeing him and our newborn again fueling me through the finishing touches of the surgery. As the doctors finish up, they move me out of the operating room and back to the familiar, comforting confines of my room.

The journey is a blur of bright lights and hushed voices, the hum of the hospital fading into the background. Relief washes over me as I'm wheeled into the room, greeted by the excited faces of friends and family. Their eyes light up at the sight of the small bundle in my arms.

Soon enough, coos and soft laughter fill the room as everyone takes turns admiring Liam. Words of how beautiful, precious, and perfect he is echo around me. Their warmth, their joy, it all feels surreal, a beautiful dream I never want to wake up from. Holding Liam in my arms, his tiny fingers curled around mine. The love I feel for him is immeasurable. It feels as if my heart could burst at any moment.

The first moments with baby Liam were nothing short of a miracle. His tiny little form, swaddled in a soft blanket, is nestled perfectly in the crook of my arm. His skin is a rosy bloom, new, warm to the touch.

Reid and I can't help but watch in wonder as his tiny chest rises and falls in rhythm with his gentle breaths. His wide grey eyes, innocent and clear, blink up at us. Each tiny breath and gurgle he makes is another note in the symphony of joy that filled our hearts.

Reid's large hand, so gentle and tentative, traces the curve of Liam's cheek, eliciting a tiny yawn from our baby boy. The love in Reid's eyes as he gazes at Liam is overwhelming, a testament to the bond that is already forming. These first moments are a beautiful, shared experience, etched in our hearts forever, the beginning of our journey as a family of three.

The day winds down with the soft murmur of family voices and the gentle rustle of nurses moving about. The excitement of the day ebbs, replaced with a warm, contented quietude. Our families linger, soaking up the peaceful joy of the moment, until a nurse finally sends them out, reminding them I need rest. Reid, however, remains steadfast by my side. He pulls out the couch, making himself comfortable, and sets up a small, makeshift bed.

We spend a little more time nestled in our own bubble, watching some television, though our attention is more often drawn to the tiny, beautiful life that keeps making soft sounds from his crib. Liam, our son, commands our attention in the most delightful way. Yet, as the long day catches up with me, I find it increasingly hard to keep my eyes open.

"I'm going to get some sleep," I tell Reid, my voice barely above a whisper.

Understanding flickers in his eyes as he rises from the couch and walks over to me. He takes my hand, the warmth of his enveloping mine, as he looks into my eyes with so much love, it makes my heart swell.

"Amelia," he starts, his voice filled with admiration. "You did something amazing today, love. Get all the rest you need."

His reassurances comfort me, reminding me we're in this new chapter of our lives together. He points out the little bottles of formula the nurse had left us, assuring me it's okay to rely on them if I'm too tired for breastfeeding.

I smile at his thoughtful words, feeling a profound sense of love and gratitude for this man who is now the father of my child. He leans down to place a tender kiss on my forehead. It's the last thing I remember before sleep pulls me under its restful wave.

Reid returns to his makeshift bed on the couch, and I know he'll be there, watching over us. As my eyes close, I can't help but think how wonderfully complete our little family feels.

"In the garden of young love, where hearts are tender and dreams are bold, the joy of producing life is a testament to the resilience of love. Despite the circumstances, the arrival of new life becomes a celebration—an affirmation that, in the tapestry of youth, even amidst challenges, love prevails, painting the world with the hues of joy."

Those first few days after giving birth were tough and I won't sugarcoat it. I had this amazing little creature, Liam, in my arms, but everything else was a whirlwind. I was learning to breastfeed with the help of a lactation consultant, which, let me tell you, is not as straightforward as you might think.

Breastfeeding, while a natural process, can present its own unique set of challenges that can be quite daunting for a new mother. For starters, it's not always as instinctive as one might assume. Ensuring the baby latches on correctly can be tricky, and an improper latch can lead to sore, cracked nipples. Then there's the question of supply. Every mother's body is different, and while some may produce more than enough milk, others might struggle with a low milk supply.

This can lead to feelings of inadequacy and stress, which, ironically, can further impact milk production. It's an exhausting cycle. But it's important to remember, it's okay to ask for help. Lactation consultants, midwives, or even a supportive friend can offer guidance and reassurance during this journey.

Then there was the pain. I had this overall soreness. I felt like a semi-truck had hit me. But those doctors and nurses didn't let me wallow in it. No, they got me up and moving, said it would help things shift back into place and aid in the healing process.

It felt like a thousand tiny razors slicing through my abdomen with each slight movement. I could barely stand upright; my body was hunched over as if protecting myself from some unseen threat. And sitting up? Forget about it. Even the simple act of laughing or coughing was a torturous endeavor.

It felt like my insides were going to burst out of the surgical incision, a thin line that signified where my body was cut to bring Liam into this world. But despite the discomfort, the sleepless nights, and the unfamiliarity of it all, I'd do it all over again. For him, for that tiny bundle of joy with his father's eyes and my stubbornness, it was all worth it.

Caring for Liam, my little bundle of joy, is an experience unlike any other. A symphony of pure, unadulterated love, punctuated by moments of exhaustion, worry, and a joy that overflows from the heart. His tiny fingers curling around mine, his dazzling smile, the way he snuggles into the crook of my arm - those are the moments that make everything else fade into insignificance.

Reid, my rock, has been incredible with Liam. He's taken to fatherhood like a duck to water, effortlessly shifting into the role of a diaper-changing, baby-soothing superhero. His quiet patience during those middle-of-the-night diaper changes, his seemingly innate ability to soothe Liam's cries, and the adoration in his eyes, whenever he looks at our son. All of this warms my heart in ways words can't describe.

Then there's Destiny. Her love for Liam is extraordinary. She's become his second mother, always eager to hold him, comfort him, and shower him with affection. She reluctantly hands him over only when it's time for feeding, and, the moment he's done, she's all too ready to scoop him back into her arms.

My mom, her support, has been invaluable. She steps in to care for Liam, allowing Reid and me to catch up on some much-needed rest. Her experienced hands and soothing voice comfort Liam, and the love between grandmother and grandson is a beautiful sight to behold.

It's in these moments, amidst the sleep deprivation and soreness, that I realize how incredibly lucky I am. For Liam, for Reid and his family, for Destiny, and for my mother. Health, love, and family. Truly, what more could I ask for?

Motherhood, while brimming with joy and love, also brings with it a rollercoaster of emotions. One moment, I might feel overwhelmed with the sheer enormity of the responsibility that comes with caring for a tiny, dependent human being. It's a mix of awe, fear, and wonder.

I frequently question if I'm doing it right, if I'm good enough, and these insecurities can be a hard pill to swallow. On the other hand, there are times when my heart seems to burst with love as I watch my little one sleep peacefully or flash me a toothless grin.

It's a beautiful, challenging, exhilarating journey filled with highs and lows. The emotional challenges are real and often overlooked amidst the physical demands of motherhood. It also shapes me, teaches me about my strengths, and deepens my capacity to love. In the end, every sleepless night, every worry, every tear shed in exhaustion or frustration becomes a testament to the incredible love I bear for my child.

The moment Reid and his family walk in, the room is filled with infectious excitement, a kind of joy that only grandparents can bring. Reid's mom is all smiles as she takes Liam in her arms. It's as if she's meeting her grandson for the first time all over again. Her eyes twinkle with happiness as she cradles Liam, gently rocking him to sleep.

And then, much to our delight, she strolls down memory lane, regaling us with stories from Reid's infancy. She holds up Liam and points out his jet-black hair, those deep-set eyes, and the curve of his lips, all undeniably Reid's.

"He's the spitting image of his father," she says, her voice filled with love and nostalgia.

Reid gently pulls me away from the family and the chaos, guiding me over to a quiet corner of the room.

His eyes are filled with concern. "Amelia, are you okay? You need anything?"

I looked at him, his worry lines making him even more endearing. A smile spread across my face.

"I have everything I need, Reid," I reassure him, placing my hand on his.

We turn our focus back to Liam, lying peacefully in his grandmother's arms. Reid's eyes soften as he watches our son, a quiet reverence in his gaze.

"He is beautiful, isn't he?" he whispers, a touch of awe in his voice.

"Absolutely perfect," I agree.

We stand there, lost in our little world, our hearts flooding with love for the tiny life we had created. Reid pulls me closer, his arm wrapping around my waist.

"Amelia, I couldn't have done this without you. You are incredible, and I... I love you more than words can express," he says, voice low, full of emotion.

I turn to face him, tears pricking at the corners of my eyes.

"I love you too, Reid, and together, we'll give Liam the best life possible," I tell him, leaning into his warmth.

As the days flow into weeks, life takes on a familiar rhythm. A routine settles in, making parenting Liam a little less daunting day by day. We've coordinated schedules between Reid's house and mine, establishing a harmonious balance that keeps any chaos at bay.

Mornings start at my place with Liam's bright eyes and infectious giggles. After breakfast and a bit of playtime, I pack up Liam's things. A bag full of diapers, wipes, a change of clothes, and that special blanket he just can't doze off without. By mid-morning, we're at Reid's, ready for a day full of father-son bonding.

Reid takes over them, feeding Liam his bottle, changing diapers, and maneuvering the stroller on their afternoon walks. I step back, allowing their relationship to flourish. The father-son bond is just as important. Meanwhile, I take advantage of the break to get a bit of rest.

In the late afternoon, I rejoin the duo, taking over the reins for the evening. Dinner, bath, and finally, putting Liam into bed with a lullaby. These are sacred rituals I cherish. Throughout it all, the strong connection between our households remains clear. Despite the physical distance, we're united by the love we have for Liam and the desire to give him the best upbringing possible.

Routine, while rewarding, certainly presents its unique set of challenges. Top of the list is the necessity for consistent communication. Keeping each other apprised of Liam's progress, changes in routine, or health concerns requires dedication and open dialogue. Ensuring that both households follow the same rules and routines can also be a struggle.

Balancing consistency and flexibility is key to a parenting relationship. The logistics of shuttling between two homes can be taxing, both emotionally and physically, for all involved. Despite these challenges, our love for Liam fuels our determination to make this work until we can find a place of our own.

After weeks of non-stop parenting, an unexpected opportunity for some alone time with Reid presents itself. His mom, ever the doting grandmother, offers to take Liam for the evening, encouraging us to take some time for ourselves. My initial hesitance gives way to excitement. This will be our first night out since Liam was born.

Reid and I decide on a quiet dinner at our favorite Italian restaurant, a place where we had shared countless memories at the beginning of our relationship. As we walk in, the familiar aroma of fresh garlic and simmering sauce brings back a rush of nostalgia. It feels like a lifetime ago that we were here without the worry of diaper changes and feeding times.

The evening flows smoothly, filled with laughter and intimate conversations. We reminisce about our time together, from our first awkward date to the joyous birth of Liam. There, under the warm glow of the dimmed lights and amidst the lively chatter of other diners, we reconnect, reminding ourselves of the deep bond that brought us together.

As we clear the last remnants of our quiet dinner, my heart flutters with anticipation. The drive back to Reid's house is filled with an electric tension that we both choose not to acknowledge verbally. Reid parks and we walk into the house quietly, not wanting to alert anyone that we're back, wanting time to ourselves a little while longer.

We walk to his room and quietly close the door. His gaze is filled with hunger as she looks at me. They reflect the desire I feel coursing through my body. Our need fills the air. It's all around us, and I feel it with every breath that I take. My heart beats faster, as this will be the first time we have sex since I gave birth to Liam. His gaze is so intense it feels like electricity is flowing through my body, creating waves of lust that have me dripping wet.

Reid stalks toward me and cradles my face. He kisses me, slow and sensual, making goosebumps form on my skin. My lips move against his as I thread my fingers through his hair to hold him against me. He walks me back until my legs hit his bed, and we fall back, never breaking our kiss. I can feel him, thick and ready, between my legs, and he pushes against me. He swallows the moan that I can't stop.

We break the kiss, and he stares at me as he slowly lifts my shirt, exposing my swollen breasts. He pulls the cups down and bends to take a nipple in his mouth. He moves on to the other one, sucking the nipple into his mouth, but he doesn't lap at them for long, knowing they're sensitive from breastfeeding. Reid pulls my shirt over my head and removes my bra before peppering kisses between my breasts and going lower until he stops at my stomach. He kisses my c-section scar before moving back up.

Our lips meet again, and this time, it's urgent, like he can't wait to get inside me. He pauses to strip out of his clothes and cover my body with his. I grab his face and kiss him as he thrusts inside me in one hard, long thrust. We moan in each other's mouths, marveling at the ecstasy we both feel. He thrusts at a steady pace, his eyes close as he's lost to the feeling.

"Baby," he says against my lips. "You feel so good. It's been too long. I'm not going to last."

He grabs my hips and starts hammering inside me. He's hitting so deep that I will not last long, either. The only sound in the room is our heavy breathing as we try to keep our moans down. He leans down, fitting his body closer to mine as he grinds his dick into me. Every time he hits deep, his pelvis rubs against my clit.

After the third time, I explode around him. My orgasm sets him off, and he groans into my neck as he comes. His dick jerks violently inside me. He continues in quick thrusts as his orgasm seems to go on and on. It's been a more that eight weeks since we've had sex, and he's coming a lot. I made sure to get a more effective birth control before I left the hospital too.

He finally stills and pulls back to look at me. I'm still trembling in his arms as the aftershock of the sex we just had subsided. He smiles down at me and kisses me deeply.

"I love you," he says, pulling away.

"I love you, too," I tell him.

He pulls out of me, and we get dressed. We quietly make our way to grab Liam from downstairs with Reid's mom. She sees us walking into the room.

"Oh, you're here?" she says in surprise. "I didn't hear you come in."

Reid and I share a smile and thank his mom for watching Liam before we take him up to Reid's room for the night.

"In the embrace of summer's warmth, our love blooms like a sun-kissed garden, and as we bask in the golden glow, we discover the joy of a new life unfolding. It's a season where love and laughter intertwine, painting our days with the vibrant hues of shared dreams and the promise of a sunlit future."

SUMMER TOGETHER

I can't help but feel a surge of joy as I realize I'm finally fitting back into my old clothes. As I head downstairs towards the kitchen, I can't resist giving a quick twirl for Mom. She bursts into laughter at the sight, and the sound makes me smile even more. We tuck into a bit of breakfast, chit-chatting as we usually do.

Out of the blue, she casually asks, "What time is Reid coming over?"

I glance at the clock. "In about an hour," I say. "We're planning to take Liam out for a walk. The weather should be perfect, not too hot."

Mom nods her head and says, "That's good."

We then settle back into our conversation, a comfortable hum of words and laughter filling the kitchen as we continue to eat. Suddenly, in walks Destiny, cradling Liam in her arms.

"Time for my little superstar to eat," Destiny announces with a warm smile before handing Liam over to me.

I can't help but coo at his adorable face. With a quiet chuckle, I shift Liam gently in my arms and pull my breast out for him to suckle. Destiny immediately throws a hand over her eyes, feigning horror.

"Amelia! You're scaring me with your boob!" she exclaims in mock terror.

We all burst into laughter, the sound echoing around the room. As soon as Liam finishes his meal, I pat him gently on the back to burp him. Destiny's hands are a warm presence on my shoulder as she takes him back.

"I've got it," she assures me before walking out of the kitchen with Liam tucked securely in her arms.

They disappear into the other room, leaving Mom and me to tackle the aftermath of breakfast. As we're finishing up, the doorbell rings, its sound echoing through the house. Wiping my hands on a dishcloth, I make my way to the door, my heart fluttering in anticipation.

I open the door to see Reid standing on the porch, his eyes warm and welcoming. The sight of him makes my heart skip a beat, as it has done since we first met.

"Hey, baby," he says, leaning in to kiss me. The familiar sensation of his lips on mine brings a huge smile to my face. "Are you and Liam ready?" he asks, pulling back slightly.

I chuckle lightly at his question. "I have to pry Liam from Destiny's arms first, but then we'll be ready."

I tell him, the image of Destiny's fake pout already forming in my mind. Reid chuckles and moves to sit on the couch, waiting patiently as I leave to grab Liam. Destiny hands him over with a dramatic sigh, her eyes sparkling with mischief. Soon enough, we're leaving the house, the sun shining brightly as we start our day.

As Reid and I stroll around the park, Liam snug in his stroller, I can't help but feel a surge of contentment. The sun gently warms our backs, and the birds are chirping like they're putting on a concert just for us. Reid's hand is firm in mine, a silent promise of his unwavering presence.

I look down at Liam, his tiny face scrunched in concentration as he takes in the world around him and I chuckle. This kid sure doesn't want to miss a thing! Walking here, in this moment, it's as if all the noise in the world has gone quiet, replaced with the perfect tranquility of our little family bubble.

"Hey Reid," I begin hesitantly, as we continue our peaceful stroll, "Have you ever thought about us moving in together?"

He looks over at me, surprise flickering across his face. "Actually, I have, Amelia, but there's something I need to tell you. I'm leaving in a week for school. We might have to delay moving in together until after I graduate."

I feel my heart thumping in my chest. I've been waiting for the right moment to share my news, and this seems as good a time as any.

"Well, funny you should mention school," I reply, trying to keep my voice steady. "I've been job hunting around the area where you're going to school and... I've got a job offer."

Reid stops in his tracks, turning to look at me. "Wait, what? Why would you do that without talking to me first?"

His response shocks me, as I expected excitement, maybe a few tears, but this... this was not what I had in mind. "I... I thought you'd be happy," I stutter, my heart sinking. "But I guess I was wrong..."

I can feel the anger bubbling up inside me, my patience snapping like a thin thread.

"What's wrong with wanting to keep my family close, Reid? Why would you react like this? I thought you, of all people, would understand my decision." I snap, my voice taut with frustration.

Reid's face reddens, and his words come out in a sudden burst. "Amelia, you're not thinking clearly! You're giving up on your dreams just because we have a baby now. You always wanted to become a teacher, remember?"

His words sting, but there's a ring of truth to them. "We have our families. They're willing to help us with this. I'm thinking about our future, Amelia, not just about the now!" he shouts. "Stop trying to create the perfect family and focus on achieving your goals in order to have the prefect family."

There's an echoing silence after his outburst, my mind whirling as I process his words. Am I really willing to put everything I'd dreamed of on hold? Reid reaches out, his hands gently cradling my face, forcing me to meet his gaze. His eyes, usually a vibrant oasis of green, now mirror the turmoil swirling between us.

"Amelia," he begins, his voice barely more than a whisper. "I love you more than words can express."

His voice quivers, the emotional weight of the moment making it tremble. "I want this family, us, you, and Liam. I want us to brave these stormy seas together, to come out on the other side victorious."

He brushes a stray curl away from my face, his touch feather-light. "I want us to be the best parents we can be for Liam, and the best partners for each other. And I genuinely believe we can only do that if we're both living our dreams, not just surviving."

His words hang in the air between us, a vow, an aspiration, a shared dream. We stand there in silence for a moment, the weight of Reid's words lingering in the air. Liam's plaintive cry, a sharp reminder of the tiny life that binds us together, shatters the silence.

Reid leans down, placing a kiss on my lips that's both tentative and fierce, full of the love we share and the uncertainty of our future. He pulls back, the taste of him still lingering on my lips, then reaches down to lift Liam out of his stroller. He holds our son close, patting his tiny back in a soothing rhythm.

Turning to me, his gaze holds a desperate plea. "I'm leaving to pursue my dreams so that I can be who I need to be for us. I just want you to do the same, and I hope you can understand that."

With that, he turns away, his back a rigid line of determination as he walks away. I watch him go, my heart pounding in a silent rhythm of mixed emotions. His words echo in my mind, a refrain of longing, of dreams deferred and futures uncertain.

I can't do anything but follow, drawn to him as surely as the tide is drawn to the moon. His words resonate within me, a clarion call to reevaluate my decisions and rediscover the woman I'd dreamt of becoming.

The days that follow are a blur. The tension simmers between us, an unspoken elephant in the room. My mind is a whirlwind of thoughts, of uncertainties that I can't escape. Each fleeting moment is tinged with the bitter sting of Reid's impending departure.

I count down the days, each sunrise a bitter reminder of the dwindling time we have left. The smiles are fewer and further between, replaced with stiff words and avoidant gazes.

Every day feels like a battle, a test of endurance. Each night I fall into bed, exhausted not from the physical exertion of the day but from the emotional strain. I clutch onto our shared dreams, onto the hope that this storm will pass and we will find our way. But for now, all I can do is watch as the days slip away, taking with them the man I love and our shared dreams.

The sound of a familiar knock jolts me from the thoughts I'm lost in. As I swing open the door, my breath catches at the sight of Reid, standing there with the same shy smile that always used to disarm me.

"I'm here to see our son," he says.

I step aside to let him in, watching as he takes in the slight changes around the room, his eyes lighting up as they land on the playpen where Liam is looking around, oblivious to his father's presence.

Reid spends the afternoon playing with our son, the tension from our last encounter seeming to dissipate as he loses himself in the simple joy of fatherhood. I watch from the sidelines, my heart aching at the sight of the two most important people in my life. The tender sight softens the bitter sting of reality in front of me, the laughter and innocent joy from my son and Reid filling every corner of the room.

As the sun sets, Reid turns to me, his eyes mirroring the same uncertainty I feel. "Amelia... Can we talk?" he begins.

I nod, apprehension gnawing at my insides. Seated across from each other, we open up, not as two people at odds, but as two lovers who have temporarily lost their way. We retrace the paths that led us here, taking turns to air our grievances, our fears, our dreams.

Listening to Reid, I understand that though our approaches differed, our endgame was the same. We both wanted what was best for Liam, for us. Just that, I was willing to put myself on hold for the sake of our family, while Reid wanted to chase his dreams to create a better future for us.

Seeing this, feeling this, the love between us, the respect for our family... I realize that Reid and I... we're not just two individuals with separate dreams. We are a team, a family. As such, we need to support each other, to understand that our dreams aren't exclusive but part of the same tapestry. We reconcile, not just as parents, but as partners, promising to support each other, to remember that our love is the foundation on which everything else is built.

As the door closes behind Reid, I'm left with a bittersweet ache. My mother, who had been a silent observer, moves to sit beside me on the couch, her eyes soft as she watches me interact with Liam. A comfortable silence wraps around us like a warm blanket, broken only by Liam's occasional coos. After seemingly an eternity, Mom turns to me, her gaze gentle yet piercing.

"Amelia," she begins, her voice a quiet whisper in the room. "I heard your conversation with Reid." A blush of embarrassment heats my cheeks, but she simply holds up her hand to stem my apologies. "I'm glad you have him, dear. And more than that, I'm glad for him. He's a good boy."

She pauses, reaching out to lay a comforting hand on mine. "A boy who not only wants to be with you, but wants to see you succeed. He loves you fiercely and will do anything for you and Liam. It's not every day you find someone like that."

Her words hang heavy in the air, laden with truth and wisdom borne of years of experience. She gives me a tender smile, her hand giving mine a reassuring squeeze.

"I'm pleased to see you both working through this like adults. It's not the circumstances that define us, but how we handle them," she says.

With a last pat on my knee, she rises from the couch, leaving me to mull over her words. I watch her go, my mind a whirlwind of thoughts. She's right, of course. Reid and I, we're not just individuals anymore. We're a team, a family, and as such, we need to navigate these stormy seas together, supporting each other every step of the way.

"Love, like a resilient vine, thrives even in the garden of separation. As distance becomes the fertile ground, our hearts send roots deep into the soil of longing, and with each passing day, the tendrils of affection grow stronger, weaving an unbreakable bond that transcends the limitations of physical closeness."

REIDS DEPARTURE

As the days dwindle down, my heart clenches tighter. Only one day now. One day, until Reid, my rock, my confidante, my partner in crime, leaves for college. My mind whirls with a mixture of emotions. Pride, sadness, worry, and a nagging sense of apprehension. I can't help but wonder how our relationship will weather the distance and the change. I'm filled with a dread of the unknown, wondering how I'll adapt to the echoing silence his absence will surely leave.

Today, we promise each other it will be a fun day, a day of laughter and reminiscence rather than tears and farewells. Reid arrives early in the morning to share breakfast with us. Pancakes, mom's specialty, aromas wafting through the air, and laughter filling the room. It felt normal, like just another day.

During breakfast, Mom turns to Reid and asks, "So, honey, are you all set up with your classes and dorm?"

His eyes light up as he nods.

"Yes, I am all set and quite excited, too," his enthusiasm is infectious, and one can't help but feel joyous for him.

But I just sit here quietly, my fork moving aimlessly

around my plate. I put on a brave face, forcing a smile that didn't quite reach my eyes. I want so badly not to let the fear and sadness show, not to let him see how much I fear the gaping void his absence will leave in my life. But inside, my heart is shattering into a million tiny pieces.

As we wrap up breakfast, I look around, taking in the simple warmth of the scene. Reid, still laughing at some silly joke Mom made. Mom clears up the dishes with a satisfied smile, happy that her pancakes were a hit as usual. The sunlight pours in through the window, casting a soft glow over everything. I want to remember this moment, to store it away for the days when the loneliness would creep in. We decide to take Liam to the zoo. It's Reid's idea.

"He may be young, but he'll love it, you'll see," he says with that infectious enthusiasm of his.

As we arrive at the zoo, the air bristling with excitement. Families, couples, and groups of laughing children bustling around. Bright flags flutter in the breeze, and the distant roars, squawks, and cries of various creatures echoes through the air. The sun is radiant, and a gentle breeze rustles through the leaves of trees lining the pathways. The scent of popcorn and cotton candy mixes with the earthier zoo smells creates a unique sensory experience that was nostalgic and comforting.

We wander around, stopping at each exhibit. Reid holds Liam up to the glass of the penguin enclosure, his eyes wide with wonder.

"Look, buddy," Reid points. "Did you know penguins spend about half their time in the water and the other half on land?"

Liam just stares and drools as he watches the penguins waddle and dive with glee. At the lion's den, Reid holds up Liam, pointing towards the majestic creature lounging in the shade.

"You see that, Liam? That's a lion, the king of the jungle.

Despite their fierce reputation, they're actually lazy most of the day. But, when they hunt," he pauses for dramatic effect, "There's nothing faster or more powerful."

We move on, each exhibit a new adventure, each animal a new story. Reid was a natural, his voice filled with enthusiasm and wonder as he shared tidbits about each creature.

As the day unfolds, a sense of happiness seeps into my heart. It was a warm, radiant feeling, much like the sunshine that bathes us in its gentle glow. Watching Reid with Liam, our baby son, his eyes sparkling with joy and excitement as he brings the world of animals alive for our baby, I can't help but smile.

Despite the sadness and fear bubbling under the surface, I'm moved by this precious moment. I find joy in Reid's joy, in Liam's wide-eyed wonder, and in the simple but profound love that binds us together. This is happiness. Not loud and exuberant, but soft and tender. It was a moment to cherish, a memory to hold on to.

As we approach the gorilla enclosure, I turn to Reid with a teasing glint in my eyes. "You realize Liam doesn't understand a word you're saying, right?"

I chuckle, gesturing to our baby boy, who is much more interested in his own fists than the fuzzy creatures lazing in the trees.

Reid simply shrugs, his grin undiminished. "I'm trying to start him young," he says, his eyes sparkling with good humor. "I read that the more knowledge you expose kids to, the better they will be at learning things as they grow up."

He hoists Liam higher, pointing at the gorillas, who seem quite unimpressed by our presence.

With a playful wink at me, Reid adds, "Plus, our boy is smart because he's got our intellect."

I can't help but laugh out loud at Reid's infectious enthusiasm and love for our little boy. We continue our journey through the zoo, each new animal a fresh opportunity for Reid to impart his wisdom to our blissfully clueless baby. And though Liam may not have grasped a single word, I knew he was soaking up the love that flowed freely between us. That, in itself, is a valuable lesson.

As we leave the zoo, our stomachs grumble in unison, crying out for sustenance. We stumble upon a quaint little bistro nestled in a quiet corner of the city. Its rustic charm was undeniable, with its ivy-covered red brick walls and small, round tables draped in red-checkered tablecloths. The aroma of fresh bread and simmering herbs wafts tantalizingly from the open kitchen, making our mouths water in anticipation.

Reid takes charge of ordering. Before long, our table is adorned with a large Margherita pizza, crowned with lush, ripe tomatoes, fresh mozzarella, and fragrant basil leaves. The crust is thin and delicately crispy, a perfect bed for the rich, tangy tomato sauce and gooey cheese. A bowl of mixed greens is also served, drizzled with a tangy vinaigrette and garnished with thinly sliced radishes and crunchy croutons.

We each grab a slice of pizza, the melting cheese stretching deliciously. The pizza is divine, the fresh ingredients blending together in a symphony of flavors. The salad provides a refreshing counterpoint with its crisp greens and bright, tangy dressing.

We finish eating as the day is slowly drawing in. The sun had dipped below the horizon, painting the sky with hues of pink and orange. Liam, overwhelmed by the day's excitement, fusses, his tiny face scrunching up in a yawn. I gently rock him in my arms, hoping the rhythmic motion would soothe him.

"We better head home, big day for the little guy," Reid said, his eyes soft with love.

We head to Reid's parents' house, and Liam and I are

staying with him. Reid leaves tomorrow, so this is our last night until we see him next.

When we reach the house, we gently laid Liam down in his crib, tucking him in with his favorite blanket. Reid and I then settle down on his bed, the weight of the impending farewell hanging heavily in the silence. Reid turn to me, his eyes softening with a tenderness that makes my breath hitch.

"Amelia," he begins, his voice low and steady. "I know you're scared. I'm a little scared, too. College... it's a big deal. And I know what you're thinking. You're worried that things will change between us. But I want you to know something."

I swallow hard, my heart hammering in my chest as I look up at him. "Yeah?" I croak out, my throat tight with unshed tears.

Reid reaches over, gently squeezing my hand. "Yeah," he affirms, his gaze never leaving mine. "Distance... it's just a physical thing. It can't touch what we have. It can't change the fact that you're my girl, and I love you. And no matter where I am, I'll always be there for you."

Reid kisses me in desperation, eager to convey how we feel to each other through touch. As Reid's lips find mine, the world around us dissolves. The kiss isn't like the others. It's desperate, needy, and filled with the unspoken sorrow of our impending separation.

His touch is heavy with the weight of his looming departure, every movement brimming with an urgency that tugs at my heart. I can feel him clutching onto this moment, trying to etch it into memory, to take a piece of me with him.

"I need you, baby," he moans against my lips and tugs me from Liam's room and into his.

I tug him closer and kiss him deeper. Our kiss is frantic as we try to maintain our kiss and strip out of our clothes. Soon, we're naked, and he thrusts into me in one swift motion, and I moan into his chest. He fills me so full and moves in intense and hard thrusts. He grips my hips with bruising force and holds me in place as he pulls back and dives deep again and again. Harder and faster.

I whimper into his chest, as this is unlike anything I've felt before. This seems more intense, more intimate, and more sexual. Just more. Reid pounds inside my body. Our need for each other is the driving force of our actions as we desperately communicate with our bodies.

My orgasm hits so suddenly, Reid has to cover my mouth with his hand as I moan so loud. I can't help it as it's fierce and intense. My body spasms violently around him as he gives me a few more thrusts and stills, coming inside me. Once I stop coming, Reid takes his hand off my mouth.

"Amelia, I love you, baby," he says. "I need you. So much. I love you and Liam. You all are my world."

I stare at him with all the love I have for him. "I love you, too. We need you too."

He gives me a quick kiss. "Promise me this won't change us. That we'll stay together. Promise me."

"I promise," I tell him with tears in my eyes.

He leans down and takes my mouth in another kiss. Our tongues duel, and I feel him harden inside me again. He starts moving inside of me leisurely, going deeper each time he thrusts back in. The slickness from our previous organisms making it easier for him to slide in and out. We take our time this round, feeling all the sensations as Reid makes love to me. I don't think there's anyone else who fits together as well as we do. He is everything to me, just like I'm sure I am everything to him.

As we pick up our pace, I feel the familiar start of my orgasm, and I move my hips to meet his, increasing the friction between our bodies. Then, for the second time, we come undone together. Reid falls on top of me, both of our bodies covered in sweat. After a moment, he moves to the side and pulls my back flush against his front. We lay that way for a while, basking in the atmosphere of our love and commitment.

As Reid's lips find mine, the world around us dissolves. The kiss isn't like the others. It's desperate, needy, and filled with the unspoken sorrow of our impending separation. His touch is heavy with the weight of his looming departure, every movement brimming with an urgency that tugs at my heart. I can feel him clutching onto this moment, trying to etch it into memory, to take a piece of me with him.

Reid's calloused hand gently cradles my face, guiding my gaze to meet his. His eyes, an unfathomable abyss of emerald and gold, hold a softness that steals my breath.

"Amelia," he murmurs, his voice a soothing balm over my frenzied nerves. "I love you. More than I've ever loved anything in this world."

He traces the line of my cheekbone with a tenderness that sends shivers down my spine.

"We're going to be alright, you know. This isn't goodbye," he reassures, his tone filled with a resilient optimism I so desperately need to hear. "It's just... the next adventure. In a lifetime of adventures together."

At his words, a solitary tear escapes, trickling down my cheek. His thumb catches it, wiping it away, yet more follow in its trail. As the reality of his departure lingers in the air, I cling to his promise, engraving it onto my heart.

When the morning came, saying goodbye to Reid was harder than I thought it would be. As I watched him leave, with our baby cradled in my arms, I wondered if we'd survive this new adventure we were about to embark on.

MILLIE MICHAELSON
The
MIDDLE
Of
FOREVER
THE FOREVER SERIES

Parenthood is no easy feat, especially when your love story began in high school. Reid and I find ourselves on a rollercoaster ride, with our love sometimes feeling distant and strained. With Reid away at college, the chasm between us seems insurmountable. We're torn between our deep affection and new responsibilities.

The longer Reid is away, the more my trust issues and insecurities gnaw at me. I'm his first kiss, his first love, his first everything. I can't help but question if he's enjoying college life and getting new experiences. Our love used to be unshakeable, yet we're struggling to find a balance between life and our hearts.

But we know our love is strong. We work hard to create a routine and establish a sense of normalcy. During it all, we rekindle our love with newfound understanding, and we grow stronger because of it. As our lives become easier, Reid takes the ultimate step, solidifying our love. Wedding bells ring, and a new journey for us begins.

Yet, I learned that marriage isn't merely a symbolic gesture of our love. It's a commitment that requires hard work and dedication. Now, our love is being put to the ultimate test.

ACKNOWLEDGMENTS

First and foremost, I want to express my heartfelt thanks to my husband. Your unwavering support, encouragement, and patience have been my rock throughout this journey. Your belief in me and my dreams is a constant source of strength and inspiration.

A special thanks to the romance community, the readers, bloggers, and fellow authors who have shown me immense kindness and camaraderie. Your passion for the genre is infectious, and I'm honored to be a part of this wonderful community.

Lastly, to the readers who have picked up this book, thank you for giving these characters and their stories a chance. It is your support and enthusiasm that drives me to continue writing, and I hope you find as much joy in reading this story as I did in writing it.

With love and appreciation,
Millie